PAX BRIT...

DARK

D0187477

Ulysses was almost at the door to the restaurant when he hesitated and looked back.

The slowly tumbling asteroid already filled the panoramic window, the ship's running lights illuminating fissures, craters and cruelly jagged outcrops across its surface. It had to be as long as a rugby pitch, if not bigger. If something that big hit the space-liner they were all dead – there would be no survivors.

Emilia unadvisedly followed his gaze. "Shit," she gasped in a most unladylike fashion.

The ship lurched. Tables overturned, crystal glasses smashed. People screamed.

Through the view shield, the ship-killer rolled overhead, tumbling on through space. The screech of the trailing edge of the asteroid scraping across the top of the hull reverberated through the restaurant.

"Thank God for that," Emilia said as she picked herself up off the floor. "That was too close for comfort."

"We're not out of danger yet," Ulysses warned, extricating himself from the waiter-droid that had fallen on top of him, and which now couldn't stop apologising. "We must get beyond the next bulkhead or we're going the same way as the air in this compartment when those other meteors hit."

"What other meteors?" Emilia asked, glancing back at the window. "Oh. Those meteors," she said weakly as she saw the hail of stones that were following in the massive asteroid's wake.

WWW.ABADDONBOOKS.COM

An Abaddon Books™ Publication
www.abaddonbooks.com
abaddon@rebellion.co.uk

First published in 2010 by Abaddon Books™, Rebellion Intellectual
Property Limited, Riverside House, Osney Mead, Oxford, OX2 0ES, UK.

10 9 8 7 6 5 4 3 2 1

Editors: Jonathan Oliver & Jenni Hill
Cover: Mark Harrison
Design: Simon Parr & Luke Preece
Marketing and PR: Keith Richardson
Creative Director and CEO: Jason Kingsley
Chief Technical Officer: Chris Kingsley
Pax Britannia™ created by Jonathan Green

Copyright © 2010 Rebellion. All rights reserved.

Pax Britannia™, Abaddon Books and Abaddon Books logo are
trademarks owned or used exclusively by Rebellion Intellectual
Property Limited. The trademarks have been registered or protection
sought in all member states of the European Union and other countries
around the world. All right reserved.

US ISBN: 978-1-906735-85-2

Printed in the US

No part of this publication may be reproduced, stored in a retrieval
system, or transmitted in any form or by any means, electronic,
mechanical, photocopying, recording or otherwise, without the prior
permission of the publishers.

This is a work of fiction. All the characters and events portrayed in
this book are fictional, and any resemblance to real people or incidents
is purely coincidental.

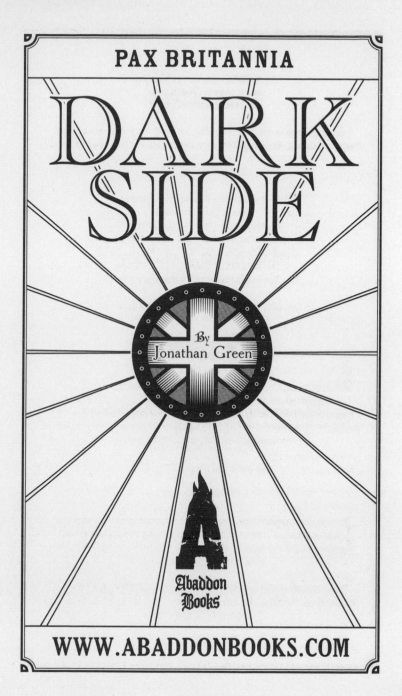

PAX BRITANNIA

DARK SIDE

By
Jonathan Green

Abaddon
Books

WWW.ABADDONBOOKS.COM

Ulysses Quicksilver Adventures
Unnatural History
Leviathan Rising
Human Nature
Evolution Expects
Blood Royal
Dark Side

Other novels from the world of Pax Britannia
El Sombra
Gods of Manhattan

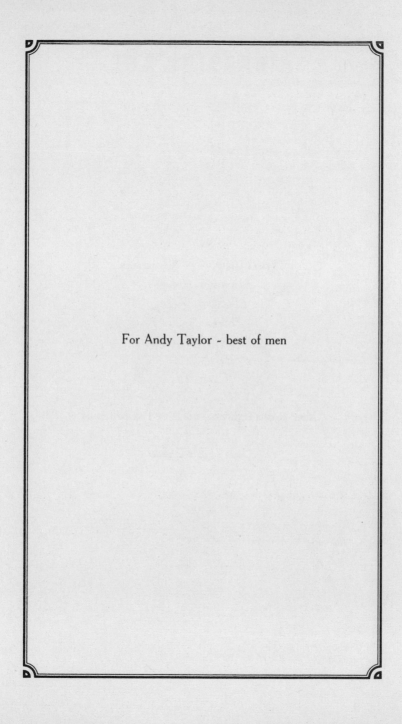

For Andy Taylor - best of men

Dear Ulysses,

By the time you read this, I'll be gone. I'm sorry I didn't say goodbye, but this letter will just have to do. I never was very good with farewells. Besides, I didn't want to hang around and give you the chance to dissuade me. This is something I should have done long ago.

Things are getting too hot for me round here. I'm an idiot, I know, but I've got myself in deeper than ever— than hopefully you'll ever know. So fate forced my hand, you might say, and it was time to leave.

I've gone off-world. Like I say, I should have done this long ago, rather than go and bring all my troubles to your door. As if you don't have enough of your own!

Anyway, don't try to come after me. After all, the empire needs you. And don't worry — I'll be alright.

We'll see each other again, when things have cooled down a little, I hope. But in the meantime, have a nice life.

Your brother,

B

P.S. — And if anyone comes looking for me, don't let on, there's a good chap.

PROLOGUE

The Time Machine

FLASHBACK...

ULYSSES QUICKSILVER REGARDED the wan, shrunken figure buried beneath the blankets covering the bed and asked, "How's he doing?"

"All right, I suppose, all things considered," Emilia Oddfellow replied, gently mopping the old man's brow with a flannel. "Anything's an improvement on being dead."

"You've got a point there. And how are you doing?"

Emilia took a moment to answer.

"Better."

In the soft candlelight of the bedchamber she looked more tired, more overwrought, more resolved, nobler and more beautiful than Ulysses had ever seen her.

He suddenly felt uncomfortable, as if he were intruding. "I'll leave you two alone."

"No," Emilia said sharply, her voice loud in the pervading stillness of the room. "Stay. Please?"

There came a muffled moan from the bed as the old man stirred.

"What's that, father?" Emilia asked, putting her ear to his mouth.

"Is he here?"

"Who?"

"Quicksilver," Alexander Oddfellow managed before his words were forced to give way to a bout of phlegm-ridden coughing.

"Yes, Ulysses is here."

Half opening rheum-encrusted eyes, the old man turned his head to look at Ulysses. A palsied hand appeared from beneath the covers and Oddfellow beckoned him over.

"Hello, old chap," Ulysses said, approaching the bed. "How are you feeling?"

"Never mind that." The irritation in the old man's voice was evident. "I must speak with you alone."

"Father?"

"Please leave us, my dear."

Emilia looked ready to protest. Tears glistened at the corners of her eyes. "Very well. I'll be out in the corridor if you need me."

"Understood," Ulysses said. He felt her pain, but he was also keen to hear whatever it was that Oddfellow had to say.

A moment later he heard the door close softly behind Emilia.

"What is it, old chap?"

"You know me of old, Quicksilver," the old man said. Ulysses nodded. "And I know you. I know for example that you're not entirely the dandy playboy you make yourself out to be. I know of your government connections, whereas, I believe, Emilia does not know how involved you are with the defence of the realm of Magna Britannia."

Ulysses smiled sheepishly. "I think you're right. It was that secrecy that drove a wedge between us."

"But now is not the time to tell her either," Oddfellow warned. "There is still action that must be taken to bring this matter to an end," he wheezed, before the coughing consumed him again.

"But it's over, isn't it?" Ulysses pressed. "You're whole again; free of the Sphere."

"Would that it were over," the old man said, gasping for breath. "Would that it were." He shot Ulysses a sinister stare from beneath hooded eyes. "You now know what that thing in the basement is?"

"Yes. I mean, it's an astonishing achievement! An experimental teleportation device. It's an incredible feat of scientific invention, Oddfellow."

"It was slow progress at first," the old man said, the suggestion of a smile shaping his mouth, "but then I got myself a sponsor and, with the necessary financial backing, I was really starting to get somewhere. But then certain things came to my attention – nothing major, just niggling doubts – and I began to suspect that... how shall I put this?" He broke off, as the coughing took hold once more.

"Go on," Ulysses urged.

"Well, that certain malign agencies had taken an interest in what I was doing and were funding the project, intent on getting their hands on the fruits of my labours. You know the accident that trapped me inside the transmat's containment field?"

"Of course," Ulysses said, one eyebrow raised in suspicion.

"Well, it wasn't entirely an accident."

"You were set-up? It was a booby-trap?"

"Something like that. I believe it was the work of..." Oddfellow paused, lowering his voice to a whisper, even though there was no one else present to hear. "An agent of the Nazis."

"Really?" Ulysses was incredulous. He knew that the Nazis were still an underground power in Europe, with their hooks in other parts of the world too, but he hadn't had anything to do with them himself within the British Isles.

"You must believe me!" Oddfellow pressed, his voice suddenly loud again. "Because if I'm right, now that I am free of the Sphere, it won't be long before they make their move."

"Who is this agent?"

"I don't know – that's the trouble. They could be here, right now, in this house!" The old man sounded desperate, on the verge of panic. "But they cannot be allowed to get their hands on my machine. I got as far as destroying all of my notes associated with the project and was preparing to destroy the machine when that so-called 'accident' occurred."

Ulysses fixed Oddfellow with a penetrating stare, the pieces of the puzzle finally beginning to fit. "What do you want me to do?" he asked, with cold purpose.

"You must destroy the Sphere, so that no-one can ever use it as a weapon or to further any evil plan for dominion."

Ulysses didn't need to be told twice. If the old man believed the device was a danger to the safety of the realm, and needed to be destroyed, then that was what would happen.

OUTSIDE THE ROOM Ulysses found Emilia pacing the corridor. She turned to him, her eyes full of questions.

"Stay with him," he told her, "and keep the door locked."

Deaf to her protestations, Ulysses raced downstairs to find the other guests gathered in the library once more.

An eerie sense of foreboding sent an icy chill crackling down his spine, turning his skin to gooseflesh. Sitting in the same leather-upholstered armchair he had favoured earlier that evening, was the corpulent philanthropist, Herr Sigmund Faustus. Dressed in a tweed suit, in the manner of a country gent, fingers steepled in front of his face, he regarded Ulysses from behind the lens of a monocle.

"Mr Quicksilver," he announced solemnly, "it would appear that you have walked into – how do you say? – something of a situation."

Ulysses tensed.

"Oddfellow truly made a deal with the Devil when he fell in with you, didn't he Faustus?"

"Oh, but you are mistaken," the German railed, double chins wobbling in indignation.

A bark of cruel laughter from the corner of the room caused Ulysses to snap his head round in surprise.

"Not as quick as you thought, are you, Quicksilver?" Daniel Dashwood sneered as he emerged from the shadows gathered within the corner of the room. Other than for the expression of dour aloofness on his face Emilia's cousin was a handsome man, athletically lean, his dark hair slicked back with lacquer. The gun he held in his hand was ugly by comparison, and trained on Ulysses.

Ulysses considered his own pistol. He was aware of the weight of it in the holster under his arm, but he left it where it was, hands by his sides. If he were to go for his own weapon now, Ulysses was under no illusions as to what would follow. Dashwood would shoot first and ask questions later, he was sure of it.

In a split second he had scanned the room. From left to right around the library, waiting in anxious anticipation, were the parapsychologist Wentworth, Sigmund Faustus, his aide, Ulysses' own manservant Nimrod, the quaking, all-but-forgotten medium's assistant Renfield, Wentworth's ghost-hunting partner Smythe, the quaking butler Caruthers and then the pistol-wielding Daniel Dashwood.

"But Herr Faustus really hit the nail on the head there. This *is* what you might call something of a situation."

With a barely perceptible nod to Ulysses to make his intention plain, Nimrod threw himself at Dashwood, displaying greater agility than his grey hair and apparent age might suggest. But before he could reach Emilia's traitorous cousin, and before Ulysses could make the most of Nimrod's diversion, Smythe, standing between the manservant and the turncoat, sprung into action himself. A vicious punch to the face floored the old prize-fighter in an instant.

Dashwood's aim didn't waiver. His eyes still fixed upon Ulysses, he gave another bark of harsh laughter and tensed his finger on the trigger.

"I believe you've met my colleagues – my partners-in-crime, as it were – Mr Smythe and Mr Wentworth."

Ulysses said nothing but continued to watch Dashwood, hardly daring to blink in case he missed the one moment's opportunity he needed.

"Very useful they are too," Dashwood went on. "Particularly when it comes to cobbling together a containment field focusing device from what little I was able to salvage from my rather ingenious uncle's notes. They're also dab hands at setting up little 'accidents', shall we say.

"Although, of course, they might not have been so hasty to arrange one in particular if they had realised that uncle had already made moves to stop anyone following in his footsteps. But now we have both the inventor and his invention intact, thanks in part to you, Quicksilver. So what need have we now of cremated blueprints?"

Obviously already considering himself victorious, the conceited Dashwood saw no reason to keep any element of his schemes secret any longer. He had revealed to Ulysses the how and the why, certain that there was nothing that the dandy could do to stop him. And unfortunately, with Nimrod out of action, he appeared to be right.

"All that remains for me to do is tie up a few loose ends."

Dashwood's finger tightened still further on the trigger, easing the mechanism back, the barrel of the gun aimed directly at Ulysses' chest.

With a cry, the flabby Faustus launched himself out of his chair with surprising speed. Startled, Dashwood turned, amazement writ large across his face, as the fat German barrelled into him.

The discharge of the gun was loud in the close confines of the library. Faustus gave a grunt and tumbled forwards onto Dashwood. It was the opportunity Ulysses had been hoping for. He went for Wentworth and sent him crashing to the floor with a well-aimed blow to the stomach, which he followed up with a double-handed blow to the back of the neck.

There was an audible crunch and Ulysses looked round as Smythe cried out. Nimrod had had his revenge. Smythe lay howling, curled in a ball on the floor, blood pouring from his broken nose.

Dashwood lay motionless, beneath the bulk of Oddfellow's sponsor.

"Nimrod, with me!" Ulysses shouted. "We haven't a moment to lose!"

Ulysses leading the way, the two of them raced back down the cellar steps and into the abandoned laboratory.

The Sphere squatted there on its claw-footed stand, as tall as a man and half that again, the machinery glowing faintly with what little power remained in its storm-charged reserve batteries. The concentric, yet incomplete, rings of the giant gyroscope remained motionless, the broken rings describing a spherical void at the heart of the machine. Thick bundles of wires sheathed in vulcanised rubber trailed from the strange sphere to the control panel of a logic engine. It was a malevolent presence in the candle-pierced gloom of the cellar. And it was still on.

The last time it had been activated – to release Alexander Oddfellow from within the confines of its containment field – had drained the potential energy collected by the directed lightning strike. But no-one had thought to turn it off again afterwards.

"We have to destroy this thing," Ulysses said, suddenly in awe of the broken sphere.

"I do not mean to sound impertinent, sir," Nimrod said, "but how do you suggest we do that?"

Ulysses scanned the control panels of the device and the stilled rings. "There must be a way to overload it. Sabotage its controls or something."

"But overload it with what?"

"Ahh..." Ulysses faltered. Hardewick Hall's generator was still down. "Don't worry, I'll think of something."

Ulysses darted to the control panel, frantic eyes searching for a solution. Shadows moved across the wall behind the device and, acting on instinct, he flung himself behind the logic engine.

The retort of the pistol was dulled by the damp stone acoustics of the cellar. There was a crack as the bullet pinged off the control console, shattering a glass dial. A second shot rang out and Ulysses heard it smack into the gyroscope itself.

He risked a glance around the edge of his sturdy shelter. The three scoundrels stood at the bottom of the steps. Smythe had a bloody handkerchief clamped to his nose. Wentworth and Dashwood were gasping for breath having both been badly winded. But Ulysses couldn't see Nimrod. He had doubtless taken cover when he heard the felons dashing down the steps into the cellar.

However, Ulysses couldn't let their presence halt his mission. It was all the more important now that he destroyed the Sphere and stopped the traitorous Dashwood and his lackeys from getting their hands on it.

Grasping the thick trunking that connected the control panel to the machine he gave a sharp tug. He heard a tearing metal sound and felt something give at the other end of the cable. Teeth gritted he heaved again and was rewarded by a spray of sparks as a bundle of wires came away from the back of the gyroscopic frame. But other cables still connected the Sphere to the logic engine, in some unnatural imitation of the umbilical cord connecting an unborn infant to its mother's placenta.

As Ulysses reached for another bundle of wires, he saw Dashwood level his pistol at him once again. Distant thunder rumbled over Hardewick Hall.

"Now I've got you," Dashwood snarled.

Scintillating electric blue light exploded throughout the laboratory as the broken rings of the Sphere began to spin. Dashwood threw a hand over his eyes against the retina-searing glare.

"Lightning never strikes twice, my arse!" Ulysses exclaimed and ran for cover.

Eyes narrowed to slits against the brilliant light pouring from the spinning Sphere, Dashwood dropped his shielding hand and searched for his target beyond the edges of the coruscating glare. The shadows there appeared even darker now in contrast to the blinding whiteness. But there was no sign of Ulysses.

"God's teeth!" he swore. Smythe and Wentworth looked at him in confusion. "Turn that thing off!" he commanded, waggling his gun at the machine.

Not wanting to inflame their employer's wrath any further, Dashwood's lackeys moved cautiously towards the sparking control console of the matter transmitter.

The machine wasn't running as it had before. Whether it was as a result of something Ulysses had done to sabotage the Sphere, or thanks to one of Dashwood's poorly-aimed shots in the dark, something was most definitely wrong with Oddfellow's invention.

There was something feral and untamed about the arcs of lightning zigzagging between the crazily orbiting rings.

"Hurry up!" Dashwood bellowed.

And that was when Nimrod struck. He caught Dashwood firmly between the shoulder blades with the wine bottle, smashing it across his back and sending him reeling. As the villain stumbled forwards, Ulysses made his move. He flung himself out of the shadows and, catching both Smythe and Wentworth around the side of the head, brought their skulls together sharply.

Smythe reeled sideways, a silent expression of pain on his face. Wentworth slumped across the control panel, stunned. As he slid down the front of the console, he fumbled for purchase with a flailing hand and caught hold of a large, gleaming brass switch, and pulled.

Ulysses leapt from the control platform, sprinting past the bewildered Dashwood, covering the cellar with long strides, as the Sphere activated one last time. There was a sound like a thunderclap, deafening within the cellar. Blinding white light flooded the lab, burning Ulysses' eyes even though they were closed. It was as if they had been caught at the very heart of a violent electrical storm, where the turbulent skies birthed their lightning progeny.

His ears hurt. His eyes hurt. His skin felt as if it were on fire.

And then the light was gone, leaving glaring after-images on his abused eyeballs, and the acrid stink of obliterated ozone in its wake.

Ulysses fought to open his eyes despite the pain. He could see nothing. The exposed skin of his hands and face stung.

He cast his gaze around the cellar, blinking all the time, and then he saw Nimrod. His faithful retainer's eyes were watering and he looked as if he were suffering from a bad case of sunburn.

Cold realisation dawned.

He could see Nimrod. He could see the workbenches of the lab behind him. He could see the cloud of smoke left by the lightning explosion.

He looked around the cellar space again, hardly able to believe what he was seeing, or rather, what he wasn't seeing. The reason he had seen nothing when he first opened his eyes, beyond the shadows sliding over his tortured corneas, was because there had been nothing to see.

Caught within the matter transmitter's zone of influence, Dashwood, Smythe and Wentworth were gone. So too was the Sphere. All of them had disappeared – villains, Sphere, logic engine, all – teleported to God alone knew where.

Considering how Oddfellow's machine had failed before, Ulysses wondered darkly whether their final destination had been anywhere within the physical realm at all.

FLASHFORWARD...

EMILIA TURNED AND, grabbing her father's hand, ran. The old man stumbled after her, grunting and wheezing.

Ahead of them, Emilia could make out a figure – a man – beckoning to them from the entrance to the crumbling chamber, one hand outstretched towards them. Ignoring the terrifying creatures that had swarmed into the chamber with him at their head, she focused only on him, for he seemed to be their only hope now.

And then she was stumbling down the steps at the other end of the twisted walkway, still pulling her father after her. She caught a passing glance of a stubbly chin and a black leather eye-patch, and then the man took her hand and pulled her after him into the maze of corridors beyond.

They ran on, she knew not for how long. But as they ran, through the flickering pools of light produced by the shaking glow-globes, she took in the man's mane of lank hair, his battered, poorly-made suit and his scuffed shoes. But still there was something familiar about him; his height, his build, even the feel of his hand in hers.

"Stop!" she shouted, as realisation dawned. "Stop!"

The man ran on, not once looking back.

"*Stop!*"

Emilia's scream echoed away into the shadowed depths of the passageway. The man came to a sudden halt, still facing away from her. He let go of her hand.

"Turn around!" Emilia commanded.

And then, slowly, he did so.

Emilia gasped, putting a hand to her mouth. A feeble whimper escaped her father's rheumy lips.

He might look like little better than a tramp, his hair long and unkempt, his chin covered with fine grey stubble and one scarred eye-socket covered by a black leather eye-patch, but it was still unmistakeably him.

The butt of a pistol thrust from the top of his trousers.

She made a mad lunge and then the gun was in her hand, the safety off, the muzzle pointed squarely at the man's face.

"Hello, Emilia," he said. "Well, I kept my promise. I came back."

Now...

ALEXANDER ODDFELLOW RUBBED his eyes and then read the result of the equation displayed on the glowing green screen in front of him again. It didn't change anything.

Behind him the infernal device throbbed with malignant power and he cursed the day, for the umpteenth time, that he ever sat down to create the matter transporter.

There was no escaping the facts, no matter how hard he might wish that he could. If they continued to run the Sphere as they were, the more the very fabric of reality would be weakened. Left unchecked, the final, undeniable outcome was inevitable.

Helter skelter. Total dimensional collapse. The end of everything. Ever.

And it would occur in twelve minutes, and counting.

ACT ONE

Apollo XIII

~ June 1998 ~

'We are all in the gutter,
but some of us are looking at the stars.'

(Oscar Wilde, *Lady Windermere's Fan*, 1892)

CHAPTER ONE

Syzygy

T minus 9 days, 23 hours, 12 minutes, 27 seconds

THREE HOURS AFTER curfew had sounded, a figure emerged from the inky blackness on the far side of the street in front of the cavorite works. The man paused and a face disguised by stubble peered up at the words painted on the wrought-iron sign over the factory gates.

Syzygy Industries
Greenwich Facility

He regarded it for a moment with his one good eye, an inscrutable expression on his lined and filthy face. The clothes he wore were just as much a mess as he was, marking him out as some kind of derelict. But a derelict was unlikely to have been carrying a crowbar and certainly wouldn't have had a rucksack full of explosives on his back.

He had been watching the plant for days. And now that he had acquired all that he needed to complete his self-appointed mission from his criminal contacts, he was ready to make his move. Tonight was the night that Jared Shurin would pay for what he was yet to do.

Pulling his cap down firmly over his unruly mess of hair, so that its brim hid his face, shooting glances both left and right, he stepped out into the street. Atop one of the granite gateposts, a camera whirred as it rotated from left to right and back again. Choosing his moment carefully, the man darted across the street, pressing his back to the gatepost as the camera panned back across the street again.

Holding his breath, he waited, his heart thumping against his ribs. The moment the gates were out of sight of the automated lens, he clambered up and over, landing in a crouch on the other side of the gates.

Glancing left and right once more, and seeing no-one, he hefted the pack onto his shoulder and, keeping low, made for the barn-like structure ahead of him.

The growl – crackling and tinny – stopped him dead in his tracks.

The man remained frozen, eyes on the shadows ahead of him, as the guard dog walked stiffly towards him from out of the darkness. Its metal body gleamed dully in the light of distant streetlamps, the *tap-tap-tap* of its paws on the cobbles sounding like ball bearings dropping onto a pavement.

The man's one remaining eye locked onto the glowing red lenses of the automaton's optical scanners. The metal dog stopped, opening gin-trap jaws filled with gleaming steel fangs, the synthesised growl issuing from a speaker located in its throat.

Moving nothing other than his arm, the man put a hand into a jacket pocket and took something out, which he then offered to the dog. The automaton studied the proffered item and immediately stopped growling. The growl died in the attack dog's throat and it promptly sat back on its haunches, wagging its brass coil stub of a tail.

"Good dog," the man whispered, reaching for something from his pack this time. "Here, hold this. And don't go anywhere."

JIMMYING THE SKYLIGHT open with the crowbar, the infiltrator took in the long drop to the floor of the manufactory fifty feet below. The sounds of clanking machinery and bubbling cavorite rose to him from the depths of the building accompanied by the asthmatic wheeze of venting pressure valves. The processing shed was bathed in an insipid amber glow. There was a greasy quality to the muggy air rising. Carefully, he stowed the crowbar in his pack.

The plant was in operation twenty-four hours a day, as a result of the current political climate, even in spite of the curfew. After all, word was that war was coming, a scale of war unheard of before in the history of not only Magna Britannia but that of the entire human race. A veritable war of the worlds.

But, as some concession to the curfew implemented across the capital in the aftermath of the Wormwood Catastrophe, the Syzygy Cavorite Works only operated a skeleton workforce during the graveyard shift. Of the few men on duty that night – security guards, machine operators and cavorite smelters – none were within sight at that moment.

Easing himself through the open skylight, the man lowered himself on his arms. He hung from the window's edge for a moment, feeling a twinge of remembered pain tug at his left shoulder.

Then, releasing his grip on the sill, he dropped the ten feet that remained between him and the suspended steel walkway, landing in a crouch, absorbing the force of the impact through his legs. Any noise he might have made was drowned by the ceaseless background hubbub of the processing plant itself.

Keeping low, the curlicue-ornamented railings of the walkway helping him remain invisible, he followed the bolted sections of the gantry as it traversed the length of the building, always heading towards the heart of the cavorite production plant.

Ten yards further on, the walkway became a flight of grilled metal steps. The man paused at the top and took something from his pack. It was hemispherical in shape, roughly the same size as half a chopped apple. Holding the black metal device against the railing with one hand, he flicked a switch with the other and the object immediately snapped flush to the metal as its mag-lock was activated. At the same time a tiny red bulb began to wink on and off repeatedly.

Giving the limpet mine one last look, just to ensure that it was working as it should, he scampered down the stairs two at a time, as quickly and as quietly as he could.

More suspended walkways and further stairs brought him at last to the steam-smothered factory floor and the cavorite production line.

The amber light was a product of the process itself – the ruddy orange glow of molten metals and other ingredients coursed along channels in the floor, or splashed in brilliant, glaring droplets from the ore buckets above.

Flicking the switch of a mag-grenade he tossed it into the air, where it abruptly changed direction, shooting sideways and latching onto the pivot of a bucket brimming with liquid metal.

He wiped a scorched and filthy sleeve across his forehead, smearing sweat and dirt across his brow. Sweat prickled on his back and soaked his armpits. Quickly, choosing between a pillar and a smelting engine for the location of the next limpet device, the saboteur finally plumped for the engine before taking shelter in the shadows on the far side of the shed, underneath another walkway secured to the rusting corrugated side of the manufactory barn.

There he waited, listening for any sounds that would betray the presence of an employee, or the *tap-tap-tap* of an attack dog's approach.

Unable to pick out anything out of the ordinary – for a cavorite processing plant at least – keeping to the wall and the shadows, the man moved from the smelting works into the ever so slightly cooler atmosphere of the house-sized laboratory, where the combination of the various molten metals and other ingredients was controlled by Babbage engine-regulated machinery. This was also under the constant supervision and critical stares of human supervisors. For, as the old adage had it: *To err is human – to really screw things up takes a Babbage engine.*

It was here that he would really have to watch himself.

He could make out two of the supervisors on the other side of the vaulted dome. They were dressed in long-sleeved once-white coats and heavy, vulcanised rubber aprons. Large-lensed brass goggles masked much of their faces.

The two men were pacing up and down in front of a bank of steel logic engines, clipboards and styluses in hand. They were wholly oblivious to the saboteur's presence within the laboratory.

Making the most of that fact, he darted from the gargantuan doorway that connected the two parts of the plant, ducking under a tangle of pipes. Using the cyclopean plumbing for cover, he approached the overseers' position, clamping another limpet mine to one of the blistering conduits as he did so.

He was only a dozen yards from the cogitator banks now. The technicians monitoring them were still unaware of his presence, thanks to the background hubbub of the factory eradicating the sound of his footsteps altogether. And, of course, no alarms had been sounded, no security posts alerted to his presence within the plant. But that would all change in only a matter of minutes.

Heart racing, every sense alert and straining, his mind working overtime, he watched and waited for the perfect moment. If he made a move for the next chamber – the one where the finished cavorite was stored – the technicians would see him. But they stayed exactly where they were and time continued to tick by, to the point that the saboteur began to worry that the placated mechanical mastiff would be found by a patrolling security guard before he was able to finish his work.

If he wanted to hit Shurin where it would really hurt, he needed to get to the cavorite store. What he needed was a distraction.

Retreating back the way he had just come, he soon found what he was looking for. Taking the crowbar from his pack he forced it into the mechanism of a pressure valve in one of the criss-crossing pipes above his head and pulled hard. The metal twisted as the valve was wrenched open. With a noisy rush of venting steam, a thick mist soon filled the chamber.

He heard the startled cries of the two overseers and them hurrying towards him, even as he doubled back and snuck round behind them, throwing a last magnet mine behind the banks of Babbage engines as he did so. And then he was through into the cavorite containment chamber itself.

An ambient heat filled the chamber, emanating from the six huge crucibles that filled the cathedral-like space. The air was redolent with the coppery stink of hot metal.

As long as cavorite was kept at a temperature above sixty degrees Fahrenheit, and it remained in a liquid state, it behaved just like any other molten alloy. It was only as it dropped below sixty degrees Fahrenheit that its gravity-shielding properties exerted themselves. It was cavorite that made space travel possible. Without it, there would not have been any colonies on the Moon or Mars.

A grim smile twisting his lips, the saboteur set to work, every one of the vast crucibles acquiring a mag-locked limpet-mine.

When he was finished he opened his rucksack again and peered inside. At the bottom of the bag lay the crowbar, just one more of the magnet-mines, and a slim, black metal device, not unlike a lighter in form. Taking these items from the bag he cast the empty rucksack aside and considered his escape route.

Footsteps echoed hollowly in the vaulted space of the cavorite containment facility.

"Hey! Who are you? What are you doing here?"

He spun round to be greeted by the shocked expression on the face of a technician.

"What are you..."

The words died on the overseer's lips as he caught the desperate glint in the saboteur's remaining eye and saw what he was holding in his hand. Cold realisation dawned and he began to scan the chamber and the crucibles with rising panic.

"Dear God, no!"

"Dear God, yes, I think you'll find," the saboteur declared.

He flicked a switch on the last device and hurled it at the side of the barn in front of him, before throwing himself behind one of the massive cavorite containers.

The black hemisphere snapped onto the rusted iron bulkhead, its tiny red bulb flicked on, and the device promptly detonated.

Smoke and noise filled the factory barn and the technician staggered backwards, putting his hands to his face, as his companion joined him.

As the smoke cleared, the roughly man-sized hole in the side of the factory shed was revealed, all ragged metal edges and smouldering steel. But of the saboteur who had made it, there was no sign.

SOMEWHERE NEARBY A siren began to wail.

He could hear shouts now and the tinny barking of attack dogs. He didn't turn back, but kept running.

The main gates lay a hundred yards ahead. To his right loomed the massive, cathedral-like structures of the cavorite works. It was time.

It his left hand he held the crowbar, in his right the detonator.

With a savage snarl, an automaton flew out of the shadows between two steel pillars, jaws open wide, its fangs snagging the sleeve of his jacket. As the man reacted, pulling his arm clear of the snapping gin-trap teeth, he lost his grip on the detonator and the device tumbled away from him, clattering across the cobbles.

For a moment, the man wondered whether the knock might activate the detonator but there was no accompanying series of detonations. And then his attention was fully back on the dog.

There was a ripping sound as the mastiff landed, much of the sleeve of the man's jacket trapped between its teeth. The automaton spun round, snarling, and leapt for the man again.

This time he was ready for it.

The crowbar, swung with both hands, caught the creature round the side of the head. The resulting clang was accompanied by a snapping metal sound and sparks burst from the rent in the robot's neck joint.

The dog howled – its synthesised yowling buzzing with static – and dropped to the ground at the man's feet. He swung again, this time bringing the crowbar down on top of its steel skull. The light in the mastiff's baleful red eyes faded.

The saboteur immediately began scrabbling around on the ground as he desperately searched for the detonator. The sounds made by the approaching security guards and yet more automaton attack dogs was getting louder. And then his fingers closed on something small and metallic. Without hesitation he found the trigger and pressed the activation switch.

Rising slowly, he turned to face the approaching security contingent, a smug smile on his lips and a manic glint in his eye.

The first explosion took out a series of skylights in the factory roof, sending sheets of flames roiling into the sky. The second was followed by a groaning crash as the great ore bucket hit the factory floor, molten metal pouring from it in a torrent that melted or set fire to much of the smeltery.

Men and dogs were sent reeling as the rest of the magnet mines touched off in quick succession. The initial detonations were soon followed by secondary booming explosions, as the processing plant began to tear itself apart.

As the initial phase of destruction came to an end, the chaos evolved in new and incredible ways.

Pieces of the factory began to rise into the air. It was only small pieces at first – shattered pipework, wall panels, chunks of rubble – but then larger sections of the factory began to ascend– roof struts, one of the massive crucibles, even some of the sheets of metal that had formed the factory floor.

In the initial explosions, liquid cavorite had been blasted all across the interior of the vaulted storage chamber. Now, as it began to cool against the surface of everything it had touched, so its anti-gravitic properties came into effect. Vast pieces of the manufactory – some of them ablaze – disappeared as they hurtled skyward, enveloped by the Smog that lay over the city like a tramp's blanket.

In a stunned state of disbelieving shock, those pursuing the saboteur focused on the one thing that still made sense to them; that the felon responsible for the attack was getting away!

The gate was only fifty yards away now. The man sprinted towards it, pursued by the security guards. A shot rang out, but the shooter's aim was off and the bullet threw a chip from one of the stone gateposts.

The attack dog that had intercepted him on his arrival at the plant was waiting just where he had left it. It turned, aural receptors detecting his approach. Seeing him, the automaton began to wag its tail.

The others were close on his heels now. The scrape of the dogs' steel claws on the cobbles sounded uncomfortably close now.

He sprinted past the squatting automaton.

"Good dog," he said. "Drop."

The mechanical mastiff obediently opened its mouth and the hemispherical metal device that had been clamped between its jaws fell to the ground, as the man threw himself at the gates and began to climb.

The detonation lifted the approaching security guards off their feet, hurling them backwards in a cloud of smoke and oily flames. The attack dogs were caught at the epicentre of the blast. What was left of the automatons clattered down around the security guards moments later.

As the smoke cleared and the men climbed painfully to their feet, the factory continuing to burn and break apart behind them – the Royal Observatory itself atop its distant hill lit up by the growing conflagration – they looked to the gates of the cavorite works. But the saboteur was gone.

CHAPTER TWO

A Trip to the Moon

T minus 5 days, 6 hours, 7 minutes, 40 seconds

UP CLOSE, THE vessel was even more impressive than it had appeared on the kinema news reels. It was truly immense, travelling between worlds like some vast leviathan whale navigating the ether currents of space. In form it appeared to be part ocean liner and part gothic cathedral.

Ulysses Quicksilver gazed up at the flank of the vessel, its control turrets towering above him like skyscrapers. The name of the craft was spelled out in letters of hammered iron thirty feet high:

APOLLO XIII

As its name suggested, there had been twelve previous vessels in the *Apollo* line – all operated by Sol Cruises (which was itself owned by Syzygy Industries), and all still in operation – but there had never been a spaceship quite like this one before.

Three years in the making, costing millions of pounds, it was the pride of the Earth-Moon spaceways, and had been in operation for two years already, with an expected working lifespan of more than fifty. It was the luxury space-liner of its day but then, as Ulysses Quicksilver reasoned, if you're going to travel, you might as well travel in style.

Looking at this prime example of the opulence the Neo-Victorian age had to offer, it was easy to put the troubles still facing London from his mind.

The capital lay ten miles and more to the east, still shrouded by the Smog, despite the former Prime Minister Valentine's best efforts to improve things for those living under its permanent pall.

But of course, the Smog wasn't the only thing Londinium Maximum had to worry about. As Ulysses knew from painful firsthand experience, there was another blight upon the city now as well.

Despite Ulysses having helped to eradicate the hive that had taken up residence in the shell of St Paul's Cathedral, there were still pockets of Locust infestation throughout the city, sealed off from those areas that had escaped the Wormwood Catastrophe by hastily-erected barricades and concrete walls thirty feet high. And it now looked as if it was going to remain that way for some time to come, as the authorities continued to struggle to clear up the mess that had been left after the Jupiter Station's launch.

Considering all that he had been through since the disaster, despite being dubbed 'Hero of the Empire', by the popular press, Ulysses Quicksilver was quite happy to let somebody else deal with the nation's problems for a change. Besides, he had been given the distinct impression that he was *persona non grata* in certain political circles, despite having saved the life of the crowned head of Russia – even if he had put a gun to the Tsarina's head in order to do so.

"You know what?" he said, gazing at the vessel resting on the tarmac of the Heathrow spaceport in front of him.

"No, sir. What?"

"I'm ready for a holiday."

"Yes, sir. I'm not surprised," Nimrod replied. "It's been quite a few weeks."

"I was thinking more along the lines of quite a few months. In fact I'd go so far as to say it's been quite a year."

"Ah, I see, sir. Yes, of course, what with Her Majesty's 161st jubilee fast approaching."

"Precisely."

"And it will be good to see Master Bartholomew again, I suppose," Nimrod added, his aquiline expression unreadable.

Ulysses looked at him askance. "Will it?"

"I thought it the appropriate thing to say, sir, given the situation."

"Ah, of course."

It had been several months since Barty had made this self-same journey, fleeing to the Moon to escape the troubles that had built up for him here on Earth. Ulysses and Barty might have had their differences in the past, as brothers are wont to do – particularly when Barty tried to have his older brother declared dead so that he might inherit their late father's entire estate – but they were brothers nonetheless, bound by blood and the tragic deaths of their parents when the two men had been little more than children.

But it had taken Lord Octavius De Wynter – Ulysses' employer, for want of a better description – to suggest that he might like to visit Barty at his new domicile on the Moon.

Barty hadn't left a forwarding address but Ulysses enjoyed enough contacts in sufficiently high up places to make the discovery of such a thing a mere afternoon's intellectual exercise.

Accompanied by wailing klaxons, the *Apollo XIII's* boarding ramps began to descend, apertures opening in the hull of the craft in order to admit those waiting to board. Those who had made the journey from the Moon to the Earth had already disembarked earlier that day.

Automaton porters poured from the ship, ready to help those coming aboard with their luggage, as the barriers that had kept Ulysses and his fellow travellers penned in until the captain and crew were ready for them to board, cantilevered upwards.

Many cheered in excitement, it being their first time on board a space-liner. Others – in general, those used to travelling in such style already – maintained a more sober facade as they walked up the gangplanks and into the belly of the beast.

Considering what London and its populace had undergone in recent months, there were still plenty able to afford a trip to the Moon. But then the realm of Magna Britannia was vast in its compass, containing an approximated three billion souls.

The Wormwood Catastrophe had been the final straw for many, prompting some to up sticks and make a permanent move to one of the lunar colonies. So it was that alongside the businessmen and the well-do-to gentry now boarding the *Apollo XIII*, were whole families, who had scrimped and saved every penny they could, selling their very homes to pay for their berths aboard the great liner, intending to start again – as Ulysses' brother had done – a quarter of a million miles away on an airless lump of rock.

Things must have been bad for them here on Earth, if moving to the Moon was the preferred choice.

Ulysses surveyed the press of people struggling with suitcases, bird cages and hat boxes. He looked at his own luggage – a few meagre packing trunks. containing only a couple of dozen changes of clothes, stacked on a trolley behind which Nimrod was labouring.

Putting two fingers to his lips, he whistled. Almost instantly one of the clockwork porters appeared at his side.

"How may I be of service, sir?" the brass and teak construct asked chirpily. The running lights of the vast liner reflected brightly from the polished dome of its cranium plate.

"Deal with these, would you? Cabin number..." Ulysses checked the number on the gold embossed tickets in his hand before glancing at the name engraved on the shield crest welded to the automaton drudge's chest plate. "Number 32A, if you would be so kind, Reg?"

"Certainly, sir," the droid chirruped. "It would be a pleasure."

As the automaton took charge of their luggage, Ulysses and Nimrod joined the press of people excitedly setting foot on the boarding ramp of the spaceship. Making their way forwards, they were funnelled towards the nearest airlock, and found themselves rubbing shoulders with all manner of individuals, from almost every strata of society – or so it seemed.

Despite his best efforts to the contrary, Ulysses found himself jostled from all sides, bumping into a young woman to his right.

"Excuse me, madam," he apologised, acknowledging the woman with a curt nod and stepping back to allow her to go first.

"Ulysses?"

Ulysses' gaze snapped back to regard the young lady. "Emilia?"

And there she was, as lovely as the day he had last seen her. Yet she looked different, somehow.

It took Ulysses a moment to realise that she wasn't wearing a mourning dress as she had been the last time he had seen her. And she was wearing her golden hair loose about her shoulders, and not tied up in a severe bun anymore. In fact the dress, waistcoat and top hat she was wearing were the height of fashion and a startling cyan, with turquoise detailing.

She blushed under Ulysses' sudden scrutiny and he felt his own cheeks redden in response. How was it that she could still have this effect on him, three years after the two of them had broken off their engagement?

It took another to break the silence that had descended between the erstwhile lovers caught within their own private universe of calm as passengers milled past them.

"Hello, Quicksilver."

The sound of the old man's voice jerked Ulysses out of his reverie and he turned to see the diminutive Alexander Oddfellow. Despite being in his seventies he looked a lot better than he had the last time Ulysses had seen him, pale and wasted, smothered beneath bed-sheets, having been missing, presumed dead, for three months.

The colour was back in his cheeks. His white hair was swept back from his forehead and alive with a lustrous sheen. The sparkle in the old man's eyes had returned as well. In fact, he looked much more like the Alexander Oddfellow Ulysses had known when he had been prospective son-in-law material.

"Fancy meeting you here."

"Fancy indeed," Ulysses replied, blinking as if coming round from a session of hypnosis. "Yes, in fact, what *are* you doing here?"

"We only went and won a competition, didn't we?"

"Really?"

"Yes! An all expenses paid luxury trip to the Moon." Oddfellow beamed.

"I can see." Ulysses smiled back at the old man. "Travelling in style, aren't you?"

"No expense spared. Travelling first class, don't you know?"

"Right. Well. That all sounds very nice," Ulysses stumbled. The jostling of those trying to barge past him to get onto the ship was getting worse.

"This way, please sir," Reg the Porter called back from the airlock, having already taken Ulysses' luggage on board.

"Right. Yes. Well, best be off."

"It's been lovely bumping into you like this, Ulysses," Emilia said.

"Yes. And you too. Well, maybe we'll bump into each other again on board," he said, his usual cool suddenly completely collapsed.

"I expect we will. Good day to you. Nimrod."

"Ma'am." Ulysses' manservant replied stiffly.

And with that, Emilia Oddfellow and her father joined the throng making their way on board. Ulysses watched her go, stunned into silence.

"Cabin 32A's this way, if you please sir," the droid called.

"What? Oh, yes, of course."

And so Ulysses Quicksilver, accompanied by his manservant Nimrod, boarded the vessel, although his mind was a million miles away already.

FURTHER BACK DOWN the line of businessmen, tourists and emigrants, another helpful droid-porter approached a young couple who were weighed down with all manner of heavy-looking packing trunks and travelling cases. Not unlike Miss Emilia Oddfellow and Mr Ulysses Quicksilver, Esquire, they too were dressed in the latest fashions – a high-buttoned full-length maroon dress and matching bonnet for her, and a three piece tweed suit, yellow crushed silk waistcoat and top hat for him. But unlike the dandy and his former fiancée they didn't appear to be comfortable asking for assistance.

"May I help you there, sir?" the porter asked, seeing the gentleman struggling to balance the trolley on which most of the black packing cases had been stacked. Meanwhile, his companion was struggling with another trunk that moved on castors of its own.

"No, I'm fine," Mr Lars Chapter snapped back.

At that moment one of the trolley's wheels decided that it wanted to go in the opposite direction to the other three and the contraption slewed sideways. As he struggled to regain control of the erratic trolley, the man's top hat tumbled from his head, a shock of blond hair escaping from beneath it. By contrast, his partner's tresses were almost blue-black in hue, and were contained within a hair-net beneath her own bonnet.

"Are you sure, sir?" the droid asked, moving to help the man. "It's no trouble."

"I've told you already, I don't need your help."

"Madame," the automaton persisted, turning to the smartly-dressed young woman instead, "may I be of assistance?"

"Bugger off and leave us alone!" Miss Veronica Verse hissed in response, her choice of words at odds with the cut-glass tone of her upper class accent. "We'll manage."

And so the pair continued to make their way up the boarding ramp.

UNSEEN BY ALL, at an adjacent boarding ramp, one jacket sleeve hanging by a thread, a roughly dressed vagabond hid himself in the press of people making for Steerage. Pulling his cap down hard, almost over his eyes, he shot furtive glances at Ulysses Quicksilver and his manservant as they boarded, as well as Mr Lars Chapter and Miss Veronica Verse, with his one good eye.

He shuffled forwards at the centre of the throng made up of the great unwashed, those hoping to find work and homes on the Moon, such things having been denied them here on Earth.

As he waved his cardboard ticket at the automaton on the gate, the man scratched at the thickening stubble on his chin. It was almost a beard now.

Start a new life on the Moon, the campaign posters had said.

Or change the course of an existing one, he considered, rubbing at the hole behind his eye-patch. *Or, even better, prevent one from ever having existed.*

CHAPTER THREE

Fantastic Voyage

T minus 5 days, 39 minutes, 2 seconds

ALL PASSENGERS HAVING boarded, the crew manifest double-checked, the embarkation ramps raised and stowed, the airlocks sealed and final checks completed, with the airspace over Heathrow cleared of dirigible traffic, *Apollo XIII* rose gracefully heavenward.

Such smooth motion and manoeuvrability were only possible thanks to the miracle alloy, cavorite. Without Dr Cavor's literally ground-breaking discovery, the final frontier would have remained out of bounds to the Victorian Empire of Magna Britannia.

Attitude thrusters fired, swinging the vast vessel's prow around as it continued to rise, the lights of London soon dwindling below it, the twisted thoroughfares of the city tangled around them, until all disappeared beneath the putrid blanket of the Smog.

"We are now clear of the terminal," the helmsman announced as a bell chimed somewhere on the bridge of the space-liner.

"Very good, Mr Goodspeed," Captain Trevelyan responded from his seat in the middle of the bridge, smiling comfortably and stroking his thick white handlebar moustache.

He was in his element here. In fact, there was nowhere else he would rather be than on the bridge of a spaceship. Nelson Trevelyan was just like his father in that respect. He had piloted countless flights from the Earth to the Moon and all this was second nature to him now.

"In your own time then, Mr Goodspeed, take her up."

"Thank you, captain." Goodspeed turned the huge ship's wheel gently to port. "Mr Wallace, half ahead full."

"Half ahead full."

Captain Trevelyan stared out of the view-shield in front of him. It was made from toughened glass, several inches thick; in reality two separate pieces of glass that formed a sandwich with a microscopically thin film of pure gold trapped between them, to protect those on the bridge from being fried by the sun when the *Apollo* left the Earth's atmosphere. It was such seemingly innocuous elements that made space-liners some of the most expensive machines in existence. And yet fleets of them made the journey from the Earth to its satellite several times a week. Of course, the flights to Mars had become seriously restricted over the course of the last year.

All that he could see now beyond the reinforced glass were banks of cloud and the occasional distant airship.

"Ensign?" Trevelyan clicked his fingers, bringing a gleaming brass automaton clanking over to his position.

"Yes, captain?" it said, saluting smartly.

"Mr Goodspeed and Mr Wallace seem to have everything in hand here, so perhaps you'd be so good as to fetch me a cup of tea. Earl Grey. Cream, not milk."

"Very good, captain." And with that the automaton trotted off to fulfil its captain's orders to the best of its ability.

Yes, Captain Nelson Trevelyan thought, as he eased himself into the well-worn indentations of his chair, this was going to be another pleasurable three days of being waited on hand and foot, interspersed with fine dining with his personally hand-picked selection of interesting guests at the captain's table. He could see no reason why this shouldn't be like any other trip to the Moon.

THAT EVENING, THE first leg of the journey to the Moon complete, the place to be was the Milky Way Bar on C deck. With the Earth's cloud-smudged southern hemisphere aesthetically framed within the bar's thirty-foot long panoramic window, with a particularly fine view of Antarctica City, and Harry 'Fingers' Malone on piano, that well-known and notorious raconteur and teller of tall tales – all of them true – the man known as the Hero of the Empire, survivor of the Wormwood Catastrophe and saviour of the Russian royal family, Ulysses Lucien Quicksilver himself, was regaling the bar's clientele.

"And so that's how I brought the bugger down, one swift, sharp poke to the brain with the tip of my blade."

"I remember seeing that on the news reels," one of the dandy's young, female admirers added, as if his story need corroborating. "It was just before the Darwinian Dawn took over the airwaves and released their ransom demand, wasn't it?

"That's right," Ulysses said, suddenly grim.

"What happened to the Megasaur after that?" a young man asked, an expression of wide-eyed awe on his face.

"You know what?" Ulysses said, taking another swig of the cognac somebody – he didn't know who – had kindly acquired for him. "I don't know."

"I heard a rumour you had something to do with that fire at the Royal Botanical Gardens," a bespectacled academic interjected.

Ulysses grunted noncommittally.

Picking up his glass again, he took another sip as he regarded the crowd of men and women gathered around him at the bar, every single one of them hanging on his every word. Thanks to his charm and natural charisma, and in no small part the many stories he had to tell, he had them eating out of the palm of his hand.

He smiled. He could get used to all this attention.

"Tell us about the time you brought down the Jupiter Station," said another.

"Well, that wasn't actually me," Ulysses said.

"But you were there, on board, with the traitor Wormwood," an older gent dressed in Harris Tweed and with a young woman – supposedly his 'niece' dangling off his arm – challenged drunkenly.

"Well yes, but I didn't set the explosives."

"I heard you met the Tsarina Anastasia," a young woman wearing a sequinned evening gown that accentuated her well-proportioned curves, interjected, leaning close. The front of her dress sagged, Ulysses feeling he could fall into her gaping cleavage at any moment.

"My, why you're a pretty little thing, aren't you?" he gasped in tipsy surprise.

His head spun. He must have had more to drink than he realised. The blonde simpered in response, looking up at him from beneath thick lashes. She stumbled and, as she recovered, one of her hands somehow ended up resting upon Ulysses' thigh.

"And yes, I've met the Tsarina."

"What's she like?" the young woman said. "Is she pretty, like they say?"

"She's not a patch on you, I'll say that much," Ulysses slurred, unable to take his eyes off the woman's décolletage.

At that the heiress laughed, her breasts joggling together in sympathy.

"Might I be so bold as to ask you your name, young lady?" Ulysses said.

"Barbara."

"Just Barbara?" he raised a flirtatious eyebrow.

"Well, Lady Barbara Mathilda Trevithick, if you want to be boringly formal."

"Ah!" Ulysses exclaimed, quickly snatching his gaze from her chest. "As in heir to the Trevithick steam velocipede millions?"

"The very same," the blonde said, with a giggle, fixing her limpid blue eyes on his. "But you can calls me Babs."

"Very well then, Baps," Ulysses slurred, taking another slug of cognac from his glass. "And what's a nice young lady like you doing on the last starship from Earth?"

"Why the Grand Tour, of course."

"Of course." Ulysses had undertaken the Tour himself, back in his youth, over a decade ago now. He hadn't been off-planet since returning from seeing the rings of Saturn all those years ago. "And you're travelling... alone?"

"Oh no, perish the thought," the young woman laughed, her ripple of mirth passing through the milk-white flesh of her breasts.

"Ah, you have a chaperone." The dandy shot furtive glances at the faces of those individuals making up the rest of the party.

"My godmother, but she's retired early. She's yet to find her space-legs. At least that was the excuse she gave."

Ulysses relaxed. "Ah, good, glad to hear it. I... I mean, I hope she feels better soon. Meanwhile..."

"I'm also travelling with my friends here."

"Your friends?"

At this point Lady Trevithick indicated another shapely young woman – a redhead, this time – perched on a stool a little further along the bar, wearing an equally daring black, sparkly number, and a raven-haired beauty, in a strappy sapphire gown, hugging a blushing young man. At being introduced to the world-renowned dandy, however, she quickly slipped her arm from around his waist and sashayed over to Ulysses, linking her arm with the blonde's and provoking all manner of wild thoughts within the dandy's brandy-soaked brain.

"How absolutely charming to meet you," Ulysses delighted. "And you are?" he asked the raven-haired beauty who was now also leaning towards him, showing off her high, pert breasts.

"Lady Fanny Fanshaw," she said, fluttering her eyelids.

"Really?"

"Really. Daddy's Lord Cecil Fanshaw, Earl of Midsomer."

"Fanny and I were at finishing school in Geneva together," Babs explained.

Ulysses turned his attention to the redhead now. Aware of his interest, the young woman made a great show of uncrossing and then crossing her legs again, her dress falling open to the thigh. Ulysses swallowed hard, unable to take his eyes off the smooth pale flesh so exposed.

"And you are?"

"Pussy."

"Yes, of course you are."

"Pussy Willow."

"And I suppose you'd be heiress to the Willow Pattern crockery company."

"You know your Who's Who, Mr Quicksilver," Pussy purred.

"So what are we going to do with you?" Ulysses said, stroking the inside of the blonde's forearm with a finger.

"I'm sure you can think of something," Fanny Fanshaw said beguilingly.

"I'll... see you later?" the young man Lady Fanshaw had begun the conversation with her arm around stuttered, but nobody was listening, least of all Fanny. Knowing that the better man had won, taking his drink in hand, he made for an empty table in front of the panoramic window, as far from Ulysses and the fickle heiresses as possible.

"Ladies, did you know there's a gravity-free pool on board?" Ulysses enquired of his female hangers-on.

"Yes, we were, weren't we girls?" Lady Trevithick replied. "But I didn't bring my swimming costume with me." This last comment resulted in a flurry of giggles from her friends.

"Oh, I'm sure that won't be a problem," Ulysses said.

"Sounds like fun," Babs said, pulling herself closer.

Ulysses found himself lost in her gaze once more. "My, but you're a pretty little thing, aren't you?"

"And it's nice to see you too."

Startled, Ulysses looked up.

Standing between Ulysses' admirers and the entrance to the Milky Way Bar was Emilia Oddfellow, dressed in a much more understated cerise evening gown, and on the arm of her elderly father.

"Emilia!"

"Good evening, Ulysses."

The trio of heiresses looked her up and down with undisguised disdain.

"Quicksilver," the old man said with a curt nod. Then his grim-set expression gave way to a broad smile. "Ladies."

"What a... pleasant surprise," Ulysses gabbled, finding himself both abruptly, and horribly, sober, and suddenly tongue-tied.

Emilia gave the women a withering look and then turned to Ulysses, a disappointed smile on her pursed lips.

"Well, it's certainly a surprise."

"Can I get you a drink?" Ulysses offered feebly. "A glass of champagne, perhaps?"

"No, it's all right. I wouldn't want to interrupt."

Emilia and her father began to make their way towards a table with a grand view of the panoramic window. "Oh, father. It really is incredible, isn't it?" she suddenly blurted out, her gasp of awe catching in her throat as she caught sight of the Earth through the inches-thick glass.

"Honestly, it's no trouble," Ulysses called after her, struggling to free himself from the women who had draped themselves across his shoulders like over-priced, gaudy ornaments. "These are just some friends of mine. Really, you wouldn't be interrupting anything."

"Yes she would," Babs interjected snidely. Emilia returned the pouting heiress's scornful stare.

"No, it's all right, Ulysses. You enjoy yourself. Good evening."

"Let's do dinner then. Another night. Tomorrow?"

"We'll see," Emilia said, noncommittally, giving the preening heiresses another disapproving look. "Good evening, Ulysses."

"Good evening, Quicksilver," old man Oddfellow added, abruptly severe again. "Ladies."

Ulysses watched as Emilia and her father made their way across the shag-pile carpet – embroidered with a needle worker's approximation of the galaxy in silver thread – and took a seat at the same table as Lady Fanshaw's erstwhile companion. The young man's mood, Ulysses noticed, improved dramatically.

"Now where were we, before we were so rudely interrupted?" Babs said, lasciviously. "Weren't you about to suggest a spot of zero-g skinny dipping?"

Ulysses stared disconsolately at the bottom of his glass. "Not tonight, ladies, if you don't mind."

"Very well," Pussy Willow said, rising gracefully from her seat, "then how about a nightcap in my cabin?"

Ulysses met her sultry gaze with a hard stare of his own. "Really. Not tonight. I'm not in the mood."

"Be like that then, Mr Quicksilver," Babs said, removing herself from about his person. "But you just missed out on the night of your life.

"You could have been an Earl," her friend Fanny added. "Come on girls."

And with that the three heiresses left, arm in arm, champagne glasses in hand and still with mischief on their minds.

"Of all the bars, on all the ships, in all the solar systems," Ulysses mumbled to himself as Nimrod emerged from the shadowy corner where he had secluded himself, making his own unimpressed appraisal of the giggling socialites, "and she had to walk into mine."

"Yes, sir."

Ulysses emptied his glass and put it down hard on the bar. "Come on, I'm ready for bed."

Nimrod raised one arching eyebrow. "Very good, sir."

In Cabin 69C, three decks down, the door securely locked, Mr Lars Chapter sprung open the clasps of the largest of the black packing cases he had struggled to bring on board with Miss Veronica Verse.

"Very impressive," Verse said, looking down at the gleaming weapon lying within the velvet-lined indentation in the box.

"A Bradshaw and Wembley Repeating Rifle," Chapter said proudly. "A hundred rounds a minute and capable of dropping a Mastodon at fifty yards."

"Open this one next," Verse said tapping another trunk, pupils dilating.

Chapter did as he was told. She watched as the man clicked open the metal fasteners and eased back the lid. Verse moaned with pleasure.

"A Maxwell and Browning Blunderbuss."

"And this one!" Verse shrieked, practically jumping up and down in excitement.

"A Klosh Gentleman's Personal Artillery Bazooka," Chapter said, and then he gasped, as she suddenly threw herself at him, sending the two of them falling onto the bed with a crash. They began kissing each other hungrily, hands fumbling with buttons and clasps, pulling each other free of their clothing.

"Now there's one weapon of yours in particular I want to get my hands on," Verse gasped and began frantically tugging at the buttons of his fly, already able to feel the bulge beneath pressing against her thigh.

CHAPTER FOUR

Mars Attacks

T minus 4 days, 14 hours, 9 minutes, 42 seconds

"I'm GLAD YOU accepted my invitation," Ulysses said, as he and Emilia took their places at dinner the following evening.

The whole of the Earth was visible now through the windows of the Restaurant Galaxia, a blue-green thumbprint against the black canvas of the void.

"And why's that then?" Emilia asked, resting her elbows on the table and her chin on her hands, fixing Ulysses with a penetrating stare.

"Well... You know." Ulysses could feel himself blushing. He wasn't usually like this around women. In fact he wasn't ever like this around women; only with her.

"Go on. I'm all ears."

In the past, he'd been the one in control. Now their roles had been reversed, it seemed.

"Well, I wanted to apologise, for one thing."

"For everything? Or just for last night?"

"Last night will do for starters." Ulysses looked down at the starched white tablecloth. "That wasn't me, last night."

"What do you mean?" Emilia didn't sound impressed.

"That's not what I'm like."

"No, I think that's exactly what you're like." Emilia frowned. "How was your evening, or daren't I ask?"

"Quiet."

"Really?"

"And expensive. Nimrod's quite the devil when it comes to gin rummy. How was yours?"

"Quiet."

"What did you do?"

"Father and I watched the patchwork of continents spin by the panoramic window, listened to the pianist and then retired for the night. You know, I've not been able to shut him up since he... you know," – now it was her turn to struggle to find the right words – "since he came back. It's as if he's realised how it could all end at any moment and doesn't want to waste a single minute of the time we have left together."

Ulysses nodded. The rattle of cutlery on bone china merged with the hubbub of murmuring voices in the quiet ambience of the restaurant.

"I'm sorry," Ulysses said, his voice sounding louder than he had meant it to.

Several diners at other tables glanced round, scowls on their faces.

Emilia Oddfellow looked back, flashing them a placatory smile. "You're sorry?"

"Yes. For not calling after the whole thing with your cousin Dashwood and the Sphere. For not being the man you needed me to be... you know... before." At last he looked up from where he had been fiddling with the tablecloth and met her gaze. "Like I said; for everything."

Emilia took a deep breath and sat back in her chair.

"That was quite some apology," she said.

"Well it's been long overdue."

Ulysses' expression relaxed then and he gave Emilia a warm smile. She, in turn, leant forward, resting her chin on her hands again.

"You know, if you carry on like this you'll have me falling in love with you all over again."

Emilia half closed her eyes as Ulysses, fully understanding what was expected of him now, leaned forward, wetting his lips with the tip of his tongue.

Beyond the nearest observation window, a million shooting stars flared, trailing flame, as they tore across the vast gulf of space.

Ulysses paused, a split second from the moment of contact – feeling Emilia's breath evaporating the moisture from his lips – and turned.

"What's that?" he muttered.

Emilia sighed and turned, following his gaze.

"They're shooting stars. That would have made the moment perfect."

"Shooting stars?" Ulysses echoed under his breath.

"Yes. They're supposed to be romantic."

"But shooting stars aren't stars," Ulysses said, his voice getting louder and more urgent by the second. "They're meteoroids. And they're heading this way!"

"WE HAVE MULTIPLE projectiles incoming, captain," Mr Goodspeed announced, trying to maintain a calm, authoritative tone, but anxiety belying his words. Myriad spots of green light painted the scanner-scope in front of him.

Emergency lighting bathed everything in a ruddy glow while a wailing siren underscored every word that passed between the bridge crew.

"How many?" Captain Trevelyan demanded, his voice like steel.

"I..." Goodspeed faltered.

"Come on! Spit it out man!"

"I don't know, captain, there are too many for the cogitator to accurately compute. And the scanner-scope keeps picking up more of them all the time."

"Size, Mr Goodspeed?"

"Varies. Looks like we've got everything from pebbles to rocks the size of locomotives."

"Saturn's rings!" Nelson Trevelyan cursed under his breath. "If anything bigger than a grapefruit hits us we could be looking at a hull breach. Source?"

"Scanning now."

For a moment the only sound on the bridge was the dull wailing of the proximity alarm and the chiming of the scanner-scope. Tense anticipation took the place of words.

"Trajectory of incoming objects suggests an origin point within the asteroid belt," Goodspeed said at last.

"Bloody Separatists!" Trevelyan hissed.

And so it had come to this, the captain thought. Mars had finally declared war on Magna Britannia.

In certain circles, political analysts had been expecting something like this to happen ever since Uriah Wormwood and the Darwinian Dawn had launched their first terrorist attack on London, fourteen months before. Ever since the first Magna Britannian colony had been built on Mars, there had been those who wanted to be autonomous of the empire that spawned them and whose influence they had left some forty-eight million miles behind them.

The situation had progressively become more and more tense, with the movement rapidly gaining support on Mars and no shortage of high-profile supporters back on Earth – some even within the current government.

But now the newly christened Martians – or some underground group acting with the colony's leaders' clandestine support – had brought the stalemate to an end with, what was effectively, an outright act of war.

It had long been mooted by government think-tank scientists that the gravity cannon technology originally used to send the first men to the Moon could be redeployed as a form of advanced, interplanetary weaponry, and it appeared that the Martians had done precisely that.

A cannon large enough could disrupt the gravitational orbit on an asteroid and then redirect it, setting it on a collision course with Earth. Of course, there was always the risk that the Moon would pull the rock off course – which would then result in it coming down on the satellite itself – but if one got through and made it to Earth, it could do untold damage.

"Mr Wallace, send a communiqué to Earth. Relay the situation to Heathrow Flight Control and get the powers that be to activate one of their agents on the red planet. Meanwhile, Mr Goodspeed, take whatever evasive manoeuvres you consider practicable and all of us had better brace for impact and pray that nothing gets through."

"Meteor shower!" Ulysses shouted, leaping to his feet and sending the table flying. "Run!"

Dragging Emilia out of her chair, Ulysses made for the exit as fast as his stumbling companion would allow.

Behind them, other diners were now rising from their chairs, staring out of the window or following the escaping dandy and his companion in bewildered panic.

Some were probably thinking that ships like the *Apollo XIII* were constructed to resist such space-borne particles, that the hull of the vessel was tough enough to resist as common an occurrence as a meteor shower. The Sol Cruises brochure had certainly said as much, but it was apparent that some of the other diners weren't sure how far they could trust the marketing spiel anymore. Unsettled by the dandy's dramatic response to the light show, rising from their tables, they were now hurrying towards the restaurant's exit themselves.

Two of those who were doing just that were a young woman and a blond-haired man, who had been seated at a table not far from where Ulysses and Emilia had sat.

"That's Quicksilver," the young woman hissed to her companion.

"Trust you to recognise that womanising dandy," Lars Chapter grumbled.

"Never mind that. I bet he knows what he's talking about. He's done this sort of thing before, I'm sure of it," Veronica Verse went on. "I think we should follow his example."

"Very well," Lars Chapter agreed, pushing his chair back as Verse got to her feet. "And we stay close."

Ulysses was almost at the door to the restaurant when he hesitated and looked back.

The slowly tumbling asteroid already filled the panoramic window, the ship's running lights illuminating fissures, craters and cruelly jagged outcrops across its surface. It had to be as long as a rugby pitch, if not bigger. If something that big hit the space-liner they were all dead – there would be no survivors.

Emilia unadvisedly followed his gaze. "Shit," she gasped in a most unladylike fashion.

The ship lurched. Tables overturned, crystal glasses smashed. People screamed.

Through the view shield, the ship-killer rolled overhead, tumbling on through space. The screech of the trailing edge of the asteroid scraping across the top of the hull reverberated through the restaurant.

"Thank God for that," Emilia said as she picked herself up off the floor. "That was too close for comfort."

"We're not out of danger yet," Ulysses warned, extricating himself from the waiter-droid that had fallen on top of him, and which now couldn't stop apologising. "We must get beyond the next bulkhead or we're going the same way as the air in this compartment when those other meteors hit."

"What other meteors?" Emilia asked, glancing back at the window. "Oh. Those meteors," she said weakly as she saw the hail of stones that were following in the massive asteroid's wake.

The rocks – the debris left over after some cosmic catastrophe billions of years in the past – hitting the reinforced glass of the view shield sounded like gravel hitting a window pane, provoking more screams.

And then there was a succession of pops, like bullets penetrating the glass, and the panoramic window exploded outwards as the air in the restaurant, and everything else, was sucked out by the hungry void into the cold, hard vacuum of space.

"THAT WAS A little too close for comfort," Captain Trevelyan said, as the shuddering echoes of the asteroid's brief contact with the *Apollo* died and the helmsman regained control of the half a mile-long vessel.

Suddenly another pinging sound joined the cacophony of klaxons and sirens on the bridge.

"What was that?" the captain demanded.

"We have a hull breach on deck seven," Mr Wallace responded.

"What's there?"

"The Restaurant Galaxia. Automatic hull breach procedures are in place. Bulkheads are sealing around the stricken section now."

"Then God help anyone still in there," Trevelyan said, the colour draining from his cheeks. "Not quite the dining experience they'll have been expecting, I'll warrant."

"HOLD ON!" ULYSSES screamed in the face of the howling gale. "Whatever you do, don't let go!"

This wasn't quite how he had imagined his dinner date with Emilia ending, he had to admit. He had considered various different outcomes – from Emilia falling into bed with him back in his cabin to her slapping his face and walking out – but he had never counted being sucked out into the cold, hard vacuum of space as being one of them.

With his left hand gripping the post between the restaurant's double doors, his right hand clamped vice-like around Emilia's wrist, their bodies at right angles to the floor as the void tried to suck them out into space, Ulysses hauled with all his might, not once taking his eyes from the two-foot thick bulkhead door sliding shut a mere twelve inches on the other side of the restaurant entrance.

The *Apollo*, like all other vessels of its kind, was divided into multiple compartments by solid steel bulkheads that could be sealed off from one another independently in case of a hull breach – as was the case now – or some other system failure.

Right now, the bulkhead closing before Ulysses' very eyes was intended to save the rest of the ship from catastrophic decompression, but at the same time it was condemning those still hanging on inside the restaurant to a premature death, as the air trapped in their lungs and the gases in their stomach expanded in the hard vacuum of space and, ultimately, their blood boiled.

And then the closing motion of the bulkhead faltered. Gears ground but the protective barrier remained open a fraction, wide enough, in fact, to let someone squeeze through.

There, silhouetted against the flashing ruddy light of the corridor beyond, on the other side of the bulkhead, was a man, arm outstretched towards Ulysses.

"No!" Ulysses shouted into the wind. "Take her first." And he hauled Emilia higher, until she was able to use his body to allow her to clamber to safety.

And then the man had a hold of her and was pulling her through the gap between the doors.

As Emilia disappeared beyond the bulkhead doors, Ulysses turned back to see if there was anyone else within reach who he could also help escape death by vacuum. Even as he watched a portly gentleman and his ostentatiously-dressed wife lost their grip on a pillar. The two of them hurtled out through the hole where the view shield had been and into the void beyond.

The only ones there was any hope for now were the young couple who had been sitting not far from Ulysses' and Emilia's own table, seemingly enjoying a romantic dinner for two of their own. The young man had his partner by the hand and was pulling himself towards the doors along the wall, the two of them using anything that came to hand to help them on their way.

"Come on!" Ulysses shouted in encouragement. "Not far now! You're almost there!"

Still clinging onto the door jamb, as the young couple came within reach Ulysses helped them past him to the waiting hands of automatons, as well as men now, that would pull them to safety as well.

It was only once the couple were through the groaning bulkhead doors that Ulysses allowed himself to be helped through.

The escaping air still battering his cheeks, as his feet crossed the threshold the bulkhead finally won its battle. Whatever override had been in operation failed and the doors slammed shut. If Ulysses had been a second slower, he would have lost both his legs at the knee.

"May I be of assistance, sir?" an automaton asked, its brass faceplate close to Ulysses' as it helped him to his feet.

The dandy quickly scanned the faces of those gathered around him, still coming to terms with what had just happened. There was Emilia, silent tears of shock running down her cheeks, her hair in disarray around her shoulders, and there was the young couple he had saved.

"Where is he?" Ulysses asked.

"Who, sir?" the automaton asked in its pre-programmed cheery tone.

"The man who saved us. The man who stopped the bulkhead from closing and who risked his own life to pull us free."

The automaton's head swivelled a full three hundred and sixty degrees about its neck joint.

"He appears to have gone, sir."

What sort of a man risked his own life to save three others and then didn't even hang around to take the credit, Ulysses wondered.

"A bally hero," he muttered under his breath. "That's who."

CHAPTER FIVE

Moonstruck

T minus 3 days, 14 hours, 21 minutes, 6 seconds

A DAY LATER, the *Apollo XIII* made orbit and limped into high dock above Luna Prime. Assisted by tugs, the half a mile-long stricken space-liner was guided down to the surface to make moonfall at the Luna Prime spaceport.

The landing pad had been cleared of all other ships, while bulbous emergency vehicles – fire engines and ambulances with spherical body units bolted to chasses with multiple large-tyred wheels – waited beside the air-tight dome of the spaceport complex itself, ready to speed into action as soon as they were needed.

Unlike embarkation on the ground at Heathrow, here on the airless surface of Earth's satellite, the concertinaed hoses of extendable boarding tubes extended from the side of the terminal building, coupling with the airlocks low down on the hull of the meteor-scarred vessel.

After all, the natural environment on the Moon was totally inimical to Man. The only place where any human being could hope to survive, without a fully-functioned, self-contained spacesuit, was within one of the bubble-like geodesic domes that housed the lunar cities, spaceports and isotope mining outposts.

Slowly, the *Apollo XIII's* passengers – many still badly shaken after the ship's encounter with the directed asteroid strike – began to disembark. Some shuffled along the exit umbilicals like zombies, barely even aware of their luggage. Others almost left the space-liner at a run, desperate to get clear of the craft as quickly as possible, while a few didn't leave at all – having already left via the shattered shield window of the Restaurant Galaxia.

Once the ship had discharged its cargo, it would be taken to one of Syzygy Industries' vast dry-dock hangers for repairs. Alternative arrangements had already been made for those agitated and disgruntled individuals who had been intending to join the *Apollo XIII* for the return trip to Earth.

Meanwhile, Captain Nelson Trevelyan would doubtless have to face a disciplinary panel, made up of the great and the good of Syzygy Industries, and answer questions concerning his handling of what would doubtless turn into a public relations disaster for Sol Cruises.

"IT'S AMAZING!" EMILIA gasped, putting a hand to her chest as she caught her breath. Ulysses followed her gaze through the glass tube of the umbilical to the monochrome lunar landscape beyond the spaceport.

"Yes. And it's good to be back on terra firma, isn't it?" he said with a heartfelt sigh as he stepped off the disembarkation ramp and into the terminal umbilical.

"After a fashion," Emilia said, offering her hand to Ulysses that he might assist her in stepping down from the ramp.

"Indeed," he said, giving her hand a squeeze. Ulysses turned to Emilia's father. "Where was it you said you were staying again?"

"The Nebuchadnezzar," old man Oddfellow said, his cheery

demeanour seemingly unquenchable. It seemed that having died once already – or at least faced death, or whatever it was that had happened to him during the three months in which he was trapped between worlds by the Sphere, a device of his own making – nothing beyond death a second time could diminish his indefatigable good humour.

"It really is no expense spared, this trip of yours, isn't it?" Ulysses flashed the old man a rakish grin.

"I know. Wonderful, isn't it?" Oddfellow returned the smile with an expression of child-like delight all of his own. "So where are you staying?"

"Well, now you mention it, the Nebuchadnezzar sounds like a suitably fine establishment. I think I'll drop by there myself; see if they've got any rooms."

Emilia looked at him through narrowed eyes. "I thought you were here to see your brother."

"Indeed I am. But I still need a place to stay. I mean, I wouldn't want to presume. Might cramp the young chap's style, if you know what I mean."

"You haven't told him you're coming, have you?" Emilia raised a knowing eyebrow.

"What, and give him the chance to run away again? Not on your nelly. Besides, after what we've been through recently, I feel that a hot bath, a hot toddy and a good night's sleep are what's in order before I even think about dropping in on my errant younger brother."

They were interrupted by a kerfuffle erupting behind them.

"I told you, bugger off! I don't need any help."

Abruptly aware of the altercation behind them, and hearing the woman's uncomely expletive, Ulysses' party turned as one. Behind them, disembarking from the liner, with what looked like a not insubstantial amount of luggage between them, were the only other survivors from the Restaurant Galaxia.

For some reason, the young woman was refusing the help of a spaceport automaton porter that was nonetheless doing its best to meet the requirements of its Lovelace algorithms by trying to assist her with her luggage. Behind her, his face set in a stony grimace, her companion appeared determined to manhandle the trolley he had procured himself without assistance of any kind either.

Veronica Verse suddenly caught Ulysses' eye and, taking in his good-humoured expression, forced her own features into a smile.

"Ah, Mr Quicksilver, we meet again."

"But under thankfully more agreeable circumstances."

"Quite."

"I would offer to get my man here to help you with your bags," Ulysses said, jerking a thumb towards Nimrod, who was already struggling to control a trolley piled high with his master's holiday wardrobe, "but I have a feeling it would only offend."

"Oh, Mr Quicksilver," the dark-haired young woman fawned. "You must forgive my outburst. It has been a trying time for all of us, has it not?"

"Indeed."

"And, besides, I would not presume. We already owe you a debt greater than any we could ever pay. I would not dream of troubling you further."

"So, what's next for you?" Ulysses asked, intrigued by this foul-mouthed young woman and her hen-pecked partner. He glanced meaningfully at the trunks and packing cases again. "Staying long are you?"

"Oh, you know. Just a few days, until our connecting flight to the outer solar system gets here."

"Ah, I see. Doing the Grand Tour, are you?"

"That's right."

"Well let's hope that you make that connection."

"What do you mean?" the woman asked, suddenly suspicious.

Ulysses smiled. "All I meant was, after what happened on our jaunt to the Moon, I wonder whether they'll still be flying."

"You think flights might be suspended?"

"I don't know. I'm not the expert. All I'm saying is that I'd find yourself a decent hotel and enjoy what Luna Prime has to offer for the time being, that's all. I hear the Island of Winds is worth a visit, and you don't want to miss the Peaks of Eternal Light either."

"Thank you," the young man puffed as he struggled past, pushing his own laden trolley before him. "We'll bear that in mind."

Ulysses gave him an appraising look. What was in those cases, he wondered.

"Perhaps we'll see you around."

"Perhaps you will," the young man replied noncommittally.

Having bid farewell to the determined young couple, Ulysses turned to his own travelling companions.

"Now, seeing as how we're all going the same way," Ulysses said, "why don't we travel together?"

"Very well," Emilia said, "and on our way you can give us your suggestion for the top ten sights we ought to see whilst visiting the Moon. After all, you have been here before, haven't you?"

The party of four made their way through the Luna Prime spaceport terminal. Much of the city was built above ground, contained within super-strong glass and steel domes, but there was always a portion of the lunar cities that was buried beneath the layers of dusty regolith, gouged out of the calcium-rich, granite-like rock of the Moon's surface.

With the material required to create the vast domes in short supply on the Moon itself – there was plenty of silicate material from which to create the glass but little in the way of iron deposits – it made sense to limit how much of the lunar colonies needed to be above ground, when the early colonists had been able to dig into the crust itself. It made even more sense in the case of the Bedford-Cavor Spaceport, when the landing pads had to be on the surface but where the support buildings, which were small by comparison, could be as unobtrusive as possible.

Beneath the spaceport Ulysses, Nimrod, Emilia and old man Oddfellow entered a vast, low cavern, cut out of the rock under the terminal itself. All about them transport vehicles – everything from steam-cabs to multi-wheeled juggernauts land-trains – were collecting the newly arrived travellers and unloaded cargos, ready to take them on the next leg of their journey. Most would doubtless be heading into Luna Prime itself, but others would be passing through, heading on to one of the other colonies, riding the transit tunnels to Tranquillity or Serenity City.

Emilia stifled another gasp.

"I know, it's quite something isn't it?" Ulysses said. "The first time you see it, I mean."

The roaring of engines and honking of horns, combined with the stink of coke and kerosene, was almost overwhelming in the restricted space of the cavern.

From the concourse in front of them various cabs and other vehicles were already setting off, following the route that would take them onto the main thoroughfare and from there to Luna Prime.

Huge droids clanked by, transferring cargo containers onto some of the larger vehicles waiting nearby – engines idling, smoke-stacks belching soot and heat into the air – while street-hawkers, who had set up shop at the entrance to the spaceport, gave those just disembarked from the *Apollo XIII* their first taste of the kind of poorly-made tourist tat that they could expect to be bombarded with during their stay on Earth's most popular emigration destination.

As they began to make their way to the cab rank, preceded by a clanking of iron feet and the hiss of leg-pistons, a massive automaton stepped into their path.

Emilia started.

"You looking for a ride?" came a female voice from somewhere in the vicinity of the droid's head.

Ulysses looked up at the twelve foot-tall Juggernaut-class droid. Sitting behind the robot's half-dome head in a cabin constructed from chipboard, canvas and corrugated iron was a young woman – practically little more than a girl, to Ulysses eyes. He wouldn't have been surprised if she wasn't yet out of her teens.

She was pretty – in a coquettish, child-like way, but not yet beautiful – but any feminine charms she might possess – other than those of her large almond eyes, upturned button nose and rosebud lips – were hidden beneath denim dungarees and an oil-stained shirt. A camel hair jacket lay on the seat beside her. The sleeves of the shirt had been rolled up to the elbows, exposing soot-stained forearms and elbows themselves stuck with sticking plasters.

The girl's hands were hidden within thick, padded leather gloves and her shock of near platinum blonde hair was currently being kept out of her soot-smudged face by a pair of goggles that had been pushed up onto the top of her head.

"We are, as it happens," Ulysses called back. "Why, are you offering?"

"Certainly am!" the girl said excitedly, lifting her heavy steel-toe-capped boots off the control console and strapping herself into the driver's seat. "Where you headed?"

"The Nebuchadnezzar. Do you know it?"

"It's all right, Ulysses," Emilia said, pulling him away from the colossal droid and its petite handler. "Our ride – as she so charmingly put it – is already here." She pointed.

The limousine was pulled up at the kerb-side, half-hidden by the bulk of the opportunistically-positioned taxi-droid. A suited and booted chauffeur waited, smiling patiently, ready to open the door to his passengers and load their luggage into the boot.

"Oh." Ulysses said, disappointedly. After all, a Rolls Royce was his London run-around. Limos he had done to death. Reconditioned salvage droids? Now that was another matter entirely.

"All expenses paid, remember? With all the frills."

"Ah, yes. Of course."

"And it looks like there'll be plenty of room for you and Nimrod, and all your luggage, as well as ours," Emilia pointed out.

Ulysses hesitated for a moment, his eyes lingering on the huge droid before giving the girl an apologetic smile. He turned back to Emilia.

"That would be very kind of you," he said. "Nimrod, give the driver a hand with our luggage, would you, there's a good chap?"

"Of course, sir," Nimrod replied, his expression of aloof disinterest never wavering for a second.

"And then it's Luna Prime, here we come!"

* * *

THE FIGURE WATCHED the Quicksilver-Oddfellow party climb into the waiting limousine, and saw the disappointment in the young girl's face.

He smiled to himself. The pieces were slowly fitting into place. It was all coming together as it should, now.

Running a hand through his mop of untidy hair and adjusting the patch over his right eye, he hefted his pack onto his shoulder and then, as the car pulled away with all safely ensconced on board, stepped out of the shadows.

Nearby, Chapter and Verse were getting into a steam-cab of their own, refusing the cabbie's help and insisting on loading their many heavy bags themselves.

He watched them for a moment, a look of resigned hatred in his eyes. Turning away at last, he wiped the grimace from his face, running a hand over the course grey stubble covering his chin, and made for the droid-cab. The robot's shoulders drooped as if in disappointment. The name 'Rusty' had been stencilled in large yellow letters across its rust-red chest plate.

"'Scuse me, miss, but did I hear you say that you're accepting fares to the city?"

The look of distracted disappointment on the girl's face was instantly transformed into a cheery smile.

"We most certainly are," she declared, beaming at him. "Where do you want to go?" she asked as she lowered a ladder to the ground, that he might climb up to the long padded seat behind the driver's position.

"Just into the city will do."

"The name's Billie," she said as the droid rose to its full height and took its first lumbering steps towards the cavern concourse's exit. Turning round she offered the man a gloved hand.

He took it and shook it firmly, feeling the girl return his handshake with a surprisingly strong grip of her own.

"And this is Rusty," she said, leaning forwards and patting the droid's head. "What's yours?"

He hesitated before answering. "Wells."

"Very pleased to make your acquaintance, Mr Wells. You been to the Moon before, only you look kind of familiar?" Billie asked as the droid strode along the thoroughfare between the chugging cabs and rumbling haulage wagons.

"Yes, I have," he replied, a distant look in his eyes. "This is my third visit actually."

"Really? And what are you here for this time, if you don't mind me asking? Business or pleasure?"

"Neither," he replied sullenly. "It's family."

"Oh, I know what you mean. Can't live with 'em, can't live without 'em," the girl chattered on over the increasing traffic noise and the chugging of the droid's own motive systems. "What is it they say? You can choose your friends but you can't choose your family."

"Indeed."

And with that the droid-cab stomped off along the Humboldt Highway, headed for the Luna Prime and a date with destiny.

ACT TWO

Moon

~ June 1998 ~

In the beginning, God created the heavens and the earth.

(Genesis ch.1 v.1)

CHAPTER SIX

Metropolis

T minus 3 days, 3 hours, 14 minutes, 34 seconds

ULYSSES QUICKSILVER WOKE the following morning to find sunlight streaming in through the windows of his penthouse suite. Of course, sunlight fell from the black void of the sky at certain times in the Moon's monthly cycle twenty-four hours a day whilst for others, the surface was left in a permanent state of darkness. It was only the self-regulating blinds and hallway lights – and, outside, the street lamps – that helped fool the body into maintaining its usual circadian rhythms.

Walking to the large, plate glass window opposite the huge bed in which he had spent a very restful night's sleep, Ulysses gazed out over the spacious parks, plazas and thoroughfares of the lunar city. It truly was a marvel of modern, Neo-Victorian engineering – an astonishing accomplishment.

There had been a thriving colony on the Moon since the 1950s, the first successful manned flights having occurred twenty years before that. With the development of cavorite, interplanetary travel had become an affordable – and hence realistic – option for the masses, rather than merely the few. Large, established businesses and canny entrepreneurs saw an opportunity to carve out a niche for themselves on this new world. Many made their fortunes in the process and the lunar billionaires were still among some of the richest individuals in the empire.

There was something reassuringly Magna Britannian about Luna Prime as well. Whereas some of the later colonies had a more cosmopolitan feel – places such as Serenity City and the uber-rich getaway of Tranquillity – Luna Prime had retained its Britishness from the get-go. Omnibuses that would not have looked out of place on any London street trundled along the wide thoroughfares. The Neo-Victorian architecture of the pale grey, mooncrete buildings was reassuringly familiar as well, as were the names of many of the shops he could see, even from here. There was even a branch of Harrods on the Moon. And, after all, where would the British Empire be without Marks and Spencers?

Luna Prime even had its own dwarf version of Big Ben – only without the Palace of Westminster attached – and a statue of Britannia that graced the painstakingly-landscaped New Victoria Park.

But this was not London. There was no ever-present pall of Smog hanging over the city for a start. The city streets were wide, the buildings new and in a good state of repair. From his window, Ulysses could not see any signs of the privation that so many millions suffered back home. This was what London might have been, had Sir Christopher Wren had his way after the Great Fire of 1666, or – heaven forbid! – Uriah Wormwood's plans for forced urban evolution been seen through to their bitter end.

Ulysses allowed himself an ironic smile. Perhaps this was what Uriah Wormwood had had in mind when he launched his potentially devastating attacks on the city. Perhaps he had planned to remodel London after Luna Prime.

And, of course, Luna Prime had avoided the disasters that had been perpetrated against Londinium Maximum over the course of the last year or more.

All in all, Ulysses could see why so many of those aboard the *Apollo XIII* had been travelling with a one-way ticket, and the intention of moving to the Moon permanently.

Gazing down on the clean city streets, he could see why a move here had been so appealing to his brother Barty as well.

But, of course, if the tide of immigrants from the Earth continued unchecked, how long would it be before Luna Prime resembled its forebears back on Earth?

He turned his focus from the already bustling streets below to the blazing white spot of the distant sun. Thanks to the filtering effects of the polarised glass of the atmosphere dome over the city he was able to look at it directly, with no worse consequences than if he had been looking at the glowing filament of a light bulb.

Possessing effectively no atmosphere whatsoever, beyond the habitation domes of the lunar cities, direct sun would burn the skin from a man's body, were he not inside a spacesuit, and, if he weren't, he would probably die of asphyxiation first.

It was like that on the Moon. It was a world of extremes. A man's blood would freeze in seconds on the dark side, and yet he would burn to a crisp from intense solar radiation on the other. If it hadn't been for the sacrifices made by those first lunar explorers – men like Clarke, Bradbury and Asimov – the Earth's satellite would have remained as nothing more than a lifeless lump of rock orbiting the Earth, rather than becoming the planet's most popular holiday destination.

Turning from the window, Ulysses retreated to the bathroom. Having washed, shaved and put on a clean suit of clothes that Nimrod had thought to put out for him the night before, leaving his manservant polishing the remaining five of the six pairs of shoes he had brought with him for his brief sojourn to the Moon, he descended to the restaurant level where a hot breakfast buffet was on offer to all of the hotel's guests.

Emilia and Alexander Oddfellow were already there, Emilia getting by on nothing but tea and toast, while the old man battled with a sugar-dusted grapefruit half.

Ulysses joined them, tucking into a full English, while he and Emilia made stilted small talk.

"So," he said at last, as he laid his knife and fork together on his egg-smeared empty plate, "what's on the itinerary today? How are you planning on spending your first full day on the Moon?"

"Father wants to visit the Lovell Planetarium," Emilia said, leaning across the table towards Ulysses, a relaxed smile on her face, "which means I'm all yours for the day, if you want me. I thought you might like to show me the sights, seeing as how you've been here before."

Ulysses took out his pocket watch and popped it open. "Sounds like a capital idea," he said, checking the time. "Besides, knowing my brother as I do, I doubt Barty will surface before luncheon. So, what would you like to see first? How about Earthrise over the Caucasus Mountains?"

"I WANT TO thank you, Ulysses," Emilia said as the dandy helped her down from the steam-powered carriage later that afternoon.

"And why's that then?"

"Why? How about Earthrise over the Caucasus Mountains, for starters." Emilia stepped down from the carriage and hugged Ulysses' arm tight as they set off along the Pascal Promenade together, their footsteps slow and measured as they dragged their heels, neither of them wanting their time together to end. "It was..."

"Yes?"

"Memorable." She smiled and squeezed his arm again. "I've simply had the most wonderful day."

"Well the Quicksilver Lunar Tour doesn't end there, let me tell you," Ulysses said, inhaling a lungful of the crisp, oxygen-rich processed air. "Tomorrow we order a luxury picnic hamper before chartering a solar yacht and heading out across the Sea of Dreams, returning in time for cocktails at Earthset."

Emilia hugged him, clasping him in a full embrace this time. "Sounds glorious. But what about Barty? I thought the whole reason you had come all this way was to see him."

Ulysses sighed. "Yes, you're quite right, and I have to admit that I am feeling a little guilty about my brother dearest. But don't worry, I'll make it up to him."

"Look, why don't you drop by his place now, at least for a couple of hours. I should really check on father anyway. We can meet again later, for dinner. How about it?"

"Sounds perfect," Ulysses agreed. "Kills two birds with one stone, as it were."

"That's settled then," Emilia said.

"You're sure you'll be all right making your own way back to the hotel by yourself?"

"Ulysses," the young woman said, giving him that oh-so familiar knowing look of hers. "I've coped fairly well without you for the last few years. I think I can look after myself now, don't you? I'm a big girl after all."

"Of course. Sorry."

"I'll see you later!" Emilia called back over her shoulder as she skipped away along the pavement, the foyer of the Nebuchadnezzar less than a hundred yards away. "Eight o'clock sharp!"

"Don't worry, I'll be there. On the dot."

"And give my regards to Barty."

Ulysses watched her go, his stomach doing somersaults. He hadn't felt like this since... since the last time she had kissed him, he thought. What was it about Emilia Oddfellow that had him acting like a love struck teenager enduring his first crush?

Certain that she would be perfectly capable of making the rest of the way by herself, Ulysses turned to face the oncoming traffic and hailed himself another cab.

"Where to, guv'nor?" the driver asked as Ulysses boarded the smoke-belching hansom.

"Milton Mansions, my good man."

ON THE WAY to Barty's apartment building on Kepler Street, over in the Rockwell District, Ulysses once again found himself pondering the possible reasons for his brother's sudden exodus to the Moon. But he always came back to the same conclusion, that it must have had something to do with his brother's inveterate gambling.

The cab pulled up outside Milton Mansions twenty minutes later. As the hansom rattled to a halt, its engine idling, Ulysses checked his watch. Six o'clock, on the dot. That gave him plenty of time to drop in on Barty, give him the shock of his life, share a few pleasantries, arrange to meet again another day, take another cab back to the hotel in time to wash and change before dinner at eight, having probably already picked up a bouquet of moon daisies from a street corner flower stall for Emilia on the way.

But what was this?

Ulysses got out of the cab, a queer, sick feeling in the pit of his stomach that was soon filling every part of him, right to the tips of his fingers. Several emergency vehicles were pulled up at the kerbside, an ambulance amongst the police cars.

The apartment block was built around a central square which opened onto the road on one side. A police cordon had been set up at this point, a tape bearing the warning 'Police line – do not cross' stretched across the iron gated entrance to the private square. Beyond this Ulysses could see half a dozen uniformed officers of the Luna Prime Police Force bustling around what he took to be the scene of the crime – whatever that crime might be.

Ignoring the authority of the police line altogether, Ulysses lifted the tape and ducked underneath.

A woman wearing the masculine uniform of the Luna Prime Police, her dark hair cut into a short bob, saw him and stepped forward to deal with his intrusion. The circle of people at the centre of the square was broken for a moment, and Ulysses was able to see, for the first time, the body around which they were clustered.

It was a man, lying on the ground, his limbs in disarray, looking precisely like a puppet that had had its strings cut. Ulysses saw the blood – so dark it was almost black – pooling around the man's head.

He pushed forwards further.

He saw the staring eyes, as cold as glass, and the terrified look on the man's rigour-locked face – on his brother's face.

Bartholomew Quicksilver was dead.

CHAPTER SEVEN

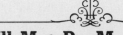

Ill Met By Moonlight

T minus 2 days, 17 hours, 3 minutes, 59 seconds

"I'M SORRY, SIR, but you can't come in here," the police officer said, approaching Ulysses, her hand out to hold him back. "This is a restricted area."

Shock and disbelief changed to frustration and anger and Ulysses fumbled in his jacket pocket, searching for his ID. Finally his probing fingers brushed the leather of the card holder and he pulled it out, brandishing it before the surprised woman.

"Sir, I must insist –"

"Look at it!" Ulysses hissed, thrusting his wallet under her nose. She glanced down and read what she found there.

"Oh. Oh, I see." The woman looked from Ulysses' ID back to his face.

A pair of jodhpurs and a close-fitting, buckled leather jacket accentuated her toned, athletic figure. Her eyes were of the darkest russet, appearing even darker given the near-white complexion of her skin. There was little discernable emotion in the hard stare she was giving him.

"I am sorry, Mr Quicksilver. I had heard a rumour that you were here in Luna Prime, but I'm afraid I didn't recognise you."

Ulysses grunted, pushing past her, unable to take his eyes from his brother's body.

Barty stared back at him, a frozen rictus of horror etched forever on his face. The blood that had leaked from his skull looked like a dark halo around his head.

Ulysses stared at his dead brother, his mouth slack with shock. The last time he had seen Barty had been before he had set off for Europe with his new ward Miranda Gallowglass and her governess, the traitorous Lilith Wishart. It was on his return from gallivanting around Asia, Russia and the Czech Republic that he had come across his brother's letter.

And now, here they were, reunited for the first time in three months, mere hours after his brother's death.

Lab-coated forensic scientists and a police photographer continued to go about their business around him.

"What happened?" he asked, suddenly sounding weary beyond belief.

"Suicide," the woman said bluntly. "Must have thrown himself from the balcony of his thirteenth floor apartment."

"No," Ulysses gasped.

"Certainly looks that way."

"No. I mean, no, he didn't kill himself," Ulysses stated firmly.

"I'm sorry, sir. Do you know something about what happened here that you're not telling me?"

"He wouldn't do that. Not Barty. I mean, why come all the way to the Moon to start again only to end it all?"

"Was the deceased known to you, Mr Quicksilver?"

"Yes. He was my brother."

The officer fixed him with a steely stare. "Then do you think you should get involved?"

"Damn right I should. In fact I should have got a lot more involved long ago." Ulysses redirected his appalled gaze back at his brother's body. "I want to see the scene of the crime."

"The scene of the crime?"

"Yes. I want to see his apartment."

"Very well, but there's no crime here, sir," the police officer persisted.

"I think I'll be the judge of that," he snarled, turning on her. "And if you continue in this manner, assuming that this case is all sewn up, just like that, then there will have been more than one crime committed in relation to this death and I'll have you for gross negligence!"

"Now, now, Mr Quicksilver, there's no need to be like that." The look in the woman's eyes was one of wary warning, rather than embarrassed guilt.

"And who are you, precisely, that you know so much about what my brother did or didn't do?" Ulysses snapped, his rage bubbling over.

The woman stood smartly to attention. "Inspector Artemis of the Luna Prime Police Force."

"Very well then, Inspector Artemis, the scene of the crime, if you would be so kind."

"Here you are," Artemis said, lifting the tape criss-crossing the doorway. Ulysses ducked underneath and entered his late brother's apartment.

Milton Mansions was nice enough, built in the Neo-Rococo style, but Barty's apartment was what an estate agent would have called 'compact' or 'bijou'. Ulysses would have called it small. There was the main living area – with adjacent kitchenette – bedroom, with barely space for a double bed, and a tiny bathroom. It was certainly a far cry from the space and luxury Barty had been used to back in London, sharing his brother's six-bedroom townhouse in Mayfair.

On the opposite side of the living space, French doors opened out onto a narrow balcony that overlooked the central concourse below. Ulysses made his way slowly across the room, taking in the glasses on the coffee table. There was little else in the way of furniture, other than for a settee and a single armchair. Papers lay strewn across the table, a copy of *The Times* (Late Lunar Edition) obscuring much of them.

Ulysses stepped through the French doors and out onto the balcony. He wasn't far from the inner skin of Luna Prime's habitation dome here; it lay only fifty feet above him. Resting an arm on the wrought iron railing he peered over the edge.

From thirteen floors up he had a bird's eye view of the enclosed square. The shape Barty's body made on the cold paving slabs made it look as if he was running from something.

Had he been running from something? And if so, what?

But then, when Ulysses came to think about it, Barty had been running from something ever since the two brothers had been reunited, after the elder had returned from the depths of Nepal, having been missing, presumed dead, for some eighteen months. He had certainly been running from something when he left London for the Moon. Ulysses only wished he knew what it was.

Whatever had driven him to leave the planet, Ulysses was certain that it had caught up with him at last, and that that was why his brother was now lying dead on the concourse below. What had he got himself mixed up in?

No matter what might have once passed between he and Barty, at that moment, Ulysses resolved that he would not rest until he had found out and laid that particular mystery to rest. For his brother's sake.

He turned from the balcony and re-entered the living room where the Inspector was waiting for him, standing smartly, arms crossed behind her back, rocking back and forth on the heels of her black leather jackboots.

She fixed him with an appraising look. "Like I said, a simple case of suicide."

Ulysses met her stern gaze. "You think so, do you?"

"And you don't."

"Then it looks like I'm going to have to prove to you that my brother was murdered and *did not* commit suicide. Barty was many things, I'd admit that – a philanderer, a gambler, a liar – but he was never suicidal."

"But all the signs indicate that he was alone when he died."

"Really? Explain."

"Very well," Artemis said. "The door to the apartment was locked when we began to investigate the scene, and there was no one else inside. There were no signs of the door having been forced. Initial signs are that there are no marks on the deceased's body, that might have indicated there had been a struggle."

"Were there any witnesses?"

"We're still looking into that, but it would appear that the suici... death," the Inspector corrected herself, "occurred between six and eight yesterday evening."

"And nobody found him until today?" Ulysses asked in amazement.

"People here keep themselves to themselves apparently. According to one old woman we interviewed downstairs they don't go out much. And apparently they don't have many visitors either."

Ulysses scanned the room again, making a point of covering every corner with his piercing gaze. "And you've found a suicide note, have you?"

"No. Not yet. But not all suicides leave a note."

"True. And, in my experience, neither do many murderers."

"I am sorry for your loss, Mr Quicksilver, really I am, but until I find evidence – or someone else provides me with evidence – to the contrary, I'm going to write this one up as a suicide."

"So I've got my work cut out then, haven't I?" A righteous resolve was burning away inside him now, reducing all other concerns to ash.

Inspector Artemis fixed Ulysses with the same needling stare as when he had first arrived.

"Go on then."

"Let's start with the door. You say it was locked when you arrived and that there was no sign of a forced entry."

"That's right."

"So, chances are, Barty knew his killer and let him – or her – in himself. Have you found a key?"

Artemis hesitated. "Not yet, but then we have yet to empty the pockets of the deceased. And just because we have not come across a key yet does not mean that we won't."

"True. But it could also mean that the killer took the key with them and locked the door on their way out. And what about those?"

Artemis followed Ulysses' gaze to the pair of brandy glasses on the table. One was half full. The other remained untouched. "What about them?"

"There are two of them, Inspector. It looks very much to me as though Barty entertained someone here before he died. I'll warrant that if you dust them for prints you'll find Barty's on both along with another set on the other as well."

"So who was this mystery visitor then?" Artemis asked, intrigued.

He had her now.

Ulysses studied the table again. Besides the two brandy glasses there was the broadsheet and, partially obscured by the pages of *The Times,* Ulysses could make out the corner of what appeared to be a card folder.

Before the woman could stop him, Ulysses stepped forward and removed the newspaper from the table, tossing it carelessly onto the settee and exposing the pile of folders haphazardly strewing the glass tabletop beneath.

Gathering them up, he began flicking through the folders to see what they contained.

"Here, careful," Inspector Artemis said in alarm, moving to stop him. "That might be evidence you're tampering with."

Ulysses gave her a dark look from beneath his knotted brows. "Evidence of what? I thought you said there hadn't been a crime committed here."

She hesitated and then took a step back again.

"Just be careful," she warned.

There were three folders, each containing a variety of handwritten notes, photographs and Babbage engine print-outs.

Ulysses arranged them into a tidy pile and then took the one from the top. Opening it he read the name printed at the top of the first sheet and studied the photographic portrait attached to it with a paper clip. He quickly scanned the information he was presented with and committed the image of the man presented in the sepia tint to memory.

The file concerned one Jared Shurin, owner and chief executive of Syzygy Industries, a company with – according to the document Ulysses was reading – interests in alternative energy sources, satellites, spaceships and cavorite production back on Earth. And of course it was Syzygy Industries that owned the space-liner *Apollo XIII.*

Ulysses had heard of Shurin just as he had heard of his company, simply from his perusal of the business pages of *The Times*, and the occasional news reel presented by the Magna Britannia Broadcasting Corporation, via the city-wide broadcast screens back in London.

Shurin was a patrician-looking gentleman, with a mane of luxurious black hair, combed back from a high forehead. Ulysses and Shurin were roughly the same age, Shurin possibly even slightly younger, although he was infinitely richer than even the well-heeled Ulysses. Shurin had built on the foundations laid by his father to create one of the most powerful businesses on the Moon, if not throughout the whole of the British Empire.

Despite maintaining various factories and production plants back on Earth – including the cavorite works at Greenwich – Syzygy Industries' true base of operations was right here in Luna Prime.

There was more to the contents of the file than merely newspaper clippings and press reports, and much of it was in his late brother's untidy hand.

Ulysses closed the file on Shurin and placed it back on the table. Working systemically, he then took up the next, this one concerning another leading lunar industrialist, Dominic Rossum – founder and owner of Rossum's Universal Robots.

Rossum looked as though he had a good twenty years on the younger Shurin, at least, appearing to be closer to sixty than forty, judging by the photograph of a jowly man with a luxurious mane of white hair and impressive silvery handlebar moustache. In the orbit of his right eye was screwed a silver-edged monocle.

Rossum was one of those early pioneers who had recognised the true market potential of robots at the dawn of the automaton age and, as a result, had made a killing in the years since. His business was also based on the Moon, with most of the droids produced at his self-contained construction plants destined to remain on the Moon; the state of the art Jeeves models destined for the condominiums of the rich, while the massive Titan construction droids went to work on one of the many building projects that were forever increasing the number of acres of lunar surface covered by human habitations.

Rossum's Universal Robots were known back on Earth as well. However, over the last decade, R. U. R. had suffered as a result of the rise of competition from China.

The last of the document bundles related to Wilberforce Bainbridge, the oxygen magnate. It was his air mills that produced fifty per cent of all the air used to maintain the ever-growing populace of the lunar cities, and, in the case of Serenity City, his company was the sole supplier.

Bainbridge still faced competition from Charles Humboldt and the Arterton Foundation but, from what Ulysses could discern from the papers in front of him, his position was secure for now.

The accompanying photograph was that of a man sporting a neatly-trimmed goatee beard, brown hair thinning at the crown and greying at the temples, and wearing a pair of glasses with various coloured-filter attachments.

Bainbridge was a self-made multi-millionaire, a rare beast indeed, practically unheard of within the rest of the empire of Magna Britannia; but then his business was one that was unnecessary back on Earth. Even the undersea cities of Atlantis City and Pacifica made use of air collected from the surface, transported to the seabed metropolises in tanks, or extracted oxygen from the very waters of the oceans themselves when necessary.

But the air mills of the Moon were a different case altogether. They created all of the oxygen required by the populaces of the lunar colonies and then maintained that air supply, continually recycling it, processing the carbon dioxide and other waste gases produced by respiration and manufacturing.

The air mills needed constant, twenty-four hour supervision and without them there could be no Luna Prime. No moonbases of any kind. No extra-terrestrial society at all.

From his fleeting inspection of the contents of the files there was nothing that leapt out at Ulysses as being strikingly unusual. So why were there whole files concerning these three men in the apartment of an inveterate gambler?

How had Barty been connected to these three? Had he been blackmailing them to pay off his outstanding gambling debts? Was this the mess he had got himself into that he had referred to in his letter to Ulysses? And if that was the case, what had he had on the men?

Was it one of those three who had been responsible for hurling Barty from the balcony of his thirteenth floor apartment?

Ulysses doubted very much that it would have been Shurin, or Rossum, or Bainbridge themselves. Such powerful men didn't stoop to dirty their hands with such minor details as getting rid of blackmailing gambling addicts. Besides, he also doubted that a man like Rossum or Bainbridge would have the physical wherewithal to get the better of Barty, even if his younger brother was no master of the martial arts or an ex-soldier, like his elder brother.

But then who was to say that Barty's killer hadn't brought the hired help with him to do the dirty deed? It might not have been one of the industrialists who had launched his brother over the railing, but getting one of his heavies to do it for him was no different from having pulled a gun and shot Barty. Both were tools with which a man could commit murder.

And who was to say that whoever the second drink had been for hadn't taken something with him when he left – such as a particular incriminating document?

But no matter what might or might not have been taken, suddenly one more potential lead presented itself.

There, lying on the coffee table, having been previously hidden under the pile of files, was a luridly red flyer, the colour of a tart's lipstick.

Like any other city the world over, Luna Prime had its own notorious red-light district, Venusville. And of all Venusville's disgracefully seedy establishments, the most celebrated was the Moon's mimicry of Paris's infamous Red Windmill – the Moulin Rouge.

Written across the flyer in gold ink, in a highly feminine hand, was what Ulysses took to be a name – 'Selene' – with a girlish love heart drawn fluidly beneath.

This only provoked more questions in Ulysses' mind. Who was Selene? And what had she been to Barty?

Ulysses felt ashamed at the thought, but the Moulin Rouge and a missive from one of the ladies who might 'entertain' there sounded much more like the sort of thing that Barty would get mixed up in, rather than business involving three powerful men like Shurin, Rossum and Bainbridge.

The whole time Ulysses had been perusing Barty's files Inspector Artemis had been watching him like a hawk.

The files in one hand, the flyer clenched tightly in the other, Ulysses now met her unremitting stare.

"Are you going to kick up a stink if I take these with me?" he challenged her.

"Whatever you think you've found, none of this proves anything."

"Not *yet*, maybe," Ulysses replied. "But I believe the evidence – when it has been properly assessed – will prove that there *was* someone else here before my brother was murdered."

"Before your brother died, Mr Quicksilver. Let's not go jumping to conclusions just yet."

"Like you, you mean?"

Inspector Artemis railed at that. "You cannot be sure that – even if someone else did call here before your brother died – that that person also killed him. Everything you've shown me so far is purely circumstantial.

"Mr Quicksilver, you've made your point. If you want to pursue your own investigation into your brother's death, using whatever means it is you have at your disposal, I don't suppose I can stop you. But I have a job to do, and, if you don't mind, I would very much like to get on with doing it."

The documents still in his hands, Ulysses reluctantly made his way towards the door.

"And if I receive reports that you have been harassing any of our most celebrated industrialists – who have helped make Luna Prime what it is today, I don't mind telling you – then I will see you removed from the Moon, royal commission or no royal commission. Do we understand one another?"

"Perfectly," Ulysses growled, his words as sharp as a knife.

And with that he stormed out of his dead brother's apartment.

CHAPTER EIGHT

Sunshine

T minus 1 day, 23 hours, 57 minutes, 11 seconds

THE EDIFICE OF white stone and mooncrete rose up before them like
some monolithic monument to the far-reaching achievements of
Syzygy Industries, the company's name emblazoned across the
front of the building in letters of arabesqued painted steel twelve
feet high.

Ulysses Quicksilver, accompanied now by his manservant,
and *de facto* bodyguard, Nimrod, strode across the white stone
plaza in front of the building and the mosaic depicting the
Sun, Earth and Moon in alignment that was the company's
corporate logo. He looked resplendent in a suit of chequered
Harris Tweed, his bloodstone-tipped sword-stick swinging from
his right hand in time with his tapping footsteps. He didn't
even break his stride as an attendant automaton opened the
great glass doors to admit the two men to the entrance lobby
of the building.

On discovering his brother's death the evening before, he had fully intended to begin his investigation into the events leading up to the murder there and then. Dinner with Emilia forgotten, he rejoined Nimrod back at his suite at the Nebuchadnezzar. But it was his ever loyal manservant who, having been filled in on all that had happened since Ulysses stopped by Milton Mansions, suggested they wait until morning the next day to pursue their enquiries. And Ulysses, having come round to the logic of Nimrod's suggestion, lost himself in a bottle of brandy instead and didn't surface until well after breakfast the following morning. And so it was that a little after eleven, the two of them arrived at Syzygy Industries.

The atrium opened out above them, rising the full height of the building. Before them stood a broad reception desk. Seated behind it was a smiling girl with a pretty face, too much lipstick and carefully coiffuered blonde hair.

Beyond the desk and its manned security screens, staircases, elevators and escalators carried those working inside the huge structure to the laboratories, offices and engineering levels above. And this was only the front of one building in a great complex of labs, testing areas and research and development zones. Here at Syzygy Industries headquarters, and making the most of the sterile environment of the moon as well as it weaker gravity, advances were being made in satellite production and interplanetary vessel design, not to mention the work undertaken with cavorite application and research into alternative energy sources.

Watched by a uniformed security guard, broad across the shoulders and with a barrel chest, Ulysses approached the reception desk, closely followed by Nimrod, a respectful pace behind.

"Good morning, sir," the girl behind the desk welcomed him brightly. "Can I help you?"

Ulysses placed his cane carefully, and purposefully, on the counter. "We're here to see Mr Shurin."

"And is Mr Shurin expecting you?" she asked, tapping a key on the typewriter keyboard in front of her.

"No."

"Oh, well I'm very sorry," the receptionist said, still beaming at Ulysses, "but Mr Shurin is a very busy man. If you'd like to make an appointment for another day –"

"So he's in then?"

"As I said, Mr Shurin is very busy but I'm sure I can arrange an appointment for next week some time –"

"Buzz him, or call him, or do whatever it is you do, and I'm sure you'll find he'll make time to see me."

Behind the woman's ingratiating smile, her expression said quite clearly, "You'll be lucky!" but she nonetheless politely went through the motions of seeing if the CEO of one of the largest corporations on the Moon was receiving guests. Judging by the grim resolve etched into Ulysses' face she wisely decided that it would take more than the "He's very busy" line to get rid of this one and so picked up the telephone handset beside her.

"Hello? Yes, reception here. I have a Mr..."

The woman looked at Ulysses, querying eyebrows raised.

"Quicksilver."

"A Mr Quicksilver here who is very keen to speak with Mr Shurin."

The receptionist was quiet for a moment as she listened to whoever was on the other end of the line.

"I'm sorry," she said, lowering the receiver from in front of her mouth, "but would that be a Mr Bartholomew Quicksilver?"

Ulysses' jaw clenched. "No, *Ulysses* Quicksilver."

The receptionist put the telephone handset to her ear again.

"A Mr *Ulysses* Quicksilver... Yes, I did explain, but he's very keen to talk to Mr Shurin today." And then she lowered the receiver again. "Who are you with, Mr Quicksilver?"

Ulysses flashed her the contents of his leather card-holder.

"Oh, I see," she said taken aback. "Mr Quicksilver's with the British government," she said. "Yes. Yes, of course. Right away. Thank you."

The woman put down the phone.

"If you'd like to take the elevator to the top floor," she said, still the same false smile locked on her face, "Mr Shurin will see you now."

"Yes," Ulysses said with grim satisfaction, "I rather thought he might."

"Mr Quicksilver, what a pleasure it is to meet you," Jared Shurin said effusively, getting up from behind his huge marble desk.

"Is it?" Ulysses asked, matching the industrialist's firm grip as they shook hands.

"But of course," Shurin said, breaking contact, whilst continuing to smile with all the sincerity of a diplomat.

"You were on the *Apollo XIII* flight, weren't you?

"Yes, I was."

"I heard there was a minor collision."

"Yes, there was."

"Well thank goodness you're all right," Shurin gushed.

"Not everyone was so lucky."

"I know. A terrible affair. Simply terrible." Shurin paused for a respectful moment before changing the subject. "So what brings you to the Moon? It is not often we are fortunate enough to receive a visit from someone of your standing and, if I might say so, celebrity status."

Ulysses looked at him, one eyebrow raised. "I thought the Moon was inundated with celebrities, minor royals, and their ilk, trying to get away from it all – especially in the aftermath of the Wormwood Catastrophe."

"Ah, you have me there. So, like I said, what brings you to the Moon, Mr Quicksilver? Is it business or pleasure?"

"It was pleasure. Now it's purely business."

"Really? How interesting."

"As if you didn't know," Ulysses added under his breath.

"I'm sorry?"

"So what is it you do here, Mr Shurin?" Ulysses asked, moving swiftly on.

"Well, I am sure you are already aware of our work in the field of aeronautics and space travel."

"Cavorite. Spaceships. That sort of thing?"

"Yes. That sort of thing. Satellite production too. If it wasn't for Syzygy satellites the Empire would not so easily receive regular updates on what's going on around the world from the news reels from the Magna Britannia Broadcasting Corporation, and the personal communicator revolution could never have taken place." The man sounded like he was making a presentation to the board as he paced before his desk. "But those areas of our business are dealt with elsewhere. The Barnes Wallace Space Station, for example – in geostationary orbit over Birmingham – and our Greenwich works."

"So what is it you are focused on here?"

Shurin took a deep breath and drew himself up to his full height. "Here we are concerned with no less than harnessing the power of the sun," he said, a look of smug triumph on his face.

"What?"

"Solar power, Mr Quicksilver. A potentially limitless supply of energy, if only it could be successfully tamed. Do you know what that means, Mr Quicksilver?"

"Why don't you enlighten me?"

"Better than that," Shurin said, still smiling. "Why don't I show you?"

THE TESTING AREA was in another part of the complex entirely, but it was only a short journey from Shurin's office via cable car and then another hundred yards by travelator.

It was housed in its own separate dome, the upper half of which was made entirely of reinforced glass. Through the criss-cross bars of the roof's construction the stars of the Milky Way glittered like ice crystals seen by moonlight. But the view was nothing compared to the machine barely contained within the dome.

At first impressions it looked like a huge telescope, but then Ulysses realised that rather than an eyepiece, it ended at what appeared to be a beam emitter of some kind. All around the chamber, carefully-angled mirrors bounced light to a polished concave surface which focused the light it collected into the aperture of the telescope rig.

"Incredible, isn't it?" Shurin said, proudly showing off his latest toy.

"If you like modern art, I suppose," Ulysses said grudgingly.

"Oh no, Mr Quicksilver," Shurin laughed humourlessly, "not modern art but a miracle of modern science."

"Oh, I see." Ulysses gazed up at the light-collecting mirror and the tubular body of the device. "So what's it for?"

"Ah, I knew you were intrigued. I could tell. But you'll be even more amazed when you hear that it's a drill."

"A drill?" Nimrod spluttered.

"Yes – a drill!"

"But I've never seen a drilling machine like this one before," Ulysses said, eyes narrowing in suspicion.

"No, you haven't, Mr Quicksilver, because there's never been one like this before. Icarus is the first of its kind."

"Icarus."

"Yes. I came up with the name myself."

"And we all know what happened to him," Ulysses muttered under his breath before adding, louder so all might hear: "Did you really? So I take it it has something to do with the sun?"

"You are quite correct," Shurin said, delight brightening his face like a new dawn.

"Would you care to enlighten us further?"

At that Shurin turned to the technicians manning the chamber and clapped his hands. As his employees set about their work, Shurin ushered Ulysses and Nimrod to the side of the chamber where he offered them a pair of polarised goggles each.

"What are these for?" Nimrod asked, looking at the goggles in his hand with disdain. "Because I think you should know that I am not enamoured of the frivolities of fashion."

At that Ulysses raised an eyebrow. "Just put them on, old chap."

"I would advise it," Shurin said, donning a pair of the tinted goggles himself. "They are a safety precaution."

With protective eye-wear in place, the three men stood back as the solar engineers worked their magic.

With a grinding of gears, the device before them was rotated so that the beam emitter was directed at a block of solid reinforced mooncrete, six feet thick. At the same time, with a succession of clattering clicks the mirrors surrounding the chamber subtly changed position to compensate as a bank of whirring Babbage engines re-calibrated the machine and made the necessary adjustments.

Ulysses watched and waited. Nothing happened.

"Very impressive," he muttered. "What does it do for an encore?"

Shurin was gazing up at the star-field beyond the glass of the dome. "We just need to wait for the satellite to come into position.

There was a sudden flare in the black sky above them and a split second later that chamber was bathed in brilliant sunlight.

"Good lord!" Nimrod gasped.

"Wait for it," Shurin giggled. "You ain't seen nothing yet."

The sudden flare of sunlight faded as the mirrors around the room collected the light, bouncing it to the focusing dish at the broader end of the telescoping body of the device, which in turn focused it into a beam of rippling light and heat no more than six inches across. But the machine wasn't finished yet.

As Ulysses watched, the light was funnelled through the cylindrical body of the machine until it emerged from the emitter at its tip as an intense beam of brilliant white light that made Ulysses wince and instinctively take a step backwards.

Even through the heavily tinted lenses of the goggles and half-closed eyes he was still able to see what happened next with perfect clarity.

The concentrated sunlight struck the block of mooncrete, cutting through it like a hot knife through butter. An acrid burning smell assailed his nostrils as flames danced around the hole where the beam had entered the rock.

Mere moments later the beam burst through the back of the block and then died in an instant as the machine was powered down.

"Impressive," Ulysses said, taking off his goggles but unable to take his eyes from the machine and the damage it had done to a block of reinforced mooncrete with nothing more than the very careful application of pure sunlight. "Very impressive."

"So, Mr Quicksilver," Jared Shurin said when they were back in his office at the top of the Syzygy Industries headquarters, "what do you think?"

"Impressive," Ulysses allowed again. As a secretary passed him a cup of coffee, he took in the woman. She might as well have been a clone of the girl at reception, so alike were they. Blondes, he decided, were obviously Shurin's thing.

"Yes, she is rather, isn't she?" the industrialist replied, his own gaze lingering on the young woman as she leant forward and offered him his own steaming cup.

"I'm sorry?"

"I mean Icarus, of course."

"Icarus is feminine?"

"Naturally."

"Naturally," Ulysses repeated, taking a tentative sip of the bitter liquid swirling in the white china in his hand. "And, I would hazard to say, just like the female of the species, potentially deadly."

To his credit, the dandy thought, Shurin's expression of innocent amiability didn't falter once.

"At Syzygy Industries we strive only to make the world, and indeed the Moon, a better place. Imagine being able to drill through solid rock without the need for explosives or using heavy machinery that burns fossil fuels at an enormous rate. A clean energy source utilised to great effect, and one that does not burden the environment with yet more pollution."

"And imagine the potential for destruction. If it fell into the wrong hands, I mean." Shurin chose not respond to that comment, but sipped at his own cup of coffee instead. "Don't tell me you haven't considered that scenario."

"And it is one that will never come to pass," Shurin growled. "I can assure you, Mr Quicksilver, that Syzygy Industries is a highly reputable company and not an arms manufacturer."

"But once Icarus is out in the public domain, what's to stop some ne'er-do-well or revolutionary tin pot jungle junta from taking your 'greatest gift to mankind' and turning it to their own evil purpose. That which has been discovered cannot be undiscovered. Once the technology is out there, someone will find a use for it."

"You are as persistent as your brother," Shurin said, and pursed his lips. "I think perhaps you had better leave."

Ulysses felt a sudden surge of blood within his veins. "So, you came into contact with Barty then?"

"Well," Shurin floundered, quickly realising his mistake, "not in so many words. But he had arranged a meeting for," – he consulted a desk diary open on the marble slab of his desk – "yes, it was for today, as it happens.

"Of course, I heard about his untimely death on the news broadcast this morning." Shurin's face suddenly assumed a concerned expression of empathy. "I was so very sorry to hear of your loss."

"You knew my brother was dead and you didn't think to offer your condolences when we first met?" Ulysses could feel his ire building inside. How could Shurin be so blasé about such a thing? How could he be so cold? "He had something on you, didn't he?"

"I beg your pardon."

Ulysses' eyes narrowed. "I don't know what it was, but I'm going to find out, you mark my words. I swear on our mother's grave that I will. And when I do... I'll be back."

"Mr Quicksilver," Shurin said, affronted, "you don't mean to imply that I had something to do with your brother's death, do you?"

Ulysses leant across the desk, keeping his sword-stick where Shurin could see it.

"I don't know. Why don't you tell me?"

His manservant, who had been patiently taking in everything that had passed between the two men without passing comment, chose that moment to intervene.

"Sir," Nimrod said softly, that one simple word advising caution.

"Mr Quicksilver," Shurin said, not raising his voice by one iota, "I do not appreciate your thinly-veiled accusations and if this is how you are going to carry on then I feel we have nothing more to discuss. I would appreciate it if you would leave. At once."

"You can't hide the truth forever, you know!" Ulysses growled. There were tears of rage in the corners of his eyes.

Nimrod put a hand on his arm. "Sir, I think we should go."

Ulysses blinked the tears away and, taking a deep breath, took a step back from Shurin's desk, putting some much-needed distance between them.

"Yes, you're quite right, Nimrod. We should go."

Suddenly he sprang forward, leaning across the marble slab until he was practically nose to nose with the lunar industrialist. "But you haven't heard the last from me, you can count on that!"

And with that, Ulysses Quicksilver turned and strode from the office, his manservant hurrying after him.

WAS IT POSSIBLE that Quicksilver knew something of their plans? Jared Shurin wondered as the door closed after the dandy and his batman. The man certainly had a reputation for unearthing mysteries and then exposing them to the world. But then how could he know anything about what they had been working on here on the Moon? It was, quite literally, a quarter of a million miles away from his daily concerns.

But it paid to take precautions, as he knew himself from bitter experience, he thought, reaching for the handset of his desktop telecom.

A minute later the call was done and he replaced the receiver in its cradle.

The sudden buzz of his office intercom made him jump. He hadn't realised how jittery just talking to the man had made him feel. It wasn't like him to be so on edge, but there was something about him – something unnatural. But then that was plain for all to see, it was just that he worked very hard to ensure that nobody did see him.

"Yes?" he snapped irritably as he depressed the 'speak' button.

"Message from reception, sir," Miss Hunt, his personal secretary, explained. "There's a Mr Chapter and a Miss Verse waiting in the lobby."

"At last!" Shurin exclaimed, smiling darkly to himself. "Then you'd best not keep them waiting any longer. Send them up, Miss Hunt. Send them up."

CHAPTER NINE

R. U. R.

T minus 1 day, 20 hours, 2 minutes, 27 seconds

ULYSSES QUICKSILVER EXITED the cab without saying a word and stared up at the imposing sign emblazoned across the automaton works, as Nimrod exited the chugging hansom behind him.

R.U.R.

The letters stood thirty feet high – even more imposing than the sign outside the Syzygy Industries headquarters half a city away. Fashioned from wrought iron and studded with light bulbs, the letters were a statement of intent of lunar domination.

Where Shurin's head office had utilised the very latest in lunar construction techniques and materials – from mooncrete to bonded regolith – and favoured the Retro-Classical architectural style, the Rossum plant celebrated all things iron and steel and brass, the very materials from which their automatons were constructed. And much of Luna Prime and the other satellite cities had been constructed by Rossum's Robots – the larger, Titan and Goliath-class droids at least – unimpeded as they were by the lack of an atmosphere or the reduced gravity.

There was something almost of the funfair about the place, from the brightly-lit sign to the brightly-dressed attendants employed to take tourists on sight-seeing trips of the unrestricted parts of the factory.

With Nimrod as ever at his side, Ulysses strode under the mighty sign and beneath arch after arch of shaped steel towards the main entrance to Rossum's Universal Robots. The steel tunnel to the complex was large enough to steer a Titan-class construction droid down.

Everything about the place spoke of great size – the scale of the labour being undertaken at the plant, the size of the workforce, the size and number of units being produced on a weekly basis, and size of the ego of the one man who had started it all, Dominic Rossum.

They passed suited clerks, overalled mechanics and errand droids – not all of them humanoid in form – scurrying in and out of the building, from one part of the complex to another. Flashing neon arrows directed Ulysses and Nimrod, and the other excited individuals visiting that day, towards the grand wrought iron doors – decorated with a bas-relief of mighty robots bestriding the lunar plains and mountain ranges and cities, all formed from the metal of the doors themselves. They looked heavy enough to keep even a Titan-droid at bay.

The amount of metal on display was testament to Rossum's power and wealth. The Moon itself had very little in the way of useful mineral resources – other than for the regolith used in the production of mooncrete – and even less in the way of usable iron ore. Much of what Ulysses and Nimrod could see must have been transported here from either Earth or Mars, or collected from captured asteroids that occasionally drifted in-system from the belt of planetary matter beyond the red planet itself.

Ulysses' dislike of the man was growing fast and he hadn't even met him yet. Rossum was obviously a blatant show off – worse even than Ulysses – for the doorman on duty before the huge iron portal was nothing less than a Titan-class droid, its vast hull emblazoned with the company crest. This alone was as good an indicator of the man's ego, power and wealth as anything; a droid designed and built for the purpose of raising vast cities from the lunar regolith, employed to open and close his front door.

Dwarfed by the vast automaton towering over it, to a height of sixty feet, it took Ulysses a moment to even register the pulpit-like reception desk positioned between the automaton's tractor-sized feet.

Before he could even open his mouth to speak, the young woman sat behind the desk – her russet hair scraped back into a bun as severe as the expression on her face and the flinty look in the grey eyes behind her horn-rimmed spectacles – put a finger to her brass and teak earpiece and got in first. "If you'd like to go through, Mr Quicksilver, Mr Rossum is expecting you."

"Is he now?"

"There's a drudge waiting to take you to his office."

The Titan-droid pushed with one huge shovel hand and one of the great doors eased open, its greased hinges not making a sound despite its immense size. Ulysses glanced warily at the towering colossus as he led the way through, memories of his various encounters with the Limehouse Golem suddenly fresh in his mind.

Beyond the doors they found themselves in a vaulted semi-circular chamber. Great arched passageways led off from this central hub to various parts of the plant. A steady stream of employees and droids were negotiating the human and mechanoid traffic filling the corridors. As Ulysses watched, something that looked like a cross between an equine automaton and a hansom cab trundled past, carrying a group of smart-suited investors to another part of the factory.

And sure enough, waiting for them on the other side of the huge doors was a droid wearing something like a bellhop's uniform, also bearing the company crest. Its cap was positioned with clockwork precision on its polished brass head at an approved thirty-two degree angle, intended to suggest a jaunty demeanour, no doubt.

"Mr Quicksilver?" the droid said in a chirpy, electronically-synthesised tone.

"Yes," Ulysses replied testily.

"This way please."

"AH, MR QUICKSILVER," the man standing at the window said, without turning round.

Even though he was only looking at the back of the man, Ulysses could still see the trumpet of a teak and brass headset clamped around the man's right ear while his left hand was sheathed in some sort of wired, leather glove.

"Mr Rossum, I presume."

Turning from the window, Dominic Rossum crossed the office with powerful strides – looking just like he did in the sepia tint in Barty's file, other than for the technological accoutrements that he was now sporting.

His stance and gait suggested that he was still a physically powerful man, and yet, according to the information Ulysses had gleaned from the file, he had to be at least sixty years old, if he was a day. Ulysses wondered whether Dominic Rossum was really half the man he used to be. And, if so, what was the other half made up of now?

The lift that had delivered Ulysses, Nimrod and their automaton guide here had emerged at the very centre of Dominic Rossum's hemispherical office. As soon as they had exited the elevator, the bellhop pressed a button, the doors closed again and the lift carriage sank back into the floor, a protective hatch sliding into place over the shaft, allowing for an uninterrupted view from the glass dome at any point in the elevated chamber, and leaving the three men alone.

From this position Rossum could look out over every part of his lunar domain, from the accounting cells to the research and development laboratories, and from the component manufactories to the automaton assembly lines a quarter of a mile away. He truly was master of all he surveyed.

Ulysses took a moment to savour the view that Dominic Rossum enjoyed on a daily basis. Begrudgingly he had to admit that it was impressive.

From the panoramic view of the plant he felt the urge to see what lay above, beyond the roof of Rossum's tower.

Through the leaded panes of the dome he could see the secondary skin that covered the entire plant and, beyond that, the complex many-layered meshing geodesic domes that covered the whole cityscape.

Rossum halted before Ulysses. The man was much taller than he would have guessed from his photograph in Barty's file, which had only shown him from his chest upwards.

Stiffly, he offered his hand to the dandy.

"Mr Quicksilver," he said. "A pleasure." There was no hint of an emotion in his voice.

Ulysses took the proffered hand and shook it, fixing Rossum's monocled gaze with a needling stare of his own. "Mr Rossum."

"And what is it I can do for you today?"

"Oh, I assumed you already knew."

"I'm sorry?"

"Well you were obviously expecting me so I assumed your co-conspirator Mr Shurin had called ahead to warn you to expect a visit."

Rossum took a step back from Ulysses, observing him, unblinking, from behind his monocle – his other eye scrunched up in a squint.

"Impressive set-up you have here." Ulysses said.

Rossum paused before answering, as if trying to fathom what kind of a confessional trap the dandy was trying to lure him into. "Why, thank you."

"It must have taken years to get it all established and build it up to this level."

"Well yes, yes it did. Almost fifty years, in fact."

"Then you're looking very spry for your age, if I might say so."

"Why, thank you," Rossum replied, still without any glimmer of emotion in his voice.

"That must have taken some work."

The older man scowled. "I'm sorry, but what are you trying to say, Mr Quicksilver?"

Was that a suggestion of anger colouring his words?

"The sort of work requiring a spanner and a welding torch perhaps?"

"Sir," Nimrod muttered, putting a warning hand on Ulysses' arm.

"I'm sorry, but are you trying to be rude, Mr Quicksilver?"

"Did you ever meet my brother, Barty?"

"I'm sorry?"

"Yes, so you keep saying. Bartholomew Quicksilver. Did the two of you ever meet?"

"N-No," Rossum stumbled over the word. "Not that I can recall. I suppose he might have run into me at some charity bash or other. Why do you ask?"

"Because he knew a lot about you," Ulysses said, joining Rossum in gazing out of the window across the factory complex.

"I am sure that there are a lot of people who know a lot about me," Rossum stated bluntly.

"Really? Is that so?"

"I expect it is, as it happens."

Ulysses took the folder from under his arm and opened it, keeping it tantalisingly out of the industrialist's line of sight.

Rossum craned his neck forwards, trying to sneak a peek.

Ulysses raised the folder so that his body obscured the papers he was perusing.

"Hmm... This makes for interesting reading, I must say." Ulysses snapped the folder shut. "What did my brother have on you?"

"What?"

"What was your association with my brother?"

"There was no association, as you put it," Rossum said. "Why are you asking me all these questions?"

"Because he's dead, and I found files on you, Shurin and Wilberforce Bainbridge in his apartment. So, tell me, what is the nature of your association with Jared Shurin?"

"What?"

"I'm sorry, Mr Rossum," Ulysses said, his temper rising, "but it would appear that that hearing aid of yours isn't working very well." He raised his voice still further. "What is your relationship with Jared Shurin of Syzygy Industries?"

"We are fellow industrialists," Rossum blustered. "We move in similar circles, that's all. It would seem that you are looking for a conspiracy where there is none!"

Ulysses kept the same flinty stare fixed on the white-haired, supposedly elderly man. "I didn't mention a conspiracy, Mr Rossum. Did you hear me mention a conspiracy, Nimrod?"

"No, sir," his manservant replied loyally.

"So, tell me about this conspiracy that you've got yourself mixed up in."

"There is no conspiracy!"

"And you really expect me to believe that, do you?"

"Yes!"

"Why?"

"Because it's the truth!" Rossum roared, the monocle popping free of the orbit of his eye. Ulysses had woken the sleeping beast of his rage.

Ah, Ulysses gloated to himself, an emotional reaction at last.

For someone who had supposedly never had anything to do with his brother and who claimed that there was no conspiracy involving him and the other industrialists, the previously unemotional Rossum was getting very hot under the collar.

"I think you should leave now, Mr Quicksilver," Rossum seethed, screwing his monocle back into place.

"But I'm not done yet."

"Well I am, sir!" Rossum bellowed. "And if you don't leave," he said, touching the trumpet-device in his ear, "I shall be forced to call the police."

Nimrod's grip on Ulysses' arm tightened. "Sir, it's time to go."

Ulysses suddenly turned on Nimrod, his eyes wild. He shook

himself free of the older man's grip and opened his mouth to speak. But then something made him think better of it and he relaxed, shrugging his shoulders and smoothing his jacket into some semblance of order.

He was sure now that Barty had had something on both Shurin and Rossum, and so, by extension, it made sense that he had also had something on Wilberforce Bainbridge. But what was it?

"Very well, Mr Rossum, perhaps we are done here."

He reached inside a jacket pocket. Rossum flinched. When he took his hand out again, there was a small piece of card held between two fingers. He flicked it towards Rossum.

"If anything you think I might be interested in hearing more about comes to mind – anything at all – give me a call. You can find me at the Nebuchadnezzar."

Rossum snatched the card out of the air with startling speed, keeping his eyes on the dandy the whole time.

The lift shaft in the middle of the office floor suddenly irised open again and, with a chiming ping, the elevator returned. The doors slid open with oiled ease and the dandy and his manservant stepped inside, to be greeted by the ever cheerful robotic bellhop.

"Remember, Rossum, anything at all."

The lift doors slid shut again and the elevator departed. Dominic Rossum was left alone once more.

He pressed a button on his earpiece.

"Yes," he said gruffly, as the switchboard acknowledged him, "get me Bainbridge."

The line buzzed. It was a moment before his call was answered and the line connected."Bainbridge? It's Rossum. We need to talk."

CHAPTER TEN

Breathless

T minus 1 day, 18 hours, 15 minutes, 20 seconds

"So, WHERE NOW, sir?" Nimrod asked as he and his master made themselves comfortable aboard a robotic sedan chair outside Rossum's Universal Robots.

"Last on Barty's hit list is Wilberforce Bainbridge," Ulysses said, the third file open on his lap in front of him. The sternly patrician image of the oxygen mill owner looked up at him from out of the attached photograph.

Ulysses leant forward and tapped the small window between them and the driver's position with the tip of his sheathed sword-stick.

"Driver?"

"Yes, sir?" came a muffled voice from the other side of the glass.

"Have you heard of Wilberforce Bainbridge the air mill magnate?"

"Course, sir. Everyone's heard of 'im. We'd all be a little short of breath round 'ere if it wasn't for Bainbridge, if you catch my drift, sir."

"Good. So where would I find him?"

"Bainbridge Tower, of course."

"Then take us to Bainbridge Tower forthwith, my good man."

The dandy eased himself back into the leather-upholstered seat and returned to perusing the file on his lap. Even after closer, and repeated, inspection, the information Barty had managed to put together in the dossier was nothing out of the ordinary. In fact it was what anybody could have found out about the industrialist with some judicious scouring of the ether-ways.

His manservant fidgeted on the seat beside as the sedan chair trotted away from the kerb, out onto the main thoroughfare outside the robot manufactory.

"What is it, Nimrod? You're making me feel uncomfortable."

"If you don't mind me asking, sir, what do you intend to do upon reaching our destination?"

"I intend to get to the bottom of whatever it is that connects Bainbridge, Rossum and Shurin with my late brother. Then, in the fullness of time, I intend to make them pay for what happened!"

"Only we still don't know that any of them had anything to do with his de–" Nimrod checked himself just in time. "With the unfortunate incident at Milton Mansions. It hasn't even yet been proved that Master Bartholomew didn't die by his own hand."

"You don't mean to tell me that you agree with that incompetent Inspector Artemis now, do you, old chap?"

"I'm not saying that at all, sir." Nimrod sounded pained, hurt by his master's accusation. "I am only advising caution in this matter." He hesitated before going on. "Permission to speak freely, sir?"

"Granted."

"So far your somewhat bull-headed approach hasn't got us very far. In fact it could be argued that it has done nothing but make us more enemies."

Ulysses looked at Nimrod, cold fury blazing in the black pits of his eyes.

"If you were any other man..." he growled. "Doesn't Barty's de... what happened to Barty bother you?" he railed.

"Of course it does, sir. He was your brother, and I know how you felt about him, despite all he did to try and have you disinherited, and his wastrel ways. And I can see how much his death grieves you."

Ulysses turned away and stared out of the window of the sedan at the passing mooncrete edifices. The atmosphere inside the transport was suddenly as frosty as the Himalayan peaks.

Neither of them spoke again for the rest of the journey.

BAINBRIDGE TOWER WAS as impressive as any of the domains of the other industrialists Ulysses and Nimrod had already visited. It rose above the acres of the Moon's surface covered by the great mills that worked constantly to recycle the air contained within Luna Prime's habitation domes – removing waste gases and pollutants, which were then ejected into the airless void surrounding the Moon – as well as producing more oxygen as required as well. The mills were unable to recycle all of the air, thanks to the steam-powered nature of most things on the Moon and so a steady supply of breathable atmosphere had to be continually generated to allow life on the Moon to continue.

The tower itself formed the hub of all operations. From underneath it a network of wide pipelines spread out beneath the metropolis, constantly pumping freshly processed air into the hermetically-sealed domes, huge fans drawing the air into the domes as suction vents extracted the waste in a ceaseless cycle. The tower extended high above Luna Prime, its peak even rising above protective geodesic dome of the city itself, allowing Bainbridge to travel by personal shuttle from his own landing pad to the other lunar cities that utilised his company's life-giving product.

Even as Ulysses and Nimrod entered the cathedral-like vault of the tower's reception area they were hurried through security to a gleaming brass and glass ascending carriage that traversed almost the entire height of the tower.

The dandy was getting used to his visits being anticipated. He had half expected Rossum – or perhaps it had been Shurin – to have tipped Bainbridge off about their imminent arrival. But it unnerved him nonetheless. It made him feel as if he wasn't entirely in control. And it was only the feeling of being in control that was enabling him to hold himself together.

Ulysses stared past the glass wall of the elevator but failed to appreciate the amazing vista it offered him, lost as he was in his own thoughts. The carriage continued to grind its way ever upwards, the skin of the city dome drawing nearer all the time. Before the elevator reached the apex of the multi-layered dome the lift shaft was absorbed into the upper levels of the almighty edifice. But the carriage maintained its steady pace, proceeding through the dome itself as it entered the uppermost floors of Bainbridge Tower.

With a ping the lift doors opened and Ulysses and Nimrod stepped out into a large foyer, the adjacent wall of which was made entirely from glass. Beyond it lay the featureless grey desert of the Moon's surface. Stars twinkled in the inky blackness of the void, some of them the landing lights of space tugs and orbiting satellites.

A young man and a young woman ducked past them, heads down, catching the lift before the doors closed and it made the return journey to ground level.

"We're here to see Mr Bainbridge," Ulysses said, approaching the desk beside a pair of mahogany-panelled double doors bearing the company logo and the customary secretary sat behind it. The girl was typing something into her desktop Babbage unit, an aloof expression on her face.

"If you'd like to go right on in, Mr Quicksilver," the secretary replied without looking up. "Mr Bainbridge is expecting you."

"Yes, I rather thought he would be."

Ulysses gave her a look that told her exactly how he felt about her poor manners, but his look of sour disdain was wasted on her as she stubbornly continued to refuse to make eye contact.

Nimrod hastened to open the double doors for his master, then stood aside to allow Ulysses to enter the office first.

Beyond lay a room that looked not unlike a gentlemen's club, decked out as it was in more mahogany panelling, green baize and carpets bearing the Bainbridge crest. It was empty.

"Hello?" Ulysses called, Nimrod pulling the doors closed again after them. "Mr Bainbridge?" He took a few more steps into the room. "Anybody?"

There was no reply.

Picking up the pace, Nimrod joining him at his side, Ulysses crossed the expanse of the office to the huge desk, which seemed small compared to the vastness of the office itself. The luxurious high-backed chair was rotated so that its back was to the two men.

"Mr Bainbridge?" Ulysses said, a note of uncertainty in his voice. Warily he reached across the desk and turned the chair to face them.

It squeaked round on its bearings.

It too was empty.

Ulysses turned to Nimrod, his features knotted in confusion. "If Bainbridge is expecting us, then where is he?"

"Sir," Nimrod said, pointing at a door on the other side of the elegant office. The door was slightly ajar, as if someone had failed to close it properly behind them.

Ulysses was first through, Nimrod close on his heels.

"Bainbridge! Bainbridge!" he shouted as he ran down the lushly-carpeted corridor beyond.

It was clear to Ulysses that the man was trying to escape, but he wasn't going to let him get away that easily. To Ulysses' mind, the mere action of trying to run expressed his guilt as effectively as if Bainbridge had signed a written confession before his very eyes.

At the far end of the print-lined passageway Ulysses threw open another door and burst through it, finding himself in a hemi-spherical dome as thick as those that supported life in Luna Prime itself.

Through part of the dome Ulysses could see the industrialist's private shuttle pad. Berthed on the pad was a Lunar Cutter.

The private boarding lounge was decorated with moonscapes by the renowned landscape painter Phoebe Hunter, along with settees, casually, yet no doubt very carefully, arranged armchairs and large potted aspidistras.

On the far side of the dome, set within a solid steel frame two feet thick, was the first in a series of airlock chambers that should have joined the shuttle craft to the top of the tower, if the umbilical used to connect the vessel to the boarding lounge hadn't been disconnected.

A nauseous knot of uncomfortable realisation formed within the pit of Ulysses' stomach as he caught sight of the red smear on the other side of the circular pane of glass set into the centre of the airlock door. Beside the airlock a fatal warning light blinked red.

In desperation, knowing in his heart of hearts that he was already too late, Ulysses punched the door release mechanism. There was a hiss of changing air pressures and the light beside the door cycled from red to orange. With what felt like painful slowness, the atmospheres inside the airlock and the boarding lounge equalised.

The light turned green. There was an accompanying metallic click and the airlock door swung open on heavy steel hinges.

Blood dripped from the door onto the plush carpeted floor of the lounge, the viscous fluid slowly sinking in the shag pile.

"Oh my lord," Nimrod gasped.

"I think you'll find," Ulysses said, staring at the crimson mess covering the interior of the airlock, "that's what's left of Wilberforce Bainbridge."

The door to the private boarding lounge banged open behind them.

Ulysses turned to see Inspector Artemis lead a squad of armed police into the chamber.

"Mr Quicksilver. We meet again."

Ulysses took a step away from the airlock towards the jack-booted officer. "Inspector Artemis, what a pleasure."

"Don't move a muscle!" she snapped, training her gun on the dandy as her squad fanned out into the room behind her. Between them, the police had Ulysses and Nimrod well and truly covered.

Ulysses briefly considered the pistol in the shoulder holster and the rapier blade sheathed in the bloodstone-tipped cane. Then he thought better of both. That way led to a premature demise.

He could see how the situation he now found himself in might look to the agitated inspector, observing the growing look of horror on her face as she took in the details of the scene.

There was nothing else for it. It was time to pull out the really big guns; it was time to talk his way out.

"Ulysses Quicksilver, you're under arrest," Artemis declared.

"Might I ask what the charge is?"

"Murder. Cuff him," she ordered the men under her command. "In fact, cuff both of them."

Realising that here and now was neither the time nor the place to attempt to resist arrest, Ulysses helpfully held out his hands in front of him, wrists together.

As a pair of cautious constables moved to act on the inspector's orders, Artemis read the dandy and his manservant their rights.

"You do not have to say anything, but it may harm your defence if you do not mention, when questioned, something that you then later rely on in court. Anything you do say may be given in evidence..."

"Look there's really no need for this," Ulysses said.

"Why? Been arrested before, have you?" the constable securing the bracelets around Ulysses' wrists asked.

"What I mean," Ulysses said, pointedly addressing the organ grinder rather than her monkey, "is that we're innocent. We only just got here ourselves."

A shrill scream rang out from behind the police officers.

Suddenly everyone's attention was on the short-skirted secretary standing at the entrance to the departure lounge, hands to her face in horror, as she too stared at what remained of her employer dripping from the sill of the airlock.

"Get her out of here!" the inspector snapped, giving the shocked young woman only the most cursory of glances.

She turned her attention back to Ulysses, lowering her gun.

"You had all the time you needed to do the deed. That poor cow told us that much when we arrived."

"And how, pray tell, did you know to turn up here only a matter of minutes after us, when we hadn't even made an appointment to gain an audience with Mr Bainbridge?"

"Whose investigation is this?"

"Humour me."

Inspector Artemis thought for a moment.

"Well, I don't see how it'll hurt. You're bound to find out sooner or later. We were acting on an anonymous tip-off."

"From the real murderer," Ulysses said, nodding to himself.

"And how *do* you explain your presence here, Mr Quicksilver?" Artemis fixed him with that no-nonsense, flinty-eyed stare of hers.

"I was carrying out my own investigation into the events surrounding my brother's death."

"Investigation or revenge killings?"

"What?"

"You have to admit, from where I'm standing that's a very realistic possibility. Of course, if that's the case, it's a most unfortunately misguided revenge, considering that there isn't actually any evidence to suggest your brother was murdered at all, *or* that the three men you have been harassing had anything to do with his death in any way whatsoever."

Ulysses bristled. "And where's the evidence that Wilberforce Bainbridge was murdered then? Where's the murder weapon? Where the motive?"

"Murder weapon – airlock," Artemis said, jerking her head towards the open steel hatch. "Motive – like I said – a deluded desire for revenge."

"You don't even know that's his body – or rather, what's left of it – in there," Ulysses persisted.

"True, but such things can be ascertained."

"Have you considered the possibility that the death we see the aftermath of here was an accident?"

"Mr Quicksilver," Inspector Artemis said, "you don't die from fatal decompression in an airlock by accident. This was a premeditated act. Mr Bainbridge was murdered."

"Either that or he committed suicide."

"Like your late brother, you mean?"

"No! Not like my brother! Barty was murdered, I'm sure of it."

"As you keep saying. And as was Bainbridge. Question is, by whom?"

"Well it wasn't me... Don't you see? This proves that Barty's death couldn't have been suicide!"

"Does it?"

"Of course! Whoever's responsible knows I'm onto them and is trying to cover their tracks."

"So what you're trying to tell me is that this wasn't a revenge killing perpetrated by an emotionally overwrought grieving brother?"

"That's precisely what I'm trying to tell you."

"Save it for the judge." Artemis turned to her constables who now had both Ulysses and Nimrod in their custody. "Take them away."

The constables began to pull the dandy and his valet towards the door.

"Who said we'd been harassing them?" Ulysses suddenly asked, intrigued.

"One Jared Shurin, CEO and owner of Syzygy Industries."

"And this information wasn't relayed at the same time as the 'anonymous' tip-off you received?"

"No. By the time we received the tip-off that the two of you were here, we'd already been to see Mr Shurin."

"Well I'd like to have another word with Mr Shurin myself."

"So would we but I'm afraid that won't be possible."

"And why would that be?"

"Because," Artemis said, turning her cold grey eyes on Ulysses, meeting his intense look with the cold fire of her own furious gaze, "when we stopped by at the headquarters of Syzygy Industries, he was already dead."

"Dead?"

"But he can't be," Nimrod gasped.

"Burnt to a crisp, as if you didn't know, in what, at first glance, appeared to be an industrial accident involving a sunlight-focussing mirror, or some such thing."

"Icarus!" Ulysses gasped. He felt cold from the tips of his fingers to the pit of his stomach. And in that state of shock his mind began to work nineteen to the dozen. "But don't you see? There's a pattern forming here! Someone *is* following us, clearing up the loose ends surrounding Barty's murder and trying to implicate us in the killings at the same time."

"Is that so?"

"Yes! Shurin was very much alive the last time we saw him. As was old man Rossum."

"Rossum?"

"Dominic Rossum. Of Rossum's Universal Robots."

"Yes, I know who you mean," Inspector Artemis said. "You mean to say you paid a call on him too?"

"Y-Yes," Ulysses stammered, feeling the nauseous knot in his stomach tighten.

Artemis led the way out of the boarding lounge and back through the plush office, into the foyer beyond to the elevator at the top of Bainbridge Tower, talking into her short-wave radio the whole time.

"Get a unit over to R. U. R.... You heard me! Rossum's Universal Robots. We may have another homicide on our hands... I know, tell me about it. One dead industrialist on our hands might be considered an accident. Two smacks of carelessness. But three...? That would be a bloody disaster."

CHAPTER ELEVEN

Short Circuit

T minus 1 day, 17 hours, 13 minutes, 29 seconds

"WHAT IS THE meaning of this interruption?" Dominic Rossum blustered, his handlebar moustache bristling in indignation. His rage echoed from the walls of the robot storage shed – a great vaulted barn of a place where the industrialist was inspecting the latest batch of completed Titan-droids.

"I'm sorry to disturb you, Mr Rossum," Inspector Artemis began.

"Not *him* again!" Rossum pronounced, looking down from his perch atop the robotic walking device he was using and seeing Ulysses paraded before him, hand-cuffed and bowed.

"I know you'll find this hard to believe," the dandy said, "but I never thought I'd be so pleased to see you again either."

"I can't say the feeling's mutual."

"No. I didn't think it would be. But that doesn't change the fact that your continued existence and excellent state of health gets me off the hook."

"Now steady on. I wouldn't go that far." Artemis said. "The fact that Mr Rossum is still alive doesn't exonerate you of the other murders."

"What happened to innocent until proven guilty?" Ulysses protested.

"Oh, come on, Mr Quicksilver. What kind of a world do you think you're living in?"

"What murders?" Rossum looked suddenly shaken.

"I understand you had dealings with Jared Shurin of Syzygy industries and Wilberforce Bainbridge of Bainbridge Mills," the inspector said, turning back to the industrialist.

"Business dealings, yes," the automaton magnate confirmed cagily. "But what did you mean by 'other murders'?"

"When was the last time you had any contact with Shurin or Bainbridge?"

"Look, who is it that's under suspicion here exactly? Am I to assume that Shurin and Bainbridge are dead?"

"I'm afraid so, sir. So, if you wouldn't mind answering the question...?"

"Well, let me think..." Rossum trailed off as he tried to come up with a suitable answer, Ulysses supposed.

With Bainbridge and Shurin dead, was Rossum the one behind it all; his brother's death, and those of the other two industrialists? But, if so, what possible motive could he have had? What did he have to gain by their deaths?

As he struggled with these thoughts, his gaze began to wander.

He stared up at the towering Titan-class droids. Like ancient cyclopean idols they loomed over the humans; dormant gods, waiting for the invocations of their worshippers to rouse them from their sleep of ages.

In the gloom at the far end of the vast shed, a spark of actinic light flashed like a burst of miniature lightning.

Ulysses was only dimly aware that the inspector was speaking again, his attention now fully focused upon what was happening at the rear of the barn.

"Inspector? I think we should get out of here," he said, trying to remain calm.

"Mr Quicksilver," Artemis replied testily, breaking off from her interrogation of Rossum. "I thought you were keen to establish your innocence in this matter and find some link between the dead men and Mr Rossum. Now we will stay here until we have managed to achieve that or not, as the case may be."

The echo of a metallic groan rang from the far end of the barn.

"I realise that, but we really need to get out of here now," he said, trying to back away from his armed police escort.

"Sir?" Nimrod looked at him, concern apparent in his eyes.

"Mr Quicksilver, I am currently investigating a double homicide. Now if you would just –"

"Yes, I know. But I'm trying to prevent another one from happening right now!"

The iron clang of the heavy footfall reverberated from the steel walls of the barn, echoing from the hulls of the other colossal automatons standing motionless in their serried rows.

"Now you all heard that, didn't you?"

Ulysses regarded the shocked faces of Inspector Artemis, the other officers present, Dominic Rossum, the two technicians attending the industrialist, and even his own manacled manservant.

"Right. I thought so. And now that I have everybody's attention, might I make a suggestion? Run!"

Before any of them could make a move, a shuddering shockwave rippled through the floor of the shed, pitching one clumsy-footed policeman onto the ground.

At the other end of the shed a colossal figure, like a walking city block, stepped out of the shadows, picking up speed with every shuddering footfall as it moved towards them.

Ulysses continued to back away, unable to take his eyes off the iron giant for even a moment. Despite his run in with the Limehouse Golem and various other droids over the years, he had never realised just how quickly something sixty feet tall, and weighing several tonnes, could move.

With pistoning steps the Titan-class construction droid ran towards the fleeing gaggle of panicking people.

"Split up!" Inspector Artemis shouted.

Policemen and Rossum's employees scattered. Rossum turned his walking carriage towards the shelter of another droid then seemed to think better of it – uncertain whether any more of the giant automatons would activate as soon as he got too close – and turned back towards the centre of the shed.

All the time the lumbering construction droid was closing on them. It made no vocalisation of any kind, but that only made its cold-blooded determination to catch up with the fleeing humans all the more terrifying.

Ulysses sprinted after the inspector.

"What are you doing? I said split up!"

"And I'm still in hand-cuffs. I need you to release me!"

"Now is hardly the time or the place and besides, you're still under arrest!"

The two of them stumbled as another juddering footfall sent a tremor through the ground.

"I'd rather hoped that this attempt on Rossum's life would have exonerated me of having anything to do with the murders," Ulysses panted.

"How do you know this isn't another –"

"What? Industrial accident? Rather a coincidence don't you think? Two in one day, in entirely different plants, the man in charge the victim on both occasions?"

"In case you hadn't noticed," Inspector Artemis said breathlessly, throwing a sidelong glance at the panicked Dominic Rossum hanging onto the controls of his striding chair for dear life, "old man Rossum isn't dead yet."

"And if his survival ensures my freedom, I'd rather like to keep it that way," the dandy countered. "Un-cuff me and I can stop that thing. I'm sure of it."

"You've dealt with this sort of problem before, have you?"

"Not on this scale, but I know what I'm doing."

The inspector ran on, saying nothing more.

Feeling another juddering tremor, Ulysses risked a glance back over his shoulder.

The droid was closing on them. With a stride seven yards long, it wasn't hard.

Ulysses saw a policeman – who was rather broad around the middle and obviously not used to having to run any distance for any length of time – stumble before the automaton's advance. He landed hard on the mooncrete floor. Ulysses could hear his plaintive cries as he struggled to get up again but there was nothing that he could do for the man. To turn back and go to his aid now would be to condemn himself to death as well.

Even as the policeman made it onto his hands and knees, a foot the size and weight of an earthmover descended on top of him. There was the briefest shrill cry of unimaginable agony and then nothing. The robot lumbered on.

"McCormack!" the inspector gasped in horror. "This way!" Artemis turned and, grabbing hold of Ulysses, dragged him into cover between the feet of another of the Titans. Pulling out a set of hand-cuff keys, anxious fingers fumbling with the lock, she managed to free Ulysses of the manacles.

"Don't make me regret this."

"You won't, I guarantee it," Ulysses said, his face alight with relief.

The two of them peered from between the statuesque robot's legs at the advancing droid. It was bringing one of its shovel-tipped arms to bear now, swinging it round with slow yet fatal purpose.

"You really think you can stop that thing?" Artemis asked.

"I think so." Ulysses said.

"You *think* so!"

"All right. Yes, I can stop it. Does that make you feel better?"

The inspector scowled. "And how are you planning on doing that exactly?"

Ulysses flashed her a devilish grin. "Oh, I don't know. I'll think of something. I usually do."

And then he was gone, sprinting across the floor of the barn, between the avenue of iron giants, towards the lumbering Titan.

As the dandy ran towards the advancing droid, Artemis emerged from her hiding place, running after the industrialist and his cantering chair. "Come on! Move it!" she bellowed. "Everybody out of here!"

The scattered officers, factory employees, industrialist and hand-cuffed butler began to converge again as they made for the small door set into the vast hangar doors of the storage barn.

The droid did not appear to have registered Ulysses' presence as the dandy came at it from out of the shadows. At least it didn't act to deal with him as it powered on between the avenue of robots after the fleeing Rossum.

Ulysses drew level with the droid as its left foot made contact with the ground again. With an extra burst of speed he made it to the side of the foot and threw himself at the access ladder running up the side of the robot's leg. Rungs were embedded into the side of the Titan, running all the way up to the droid's head and the driver's cockpit. Ulysses clung on as the automaton took another step forward and a huge shovel-hand swung past like some colossal pendulum. Then, having got a firm grip on the ladder, he started to climb.

As he climbed he began to formulate a plan. For someone to have activated the droid remotely they had to either be relaying a signal to the droid's Babbage core or have already downloaded a Lovelace algorithm into the robot's operating system. Either way, if he could de-activate the Titan's reasoning engine he could bring its rampage to an end. And of course, if Artemis's assumption was correct, and the robot's behaviour was the result of a short circuit, then removing its brain would still be the most effective way to turn it off.

Despite the swaying motion of the droid, Ulysses was actually making good progress. As he neared the automaton's shoulder he could see the others making for the open door and safety. They were almost there now – Rossum in the lead, atop his galloping carriage, with Nimrod not far behind him.

Making it to the railed walkway that ran from the shoulder to the automaton's head, Ulysses darted along it, keeping his hands on both rails as he ran, just in case. Reaching the end, he threw himself inside the driver's cabin that formed much of the robot's steel skull.

The massive robot veered suddenly sideways, one huge hand smashing into a line of motionless droids. The first robot to bear the full force of the collision began to topple sideways with what felt like tectonic slowness. With a dull boom it collided with the Titan next to it, which also began to fall. One by one the line of giant automatons toppled into one another, like felled sequoias, the noise of their collisions filling the shed with a cacophony of crashing metal.

The robot suddenly lurched the other way and Ulysses fell into the driver's seat. Instinctively he made a grab for the controls in front of him, pulling back hard on the steering paddles.

Through the smeared glass of the cabin's windows he watched as Nimrod, Rossum and the others piled through the door, chased by oily flames as fire blossomed in the darkness of the storage shed.

As Ulysses had feared, pulling on the controls made no difference to the motion of the runaway droid. The controls had been locked out.

Now, more than ever before, Ulysses was certain that this was no industrial accident. He was going to have to go with his original plan.

He turned in his seat and saw the panel behind which the droid's cogitator core resided. But his heart sank as he saw the bolts holding it in place.

He started to scour the cabin for anything remotely resembling a spanner or a wrench. Without a toolkit he didn't have a hope of removing the panel and getting at the robot brain beyond.

As the robot took another lurching step towards the closed hangar doors, with a metallic *clink* something fell onto the sheet steel floor of the cockpit.

Ulysses snapped his head back round to the panel. The bolts were loose. In fact one of them was now rolling around at his feet.

That was all the evidence he needed. Someone had been in here before him and tampered with the automaton's Babbage engine directly, only they'd been slack in securing the panel, obviously assuming that no one would ever be so foolhardy as to attempt what Ulysses was attempting right now.

Twiddling the three remaining bolts free with his fingertips, Ulysses ripped the panel open and hurled it aside. Beyond, in a space no larger than a rabbit hutch, lay the Babbage core, fairy-lights twinkling in the darkness.

NIMROD STUMBLED THROUGH the door, panting for breath, his heart racing. The police inspector stumbled through behind him a moment later. Ahead of him, Rossum brought his cantering walker to a halt in front of the looming hangar doors.

As the rest of Artemis's officers and Rossum's lab-coated technicians joined them, all of them struggling to catch their breath, Nimrod stood up straight, head turned to one side.

Registering his hawkish pose, Artemis raised a questioning eyebrow. "What is it?"

"Do you hear that?"

The inspector listened, concentrating on filtering out the panting of her officers, whilst trying to work out what it was Nimrod could hear and that she couldn't.

"I can't hear anything," she said.

"Precisely."

WITH A SUDDEN clattering crash, and a groan of metal, the hangar doors buckled and bulged outwards, the steel shutters splitting open as the colossal construction droid careened into them, then, with terrible slowness, it toppled to the ground.

Nimrod watched as, at the last possible moment, his employer flung himself free of the cranial cabin of the Titan, dropped the last twenty feet to the ground and, curling his body into a ball, hit the ground. He bowled across the mooncrete, landing in an awkward sprawl twenty feet away.

At the same time the Titan hit the ground with seismic force, sending everyone present reeling and tumbling. All except for Dominic Rossum and his now stationary strider.

There was nothing any of them could do as the droid's head-cabin came down on top of the industrialist, crushing every bone and bionic component in his body, and pulping every organ, as surely as if he had been run over by a steam roller.

ULYSSES QUICKSILVER GOT painfully to his feet as the last echoes of the Titan's fall faded and the dust cloud thrown up by it settled back down to the ground. His elbows, shoulders and knees hurt, his suit jacket and his trousers were scuffed and torn.

He staggered painfully towards the others – some vital component of the droid's cerebral cortex clutched in his hands – as they slowly got to their feet.

Ulysses was met by staring faces, slack with shock, that looked from him to the toppled Titan and back again. With the off switch having effectively been thrown, with Ulysses' removal of its Babbage brain, the droid had shut down immediately, mid-stride. Momentum had done the rest, sending the droid crashing through the hangar doors of the storage shed.

Misreading the appalled expressions of those gathered around him, Ulysses glanced back over his shoulder.

"I know," he said, almost laughing with the relief of it all. "The bigger they are... Is everyone all right?"

Receiving no answer from the rest of them Ulysses began to count heads himself. Nimrod was safe, as was the inspector and her men – apart from the one who had been crushed by the droid back in the barn, of course. There were the two technicians, and...

Ulysses' face fell. "Oh," he said, crestfallen.

CHAPTER TWELVE

The French Connection

T minus 1 day, 16 hours, 17 minutes, 10 seconds

THE DANDY HAD withdrawn to a quiet corner of the robot marshalling yard from where he watched as a pair of Juggernaut-class droids, with human handlers in their driving seats, lifted the debilitated Titan clear of the crushed smear on the mooncrete that was all that remained of Dominic Rossum.

Ulysses had been so determined to save Rossum's life, in order to prove his innocence, that his actions had actually resulted in the wretched man's death.

The inspector broke away from a circle of policemen and forensic scientists, leaving them to their work, and made her way over to where Ulysses sat, disconsolately, with his head in his hands.

"You're off the hook; you know that, don't you?" she said.

Ironically, in the eyes of the law – at least the law as represented by Inspector Artemis – he was now exonerated of all crimes, despite having ultimately inadvertently killed Dominic Rossum himself.

"Am I?"

"Well, not completely. Make no mistake I'll still be keeping a close eye on whatever you get up to as long as you remain in the city. I'm not telling you anything you don't already know here, am I?"

Ulysses shook his head.

"But as far as I can see, unless this is some highly elaborate subterfuge, you weren't the one behind the murder of Jared Shurin, or that of Wilberforce Bainbridge, and nor were you responsible for the attempt made on Dominic Rossum's life – in spite of its tragic outcome."

Ulysses said nothing, but looked at her with a haunted expression on his face.

"You only discovered your brother's death yesterday," the police officer went on, "and the only likely co-conspirator I see around here is your man who, until only a few moments ago, was cuffed just as you had been.

"I don't believe either of you was really in a position to set that trap for Rossum. So, ironic as it may sound, I don't hold you responsible for Rossum's death, even though it could be argued that you were the one that did for him in the end."

She cast him a wry smile.

"Unless of course it was all part of an elaborate ruse to make you believe my innocence," Ulysses said.

"Don't push your luck," Artemis laughed. "Besides, when did you have time to set all this up? And why would you put yourself at risk, exposing yourself in such a way? You don't strike me as the sort of man to sacrifice himself unduly. And you've been under armed guard ever since we got here. No, I'm going to let you off this one, but don't think that means I'm not still going to keep a close eye on you."

Ulysses fixed her with a cold, flinty stare.

"Let me guess... Your train of thought goes something like this. If you let me go and keep tabs on what I'm doing, I might lead you to the ones actually responsible?"

Artemis laughed again. "What, you think I've got nothing better to do all day other than run around after you?"

"I'm a charmer, you know? The ladies can't keep away."

"I'll be seeing you later, I'm sure," she said, as she began to walk away.

And then she hesitated.

"Unless you know of any other potential leads, avenues of enquiry that you'd like to share with me now?"

"No. Nothing," he lied. "There were the three industrialists and that was it, and I'm still none the wiser as to what they had to do with Barty or what he might have had on them."

The lurid pink flyer loomed large in his mind's eye. It was all he'd been thinking about for the last few minutes, since he had averted the crisis at the robot factory, and yet not really averted it at all.

"Well, if you do happen to think of anything..."

"I'll give you a call," Ulysses lied again.

As Inspector Artemis left to pursue her own lines of enquiry, a familiar and most welcome figure approached Ulysses, rubbing at the sore skin of his wrists.

"Might I enquire as to – I believe the phrase is – how you are doing, sir?" Nimrod asked stiffly.

"I've been better," Ulysses sighed.

"We're free to go."

"Are we?" Ulysses asked, fixing his old friend with a weary look. "I'm not free of the knowledge that my brother's murderer still walks abroad. I am not free of the guilt I feel at my part in all this."

"Your part, sir? You mean Mr Rossum's death, I take it?"

"I actually meant my part in Barty's self-imposed exile to this godforsaken rock."

"That was nothing to do with you, sir!" Nimrod contested with surprising vehemence. "You are wholly blameless in that regard!"

"Am I?"

"Of course, sir! One hundred per cent."

"Well, whether that is the case or no, Barty's killer is still at large. And it looks as though the only people on the Moon capable of solving this mystery are the two of us, old chap."

"In that case, sir, am I to take it that you have a stratagem as to how we proceed from here on in?"

"Indeed you are, Nimrod. Indeed you are."

"So you were being, shall we say, economical with the truth when you were conversing with the inspector?"

"Right again, Nimrod!" Ulysses said, a spark of triumph in his voice and something like an ember of the old fire glowing in the black pits of his eyes.

Ulysses suddenly sprang to his feet.

"So, sir, where next?"

"Petit Paris, Nimrod. Venusville," he said, taking the folded flyer from his pocket and opening it up in front of him. His manservant's nose wrinkled in disgust, as if he had just caught a whiff of something noxious and undesirable. "More precisely, The Moulin Rouge in Venusville. I rather think it's time we dropped in on Miss Selene, don't you?"

ACT THREE

Sin City

~ June 1998 ~

'I can resist everything except temptation.'

(Oscar Wilde, *Lady Windermere's Fan*, 1892)

CHAPTER THIRTEEN

Moulin Rouge

T minus 1 day, 10 hours, 29 minutes, 7 seconds

WITH STANDARD IMPERIAL Time reading close to midnight, the rest of Luna Prime was settling down to sleep for the artificially-managed night; but not Venusville. Venusville never slept. While the rest of the populace were retiring to bed, many of those who either worked in the city's notorious red light district, or who were visiting it at that late hour, were also going to bed, although with something other than sleep on their minds.

The rust-coloured droid clanked to a halt and slowly relaxed, sinking down on its piston legs as steam vented from its joints.

"There you go, gents," the girl in the driver's seat said, pushing her goggles up onto the top of her head and giving them a cheery smile. "Venusville, as requested!" The white rings around her eyes and the soot smearing the rest of her face gave her the appearance of a panda.

"Thank you...?"

"Billie, sir."

"Thank you, Billie. You have been most helpful."

"Not a problem, sir. Are you sure I can't take you anywhere in particular? How about The Last Resort or the Automaton Arena? They do say there's something for everyone in Venusville, especially a couple of discerning gents like you."

"That won't be necessary, thank you," Nimrod said dismissively.

"No, here's just fine," Ulysses added, with rather more tact.

The dandy knew that there was something for everyone in Venusville from personal experience, although he had been a young man the last time he had stopped by here.

You could walk past the canal-side brothels of New Amsterdam, take in an exotic dancing extravaganza in one of the vaudevillian theatres of Petit Paris, partake of the rough pleasures of a Turkish bath or wile away hours – or even days at a time – in the opium dens of Chinatown.

If you could afford to pay for it, in Venusville you could buy it.

The place was a celebration of gaudiness and depravity, all under one dome. Here private shops, selling clockwork sex toys, and brothels rubbed shoulders with Italian ice-cream parlours and Oriental drug dens. Casinos, along with every other form of gambling imaginable, proliferated here with the result that some people never left – arriving as optimistic, nouveau riche parvenus on the up and reduced to begging on the streets after literally losing the shirts off their backs in one of the many iniquitous poker dens before the day was out.

He wondered how many of those who came to the Moon to start a new life found themselves trapped here, as destitute as they might have been had they stayed on Earth, ruined by greed; their own as well as that of the bookies.

He wondered if Barty had ever visited any of these places. Then he stopped wondering. Of course he had. He must have done. But had it been this place that had led him into trying to blackmail three of the most powerful men on the Moon? Had Barty stumbled across their combined secret in one of these seedy backstreet flea pits?

The girl looked at Ulysses with brows furrowed. "I hope you don't mind me asking, sir, but do I know you?"

"We almost took your cab when we arrived at the Bedford-Cavor Spaceport two days ago."

"Ah, that must be it. I thought it was from somewhere else, a more recent fare, but that must be it. You had a lady and an old guy with you."

"That's right."

"See, I never forget a face."

"Well, that's excellent. Well done. Perhaps we'll see you around again some time," Ulysses said, nonchalantly turning his attention from the girl and her droid to the gaudily lit-up club on the opposite side of the street. "Pay the lady would you, Nimrod?"

Nimrod did as he was bid; peeling one bill off from the bundle of notes that suddenly appeared in his hand, as Ulysses disembarked. He clambered down from the shoulders of the Juggernaut-class droid via the passenger ladder, having already passed on the option of having the droid lift him down.

"I'm surprised you wanted to travel by automaton after what happened at Rossum's Universal Robots," Nimrod said as he joined Ulysses on the ground.

"Nimrod, you really can be such an old woman sometimes," Ulysses said with a mirthless chuckle.

His manservant said nothing but gave a snooty huff.

"Come on, Rusty. Time we were on our way."

Behind them, the girl pulled on a series of levers and she and the droid departed in the direction of the nearest cab rank, ready to make the return journey to Luna Prime's main dome courtesy of another paying customer.

Nimrod looked at the facade of the building in front of them now with the same aloof expression of disgust with which he had greeted his master's suggestion that they should pay a visit to Luna Prime's red light district in the first place.

"You think the answers you seek lie within this den of iniquity?"

Ulysses nodded. "I think the means to getting them might."

Above the entrance the sails of a red-painted windmill turned, each one picked out in lurid electric light. The tinkling of a pianola was vying for attention with a wheezing steam organ that hissed and groaned somewhere nearby.

The place had obviously seen better days. The lights and lurid pink drapes that adorned the exterior of the club did nothing to hide the peeling varnish and scuffed paintwork, if one bothered to look, which, to be honest, Ulysses doubted many of the club's clientele did. The state of the decor wasn't the thing uppermost in most people's minds when they paid a visit to the Moulin Rouge.

Like its original Parisian counterpart, the Moulin Rouge was notorious – even by the laissez-faire standards of Venusville.

Recognising Ulysses for the dandy he was – a man of substance and class with, at best, a loose attachment to his morals in certain areas – a thickset doorman, wearing a straining black tuxedo, stepped aside to let him and his manservant enter.

"Tip the man, would you?" Ulysses said coolly, his sword-cane swinging in his hand.

He looked for all the world like a casual tourist, visiting Venusville for a little light relief, come to fritter away his fortune on loose women, cheap champagne and over-priced cocktails. He certainly did not look like a man still mourning his dead brother; but then that was precisely the impression he didn't want to cultivate in others.

It wasn't the real him. It might have been once, but not now.

He *was* still grieving for his late, lamented brother, but it was that very grief that now allowed him to maintain such a convincing facade, his mask of nonchalant playboyish-ness. Below the veneer of his devil-may-care attitude, he did care – very much. Circumstances had forced his hand and he was now determined to avenge Barty's death, and it was that focus alone that enabled him to give the impression that, right at that moment, there was nowhere he'd rather be than the Moulin Rouge in Venusville's French quarter.

They passed through a gloomy lobby, decked out in blacks and deep purples, and lit only by a few latticed oil-lamps, circumvented the coat check, and passed through a set of swinging double doors into the heart of the club itself.

The air was thick with the blue fug of tobacco smoke, stale liquor and cheap perfume. Ulysses took a deep breath.

"Ahhh... Can you smell it?"

"Smell what, sir?" Nimrod said, nose wrinkling in disgust.

"Vice, Nimrod. The smell of dodgy deals done, lascivious liaisons shared and vices partaken of. Sin, old boy. We're in Sin City now."

"Hmm," Nimrod grunted, noncommittally. "The air is redolent with a distinct lack of taste and decorum, if you ask me. The sort of place..." He suddenly caught himself.

"The sort of place my brother would frequent, you mean?"

Nimrod looked at the floor, cheeks reddening in mortified embarrassment.

"I meant no disrespect, sir."

"None taken. But you forget that I've seen my fair share of stews and drug dens the world over. A life lived before it began to mellow with age."

"I do not forget, sir," Nimrod corrected him. "It is rather that I try hard not to remember."

"Very well, have it your own way. Now get the drinks in while I find us a table."

As Nimrod obediently made his way towards the lurid lights and noxiously coloured bottles on display behind the neon-lit bar, Ulysses navigated the network of tables laid out before the stage.

He made slow progress, as much thanks to the distracting spectacle that was being revealed on stage, as by the close packed nature of the furniture.

She was tall, her elegant, shapely legs made all the longer by the frankly obscene heels she was wearing. And she was as good as naked. A few strips of sparkly material and what looked like little more than a few pieces of black cotton protected what little modesty she had left, while a glittering black feather boa did little to hide the pertness of her exposed breasts or the erect studs of her nipples. The whole ensemble – what there was of it – was finished with generous amounts of powder, lip-gloss, eye-liner and mascara.

Ulysses assumed that she had had a little more on when she had first taken to the stage but the end result was what mattered in a – for want of a better word – strip joint like the Moulin Rouge.

He sat down, resting his cane on his lap and stretching out languorously, teasing out the knots in his aching muscles. The skin of his elbows and knees still stung from his tumble across the robot marshalling yard. But at least he had survived his encounter with the Titan-droid, unlike the unfortunate Rossum.

An up-tempo tune permeated the atmosphere of the club and as the black-haired beauty on stage brought her performance to an end – embellishing the bounteous gifts Mother Nature had supplied her with with a few flicks of her hair, spins around a conveniently positioned pole and modesty-risking high kicks and splits – Ulysses did his best to concentrate on his surroundings and select the best escape route, just in case, as much as the club's almost entirely male clientele were concentrating on the delightful young woman on stage.

The bar curved around one side of the elliptical space that enclosed the stage. To either side of the dancers' podium, a flight of stairs curved around the walls to the floor above, joining with a balcony that formed a complete ellipsis around the tabled area beneath. The faces of rouged young women – some barely in their teens – and the whiskered faces of the much older gentlemen they were entertaining peered down through the fug, also watching the burlesque act.

Ulysses had been to enough clubs like this one to know that leading off from the balcony would be the myriad rooms where the working girls of the Moulin Rouge ensured that the oldest profession was still alive and kicking at this furthest of the British Empire's frontiers. There had been bawds in tow when the Romans invaded Britain two millennia before, just as the soldiers fighting for queen and country in the many notable conflicts of the nineteenth century had found female companions readily to hand to offer relief from the stresses and strains of battle, and one of the first flights to the newly erected Luna Prime, more than forty years before, had brought with it its own 'monstrous regiment' of women.

He took the folded flyer from his jacket pocket and opened it. He sniffed the scented paper, the heady smell of jasmine flowers waking the suppressed memories of a rebirth in the hidden valley of Shangri-La, a quarter of a million miles away. But where would he find the fragrant Selene? On stage? Behind the bar? Or upstairs, already otherwise engaged?

"Your drink, sir," Nimrod said, placing a glass of brandy on the table in front of him.

Ulysses took the glass in his hand, resting it in his upturned palm, its stem between his third and fourth fingers. He held it under his nose and inhaled deeply, the heady vapours of the alcohol raising their own not unwelcome ghosts from his subconscious. He took a swig, savouring the honeyed sweetness and fiery aftertaste of the liquor as it slipped like melted chocolate down his throat.

"Thank you, Nimrod." He cast his manservant a sideways glance. "What are you drinking?"

"Aqua mineralis. On the rocks."

Ulysses smiled. The older man, prim and proper in his butler's attire, was sitting perched on the very edge of his seat, straight-backed, and looking as uncomfortable as a serial killer about to be interviewed by the police about the bodies they'd just turned up under his patio.

"So – if I might ask, sir – what now?"

"Now, Nimrod? Now we relax, kick back, blend in, enjoy the show."

A shudder of revulsion passed through his manservant's body.

"It's all part of the act, Nimrod, that's all. We're doing this for Barty."

Nimrod sighed, resigned now to the fact that they were going to have to wile away some time in this bordello. "Very well, sir. If we must."

Ulysses' attention drifted from his companion's unease to the arrival on stage of a new performer, greeted by a chorus of whoops and cheers, as the boa-draped nymph slipped away backstage.

She was older than the nubile girl who had preceded her but she wore her age and experience about her like a mantle. She was decked out in thigh-length patent leather boots, stockings, a suspender belt and French knickers. A scarlet taffeta whalebone corset was sorely failing to keep her swollen bosoms contained and looked in danger of giving way under the force of her Amazonian assets at any moment. She wore a feathered plume atop her carefully coiffured dyed-red hair and received the spectators' cheers and applause with arms outstretched and a saucy smile on her rouged lips.

The audience's appreciation of her not inconsiderable charms was marked by a series of shrill wolf whistles and cries of "Emmanuelle!"

The house band struck up a new tune, one ripe with fruity brass notes and trombone slides as the stripper set about wowing the crowd all over again.

Ulysses knocked back the rest of his brandy, swirling the glass to release the last of its alcoholic aromatic fragrance.

"Much as I'm sure I would relish Emmanuelle disrobing," Ulysses said, "time's a-wasting. We need to track down Selene."

"*We*, sir?"

Ulysses chuckled. "Good point. You stay down here, watch the exits. *I'll* look for Selene."

Nimrod gladly vacated his seat, retreating into the shadows beyond the bar. Ulysses left it a few moments longer, waiting until Emmanuelle's heaving bosom had at last been freed of her corset – although a pair of resolute tassels defied the men's expectation. Then, the brandy and the enthusiastic display of naked flesh warming the cockles of his heart, he too rose and made his excuses as he crossed the room accompanied by a chorus of tuts, grunts and outright cries of "Out of the way!" and "Move!"

As he left the tables and reached the foot of the stairs he was met by a woman – who was barely more than a girl – in lavender chiffon skirts and a lilac bodice. Catching his eye, she threw him a practised – and yet still utterly captivating – smile.

"Well, good evening, sir. Or is it tomorrow morning now?" she purred.

Placing a hand on his shoulder she descended the last step and draped her other slender arm around his waist.

"And what can I do for you?"

Ulysses deftly ducked a hand inside his jacket and pulled out a bundle of notes. The girl's eyes lit up like the sign above the club.

"You can tell me where I'd find Selene," he whispered into her ear, placing one of the notes into her open palm.

The girl quickly stuffed it inside her bodice and out of sight, between her heaving breasts. Her ready smile became a look of blunt disappointment.

"Up the stairs, second door on the left," she said, already walking away towards the bar, hips rolling, ready to reel in another, more willing gentleman companion for the night – or for the next hour at least.

Following the wide sweep of the stairs to the balcony, Ulysses passed a brunette dressed in a French maid's outfit – but which looked like the most impractical thing to wear if the girl was actually intending on doing any cleaning – and a blonde made-up to look like a very strict school ma'am. The men who had already sought company upstairs discretely turned the other way as Ulysses passed by.

He stopped outside the second door on the left which was upholstered in pink chintz, the traditional Valentine's image of a love heart picked out in appliqué at its centre.

He paused, listening – but hearing nothing – before knocking three times.

"*Entre*," came an accented feminine voice. "It's open."

Ulysses' first impression of the small bedchamber was that it had been set-dressed to look like something out of the Palace of Versailles, before the French had revolted, but even tackier than the real thing.

At the heart of the boudoir, a girl – of no more than twenty-one, if Ulysses was any judge – was knelt on the bed. Her skin was like porcelain. Her platinum blonde hair was piled up on top of her head, making her look like some sort of French courtesan or Wild West frontier town whore, her dress hanging off her slight frame, her less than ample bosom squashed almost flat by a whalebone corset.

"Good evening, monsieur," she said sweetly.

"Good evening," Ulysses replied, suddenly feeling uncharacteristically uneasy. "Do I have the pleasure of addressing the lovely Selene?"

"You do, *monsieur*. And how might I help you this fine evening?" she asked, stepping off the bed and making her way across the room towards him as he closed the door, turning the key in the well-oiled lock without drawing undue attention to the fact.

She stopped in front of him, her slender fingers caressing his cravat and lingering on the diamond pin.

"No, you misunderstand me, mademoiselle." Ulysses blushed. "I do not wish to sleep with you."

"You do not?" the girl said, pulling away from him aghast, utter disbelief writ large across her delicate, captivating features.

"No, I only want to ask you some questions."

"Questions?" The girl dropped her pert posterior onto the bed.

"I have money. I am happy to pay you for your time."

Selene looked at him, a childish pout on her lips. "Go on, then."

"Am I right in thinking that you knew one Bartholomew Quicksilver?"

The girl gave a gasp, her face contorting into an expression of appalled horror. Quick as a flash, she shot a hand under the plumped pillow beside her and pulled out a small ladies' pistol, its stock and barrel inlaid with glistening mother-of-pearl.

Holding the pistol in both hands, she pointed it at Ulysses' face.

The dandy swallowed hard. "*Sacre bleu!*"

CHAPTER FOURTEEN

An Inconvienient Truth

T minus 1 day, 10 hours, 13 minutes, 12 seconds

"So I TAKE it you know him then," Ulysses said, trying to remain calm.

"What's it to you?" The girl was shaking, the gun in her hands trembling.

He had seen pistols like hers before – they usually only held one round, two at most. Trouble was, she was so close that if she were to pull the trigger, chances were that the shot would still kill him, or at least leave him in a vegetative coma and as good as dead.

Ulysses gave a weary sigh. "Look if he owes you money or has upset you in some way, I'm sure I can square things with you on his behalf, but whatever the truth of the matter I could really do with your help right now."

"He warned me about people like you," Selene hissed, keeping her pistol pointed at Ulysses' forehead.

"People like me?"

He either needed to call her bluff and make a grab for the gun or, alternatively, a two-handed upper cut might knock it out of the way.

"People asking questions!" the girl spat.

"But I only asked if you knew him."

"Where is he?" There was the rumour of tears to come in the corners of her eyes. "What have you done with him? Is he all right?"

"Then you haven't heard," Ulysses said.

"Heard what?"

"You might want to sit down first," Ulysses suggested.

"What is it?" Selene shrieked, her platinum curls quivering. "Tell me!"

A sudden knock at the door made both of them start.

"Selene?" came a muffled voice. It was gruff and male. "You all right?"

The shaking courtesan looked from Ulysses to the door and back again, her eyes wide, not knowing what she should do.

The door handle turned. And then the lock rattled.

"Selene?" the gruff voice came again, more anxious cadences apparent in its tone.

"Open that door and you'll learn nothing more from me," Ulysses hissed.

The girl hesitated, eyes darting backwards and forwards.

The someone on the other side of the door gave it a push.

"Selene! What's going on?"

The girl gave Ulysses an imploring look, but kept the gun on him all the while. She took a deep breath, struggling to compose herself, and then called out, "It's all right, Harry, I'm with a client."

"Are you sure you're okay, though? He's not roughing you up is he?"

"*Non*. It is nothing like that. Just a bit of... role-play."

"Oh, all right then. Sorry to disturb you, sir."

The tension on the door handle released and Ulysses breathed a sigh of relief.

"Now," hissed Selene, "tell me, what have you done with Barty?"

"I haven't done anything with him," Ulysses replied, muscles tensing, ready to leap into action in a moment. "You have to remember that. It wasn't me."

"Tell me!"

"I'm afraid Barty's dead."

For a moment Selene did nothing. She simply stood exactly where she was, gun trained on Ulysses, mouth agape in shock, eyes wide with disbelief and glistening with moisture.

"You killed him!" she hissed, and Ulysses heard the ratcheting sound that came of her tightening her finger on the trigger.

"I didn't kill him! I wouldn't do that."

The girl's hands began to shake again, more violently than before, and she sank down onto the bed, her whole body wracked by silent sobs.

"*Mon dieu*! What am I going to do without my precious Barty?"

In that instant Ulysses made his move. In one fluid motion he grabbed the pistol and angled the barrel towards the wall before the girl knew what was going on. She gave a startled cry of panic.

"Quiet!" Ulysses hissed, turning the mother-of-pearl pistol on her now.

She looked at him with that same open expression of dread. "Are you going to kill me too?"

"No, I'm not going to kill you," he said, throwing the gun onto a white wicker chair in the corner of the room. "I haven't killed anyone," he said with a weary sigh. "Well, that's not entirely true, but I'm not going to kill you. And I didn't kill Barty either." He was quiet for a moment. "Barty was my brother; an idiot, a gambler and a fool, but my brother nonetheless."

"Then you must be Ulysses," Selene said, a faraway look in her eyes now.

"He mentioned me then?"

"A few times."

"And what was he to you?"

"He was my boyfriend," was all she could manage before she was overcome again.

"Here," Ulysses said, passing her a monogrammed handkerchief. He sat down on the bed beside her. "I loved him too, you know, despite everything."

Selene said nothing but buried her face in the handkerchief, her shoulders shaking.

"I swear that I will make whoever's responsible pay – in blood."

"How did it happen?" Selene asked, looking up at him, her eyes red and puffy.

"He fell from his thirteenth floor apartment. Broke his neck. Died instantly, thank God."

Selene gave an agonised wail of grief.

"I'm sorry. I shouldn't –"

"No," Selene interrupted him, "I want to know. I need to know."

"The police are convinced it was suicide."

"No, never!"

"Then you and I have something else in common. But if Barty didn't end his own life, someone else must have ended it for him."

"It must have been one of them," Selene replied, her voice barely more than a whisper.

Ulysses' heart suddenly leapt. She knew something. "Who?"

She looked at him, as if attempting to read his face. And then she was suddenly shooting anxious glances around the room, as if she had just remembered something discomforting yet important.

"No," she said, leaning forward and whispering into his ear. "Not here."

Ulysses followed her agitated gaze into the corners of the room. The room must be bugged – possibly for no more sinister a reason than for the protection of the girls working at the club. "Where then?"

"Do you know the arena down the street?"

"Not yet, but I'll find it."

"I'll see you there in time for the Clash of Steel bout. Now go."

He took her hands in his and gave them a gentle squeeze, along with what he hoped was a reassuring smile. Then he turned, unlocked the door, and slipped out of her boudoir.

Keeping his eyes down and trying not to draw attention to himself, Ulysses descended the staircase and made his way towards the exit. As he passed the bar, Nimrod emerged from the neon-formed shadows there.

"We're leaving," Ulysses said under his breath as his manservant dropped into step beside him.

"Am I to take it that you found Miss Selene?"

"Yes, thank you."

"And did you pump her for information?"

Ulysses halted mid-stride. He turned to his manservant, a snarl forming on his face. "She was Barty's girlfriend," he growled, stabbing Nimrod in the chest with his index finger. "The girl's in bits."

Nimrod blushed and looked down at his immaculately polished shoes. "Sir, please accept my apology. I don't know what came over me."

"Apology accepted." Ulysses quickly picked up the pace again. "Now let's get out of here. The arena awaits."

"THEY'RE ON THE move again," Veronica Verse said, dropping the binoculars from in front of her face.

Beside her, in the driver's seat of the automobile, Lars Chapter finished packing the rucksack open on his lap. "They weren't in there long."

"No. But then I find most men don't take as long about these things as they claim they will." The young woman turned and grinned, seeing her companion's disgruntled expression. "Apart from you, of course, my cherry pie," she said, patting his thigh.

"So, what now?"

"Now, my little apple crumble? We keep close on their tail and see where they're going. Nice and simple, just like the boss wants."

Lars started the car and pulled out from the kerb, following the two men as they strode purposefully along the pavement, the car's tyres crunching on the mooncrete surface of the road, safe in the knowledge that in the boot of the car there was enough ammunition to take down a Titan-class droid.

CHAPTER FIFTEEN

Gladiator

T minus 1 day, 9 hours, 41 minutes, 36 seconds

INSIDE THE ARENA all was noise – the blaring of klaxons, the brass trumpeting of horns, the excited roar of the crowd, the clatter of heavy machinery and the steam-piped musical fanfares being broadcast over loudspeakers.

Outside, the building looked like little more than a steel cube; a prison, draped with greasy chains and adorned with blunted cutting blades. Empty oil drums, shredded tyres and all manner of scrap metal detritus filled the alleyways surrounding the structure, where they merged with the workshops that catered to the kill-bot support crews.

The entrance was wide and gaudily-decorated, draped with circus tent canvas door flaps, between which those attending the gladiatorial bouts had to pass. Above it, atop the rusted teeth of mock crenulations, the carcass of a decommissioned Goliath-class droid hung suspended from a winch-crane. The dead robot had long ago had its guts ripped out and recycled, its pitted shell having nonetheless been given a fresh paint job that made it look like a mechanised harlequin in the swinging beams of rotating search-lights.

Ulysses and Nimrod joined the heaving tide of humanity entering the arena.

Having paid a girl, dressed as a tin woman, at a ticket booth, Ulysses led the way through the broad arch, circumventing the bookies declaring the odds on the upcoming fight with much frenzied arm-waving. Their frantic tic-tac-toe made them look like they were suffering from St Vitus' Dance, as if capering to the accursed disease's tune.

From a holding bay area – surrounded by merchandising stands and hot food vendors – they followed the clamour of the crowd and the smells of hot metal and axle-grease to the arena floor.

Inside it was a riot of colour, from the rust-red of the wall panels, to the sodium orange glow of the arc-lamps, the fluorescent pinks and greens of neon signs to the garish outfits of those employed by the arena. Even the gun-metal grey of the sentry droids' armour had been masked with copious amounts of bright blue paint and the addition of crazed black and white hazard markings.

The combat area itself was a square, measuring some thirty yards across on every side, a raised wall of steel plates keeping the audience and the combatants a safe distance apart. The gladiatorial pit so created was surrounded on three sides by tiered rows of seating. The fourth side of the square contained the portcullis gate by which the combatants entered the arena under their own steam, and through which many of them would be carried out later in pieces.

Above the heavy medieval portcullis a grille-enclosed balcony jutted out over the arena. From this elevated position the master of the games would see that all bouts were conducted fairly, all from behind a pane of wire-mesh-reinforced, bullet-proof glass.

While Ulysses and Nimrod were still looking for a seat, the last unfortunate to lose a fight was being winched out of the arena on the end of a large steel hook, internal pipework dangling like intestines from the hole that had been torn through the steel plate of its simulated midriff.

During this brief hiatus in the otherwise unending rounds of combats, some of those in attendance were making a dash for the public conveniences or taking the opportunity to get something to eat from one of the eateries positioned just outside of the main arena.

The Automaton Arena was not on any of the officially-sanctioned tours but it was one of the most popular and well-attended event locations within the whole of the teeming future metropolis of Luna Prime.

Ulysses went from scouring the crowds for any sign of Selene to checking his fob-watch, to see how many minutes had passed since they had last spoken.

"Any sign of her, sir?"

"No, not yet. But then she's still got another few minutes to go before the next bout by the look of things. You need to be keeping an eye out for a slight girl with long, platinum blonde hair and skin the colour of milk."

"Very good, sir."

The two of them returned to scouring the crowd, trying to catch sight of Selene as she made her entrance.

"Look," Ulysses said after only another sixty seconds or so, "and I don't know about you, but I'm feeling a little peckish. In fact, I can't remember when I last ate. Run and get me some popcorn or something in a bun would you, before the show starts? There's a good chap."

A FEW MOMENTS later, Veronica Verse and Lars Chapter joined the steady stream of people entering the robot arena.

"Which way did they go?" Lars asked, adjusting the position of the loaded pack on his back, as Veronica tossed a ticket booth attendant a handful of coins.

"They're inside."

"What? In the audience?"

"Yes," Verse replied as she bustled her way past the food stands and past the entrance to the main arena, making her way towards a gaggle of people surrounding a cage in which two robot avians were clawing and pecking the clockwork innards from each other.

"Then why aren't we following them?" Chapter said, hurrying to keep up with the trotting footsteps of his companion.

"Because it's too public, you silly pudding. We need to be more subtle than that if we're to keep our cover. You've still got another of those remotes in your bag, haven't you?"

"Oh, I see," the hitman said, as they ducked past the robocock fight, those eagerly absorbed in the match ignoring them completely. "You mean like the number we did back at the Ros –"

"Shhh!" she hushed him, grabbing him and pulling him into the shadows behind an iron pillar. "Not here!"

They waited as a burly engineer emerged from behind the curtain that led backstage, carrying a heavy spanner over one shoulder, whistling tunelessly through his teeth.

"But yes," she admitted once the engineer was out of earshot. "Like that. And you've still got that portable Babbage engine?"

"Yes."

"Good. Then follow me, sugar cakes. We're going to sabotage ourselves a robot."

"LADIES AND GENTLEMEN," the voice boomed from speakers suspended from the spider's web of walkways above the fight floor.

All eyes turned to the balcony. Standing there in a motley top hat, floor length multicoloured coat and matching waistcoat, stood the Master of the Games himself.

He was flanked by a pair of youthful lovelies – young enough to be his granddaughters – and twins by the look of things as well, and dressed even more outrageously than the Master of Ceremonies. They wore black tutus that might as well have not been there at all, considering how well they showed off their legs, their torn fishnet stockings and their thigh-length leather boots. Their blouses were open provocatively low at the front and the pair's ensemble was finished with brass-rimmed goggles and a shock of short-cropped, peroxide blonde hair.

The Games Master was tall – six feet at least – and thin. He could have been in either his fifties or his sixties but, even from his seat in the crowd, Ulysses could still discern the mischievous, youthful twinkle in his eye. His shoulder length hair and showman's goatee beard had both been dyed a variety of colours to compliment the rest of his look, and in one fingerless-gloved hand he was holding onto the flared end of a speaking tube.

His rich baritone swept through the arena and over the heads of the eager spectators. "It's past the witching hour which means it's time for... Midnight Murder Machines!"

The roar of the crowd became a fever-pitched scream.

This was the main event.

"This is what you've all been waiting for. The fight of the night! Pure mechanoid mayhem! No quarter asked and none given. Kill or be killed. A battle to the death between our champion and a new challenger!"

The crowd went wild.

"Sorry," came a feminine French voice from besides Ulysses, making him start. "It took longer to get away than I thought it would."

"Never mind," said Ulysses, his racing pulse slowing again. "You're here now; that's all that matters."

The girl looked much as she had when Ulysses had last seen her in her boudoir, only she was wearing a travelling cloak over her clothes now.

"Ladies and gentlemen! Fight fans! Please put your hands together for five times champion, undefeated in this ring to date – the Slayminator!"

The crowd cheered as a brassy fanfare trumpeted from the speakers over their ringside seats.

"So, what did you want to tell me that you didn't want to risk telling tell me back at the Moulin Rouge?" he asked, having to raise his voice to be heard over the noise of the crowd.

She leaned in closer. "I know who Barty was working for."

"And now," the Games Master's voice bellowed from the public address system, "give a big Automaton Arena welcome to the carborundum-bladed menace, the mech of misery, the robot revolutionary – Lockjaw!"

This time the ever-growing audience responded with as many boos as huzzahs.

"He was working for someone?"

"Yes."

"What do you mean? I can't imagine Barty ever having anything like a conventional job."

"I mean I know what he had got himself mixed up in. I knew it was dangerous. I told him he was playing with fire. But the way he spoke about it... I don't think he really had a choice."

"What was he mixed up in, Selene?"

She opened her mouth to speak again.

"Gladiators!" The roar rang from the steel walls of the gladiator pit. "Prepare for battle!"

Horns blared and klaxons sounded. Having loosed the chains securing the droids' weapons, the hulking, battle-upgraded automatons' attendants hurried to safety, retreating beneath the great spiked portcullis gate which lowered behind them with a reverberating clang.

"Let the mechanoid mayhem begin!"

A strident horn blast sounded and battle was joined.

The furnace roar of steam engines, the grinding of chain weapons, and the pumping of pistoning pile-driver fists – along with the crash of iron on steel as the robots charged each other – even this white noise of battle was almost drowned out by the hysterical screams of the hyped-up crowd.

"Say that again?" Ulysses bellowed over the clamour.

"Your government. The British Government!" Selene repeated, her voice suddenly sounding louder than even the clash of steel booming from the arena below.

Ulysses turned away, his brow crumpled in consternation, his attention falling on the spectacle unfolding beneath them.

The Slayminator was like an industrialised suit of armour built for an ogre, its head a grilled knight's helm, one arm a whirling flail, the other a whirring chain-blade. Lockjaw was shorter, squatter and more compact, with tracked caterpillar treads rather than pistoning legs, its head little more than an endlessly snapping gin-trap maw lined with diamond-hard carborundum teeth, both its telescoping brass arms ending in snapping pincers. The two robots powered towards each other, trailing steam and sooty smoke, their mechanised actions generating their own monstrous bestial battle-cries.

Surely if Barty had been employed by Department Q, the same agency he worked for, he would have been informed. Surely Barty would have told him. But then perhaps he was working for another faction within the government, one with its own shadowy puppet-masters with their own agenda – one at odds with the powers that be. Or whoever had got their claws into Barty had lied. Perhaps they had merely been masquerading as a government agency. Or perhaps Barty had lied to his new girlfriend to make himself appear to be something other than he truly was.

A scream of metal sparks flew from the carapace of the beleaguered Lockjaw as the favourite, Slayminator, buried its whirling chain-blade in the robot gladiator's treads. Another cheer went up from the crowd. The underdog spun on the spot, its motive systems crippled. The hulking, adapted Goliath-droid pulled its blade free, bringing the Morningstar mace-heads of its flail crashing across the crown of its rival's head.

The clacking gin-trap jaws snapped shut on a steel ball. The crowd started to boo. The Slayminator, finding itself trapped, raised its screaming chain-blade again. The champion's supporters cheered and waved banners.

Ulysses was only half aware of what was taking place in the fighting pit below. He barely even noticed when a smear of oil burst into purple-orange flame, ignited by a stray spark.

During the course of the last forty-eight hours his world had been turned upside down. His brother was dead, so were the three industrialists he appeared to have some (as yet unexplained) interest in, and now Barty's girlfriend had just told him that his brother had been working for the British Government. If that was truly the case, was that the trouble that had driven Barty into hiding on the Moon, the problem that he had claimed even Ulysses, with all his contacts, couldn't help him with?

"Hmm?" Ulysses asked, aware that Selene was speaking to him again. Nimrod sat on the other side of him, gazing with disinterest at the gladiatorial combat.

Selene looked at him, sorrow etched deep on her young face. "I said what do we do now?"

"Now? We find my brother's killer, that's what."

"But we already know who..." She broke off as the tears came again.

"I don't believe it," Ulysses said, his tone one of insistent denial.

"Who else is there? Who else would have done such a thing?"

"It has to have something to do with the three industrialists."

The scream of metal on metal rang from the fighting pit as the Slayminator's chain-blade grated across the carborundum teeth of its challenger.

"Did you know about them as well?" continued Ulysses.

"Barty did say something. You know who these men are?"

"Were. But yes, I do."

"Were?"

"They're dead as well, now. All within the last twelve hours."

Selene stared at him, utterly bewildered. "They were murdered too?"

"It rather looks that way."

"Then how can they be behind..." She couldn't bring herself to finish the sentence.

"They've still got something to do with it, I'm sure of it. Just because they're dead doesn't mean one of them didn't see Barty bumped off before someone got to him in return."

She fixed him with an accusing stare. "And that wasn't you?"

The crowd shared a sharp intake of breath as the Slayminator wrenched its rival's head from its armoured body.

"What? You think I killed them?"

"Well, did you?" Selene asked.

"No, I did not! Well, one of them, but that was an accident. I wasn't the one who let a rogue droid loose in his robot factory!"

"What?"

"It's a long story." Selene's accusing stare didn't waver. "And it would take too long to go over again now. Just believe me when I tell you that I didn't set out to do away with any of them. I only wanted to get to the bottom of who it was that had Barty killed!"

Registering the horrified look in the girl's eyes Ulysses turned away, as he concentrated on bringing his temper back under control. He hadn't meant to fly off the handle at her like that, but then grief affected people in different ways.

He looked up sharply. Something was wrong. It took him a moment to realise what it was.

It was the voice of the crowd. He could hear screams as well as shouts rising from the throng of spectators – and not screams of excitement either. They were screams of fear and the primal screams of mass hysteria as panic began to spread its insidious tentacles throughout the audience.

Ulysses stood up.

"What is it, sir?" Nimrod asked, rising from the bench.

"Something's wrong."

The crowds of people were parting like the Red Sea before Moses' staff as a tidal wave of terror surged ahead of them.

Ulysses stood on tiptoe, craning his head to see what lay to the rear of the panicking throng.

The first object his eyes alighted on was the smoking wreckage of the machine known as Lockjaw, now missing its head and one pincer limb, the ruined robot's torso still whirling like a dervish about its central gimbal.

It took him a moment to find its conqueror, the Slayminator. The gladiator-automaton was up to its chain-blade and flail in bodies, arterial blood spraying across its armour-plating, a furious red glow behind its eye-visor. People were gutted, bludgeoned and crushed beneath its relentless advance as the robot waded into the defenceless crowd.

Beyond the barricade of the portcullis – which, Ulysses noticed, remained down and locked in place, no doubt – technicians were desperately punching at remote controls, shouting at each other in desperation as their efforts to shut down the Slayminator from afar failed spectacularly.

The Games Master and his girls were staring in horror at the massacre being committed in the arena below, their shock-white faces pressed up against the reinforced glass of their booth.

"It's gone haywire, sir!" Nimrod exclaimed with a burst of uncharacteristic emotion that surprised Ulysses almost as much as the murderous actions of the droid.

"I wouldn't say that exactly," Ulysses muttered, his eyes following the Slayminator's homicidal advance. "I think if you look again, you'll see that it's heading straight for us."

Selene gave a heartfelt cry of, "*Merde!*" and was on her feet in an instant.

"That's a very succinct way of summing up our situation," Ulysses said. "Now if I might make a suggestion? Run!"

CHAPTER SIXTEEN

Robots

T minus 1 day, 9 hours, 29 minutes, 18 seconds

"WHAT'S GOING ON?" Selene shrieked as Ulysses pulled her after him through the panicking crowds.

"I know," Ulysses managed between breaths, "you're wondering why we're running when we should be standing up to that thing and taking it down."

"No, that's not what I was thinking, actually!"

"The situation is that that thing's targeting us," Ulysses explained as he and his manservant forced a way through the throng.

"What?"

"Well, one of us. You or me."

Selene looked even more confused and uncertain than before Ulysses' revelation. "How can you be sure?"

With a rending crash of steel, the Slayminator burst from the arena between them, tearing down a sheet metal wall with one swipe of its whirling chain-blade, its attack bolstered with the additional momentum of the weight of its massive body. Selene screamed.

"Is that enough evidence for you?"

People scattered behind them, but still the huge gladiatorial robot thundered after them, flail whirling, chain-blade shrieking.

The air around them was redolent with the smells of engine oil, hot metal, burning coal and fear.

"And if that isn't enough evidence for you, put it this way." Ulysses dodged past an abandoned food stall, dragging Selene after him, as Nimrod brought up the rear. "First the three men that my brother has files on in his apartment are killed within the space of a day. Then I follow up the only other lead Barty left me and find you. We then meet to talk and it just so happens that that's when an eight-foot tall kill-bot decides to go haywire and lays into the crowd, whilst heading in our direction. Coincidence? I think not."

The main entrance to the arena was in sight now. Behind them the Slayminator swept a hot dog stand out of the way with a swipe of a massive arm, crushing the wretch who had been manning it under a heavy steel hoof.

The two sentry droids came to life, rotating about their wheel bases and, moving as one, converged on the escaping gladiator-droid.

The battle between the three automatons, such as it was, was brief and yet would have been the stuff of mechanoid-mangling legend, had it taken place within the ring. But in the time it took Ulysses, Nimrod and Selene to cross the holding bay the conflict was over, the gladiator emerging with its armour scarred and dented, but unbowed. What was left of the sentry-droids, however, would have to be collected in barrows and wheeled to the nearest scrap heap.

"We get clear, we draw it away from other innocent bystanders and we limit the loss of life," Ulysses explained. "Then, when we've got it out in the open, we take it down."

"And how do you plan on doing that?" Selene pressed, still in a state of shock.

Ulysses turned and flashed her a manic, devilish grin. "Don't worry, I'll think of something. I usually do."

"THEY'RE LEAVING THE arena!" Lars Chapter exclaimed as he kept a hand on the joystick of the remote control.

Crouched behind an upturned droid, lying over an inspection pit in the repair shop backstage at the Clash of Steel, Chapter and Verse followed the droid's progress via a grainy image on the tiny screen in front of them, piggy-backing on the signal transmitted by the automaton's own optical relays.

"Is the 'bot still in range?" Verse demanded.

"At the moment, but it won't be for long. This kit's only got a short range transmitter."

"Why, for God's sake?" Veronica Verse shrieked, her face contorted into a demonic manifestation of rage.

"Because anything with a longer effective range wouldn't fit in a backpack!"

"Then get after them!"

"But someone might see us," Chapter protested, still trying to direct the killer robot at the same time as holding up his end of the argument.

"What would you rather risk? Someone seeing us, or our bloody reputation? Answer me that!"

NIMROD AND ULYSSES ran on – with Selene still in tow – and out of the confines of the Automaton Arena.

Even though it was close to one A.M., Venusville's Petit Paris was still bustling with tourists, gamblers, gentlemen in search of companionship for what remained of the night, and young ladies of questionable virtue looking to give those very gentlemen the benefit of their company for significantly less time, and considerably more money, than the gentlemen would really have wished.

But it was clear to even the most casual of onlookers by now that something was wrong. Underscoring the melange of card-programmed steam organs, the cheery tunes rising from the many vaudevillian establishments that lined the street and the cries of bunko booth artistes, were the cries of the crowd now pouring through the arena gates, heedless of their own safety in the face of the chugging hansoms, omnibuses and steam-velocipedes already struggling to navigate the packed central thoroughfare of Petit Paris.

Ulysses skidded to a halt as a hansom cab hurtled past, missing him and his two companions by only a matter of a few inches, horn blaring angrily.

The dandy quickly scanned the street in front of him. He was met by lurid neon-lit signs, crowded omnibuses and the scattering survivors of the arena massacre.

Behind him he could hear more screams accompanied by the screech of rending metal and the furious roar of the Slayminator's weapons.

And then, to Ulysses, it seemed as if a curious hush fell over the scene.

He turned, his right hand still tightly gripping the girl's, his knuckles white, not daring to let go. And then Nimrod was gone, swallowed up by the escaping masses.

Ulysses looked back at the advancing automaton. Eight-feet tall, and almost as broad across its shoulders, it was covered in armoured plate three inches thick, intended to protect it against the worst the robo-arena could throw at it. Each piston-driven leg could deliver several tons of pulverising pressure while its whirling flail and chain-blade attachments were designed to remove the head or limbs from a fully-armoured counterpart – as it had proved to such great effect against the unfortunate Lockjaw. Flesh and bone would be as rotten fruit and cardboard against their crushing metal might.

Ulysses was reminded of his various run-ins with the Limehouse Golem in the rotting docklands of the East End of London. Nothing less than an explosive charge had been required to take that down in the end – and, even then, the technologically-adept vigilante Spring-Heeled Jack had been able to reconstruct it and bring it back from the dead.

The Slayminator's scratched and dented carapace glistened with an unearthly iridescent green and purple sheen in the sinful lights of Petit Paris' seedy illuminations.

With less than ten yards between them, the automaton tore down the circus-tent drapes of the arena entrance, stepped through onto the street and came to a grinding halt.

"WHAT'S HE DOING?" Lars Chapter's tone was one of utter disbelief, as Veronica Verse dragged him into cover behind an overturned food stall in the entrance lobby.

"What is it? What's the matter?"

"He's just standing there, looking at us..."

"Looking at *us*?"

"The robot. I mean the robot."

"Then take him down!"

Chapter hesitated, his hand hovering over the joystick control. "Perhaps he knows something we don't. What trick's he got up his sleeve?"

"None that he's going to have time to use if you take him down now!" Verse hissed, daring to poke her head above the rim of the toppled cart. "I can see him. Him and the girl. Take them out. Both of them. Now!"

Lars Chapter took hold of the control lever. "Very well. If you're sure."

WITH A HISS of steam and a grinding of gears, chain-blade revving, the Slayminator resumed its advance.

"*Monsieur?*" Selene said weakly, giving Ulysses' hand a squeeze. "If I might make a suggestion, I think now might be a good time to run, *non?*"

A shrill steam-whistle blew behind them. Ulysses shot a glance over his shoulder, some unknowable instinct inside him meaning that he was already moving out of the path of the accelerating vehicle before his conscious mind had registered what was going on.

As the robot powered towards them, trailing clouds of smoke and steam after it, the omnibus hurtled across their path, and slammed into the automaton.

An empty omnibus ploughed on up over the edge of the pavement – the automaton's heels kicking up sparks from the mooncrete as it was pushed ahead of the speeding vehicle – and into the side of the arena palisade before coming to an abrupt halt, its windscreen fracturing under the force of the impact.

For a moment the crowd was silenced. Then the hubbub began to rise in volume again as the scattered onlookers began to jostle around, morbid fascination dragging their steps back across the street, wanting to see for themselves precisely what fate had befallen the gladiator droid.

A tangle of piston-limbs and twisted weapon attachments protruded from the buckled bonnet of the omnibus.

The driver's door creaked open, making those leading the line of the curious start, and a dazed Nimrod half-fell out of the cab onto the street.

Slipping free of Selene's hand, Ulysses was the first to reach his reeling manservant.

"Nimrod, are you all right, old boy?" he said, putting a steadying hand around his companion's shoulders.

Nimrod looked at him sheepishly and nodded.

"That was a damn stupid thing to do, you old fool!" Ulysses clapped a hand on his back. "That's just the sort of foolhardy thing I would've done. Well done!"

"I learnt from the best, sir," Nimrod said, the rumour of a smile creasing his lips momentarily.

"Come on," Ulysses said as Selene joined them, one shock after another compounding the look of utter bewilderment on the girl's face. "Let's get you a stiff drink. Or do you think you need to see a doctor?"

"No, sir, I'll be fine. I'll be right as rain in a minute. If I could just sit down for a moment..."

"Of course," Ulysses said, "and we'd better make that drink a double. And one for you too, old boy," he quipped.

The murmurs of the gathering crowd were suddenly drowned out by the tortured groan of twisting steel coming from behind them. The crowd gasped.

"Now that doesn't sound good." Ulysses surveyed the spot where the omnibus had ploughed into the exterior wall of the arena.

It shifted on its wheels and then bumped backwards on its tyres. With a scream like an over-revving engine the Slayminator's chain-blade started up again.

Rusty water sprayed from the ruptured boiler of the cab in a geyser of super-heated steam as the robot cut itself free.

The gestalt entity that was the crowd was backing away now, parts of it at a stumbling run, knowing what the killer-bot was capable of, other parts screaming as hysterical panic seized hold of them.

Ulysses and Selene began to do the same, half-carrying the woozy Nimrod between them. Ulysses wondered if he was concussed after the crash.

As he watched the Slayminator extricate itself from the wreckage of the omnibus, he really didn't know what they were going to do.

The droid stumbled free, almost losing its balance straight away. Ulysses could see that its right foot had been almost sheared clean off by the collision, crushed as it had been between the cab of the omnibus and the steel wall of the arena, which now bore a massive indentation in the shape of its hulking mechanoid form.

The robot's head rotated left and right as its optical sensors struggled to locate and lock on to its original target.

The head abruptly ground to a halt mid-rotation, the angry red glow pulsing from behind its visor fixed on Ulysses' face.

The droid limped towards the dandy's party, still managing to cover several yards with every stride. Its flail twitched ineffectually on the end of its right arm but – as had already been proven by the Slayminator's escape from the wreckage of the omnibus – its devastating chain-blade was still in lethal working order.

Ulysses was quietly confident that he could move faster than the robot, now that it had been crippled, but Nimrod was in no condition to run anywhere, and the dandy wasn't about to leave him to the mercies of this killing machine. He was pretty sure the girl wouldn't get far without him either. He couldn't risk leaving either of them. He still wasn't entirely sure which of them – him or the girl – was the actual intended target. There was always the possibility that it was both of them.

No, he thought, this had to finish and it had to finish now. The only question was what suitable weapon was there available to him that could stop the Slayminator when it had managed to walk away from a high-speed collision with a six-ton omnibus?

Ulysses steadied himself as a series of tremors passed through the mooncrete-surface of the road. A second later he could hear the crash of pounding footfalls as well as feel them through the trembling ground.

"What now?" Ulysses exclaimed, snapping his head in the direction of the new wave of screaming emanating from the other end of the street. Had another droid been sent after them?

A shadow passed over them as the Juggernaut stepped between them and the goliath-class automaton.

The Slayminator had been an intimidating presence, a good two feet taller than Ulysses and many, many times heavier. But even this champion of the Automaton Arena was dwarfed by the statuesque Juggernaut, looking like some primitive idol come to life in response to the prayers and entreaties of its cowed followers.

The rust-red monster clomped towards the gleaming but battered Slayminator, fists the size of forty-four gallon oil drums pulled back, piston-muscles ready to pound the battle-bot into the ground.

With a furnace roar of fury, the kill-droid engaged the Juggernaut, chain-blade raised.

Ulysses and Selene continued to back away, making for the other side of the street, taking Nimrod with them.

The Juggernaut had its back to them but even in the strange, pooling neon light of the whorehouses and casinos, Ulysses could still make out the tattered remnants of playhouse bills and advertisements for the oxygen mills plastered to its hull. With the colossal droid standing between them and the berserk killing machine, Ulysses could see little of the fight that ensued but of a couple of points he was certain. It was brief and it was brutal.

He heard the scream of the chain-blade. He heard the crunch of a fist – designed for pulverising moon rock repeatedly for days on end – connect with armour-plating three inches thick.

The scream of the blade became a screeching – like the cry of a wounded animal – and then died altogether. There was the crump of a boiler imploding and the fingernails-on-a-blackboard sound of separating metal vertebrae, before a nerve-shredding unnatural silence descended over the street.

The rust-red hulk in front of them rotated about its waist-bearing and Ulysses found himself presented with the head of the Slayminator, held in the shovel fingers of the victor, spools of copper wire and leaking hydraulic pipes trailing from the dead robot's severed neck. As he watched, the furious red light behind its visor grille faded and died.

Ulysses looked from the disarticulated head up, past the juggernaut's colossal chest-plate, to the driver's cab atop its shoulders and the grinning face of the girl.

Blue eyes and a shining smile beamed down at him from beneath a shock of bleach blonde hair, a pair of grease-smeared goggles pushed up on the young mechanic's panda-eyed face. Ulysses smiled back at the girl and her droid.

"All right, gents?" Billie said. "Looked like you could do with a hand, didn't they Rusty?"

The rumble of a steam engine rose from inside the boiler-chest of the juggernaut, and in that moment Ulysses could have believed that the robot was chuckling to itself.

CHAPTER SEVENTEEN

Pretty Woman

T minus 1 day, 8 hours, 8 minutes, 51 seconds

"WELL I DON'T know about you lot," Ulysses said as he helped ease Nimrod onto one of the cream-upholstered sofas back in the suite they shared at the five-star Nebuchadnezzar, "but I could do with a drink."

"Here, let me," the French girl said, bustling into the apartment and making her way over to the room's drinks cabinet with unerring accuracy.

"Cognac please. Two." Ulysses looked at the still woozy Nimrod with genuine concern in his eyes. "And you'd better make them doubles."

"*D'accord.*" With that Selene set about pouring the drinks from a crystal decanter from a silver tray on top of the cabinet.

"Come in, Billie," Ulysses said, addressing the open door of the hotel suite. "Come in. You've earned your right to be here just as much as anyone else. If it wasn't for you we probably wouldn't be here at all!"

The smudged face of the youthful cab driver appeared from around the edge of the door.

"Blimey O'Riley!" she gasped, her eyes wide with shock. "I ain't never been in a place like *this*!"

Slowly the girl entered the room, struggling to take in the sheer opulence– from the crystal chandelier, the polar bear skin rug on the floor, to the lead crystal glasses of the drinks cabinet and the home kinema screen on the far side of the living room.

"Bloody Nora!" she exclaimed, her voice barely more than a whisper. "My five brothers and I grew up in a place less than half the size of this one room!"

She looked as if she was about to take a step over the threshold into the suite when she hesitated again.

"Are you sure they'll be all right with me leaving Rusty downstairs in the car park?"

"They should be. After all, I tipped them handsomely enough," Ulysses said. "Which brings us rather neatly to the question of your fee. Come on in and we can discuss how much over the odds I'm going to end up paying you. Give me a hard time, mind. I'm not a pushover you know."

Cautiously the young cabbie-cum-mechanic took half a dozen wary steps into the hotel room. She suddenly stopped and looked down at her feet.

"Oh Lordy," she said, as she saw the dirty black footprints the soles of her boots had left on the pristine, ice white carpet.

"Don't worry," Ulysses laughed. "Come on in. Have a seat. Take the weight off. You'll have a drink with us, of course, won't you?"

"I can't," the girl said, suddenly coming across as mousey and nervous, the bravura she had demonstrated back in Venusville having evaporated.

"Oh, I see, I'm sorry," Ulysses backtracked. "Of course, how foolish of me." Billie looked crestfallen. "You're quite right; you shouldn't drink and drive."

"What?" A snort of laughter erupted from the cabbie. "Many's the time I've taken Rusty out after a skin-full the night before when I've probably still been drunk as a skunk. No, I'll drink your health, sir. I was just worried about the furniture. I can't sit on that." She pointed at the cream covering of the sofa.

"Oh, I see."

"Quite right too, Miss Wilhelmina," Nimrod said, making all sorts of strange faces as he struggled to bring his eyes into focus.

"Here, I don't suppose I could ask a cheeky favour, could I?"

Ulysses smiled at the young woman. "I have a feeling you're going to ask me anyway."

"Would you mind if I stepped into your bathroom to freshen up, only I don't often get to take a shower under anything other than the leaky gutter out the back of the garage Rusty and I call home. Only, seeing as how we stepped in at the last minute and saved you-"

"It's all right, go ahead," Ulysses said. "You don't need to justify yourself to me. You deserve it. Run yourself a bath if you fancy it. It's that way."

"Thank you kindly," Billie said, kicking off her boots and scampering across the vast suite, already starting to strip out of her greasy overalls as she did so.

Selene gave her a severe look as she passed her, two half-full glasses of brandy in her hands, as much as to say, "Don't start treading on my toes; flirting is my stock in trade."

Ulysses found himself unable to wipe the satisfied smile off his face as his eyes followed the young woman's skipping steps to the bathroom, the oily overalls already pulled down as far as her hips.

She ducked through the door to the bathroom - leaving greasy finger marks on the gleaming brass handle - and closed it quickly behind her.

Ulysses, his pulse racing, realised he had been holding his breath and now let it out in a breathy whistle.

Handing the dandy and his butler their drinks, the courtesan sat down beside Ulysses on the sofa, folding her legs under her, the sliced fabric of her dress separating to expose the milk-white flesh of her thighs.

Now that she was so close to him, Ulysses inhaled, catching the lavender and lilac scent of her perfume, and his felt his pulse quicken for the second time in as many minutes.

He caught himself at that point. This was his brother's grieving girlfriend – his *late* brother's girlfriend – and a harlot at that. Not that that bothered Ulysses. He had enjoyed the company of the ladies at the Queen of Hearts' Temple of Venus in Belgravia on plenty of occasions, but he wondered if it had bothered Barty, knowing that she was going with numerous different men on a daily basis, between their own stolen moments. The evidence provided by the Moulin Rouge flyer suggested that Barty had probably met Selene the same way most men had.

She seemed much calmer now, their encounter with the Slayminator having ended in such a pleasing fashion – at least as far as Ulysses' was concerned. After the adrenaline come-down following his encounter with the robot gladiator, he needed something to distract his weary mind from the traitorous suggestions his body was implanting inside his mind, now that his ability to fight temptation was at its weakest.

"So," he said, with forced enthusiasm. "Where were we, before we were so rudely interrupted by that berserker bot?"

She sat there for a moment, nursing her glass of brandy, peering at Ulysses from beneath a tumble of platinum curls that now hung in disarray, giving her a somehow appealing, dishevelled look.

"How many died, do you think?" she asked.

"I'm sorry? When?"

"At the arena. The robot. How many do you think it killed trying to get to us?"

Ulysses broke eye contact, turning his gaze, instead, to the glass in his hands. "I don't know."

"I'll tell you how many. *Too* many! And before that how many others?" Then the tears came again. "What am I going to do without my poor, dear Barty? He promised me that we would escape this place together."

The girl's slight body was wracked by great silent sobs, salt water splashing her dress.

Just like Barty, Ulysses thought, always trying to run away. Only trouble was, trouble always followed him because the one thing a man couldn't run away from was himself.

From beyond the door to the bathroom came the sound of a bath being run and the tuneful humming of the other girl.

"Think not of how many have already died but think of how many more will die if the arch-manipulators behind this dark scheme – whatever that may be – are not stopped," Ulysses said, putting down his glass and taking her hands in his. "Tell me everything you know, and I promise you that I will do all I can to bring Barty's killer – or killers – to justice."

Selene sniffed loudly and Ulysses dipped a hand into a pocket, passing her a crumpled handkerchief.

"What did Barty tell you about the three industrialists?"

It seemed even more likely now to Ulysses that one of the mysterious trio of Shurin, Rossum and Bainbridge had had Barty killed. Perhaps all of them had been in on the plan, having found out, via their own agents no doubt, that Barty was spying on them. But that didn't tell him who had had the three of them killed, or why. Had it been another of the operatives from the agency Barty had been working for, or was there someone else involved? Someone Ulysses had not yet run into?

Selene took another swig of brandy, took a deep breath to compose herself, and then began. "He told me there were three of them. He didn't tell me their names, just that I'd be amazed if I ever found out; that I wouldn't believe him if he did tell me."

"Well I can tell you who they were," Ulysses said. "Jared Shurin, owner and CEO of Syzygy Industries, Dominic Rossum, of Rossum's Universal Robots, and Wilberforce Bainbridge, the air mill magnate."

Selene stared at him, her mouth agape in shock. "I don't believe it."

"Then Barty was right, wasn't he?"

Selene rolled the cut-glass crystal between her palms, but said nothing.

"Did he tell you anything about them? Such as why they might have attracted the interest of his employers?"

"He said they were all working together on the same secret project."

"What project?"

"I don't know. Only that it had something to do with the dark side of the Moon."

"Damn!" Ulysses cursed. "It looks like the only way we're going to be able to find out any more about this clandestine venture of theirs is if we break into one of their private offices and take a look inside their Babbage memory cores." Ulysses was on his feet in seconds. "Right, Nimrod, I want you to do your thing and find me someone local with the ability to break into a centurion-level protected Babbage network. Got that?"

"Yes, sir. Right away, sir," Nimrod groaned, struggling to get to his feet.

"Or you could just talk to the fourth member of their little group," Selene suggested.

Ulysses turned to her, a startled look on his face. "Fourth man? What fourth man? There were only three files in Barty's flat."

"There was another name that Barty did mention, once or twice. It stuck in my mind because I am sure I had heard it before."

"What was the name? Who is the fourth man, Selene?"

"Jules Verne."

Ulysses' face froze at the moment of surprise. Then his features softened and he couldn't help but laugh, despite himself.

"What is it? What is so funny? Do you know this man?"

"Jules Verne?"

"Yes. Jules Verne. You know him?"

"Yes and you should too."

"*Pardon?*"

"Only his name has another connotation here on the Moon."

"Please explain," Selene pleaded.

Ulysses relented, seeing how tired and emotionally wrung out she was. "You're quite right, my dear. Jules Verne is the name of a famous French writer of scientific romances, tales of exploration and adventure, but he also happened to give his name to a crater located on the far side of the Moon."

"Oh. I see."

"So, we have an alternative energy pioneer, with a hand in everything from cavorite production to spaceships – not to mention a brand new sunlight-powered cutting tool – a manufacturer of construction automatons, and an air mill magnate, all working together on something – some secret project or other – on the dark side of the Moon. Now what could that 'something' possibly be?"

"It would seem to me," Nimrod chipped in, "that that is the exact combination of industries you would need to build your own base on the Moon."

"Precisely what I was thinking. And on the dark side too, away from habitation, away from prying eyes. But for what purpose?"

"And by whom, sir?"

"Indeed. I doubt the three of them would have initiated such a plan. I suspect that there was a 'fourth man' involved, for want of a better phrase, somewhere along the line."

"Right," he said, jumping to his feet. "Well this changes everything."

"It does?" Selene said, staring at Ulysses in bewilderment.

"Of course it does. We no longer need to break into a maximum security data vault to extract the information we need since we now know where we're going – to the Jules Verne Crater."

"We?" Selene said.

Ulysses grinned at her. "I mean Nimrod and me. You, my dear, are staying here. After all, we don't want any other unpleasant accidents befalling you now, do we?"

Ulysses turned to Nimrod.

"Okay, change of plan," he announced, a look of glee on his face. "All we have to do is get ourselves some lunar transport and take a trip to the dark side. Now where could we acquire something like that?"

"I'll get onto it right away, sir," Nimrod said. He suddenly looked faint – his skin acquiring an unhealthy grey sheen – and sat down again quickly.

"I think that can probably wait until the morning," Ulysses said, obvious concern in the look he gave his old friend. "You're not going anywhere other than to your bed."

Ulysses helped Nimrod to his feet, putting the butler's arm across his shoulders and then guiding him with cautious steps to another of the white doors leading off from the living room.

"I could help you with that, if you like."

Billie stood at the door to the bathroom, the towel of finest Egyptian cotton wrapped around her torso only just covering her breasts and buttocks.

Ulysses felt his heart skip a beat again. He had never seen her looking so clean. And now that she was free of the grease and soot, her short cropped blonde hair a tousled damp mop, Ulysses could appreciate just how pretty she was.

"I won't argue with you there," Ulysses muttered under his breath, unable to help himself.

Selene scowled at him, unimpressed.

"Sorry?" the girl asked. "I didn't catch that last bit."

"I said that would be most kind," Ulysses said, blushing. "You know where we could acquire a lunar transport then?"

"You could say that. I'll have it here by morning. Will that do you?"

Ulysses smiled broadly, his senses thrilling as she brushed past him. "That would be most helpful. You smell simply divine by the way."

Billie laughed – a sound like sunshine given voice. "I can do girly too, you know."

"Yes. Yes you can," Ulysses mused, drinking in the heady aroma of shampoo and bubble bath. "And in that case, by way of a small thank you, we'll give the hotel boutique a call and see if they can't rustle you up something 'girly', shall we?"

"That would be very good of you, sir," Billie said. She wavered for a moment, and then, putting one hand on his shoulder, stretched up on tiptoes to plant a soft kiss on his cheek. Selene's frown deepened.

"Let me just get Nimrod into bed and then we can make all the necessary... er... arrangements."

With that, Ulysses pushed open the door to his manservant's room and helped the still woozy Nimrod inside.

There was a knock at the door to the suite.

"Don't worry." Billie called, "I'll get it."

She skipped over the silk-soft carpet, delighting at the sensation of it tickling the soles of her feet, and opened the door.

"Oh, hello. You here for his nibs as well, are you?" Billie asked the woman standing at the threshold.

"His nibs?" Emilia Oddfellow echoed, staring at the near naked girl in disbelief.

"Come on in. He's won't be a minute. He's just in the other room."

As if sleep-walking, Emilia took a few stumbling steps into the luxurious suite.

"*Bon soir.*"

Emilia turned on hearing the accented voice to see a second stick-thin young woman stretched out on the sofa in what appeared to be her undergarments.

Emilia remained exactly where she was, not knowing where to look next for fear of what she might see.

It was at that moment that Ulysses Quicksilver reappeared.

"Right, shall we get started then? By the way, who was at the door?"

He stopped abruptly as his wandering gaze answered his question for him.

Emilia returned his horrified stare. "Ulysses?"

"Emilia!" he said, surprised and delighted. But then, registering her expression of consternation, he looked around the room, taking in his two female companions, and suddenly saw things through Emilia's eyes. He could feel his cheeks reddening again.

"Ah, Emilia... Can I just start by saying that things aren't as you are probably imagining them to be right about now?"

"Ulysses Quicksilver!"

"So," he said weakly, "what brings you here?"

An uncomfortable hush fell over the room.

"What brings me here?" she snapped, her exclamation shattering the silence. "Why would I stop by your hotel room, you mean? Well, I'm beginning to wonder. I hear your brother was found dead twenty-four hours ago and then the next day you take yourself off, and I don't hear anything from you. Perhaps I was worried about you. Did you think of that, did you? Perhaps I thought you might need someone to talk to, but it looks to me like you've got plenty of shoulders to cry on already."

"Look," Ulysses said. "This is Miss... Selene," he said nodding towards the waif on the couch, "and you've already met Billie. She's –"

"I don't want to know what she is!" Ulysses shut up immediately. "If this is how you deal with grief then so be it, get it out of your system, but don't expect me to still be here when you're done!"

Turning on her heel, she strode out through the open door and away down the corridor.

"Emilia, wait!" Ulysses called, running after her.

By the time he reached the corridor, she was already entering the lift. The sounds of her sobs echoed back to him.

"Emilia!" he tried again, moving out into the corridor uncertainly.

And then he stopped. She wasn't in any mood to listen to what he had to say right at that moment.

"Go after her," Billie called from the room behind him.

"No," he said, his voice a deadened monotone. "It's probably best this way."

"What do you mean?"

"I mean I don't think I'm the safest person to be around right now, do you?"

The two women looked at him, and then each other, an appalled expression on their faces.

"I mean we've just gone toe-to-toe with a crazed killing machine and I'm about to go in search of some nefarious villain's secret moonbase. No, it's best this way. It's better she's not anywhere near me, right about now. She'll be much safer if she stays here at the hotel. I can sort everything out with her later, after this has all been cleared up and I've brought Barty's killer – or killers – to justice."

Ulysses walked back into the room, pushing the door shut behind him. "It's Earthrise in about four hours and preparations need to be made."

*　　*　　*

BY THE TIME she made it back to the more modest suite she was sharing with her father three floors down – some expense having apparently been spared despite the fact that the publicity for their prize-winner's trip to the Moon had boasted that there was 'no expense spared' – Emilia's tears of anger had become simple tears of sadness and self-pity.

Ulysses Quicksilver had done it again. As soon as she had let herself get close to him once more, he had gone and let her down, just as he had when they had been engaged three years ago. What a fool she was, she told herself; she had been certain that things would be different this time.

Fumbling with the key in the lock, wiping the tears from her eyes, she let herself into the room.

Her father, Alexander Oddfellow, was waiting for her. As was the young man holding him in an arm lock with the barrel of a brutal-looking handgun pressed against the side of his head.

"Father!" Emilia blurted out before she could stop herself.

She let out a gasp, feeling the rough metal of another pistol press into the sparse flesh at the back of her head. The owner of the gun pushed harder, forcing Emilia into the room and shutting the door firmly behind her.

"Good evening, Miss Oddfellow," came a woman's voice from behind her. "Or should that be, good morning? It's time we had a little chat."

"Want do you want?" Emilia said, her voice hard.

"It's time you learnt the truth about your all expenses paid trip to the Moon."

"What?" Emilia could feel the sweat beading on her brow.

"You know how they say there's no such thing as a free lunch?" Emilia said nothing. "Well, turns out there's no such thing as a free trip to the Moon either. And right here's where you start paying."

She felt the sudden change in air pressure behind her then crumpled as the butt of the pistol came down hard on the back of her head, and her world exploded into cold oblivion.

CHAPTER EIGHTEEN

Silent Running

T minus 1 day, 2 hours, 34 minutes, 49 seconds

BY EIGHT A.M., Greenwich Mean Time, Ulysses and his companions had relocated to what appeared to be a scrapyard and were staring up at the bulbous cockpit of a decrepit Lunar Exploration Vehicle. The LEV's name was still just about visible, etched onto a brass plate, green with verdigris, secured to its hull.

COPERNICUS

The rover looked like a Pullman carriage with a giant goldfish bowl bolted onto one end and six giant rubber-tyred wheels, each as tall as a man.

"You're impressed, aren't you, I can tell. I've done well, haven't I?" Billie said, staring with intense scrutiny at Ulysses' dumbfounded expression. "I told you I wouldn't let you down."

The black boiler suit with tailored jacket look suited her,

Ulysses thought, with an almost paternal tug of the heartstrings. But so much for her proud boast that she could 'do girly'. Her droid-cab Rusty squatted on the other side of the yard, rumbling contentedly to itself.

Nimrod – who was obviously feeling much better after a few hours' sleep – approached the LEV with caution, as if he were worried it might crumble to dust in front of his very eyes, and ran a critical finger along the hull. He peered down his nose at the line he had traced in the regolith dust covering the vehicle. The smell of gunpowder lingered about the LEV.

"I would have gone for something a little cleaner myself," he said. He turned to Billie. "Miss Wilhelmina, are you sure it's... surface worthy?"

"The seals are good," she said, giving one of the huge grey tyres a thump, "and the engine's an early re-condenser so it'll keep running 'til the Moon explodes."

"That's not likely to happen any time soon, is it?" Ulysses asked. "You don't know something we don't, do you?" He flashed her a knowing grin.

"No." She laughed, punching him on the arm. "Unless there's something you're not telling *me*."

"So we're good to go?"

"There's a week's supply of ration packs and water – although the onboard aquifer will keep giving you a not so fresh water supply, but good enough, for up to a month. There are also a couple of atmosphere suits in one of the storage lockers. Basically she's ready to go when you are."

Ulysses considered the *Copernicus* again. The convention that vehicles should be feminine had always intrigued him, especially when the vehicle in question happened to have a masculine name.

With droids he could understand it. An entirely different convention had it that they should be made to appear human. Even hulking monsters like Rusty and the late Rossum's Titan-class construction droids were constructed based on a recognisably humanoid template. And in the case of droids, they were often referred to as being of the male persuasion, apart from in the case of some of the new rubberized Geisha models Ulysses had heard were being developed in the Far East. Those were most definitely female. But vehicles?

"Right, Nimrod, ready to get on board and suit up?"

"After you, sir."

Unable to hide the thrill he felt at their impending expedition outside the dome of Luna Prime, Ulysses put a hand and a foot on the ladder leading up to the rover's rear boarding hatch.

"So this is *adieu*?"

Ulysses paused, then climbed back down – signalling that Nimrod should ascend and board the rover first – and strode across the scrapyard to where Selene stood beside the Juggernaut, her travelling cloak wrapped close around her meagre frame.

"No, my dear," Ulysses said, taking her hands in his and bending to plant a kiss on her forehead. "Think of this only as *au revoir*. We *will* see each other again, have no fear. I'll be back."

As Nimrod entered the *Copernicus* and took his place in the driver's seat – clearly visible now through the reinforced glass bubble of the cockpit – Ulysses turned to Billie, a useful person to know if you were ever in a fix on the Moon, it would seem.

"And thank *you*," he said, not knowing whether to kiss her, hug her or shake her hand, so he gave her a punch on the arm instead.

"And you promise you'll keep an eye on her?" He nodded towards Selene.

"Cross me heart and hope to die," the girl chuckled, drawing a finger across the front of her boiler suit twice. "You won't find a better bodyguard than Rusty this side of the Caucasus Mountains."

"Good girl! But hang on; I thought he was a cab."

"He's a girl's best friend, that's what he is."

Ulysses sprang back up the ladder to the *Copernicus*'s airlock.

"And don't forget, give us a few hours' head-start from when we leave the dome before you put that call through to Inspector Artemis of the Luna Prime Metropolitan Police and tell her where we've gone and why."

"Will do." Billie called back. "What about your girlfriend?"

Ulysses hesitated. "Emilia's... She's not my girlfriend," he blustered.

"Yeah. Course she isn't. Just like Rusty's not an ex-military grade robot." Ulysses blushed. "So do you want a message passed on to her as well?"

"No. Don't worry about Emilia. I left her a note with the receptionist back at the hotel." Ulysses hoisted a hand in their direction. "Farewell then, ladies. Rusty."

With Selene waving her own farewell, he disappeared inside the LEV, sealing the airlock behind him.

IT WASN'T FAR from the scrapyard to East Gate Six. It wasn't the norm for tourists and everyday Joes to leave the habitation domes on their own, and traffic through the dome skin was carefully monitored. However getting out onto the surface wasn't a problem if you knew the right people, or you had the right level of clearance.

Having fully recovered from the knock to the head he received during the crash, Nimrod skilfully steered the *Copernicus* out of the yard and joined the queue of mining vehicles trailing back from East Gate Six. There was no other traffic; the guided tours so beloved of tourists set off from North Gate Two or over at West Gate Eight, where the paying passengers were afforded much more appealing views of the lunar landscape, rather than the steady stream of scrip-miners and haulage trucks that traversed the plains in ceaseless toil over on the borders of the Mare Nectaris.

Finally the last truck in front of them entered the complicated series of airlocks that kept Luna Prime's carefully-created atmosphere in, and then it was their turn.

A judicious reveal of Ulysses' 'By Royal Appointment' ID, pressed up against the inside of the *Copernicus*' goldfish bowl cockpit, and the gate guard on duty initiated the opening of the massive airlock. With a nod from the guard, Nimrod drove the clanking bucket of bolts inside the shielded tunnel.

The two of them sat there, a smell of old leather seeping into the stale air of the cockpit. Within the gloom of the gate they waited for the inner door seals to lock before the next set would open. As each set of doors did just that, one after another, Nimrod rolled the rover slowly forwards.

Ulysses' pulse was racing in excitement. They were leaving the protection of Luna Prime's environment dome in pursuit of the mysterious Fourth Man – who doubtless held all the pieces of the puzzle, ready to face him in his lair on the dark side of the Moon.

And then, with a final hiss, like the last gasp of a dying man, the last of the air in the airlock was sucked out by huge compressor fans. A halo of hazard lights slicing the darkness, the yellow and black zigzags on the circular reinforced steel portal parted as the gate ground open.

A simple push on the lever in Nimrod's right hand and they were through. The massive wheels of the rover crackled over the compacted regolith of the track way that led from Luna Prime to the strip mines of the Mare Nectaris to the east as the LEV's engine throbbed beneath them.

With the lunar longitude and latitude entered into the rover's navigational control, Nimrod steered the *Copernicus* off the well-worn and dusty road, heading for the far horizon and the dark side of the Moon.

ACT FOUR

The Dark Side of the Moon

~ June 1998 ~

And we are here as on a darkling plain
Swept with confused alarms of struggle and flight,
Where ignorant armies clash by night.

(Matthew Arnold, *Dover Beach*, 1867)

CHAPTER NINETEEN

Black Moon

T minus 18 hours, 57 minutes, 6 seconds

THREE HUNDRED AND fifty miles out from Luna Prime, and seven hours, later the *Copernicus* came to a stop, jolting Ulysses out of the dream he'd been having – in which he, Billie and Selene had been battling the evil robot minions of an Emilia-lookalike Queen of Villainy.

"Where are we?" he mumbled, taking out his fob watch to check how long it had been since they had left Luna Prime.

Nimrod lent over to the navigational control, turning a knurled knob on the side of the device.

"Just shy of the terminator, sir."

Ulysses sat up and peered out of the glass bubble of the cockpit. Some miles ahead of them, he could see the line where the light of the sun gave way to complete darkness.

"Why have we stopped?"

Nimrod pointed beyond the windshield.

"Tracks, sir." Ulysses could see them quite clearly now, the fresh tyre-marks, clear to see in the regolith. "We're not alone out here."

"Good." Ulysses said with a smile.

"Good, sir?"

"Well," Ulysses said, a devilish grin on his face, "I'd hate for us to be wasting our time on some wild goose chase."

Fully awake now, Ulysses looked from the tracks to the ominous, oppressive darkness before them.

"Where are they heading, as if I really need to ask?"

"They're on the same bearing as us, sir."

"I knew it!" Ulysses declared.

"But who are *they*, sir?"

"That is the sixty-four thousand guinea question, isn't it, old boy? And to be honest with you, I have no idea. No idea at all. But then that's why we're driving half way round the Moon, isn't it? To find out."

THE *COPERNICUS* TRUNDLED on its way, Ulysses paying full attention as his butler and driver negotiated the myriad craters and basalt boulders that littered the Moon's surface, like the aftermath of a giants' game of knuckle stones.

Amidst the craters and the splintered ridges illuminated by the rover's arc-lights they saw other things too that reminded them of how human life on the Moon had begun, leaving the two companions in a melancholic mood.

The great hulks of the great gravity cannon shells that had been used before cavorite had been successfully produced on an industrial scale – preserved by the airless and waterless conditions that existed on the Moon's surface – stood as sentinels to another, darker time; to the thousands of lives lost in the Empire's drive to become the first nation to colonise Earth's satellite and turn it into yet another outpost of the British Empire.

Thousands had died all those decades ago, as the ruthless masters of Magna Britannia continued to expand the realm of Her Majesty Queen Victoria beyond the limits imposed upon it by the Earth and the burgeoning empires of the Far East. Thousands had been forcibly transplanted from their homes in the Sudan, Uganda and the British Empire's other African colonies.

The price paid for Magna Britannia's dominance of the Moon had come at too great a cost for anybody's moral conscience to deal with, paid with the lives of thousands of men, women and even children – all of them transplanted from the heart of the Dark Continent.

"Will you look at that?" Ulysses gasped, in dreadful awe. "Think of all the lives lost."

The only memorial that now stood to the memory of those first lunar travellers – so many of whom died so that that the great and the good, and every ticket-buying tourist could see Earthrise over the Caucasus Mountains for themselves or charter a solar yacht to travel in style across the Sea of Dreams – were these lifeless hulks. And none of the tourist transports ever came out this way to see them.

The gravity cannon shells lay, like the bones of those first lunar travellers buried just below the regolith, discarded and abandoned, conveniently forgotten about by all those who should have thanked them with every iota of their being and made the pilgrimage to their mass graves to give thanks for their sacrifice.

ANOTHER FOURTEEN HOURS later and the *Copernicus* ground to the top of a steep incline that had brought the rover to the lip of a vast geological feature in the otherwise grey desert. They had crossed the terminus, passing over from the near side of the Moon into the dark beyond, some hours previously. The crater that now stretched out beneath them lay in total darkness. The LEV was already descending the inner wall of the ridge before either of them spotted the tiny pinpricks of light visible within the distant dome, looking like a gleaming carbuncle of steel on the far side of the featureless crater.

Ulysses punched the air in delight. "I knew it!"

"Well done, sir," Nimrod said, in his usual emotionless way.

"How far away are we?" Ulysses asked, leaning forward anxiously in his seat.

Nimrod turned the knurled knob on the navigational control again. "Roughly thirty miles, sir."

"And there's no sign of the other vehicle? I can't see it, can you?"

"No, sir. Only the tyre tracks we've been following."

"Then I suggest you kill the lights and we proceed at half speed from here on in, using the navi-con alone to guide us."

"Very good, sir," Nimrod replied, calmly pulling a lever, the note of the LEV's engine changing in pitch accordingly.

Ulysses flicked a series of switches on a panel above his head and the lumin-lamps inside the cabin died. The view beyond the cockpit melted into darkness.

"Steady as you go," Ulysses instructed, his voice becoming a low whisper.

The only visible light came from the distant twinkling pinpricks dotting the distant dome, a smattering of stars an impossible distance away, and the glowing green screen of the navigational control.

And so they proceeded down the side of the great basalt ridge and across the bottom of the Jules Verne crater.

ULYSSES STARTED SUDDENLY. "Did you feel that?"

"What, sir?" asked Nimrod, the vibration of the LEV's engine and the vehicle's jolting progress over the uneven floor of the crater bouncing him around in his sprung seat.

"A tremor." It had been barely perceptible, but Ulysses had felt it just the same.

The rover suddenly lurched and tipped sharply to port. Nimrod fought to control the steering column.

"What was that?" Ulysses said.

Nimrod glanced at the instruments. "Some sort of fissure, sir. It just opened up beneath us."

Ulysses waited until the *Copernicus* had pulled itself out of the fracture that had formed in the Moon's crust, allowing Nimrod to proceed for a good hundred yards, before calling a halt.

"Turn the engine off," he said.

"Sir?"

"Just do it."

The engine died with a rattling cough. The continual shuddering motion that had been with them ever since they had set off from the scrapyard ceased. All was still. Ulysses peered out of the cockpit at the shadowed crater beyond and the unobscured star field above.

The distant lights of the curious moonbase still twinkled in the dark, like reflections of the stars. There was no other sign of anybody else being out here.

This time they both heard the tremor as well as felt it.

It was as if they had parked on the back of some lunar leviathan – like the sailors of old who had supposedly mistaken the backs of basking whales for dry land – that was even now stirring from its eons old slumber and shaking to rid itself of some irritating parasite that had taken up residence while it slept.

The *Copernicus* bounced and jerked around them as, beyond the bubble of the cockpit, Ulysses saw the powdered grey sand covering the floor of the crater dance like iron filings on a taut, vibrating drum skin.

As the shuddering passed, Ulysses turned to Nimrod, a horrified look on his face. "I was stupid! Start the engine. We have to get out of here now!"

Nimrod didn't need to be told twice. Punching the ignition switch, activating the headlamps, he put the LEV into gear and his foot to the floor. Kicking up a spray of regolith from its back wheels, the rover took off, bouncing over the crater floor at a giddy fifty miles per hour.

Ulysses didn't care now that they might be spotted. Whoever awaited them inside the moonbase either already knew that they were coming or were about to find their day taking a most unusual twist. Besides, Ulysses decided he would rather take his chances with whoever was lurking in their lair than end up plunging into some newly-opened chasm God alone knew how many feet deep.

Nimrod jinked and wrestled the vehicle as it bumped over the lunar surface – the LEV sometimes losing contact with the ground entirely in its hurtling flight while Ulysses clung on to the edges of his seat. The surface of the Moon seemed to be fracturing all around them, making it harder and harder for Nimrod to navigate a safe way through the tectonic turmoil.

The was a terrible crash and then Ulysses was tumbling about the cabin as the *Copernicus* was bowled over sideways and started to roll. The battered LEV bounced over the fracturing crater floor.

It was too late to regret not fastening his seat-harness as he was thrown free of his seat, the side of his head making contact with the navi-con, and before Ulysses knew what the ultimate fate of the *Copernicus* was to be, he lost consciousness.

CHAPTER TWENTY

Tremors

T minus 4 hours, 1 minute, 56 seconds

As the tremors subsided, Nimrod opened his eyes to near total darkness. He was still in his seat, thanks to his pilot's harness. Below him he could just make out the motionless form of his master, Ulysses Quicksilver, lying against the inside of the cockpit bubble. The rover was lying at an angle of forty-five degrees, with its nose pointing downwards, the main body of the *Copernicus* extending behind and above his current position.

The time for stealth was over. They were already in about as much trouble as you could ever expect to be on the Moon, and yet still be alive. Unclipping his harness, he leaned across and flicked the switches that activated the cabin lights. The dull lumin-strips began to glow, suffusing the cabin with a dirty nicotine-yellow light.

His master didn't move. Blood oozed from a bruised cut on the side of his head. Carefully, Nimrod climbed out of his chair and down into the reinforced glass bubble. Putting two fingers to the artery in the man's neck he breathed out with relief as he found a pulse.

"Sir?" His voice sounded strange in the confined space of the LEV. "Sir!"

Still there was no response.

Nimrod looked about him, carrying out a more detailed assessment of their condition.

His master was unconscious, but alive. The *Copernicus*, however, was as good as dead. It was stuck, nose-down, in a crevasse and the only way it was ever likely to get out again was if another, larger vehicle winched it out.

They still had water and food for six days, and, as long as they had power of some description, the air would keep being recycled too. The lady inspector would have doubtless sent a party to look for them by now and, if he activated the LEV's emergency beacon, they would probably be rescued within a day, two at most.

All they had to do was stay put and wait for help to arrive.

Nimrod's attention was drawn to a blinking red light on the control panel above him. Pulling himself back up into the driving seat, he studied the bank of lights.

"Oh dear," he said to himself.

The blinking bulb was labelled 'ATMOSPHERE BREACH'.

"Vacuum suits it is then," Nimrod added, keeping quite calm.

Without the slightest modicum of fuss, but with efficient, economical movements, Nimrod set about accessing the locker containing the two environment suits they had brought with them.

Had the LEV still been horizontal, it would have been a straightforward process that would only take a matter of seconds. However, with the *Copernicus* half buried, and with his master in a state of persistent unconsciousness, it was touch and go whether Nimrod would be able to get them both into their sealed suits before oxygen levels in the LEV reached a critical point and he too blacked out.

He climbed up through the body of the rover, using pipework and storage cupboard handles for support. With one hand, he managed to yank open the cupboard containing the two vacuum suits and the associated paraphernalia that went with them, including two pairs of heavy, lead-soled moon boots.

Carefully, he dropped the articles of clothing into the cockpit, taking care not to drop anything heavy on his master or on any of the devices on the control console. He didn't want to add to the damage that had already been caused during the crash.

Having made his way back down to the cockpit, he first set about putting on his own environment suit before attempting to help his master into the other one.

Ulysses moved and mumbled something groggily, his words slurred and unintelligible, his mouth not even open, as Nimrod pulled the vacuum suit up over his shoulders.

"It's all right, sir. I'm just helping you on with your suit."

There was more mumbling and then his master's body went limp again.

Nimrod took another look at the graze on the man's head as he gently guided it through the suit's heavy metal and rubber neck seal. It had stopped bleeding, a red-black crust starting to form as the blood matting the greying hair at his temple hardened.

Nimrod was starting to feel breathless. The air inside the LEV was running out more quickly than he had hoped it would.

Hurriedly he secured his own helmet and locked the seal shut tight. As he activated the suit's integral air supply, the sound of rushing gas filled his ears and he took a number of luxuriously deep breaths.

He quickly secured the second helmet over his master's head, twisting it to lock it, flooding it with oxygen.

Nimrod himself had checked that the suits' air tanks were full before setting out from Luna Prime. As a result, if their kept their exertions to a minimum, their air supply would last upwards of four hours. If Inspector Artemis's team were already nearby there was nothing to worry about. However, if they were more than four hours away – which seemed far more likely, unfortunately – Nimrod and his master were doomed.

Nimrod reached up to the control panel above his head and flicked the protective shield off a large, red button marked with a hazard symbol, and depressed it fully. A repeating chiming note began to sound inside the cockpit.

With the onboard emergency Mayday signal active, Nimrod prayed that someone would find them and pull them to safety before the oxygen ran out.

ULYSSES OPENED HIS eyes to be met by the dimly illuminated up-ended interior of the LEV and the concerned face of his manservant.

"I don't suppose there's much point asking what happened?" he said, taking in the state of his surroundings.

"We were hit by a landslide triggered by the moonquake," Nimrod replied, his voice coming to Ulysses through the short-range comm built into his helmet. "It knocked us into a fissure. The LEV's air supply was compromised and so here we are."

"But what caused the quake in the first place?"

Ulysses eased himself up into a sitting position and winced, automatically trying to put a hand to the bump on the side of his head but finding half an inch of reinforced glass helmet between the wound and his own gloved hand.

"How long have we been like this?"

"About thirty minutes," Nimrod replied without checking the chronometer built into the wrist panel of his suit's left arm.

"So help should be here – what? – within about an hour or so?"

"We can only hope, sir."

"Indeed." Ulysses looked from the main body of the LEV rising to the sealed airlock at the rear of the cabin, and then down at the bubble of reinforced glass on which he was lying. He immediately wished he hadn't.

Knowing that the glass had survived the landslide as well as being bowled across the Moon's surface without sustaining so much as a scratch still didn't fill him with reassurance when he gazed down into the black void beneath them.

"How far down do you reckon that goes?" he asked, as nonchalantly as he could manage.

"Far enough, sir," came Nimrod's blunt reply. It was said that some of the cracks in the Moon's surface were as much as fifteen miles deep.

"And how long did you say we're likely to be stuck down here?"

"Long enough."

Putting a hand to the armrest of the seat above him, Ulysses pulled himself into a standing position. "I think I might just have a sit down up here, if that's all right."

A tremor passed through the *Copernicus*, causing the LEV to shift and drop by several inches, and Ulysses fell back onto the glass of the cockpit.

"Was that me?" he gasped.

Another shuddering aftershock rattled the rover, setting cupboard doors swinging open and sending their contents raining down on the two men.

"More tremors, sir," Nimrod said, an anxious look replacing the more usual expression of aloof disdain.

"But what's causing them?"

"A moonquake, sir?"

"But caused by what? The Moon's been dead, geologically, for the last three billion years!"

Another tremor juddered through the *Copernicus*, causing it to slip another foot further into the crevasse. A cascade of regolith showered down over the top of the cockpit, skittering off the curved glass bubble, illuminated from underneath, for a moment, by the cabin light, before vanishing into the darkness below.

"Whatever's causing them, sir, I would suggest it's time we vacated this vehicle."

"While we still can, you mean?" Ulysses said, scrambling to his feet again.

"Precisely."

"Then we'd better start climbing, hadn't we, old boy?"

"Just what I was going to suggest, sir."

"I mean that airlock isn't going to open itself now, is it?"

* * *

THE OUTER HATCH of the transport's airlock fell open and Ulysses, aided by his ever loyal manservant, emerged from the dull gloom of the LEV into the cold cloying shadows of the crater.

Nimrod dropped to what passed for ground here and then helped Ulysses down after him.

And all the while the *Copernicus* kept on sinking into the coarse grey sand and the yawning fissure beneath. Only moments after Ulysses made it to the surface, the airlock slammed shut and, as the two companions watched, the rover sank from view beneath the rippling regolith.

"Come on, sir," Nimrod's voice came through Ulysses' helmet-comm again. "On your feet. We need to get moving before we go the same way as the *Copernicus*."

Being many degrees of magnitude lighter than the heavy rover, it was considerably easier for the two men to avoid sharing the LEV's fate but, if they hung around too long, they would soon discover that the grey, broken pumice could be as deadly as quicksand.

Aided again by the ever-patient Nimrod, Ulysses struggled to his feet, his vision greying for a moment, accompanied by a stab of pain at his temple, and then the two of them were moving at a stumbling run, bounding over the lunar surface away from the site of the sinking LEV as quickly as they could.

At last the shuddering tremors subsided and the Moon's crust settled into stillness once more.

"So, now what?" Ulysses said, sitting on a slab of grey rock as he recovered his breath.

"We go on, sir," Nimrod stated. "Our transport's gone, we're a thousand miles from Luna Prime and we've only got enough air for a few hours, if we maintain a steady walking pace.

"On the other hand, I estimate the base," he said, pointing, "to be only another six miles away as the crow flies."

"Not that we'll be seeing many crows flying round here, will we, old boy?" Ulysses grinned, despite the dire nature of the predicament they now found themselves in. "Then, as you say, we go on. I mean we don't want to wait for Inspector Artemis and miss all the fun now, do we?"

THE TWO COMPANIONS – master and manservant – set off across the crater, on course for the moonbase, their heavy lead-lined boots clomping over the unstable ground. Every step over the minutely fractured surface of the Moon felt like hard work, as it gave beneath with every footfall.

As they walked they said nothing, not wanting to waste valuable oxygen when they still had several miles of hard walking to go.

It had been twenty minutes since the last tremor when the ground began to shake.

"Not again!" Ulysses complained as the regolith began to rattle around their feet. "What is it that's causing these sodding tremors?"

"I don't know, sir," Nimrod said wearily, "although I'm quite certain that if we don't pick up the pace we could quite possibly go the same way as the *Copernicus*."

The two of them quickened their steps, even though they used up great lungfuls of air with every strenuous breath.

With a sudden lurch, the Moon's crust splintered beneath them, great chunks of fractured granite-like rock rising up in jagged shards as tons of shifting sand poured from whatever it was that was now pushing its way up from below the surface.

Ulysses and Nimrod were sent tumbling backwards, head over heels, down the slope of the newly formed mound. They landed in a tangle of limbs, their environment suits and helmets thankfully still intact.

Ulysses gazed up at the massive maggot-like form blotting out his view of the star field in horror and disbelief.

The thing was as big as a whale, its undulating hide the same colour as the sands from which it had emerged. The thing twisted its shapeless body, its eyeless head flopping back down onto the regolith.

Was this what had been causing the tremors – Ulysses found himself wondering as the gigantic, slug-like beast turned its tooth-lined, leech-like mouthparts towards them, sensing them in some unfathomable way – or was it the tremors that had driven it to the surface?

Whatever the truth of it, and whatever the thing was, Ulysses knew that he and Nimrod had to get away from it as fast as possible, as it spasmed and lurched towards them, its mouth stretching to form a cavernous maw.

He kicked at the regolith with his heels but failed to get a purchase or move himself out of reach of the abomination.

Twisting, he scrambled to his feet, as Nimrod tried to do the same, and cursing his lead-weighted boots, tried to run, the wound on his head pulsing painfully with every beat of his hammering heart.

But no matter how hard the two of them ran, the ground continued to give way beneath them with ever increasing speed.

Ulysses turned, risking a glance backwards.

The slug-like beast lay there, wriggling deeper into the sand with every convulsion of its horrid form. Its cavernous mouth yawned only a few feet below them, as it sucked great quantities of the grey dust into itself with every rippling convulsion.

Ulysses re-doubled his efforts, but the more energy he extolled, the quicker the regolith slipped away beneath him and the closer he came to the creature's gaping, hungry maw.

And then Nimrod was gone, with barely a protest, the treacherous shifting sands giving way beneath him entirely and dropping him into the monster's gullet.

Ulysses gave a cry of shock, pain and desperation.

With one last herculean effort he launched himself up the cascading slope. He landed flat on his face, far from anything remotely resembling solid ground. And then he knew that he had condemned himself by his own actions.

With one last great gulping peristaltic motion, the slug swallowed one last dredger-sized mouthful of regolith and, with it, the desperately clawing Ulysses Quicksilver.

CHAPTER TWENTY-ONE

The First Men In The Moon

T minus 3 hours, 19 minutes, 5 seconds

HE WAS SUFFOCATING. The air was being squeezed from his lungs as something soft and squashy smothered him, rippling with a disgusting peristaltic motion as he was passed through the suffocating coils in the pumping, red darkness with every sphincter-like contraction of the thing.

The sphincter contracted again and he was squeezed out of the rear end of whatever it was that had swallowed him and dropped several feet to land in a drift of grey sand.

He sat up and looked around him. He was sitting in the middle of a wide crater and the ground under him was shaking again. An eerie sound, like the rumbling of rocks or the wheezy robotic laugh of the juggernaut-droid Rusty echoed impossibly from the walls of the airless crater.

And then his viewpoint changed drastically as he hurtled away from the Moon's surface and into orbit, his gaze still focused on the moonscape beneath.

The faster and the further he travelled, the more was revealed to him. First he could see the craters – scores of them, hundreds, then thousands – and the grey-white lunar mountain ranges. And still he was speeding away from the Moon, the curve of the satellite clearly visible now.

As he continued to fall deeper into the cold depths of the void, it became clear that the topographical features of the Moon were in fact the features of a huge moon-face.

Lips of basalt moved, sending tremors skittering through the brittle crust and an urgent expression furrowed a brow made of craters and lunar mountain ranges.

The Moon was trying to tell him something.

ULYSSES QUICKSILVER OPENED his eyes.

There, in front of his face, were the concerned aquiline features of the ever-loyal Nimrod.

"Sir," Ulysses heard him say, in a voice that was barely more than a whisper, "you must wake up, sir."

He sat up, blinking himself into wakefulness. "Nimrod?" he said, his tongue thick and sluggish within his mouth. "Where are we? What happened?"

"We were brought here."

Ulysses was not fully concentrating on what his companion was telling him, as he peered past him, trying to make sense of where he was through the murk.

"By what?"

They were in some sort of low-roofed cave, with walls the colour of pumice. As his eyes became accustomed to the low light he saw that what little illumination there was came from some species of luminous fungus covering the roof and walls of the chamber.

"You mean you don't remember the slug, sir?"

Ulysses turned to his friend, a look of consternation on his face.

"You mean being swallowed? That was real? I thought that

was a dream," he said, shaking the last of the sleep from him.

The memory of the suffocating darkness and the fluid intestinal tract sprang back into his mind.

"I'm afraid not, sir."

He looked at his environment suit. Something unpleasant coated it in a sticky sheen to which the dust had clung, and which was starting to harden over the fabric. He shuddered.

Ulysses was dimly aware that he had been lying on some sort of shelf, a shallow hollow easily large enough for a man to lie down in. There were others in the gently curving walls all around him but none of those were occupied. Under the palms of his hands, the shelf felt smooth to the touch.

Ulysses started, holding his hands up in front of his face. Where were his gloves? It was then that he realised that he wasn't wearing his helmet either. He gave a gasp and felt his chest tighten as his heart began to race.

"My helmet!"

"It's all right, sir." Nimrod placed a calming hand on Ulysses' shoulder. "Don't ask me how but there's a breathable atmosphere down here."

Swinging his legs over the edge of the shelf Ulysses took several, long, slow, deep breaths, savouring each and every one, feeling his lungs inflate and deflate again, watching his chest rise and fall. He was still wearing most of his environment suit; it was just the gloves and helmet that were missing. The air tasted slightly sooty – with a hint of sulphur. In fact it smelt like gunpowder.

"You said, 'down here'. Nimrod, where are we?"

"I believe we are inside the Moon itself, sir," Nimrod said, a look of baffled bewilderment on the butler's face.

"But how is that possible?"

"Like I said, sir, we were brought here."

"But by whom?"

Nimrod was about to reply when, detecting movement at the periphery of his vision, Ulysses turned to the opening that led into the cave and his question was suddenly answered.

"Good God!" the dandy gasped.

Three figures stood in the doorway – but they were like nothing

Ulysses had ever seen, and he had seen some mightily strange things in his time.

It was immediately obvious that they were not human. For a moment he wondered whether they were some form of mutation created by Doctor Galapagos' accursed serum. But there was something so unutterably alien about the creatures that he quickly dismissed that idea.

The closest he could come to a comparison was that they were like bi-pedal giant ants. They had six limbs but stood only using the hindmost pair. The uppermost pair were more like arms, projecting from the thorax on shoulder-like joints, and indeed two of the creatures were holding bone spears. Their bodies were also divided into distinctly different parts; a thorax as well as an abdomen, surmounted by a head that was more insect than human, with twitching antennae and large, compound eyes.

The aliens' bodies were coloured a khaki brown, although Ulysses could see some differentiation in hue and pattern between the three. He wondered if this was just chance, or dependent on the genes of the parent, like hair or eye colour in human beings – or whether it was more significant than that. Their carapaces provided them with a hardened exterior but two of the three were also wearing what appeared to be polished plates of black chitin in place of armour. Ulysses could have believed that they were wearing the discarded carapaces of others of their kind, perhaps even the exoskeletons of their dead.

All three were facing him, their compound eyes rippling with purple-green iridescence, like the polarised rainbows found in a drop of spilt petroleum. Realising that he was staring at them with his mouth agape Ulysses shut it, and then opened it again when the third figure – wearing what appeared to be a ceremonial necklace of shed scales and bone fragments – addressed him directly.

Welcome, Ulysses Quicksilver.

When the ant-like being spoke, its mouth parts worked rapidly and Ulysses could hear a hollow knocking sound, accompanied by a series of chirrups and clicks. But the words he heard, in perfect Queen's English, were inside his head, having bypassed his ears altogether. His mind reeled at what this meant – that the creature was communicating telepathically.

"What are they?" Ulysses hissed at Nimrod out of the side of his mouth.

We are the Cythalan'xians, the creature replied before Nimrod's mouth could even shape a reply. *But I believe your kind know us by another name.*

"Selenites," Ulysses breathed. It was the name the writer Herbert George Wells had given to the inhabitants of the Moon in his speculative work *The First Men in the Moon*, having proposed that such creatures might inhabit the satellite's interior.

That is correct, the creature responded, its mandibles making the same rapid drumming sound as the words formed themselves in Ulysses' mind. *And yet also incorrect.*

"What do you mean?" Ulysses asked, mesmerized by his conversation with the creature. Nimrod seemed to be following their exchange, looking from his master to the creature and back again as each spoke in turn, implying that he could hear the Selenite's words inside his head too.

We are not indigenous to this world. We came here long ago in our colony-barques, from far across the stars. The name 'Selenite' implies that we are of this Moon, as you call it, which we are not. But you may refer to us by that name if it is easier for your simple minds to manage.

"Aliens," Ulysses gasped.

I believe the correct term is extra-terrestrials, the creature said. Its voice felt warm and soft inside Ulysses' head.

"Bloody hell," was all he could think to say in return.

My name is N'kel'nn'kel'elk'nn, the Selenite thought-formed, *but you may call me N'kel. And now that we have been properly introduced, Ulysses Quicksilver, perhaps you would like to come with me?*

Ulysses continued to stare at the creature, dumbfounded, and remained rooted to the spot as it turned and passed back through the entrance orifice. Its two bodyguards also remained exactly where they were.

"I should do as he says, sir," Nimrod whispered.

"How do you know?"

"How do I know what, sir? That you should go with it?"

"That it's a 'he'?" Ulysses blinked several times, as if making sure that he really was awake. "Do you think we can trust them?"

Do you really have a choice? Ulysses heard the gentle voice chime inside his head.

He scowled, but the Selenite had a point.

And so Ulysses followed, unable to take his eyes off the thing as it led him and his attendant manservant out of the cave into the passageway beyond. The two looming, bone-armoured guards dropped into step alongside them, the hard points of their chitinous feet knocking hollowly on the pumice-like material that made up the floor of the carved passageway.

Other chambers branched off from the main arterial passageway they were following. Some looked like the one in which he had awoken. Some of these contained more of the curious moon-dwellers, although these individuals were coloured a paler, sandy shade of brown. Others he could not see inside, as the chambers had been sealed shut with some kind of gummy, resinous substance.

It felt like he was exploring the burrows and hollows of a giant ant's nest and he was reminded of the hive that the Locusts had constructed within the desecrated shell of St Paul's Cathedral.

His mind was full of questions. Where had these Selenites come from and how had they travelled to the Moon in the first place? How could there be a breathable atmosphere underneath the Moon's surface? Had the Selenites saved him and Nimrod from the slug or had it been in their employ, somehow? How long had he and his manservant been underground? How was it that N'kel could understand them when they spoke, and when the alien spoke, how come Ulysses heard it speaking English? Was it really the slug's burrowing that had been responsible for the tremors that had wrecked the *Copernicus*? And did these alien ants have anything to do with the events surrounding his brother's death?

There were so many questions but the most pressing was the one which now pushed itself to the front of his mind, demanding to be voiced.

"Can you at least do us the courtesy of telling us where you're taking us?" Ulysses asked, unable to contain himself any longer.

But of course, N'kel replied, demonstrating the kind of civilised etiquette that a Swiss finishing school graduate would have been proud of. *You have an appointment with Her Majesty. We are going to see the Empress.*

"The Empress? The Empress of the Moon?"

That is correct, the Selenite said, its soothing voice helping to ease his sense of apprehension. *And, for your information, our species effectively has four genders. The reproducing males and the non-reproductive drones, as well as the female worker drones and the sexually reproductive Empress. I, myself, am female.*

"Really?" Ulysses said, intrigued. Nimrod raised his eyes to the roof of the tunnel and let out an exasperated sigh.

Yes, although I am incapable of sexual reproduction.

"So, tell me about this Empress of yours."

CHAPTER TWENTY-TWO

Aliens

T minus 3 hours, 13 minutes, 27 seconds

THE FURTHER ULYSSES, Nimrod and their armed escort proceeded, the more apparent it became that the Selenites inhabited a vast network of tunnels, caves and galleries, all cut from the silicate material of the Moon's crust – although by what means Ulysses couldn't tell.

He knew that there were no natural tunnel formations on the Moon due to the lack of the eroding effects of water in a liquid state. However, he had also known that there was no breathable atmosphere of any kind on the Moon other than that which filled the habitation domes of the lunar cities and their associated outposts, and yet his continued existence had proved that assumption to be false.

But the means by which the Selenites must have constructed their hive bothered him nonetheless. Nowhere was there any evidence of metal tools or machinery of any kind. Ulysses knew that the Moon itself was poor in metals, but the Selenites – or the Cythalan'xians, as N'kel had referred to her race – had travelled here from many light years distant, or so they had been told. And if that were the case, Ulysses would have expected there to be at least some evidence of the vessel, or vessels, that had brought them here, re-utilised to enable the aliens to survive on the inhospitable Moon, either in a piece of wall-plating or section of roof support. There wasn't even evidence of cutting marks in the rock; the walls were smooth as glass. How on Earth had they made these tunnels?

There wasn't any evidence of metal in the armour worn by the bodyguards either, nor in the weapons they carried, which appeared to be made out of bone or some other calcified substance.

You are curious as to our nature. The Selenite's unspoken words intruded upon Ulysses' thoughts, making him start.

"I'm sorry?" he said.

And now you are wondering if we can read minds. If I am reading your mind right now. The Selenite turned to regard him with those sparkling inhuman eyes of hers, and Ulysses shrank back from her. *But let me assure you, we cannot.*

"Then how can I hear your voice inside my head?"

It is complicated. But let me reassure you, once again, that we cannot read your minds.

At least that was what she wanted him to believe, Ulysses considered, hoping his thoughts weren't betraying him there and then.

"So, tell me," Ulysses said, keen to move the topic of conversation away from the alien's unsettling telepathic powers, "how is it possible that your species is able to survive down here? Where does your air supply come from? Are you pilfering it from a pipeline used to supply the habitation domes on the other side of the Moon?"

Even as he spoke the words, Ulysses suspected that his guess was wildly off the mark. N'kel had said that her people had been here for a long time, probably since before Man had ever set foot on the Moon.

Nimrod continued to cast furtive glances to left and right, as if keeping an eye out for handy exits, although where his companion thought they could escape to, Ulysses didn't know.

It is thanks to the Uuhge. Without them we would perish. They chew their way through the crust guided by our sympathetic telepathic abilities.

The giant slug, Ulysses realised. And N'kel had referred to the creature in the plural; there had to be more of the monsters lurking beneath the surface of the Moon.

They are a silicon-based life-form from the Moons of Ymgall'agziss and so do not require oxygen to live. However, the process of devouring the silicate material of this world produces water and nitrogen as waste products.

He heard the names of the chemicals as he would understand them, even though he was sure the alien Selenite would never have used such specific words herself.

Other microbial processes break down some of that water into its constituent hydrogen and oxygen molecules, ultimately creating the atmosphere we rely on.

"And you brought all these different creatures and microbes with you from – from wherever it is you came from?"

Some of them. Others we acquired during our long odyssey.

"And what do you live on?" Ulysses asked, suddenly hoping that it wasn't human flesh.

Algae, the Selenite replied. *It serves many of our needs. Some strains light our city, while others provide us with all the nourishment we need.*

"Haven't you ever thought of making the last leg of the journey to Earth?"

The Selenite was quiet for a moment.

That was our intention once. Legend tells of a time when our race set its sights on the blue-green planet but now is not the time. Silence, we are here.

The party came to an abrupt halt as the tunnel they were following opened out into a much larger cavernous space.

The Empress's audience chamber, the Selenite announced, her words tinged with pride.

The ant-like creature stepped aside, allowing Ulysses to pass through the tunnel-mouth and into the cavern. He was only dimly aware of the guards standing either side of the circular opening on a ledge of slug-cut rock, so captivated was he by the splendour of the space before him.

It was like gazing upon the interior of some unearthly, giant termite mound. The chamber was as high, from floor to domed ceiling, as a cathedral and as long as two rugby pitches laid end-to-end, shaped like a squashed egg lying on its side.

He was only half way up one side of it. A dozen other openings led into the vast grotto at myriad different levels.

Ulysses was blown away by the insect artistry of the Selenites and their ability to control the slug-like creatures, that they could coerce the Uuhge into carving such beauty from the substance of the Moon.

There were soaring pillars, jutting balconies and intricately sculpted galleries. A curving flight of steps descended from the balcony on which they now found themselves. At N'kel's bidding, Ulysses and Nimrod began to descend.

As the party began its descent to the throne room floor, Ulysses could not help but gaze at the wonders all around him. He almost lost his footing more than once because he was too busy staring at the sculpted stalactite-like protrusions spiking from the roof or the higher tiers of the chamber protruding from the walls like bracket fungus on an old oak, festooned with hanging nets of bacilli that rippled with an eerie spectrum of colours.

They passed through a sculpted gallery shaped like the interior of a nautilus shell and emerged, some minutes later, close to the floor of the chamber.

Ulysses gaped, the breath catching in his throat.

"God in heaven," Nimrod cursed under his breath.

The floor of the cavern – all two rugby pitches' worth – was covered with a seething mass of the ant-like moon-men. Their mottled, sandy markings ranged from pale yellow to deep, russet brown. The Selenites were entering and exiting the chamber in seemingly never-ending snaking lines. Among the throng Ulysses saw a full phalanx of chitin-armoured guards and other castes as well, but predominantly worker drones. He could also see that there were not many coloured the same shade as their guide. Her markings and ceremonial chains of office marked her out as something special.

But more incredible than the host of ant-people was the creature they had all come to venerate, whose very word was law within the hive, whose every decree was responded to with something akin to religious devotion. And there was no danger of Ulysses mistaking any other for the Empress.

Where the worker drones were a near-white shade of tan and no taller than Ulysses, the soldiers of the colony a good two feet taller than that, broader in build, their exoskeletons coloured a rich roan, and N'kel somewhere between the two, their ruler was coloured a vibrant red.

She was also the largest, by far, of all the Selenites. She was the brood-mother of the hive. Her anatomy was markedly different from others of her kind. Where they were basically insect-like in form, she was somewhere between an arachnid and a crustacean.

Her body was segmented and had many more limbs. Her facial features – if they could be called that – were just like those of any other Selenite, although her bone-jewellery was more impressive than that worn by any of her people and had been polished to an obsidian lustre.

Ulysses felt his skin crawl as he gazed upon her awesome majesty, unable to blot the image of the savage, de-evolved Queen of the Locusts he and Nimrod had encountered within the ruins of St Paul's Cathedral not three months previously, from his mind. But that particular specimen had been an egg-laying monster; the ovipositors of the Empress of the Cythalan'xians were still. She was clearly enjoying a lull in her alien breeding cycle, and was instead holding court at the centre of the hive, mistress of all she surveyed.

Ulysses looked from the Empress to their guide and noticed, for the first time, the atrophied limbs hanging at her sides below her primary arms, and that her abdomen was slightly more swollen than those of the other Selenites he could see. He wondered what familial connection there might be between N'kel and the Empress.

As they left the carved steps and set foot on the smooth floor of the audience chamber, Ulysses felt a resonant vibration within his very bones which rose to become a sonorous trumpeting. Surprised by the sound he looked round. Soldiers were blowing into huge cochlea-shaped horns, carved from the very stone of the chamber walls, and it was these that were producing the awesome booming notes.

The throng parted and N'kel took the lead, their accompanying guards bringing up the rear, with Ulysses and Nimrod sandwiched between them. In this order the party approached the dais-throne on which the Empress squatted, like an overgrown tarantula poised in the middle of its web.

The Empress turned her head towards them, the creature's mandibles twitching, as if the Selenite queen were imagining what a tasty snack the two men might make.

Ah, brood-sister. Ulysses flinched. The Empress's voice was sharp. When she spoke it felt as though her words were being etched into his mind in acid. It was totally unlike the gentle, soothing thought-tones of N'kel. *What have you brought me?*

Two of the Earth-men, majesty, N'kel returned.

The Empress regarded them with predatory interest.

Step forward, Earth-men.

N'kel stepped aside, so that Ulysses and Nimrod might approach the Selenite ruler.

Taking a deep breath, Ulysses stepped forward, head bowed respectfully. After all, if the Empress did intend to make a meal of them, there was little they could do to stop her, surrounded as they were by the Selenite throng.

Nimrod followed his lead.

Ulysses had met royalty on plenty of occasions – most recently Queen Victoria, and Tsarina Anastasia III of Russia – but the Empress of the Selenites, on first impressions at least, had more in common with the Queen of the Locusts than those heads of state. But the way in which she spoke marked her out as being as royal as the rest of them, imperious and proud.

Ulysses genuflected before Her Imperial Alien Majesty, and bowed lower still. Nimrod followed suit. "Your majesty," he said.

"It is truly an honour to meet you." In his experience, when it came to royalty, a little flattery went a long way.

Of course it is, the Empress replied. *I only wish I could say that the feeling was mutual on meeting our first emissaries of human-kind.*

Again, Ulysses found himself considering the nature of the aliens' means of communication. He had seen no evidence anywhere to suggest that the Selenites would know words like 'humankind' or 'Earthman', or even 'mutual'. However, they obviously understood the concepts and that must be what they were communicating to his subconscious at the telepathic level, his mind was doing the rest, making sense of these communications and translating them into a form of language he could make sense of.

But this didn't lessen the shame he felt at her remark. He felt his cheeks redden as the heat of embarrassment rushed blood to his face.

"I am sorry if that is how you feel, your majesty. Can I ask what it is that we have done that might have offended you? If it is because we intruded within your realm, the only defence I can offer is that we did not know –"

Silence! the Empress demanded, and both Ulysses and Nimrod winced at the force of the telepathic pulse.

The creature rose up on her many legs, her segmented abdomen arching up over the top of her thorax like a scorpion's tail, as if preparing to strike.

You call yourself human-kind, but you show little compassion for other species.

"I cannot apologise enough," Ulysses countered, answering as quickly as he could, all too aware of the fact that the Empress might vent her fury on them in an instant. "I can only apologise and give you my assurances that we did not know we were trespassing within your –"

Stop your jabbering!

The force of the Empress's command would have brought him to his knees, if he hadn't been kneeling already.

You come to this world, assume mastery of it, and then proceed to shake our colony-city to its very foundations.

At this last comment, as if it had been planned down to the last second, a juddering tremor passed through the cavernous chamber. There were sudden chittering thought-screams of fear and panic as, with a sharp crack, one of the stalactites broke free of the ceiling and plummeted into the throng of Selenites below.

"Your majesty," Ulysses said, steadying himself as the seismic shudder continued, with no sign of abating, "I can assure you that we have nothing to do these tremors."

How can you say that? They are not the work of the Cythalan'xians. Therefore they must be the work of human-kind.

"Then they are not caused by your mining slugs? The Uuhge?"

Of course not! Do not risk my wrath, Earth-man.

"One individual cannot be held to account for the actions of another of his race," Ulysses pointed out.

Why not? They can if they are Cythalan'xian.

"But mankind is not like your race, your majesty."

That is patently clear.

"It was a tremor such as this that set us on the path that brought us here. We were lucky we weren't killed."

You might think that.

Ulysses swallowed hard and looked up into the clicking alien face of the Empress.

"Before we were diverted from our mission," Ulysses said, mustering himself again and pressing on regardless, "we were heading for the moonbase that lies on the far side of the crater above us, and believed we were closing on the source of the disturbances."

He swallowed hard, hoping that his pheromones weren't giving him away. Anyway, it wasn't a complete lie.

So you do not deny that this – the Empress pointed at the stalactite smashed on the floor of the cavern with a taloned claw – *is the work of others of your kind, a race that is no better than a parasite, and that, having despoiled your own world, you would now despoil ours, the world that we have made our home, after incalculable aeons traversing the stars? We have monitored your communications and we have seen what you have done to your own world. And now you would do the same to ours. You have brought your warring natures to this world and we will suffer as a consequence.*

There was nothing Ulysses could say to appease her and he could not deny the truth of her words, no matter how much it pained him to hear them. He was reminded of the broadcast put out by the Darwinian Dawn on the first day of their terrorist bombing campaign against the capital over a year ago. He might not have agreed with their methods, or even the ideals of men like the reactionary Jago Kane, but neither could he deny the accuracy of their allegations against the empire of Pax Britannia and, by extension, the entire human race.

"No, I cannot deny it," he said at last.

The Empress rose up on her hind-quarters, talon-arms stretched out before her, as if she were the Grim Reaper personified.

His pulse thumping in his ears Ulysses snatched a quick breath and, before the chitin-blade could fall, said, "But if a race is to be condemned by the actions of one then let it also be redeemed by the actions of another."

The Empress hesitated, the moment of execution halted, allowing them to enjoy the briefest reprieve.

Go on.

"If you have the heart to set us free, my man and I will continue with our mission and make our way to the epicentre of the disturbances and do all that we can to stop them."

His heart pounding against his ribs, he awaited the alien queen's sentence. There was no doubt in his mind now that his and Nimrod's lives were hanging in the balance.

Two Earth-men?

"Yes, your majesty. If you doubt we are capable of accomplishing such a thing then by all means send us in the company of a cadre of your finest warriors."

No! Long ago we decreed to have nothing to do with the affairs of human-kind. If you do this, you do this alone.

Ulysses waited, every muscle in his body tensed.

No sister, not alone.

Ulysses turned in surprise, hearing the thoughts of N'kel interrupt the declarations of the Empress.

Cocking her head on one side, the alien queen regarded N'kel with the same mantis interest she had shown Ulysses and Nimrod on first meeting them.

How so? The Empress demanded.

Because I shall go with them, as their guide.

Very well. Earth-men, the Empress said, turning her startling compound eyes on Ulysses, *it would appear you have been given the chance to redeem your race. You are free to go.*

CHAPTER TWENTY-THREE

Underworld

T minus 54 minutes, 13 seconds

THEIR FOOTSTEPS ECHOED hollowly in the empty darkness of the tunnels, the lamps attached to their helmets stabbing the gloom with slender beams of light. Once their path was set and the Empress had decreed their safe passage from the colony, the explorers' gloves and helmets had been collected and returned to them.

In the lull that followed the Empress giving her permission for them to leave, the air supplies in their suits' oxygen tanks had been replenished as best they could be, although N'kel told them it was just a precaution; they would not need an artificial air supply to reach the moonbase.

To Ulysses' mind that could mean only one thing – that the Selenites' sub-lunar tunnels reached as far as the armoured dome itself. If that was the case, and the Selenites knew about it, why hadn't they acted to do something about the tremors themselves?

Ulysses asked N'kel as much as they continued to negotiate the twisting miles of abandoned chambers and slug-cut passageways – the same party of five that had first entered the Empress's audience chamber together; Ulysses, Nimrod, N'kel and the two hulking, soldier-caste Selenites.

We abandoned these tunnels long ago, she thought-formed.

"Why?"

For us to maintain the atmosphere we need to survive, the Uuhge have to eat. If we stayed still for too long and starved the Uuhge, they would die, while we would dehydrate and ultimately suffocate.

"How large is the colony?" Nimrod asked.

The whole is made up of approximately thirty thousand individuals.

Ulysses was quiet as he peered at the walls and dome of the cavern, his suit-lights barely able to illuminate the edges.

This one cavern alone was vast. And there were features that were recognisably Selenite – or rather space-slug – in design, but this place had been abandoned long ago. A fine dusting of regolith sand covered the smoothed floor. There was an eerie air about the place. It was like walking through a mausoleum.

"How long have your kind been here?" Ulysses asked.

Since the passage of the comet sent us off course, two thousand of your years ago.

Ulysses didn't know what to say in response to that revelation.

N'kel suddenly broke away from the party, approaching the curving wall of the chamber with quick, darting strides.

See, she said, pointing with a claw.

Ulysses and Nimrod looked.

"Good lord!" the usually unflappable butler gasped.

The two men joined N'kel at the wall. They could see the markings more clearly now, the shadows cast by the lanterns highlighting the marks made by chitin-axes centuries ago.

The intricate carvings were not unlike those found in the Trois Frers cave in the Pyrenees – that Ulysses had visited once on a family holiday when he and Barty were children – the Nazca lines of Peru, or the Tanum petroglyphs. But at the same time there was something otherworldly and inhuman about the stone-cut images.

It soon became apparent that the carvings were a pictographic record of the history of the Selenite civilisation, etched into the undulating grey walls of the cavern.

It took Ulysses a moment of study to realise that the story was told from right to left, the more recent carvings being those they must have already passed on their way through the abandoned portions of the Selenite city.

Ulysses saw the depiction of something that looked like a seed pod, or a cluster of spider's eggs, and to the left of that a depiction of what could only be a crash or explosion. The markings that followed these were simplistic depictions of the Selenites themselves and the beasts they employed to constantly renew and expand their hive, including mantis-like spider-things that Ulysses and Nimrod had not encountered for themselves. Looking at the monstrous representations more closely, Ulysses was glad that they hadn't.

Other carvings showed ranks of what were obviously soldiers venerating a bloated arachnoid form residing atop a raised platform within a domed chamber; troops paying fealty to their Empress.

These wall-carvings were made by our ancestors.

"And how long ago were they made?" Ulysses asked.

The first ones during the time of the first Empress, N'kel replied.

"And how long ago is that, exactly? How long is a generation? I mean, how old are you?"

If you mean in terms of measuring the passage of time in relation to how frequently the Earth and Moon travel around the star you call the Sun, the Selenite began, speaking slowly, as if giving herself time to think, *then I am 114 years old.*

THIS IS THE *place,* N'kel's gentle voice spoke inside his mind, as their party came to a halt, and Ulysses could immediately see that she was right.

The Selenite tunnels showed no sign of coming to an end but something else had intruded into them from above, pillars of mooncrete and reinforced steel thrusting through from the surface like the roots of some giant alien plant.

Ulysses approached one the pillars, passing right the way around it.

"Okay," he said. "But how do we get in?"

Without any warning the ground around them began to shudder and shake. Ulysses was forced to grab hold of the pillar to stop himself losing his balance altogether. Nimrod, cat-like in his movements, kept his balance, as did the Selenites. Dust showered down onto them from the roof.

It was almost a minute before the quake subsided but Ulysses could hear N'kel's voice quite clearly over the din of the crumbling rock.

It's this way, she said. *Follow me.*

The fissure lay not much further on. It had formed between one of the pillars and the roof of the tunnel that the foundation support had been sunk into. Ulysses had no idea how far below the crust they were at this point, but it seemed likely to him that the fissure would lead up into the base above if it went anywhere at all, and N'kel seemed certain that it did.

The crack must have been formed during the construction of the base or – what seemed just as likely to Ulysses – as a result of the constant moonquakes that were afflicting this region. If it hadn't been for the Selenites' air-filled tunnels, when the crack formed, the dome above would have begun to lose its atmosphere.

Ulysses smiled wryly to himself. It was a crack in the surface of the Moon that had taken them into the world of the Selenites in the first place, and it was another crack that was going to get them out again.

"Righty-ho," he said, "last one up's a rotten egg!"

THE CRACK WAS wide enough for a man – or Selenite – to pass through, but only just. Like a natural chimney through the rock, the fissure described a zigzagging path through the Moon's crust, the rift providing the climbers with plenty of handholds and ledges for them to put their feet on. In places it was almost like climbing a ladder or a flight of highly irregular stairs.

Ulysses led the way, sending showers of grey dust down onto the heads of those following him but he was saving any apologies for later, knowing that they could all too easily be overheard by whoever it was that might be occupying the dome.

The climb took longer than Ulysses had been expecting – the foundations must have been sunk far into the Moon's crust to anchor the dome, limpet-like, to the floor of the Jules Verne Crater. But at last, Ulysses looked up and saw the glimmer of light above him. Dousing his own helmet light, he took the last ten feet of his climb very slowly until he cautiously poked his head through into the chamber above.

Wedging himself at the top of the fissure he quickly turned his head from left to right, taking in the confines of the small storage chamber in which he found himself. Other than a few cargo crates he could see nothing – certainly no signs of human life – and so he gave the signal for the others to follow him up.

Nimrod was first to enter the room after Ulysses; the armoured head of one of the soldiers was next. Ulysses had not necessarily expected the Selenites to do any more than lead them to the place where they might enter the dome, but he felt glad that N'kel and her bodyguards were coming too. After all, everyone knew there was safety in numbers.

When all five of them were ready Ulysses made his way over to the only door he could see and, moving with heightened caution, his pulse thumping in his ears, he turned the handle and opened it a fraction.

The corridor beyond was empty and devoid of any decoration, as was the one after that, and the T-junction they came to after that.

The base certainly did not appear to have been built for anything other than some entirely practical purpose. From what they had seen so far, it certainly wasn't somewhere that had been built with human comfort in mind.

Ulysses pressed on, and where he led, the others followed.

The gently curving corridors all seemed to be leading one way, towards what the dandy took to be the centre of the moonbase. The further they went into the dome the higher the ceilings of the corridors became, as if they mirrored the shape of the arching roof. If that was the case, then they were certainly steadily working their way towards the centre.

The passageways were steadily broadening too, but they were eerily empty, not only of people but of any equipment that might help them determine for what purpose the base had been built in the first place.

Ulysses began to wonder if it there was anyone here at all, or whether – with the deaths of Shurin, Rossum and Bainbridge – the project had faltered and remained unfinished. But that would have meant someone had known what they were up to and wanted to stop them before they could complete their work. Was that why Barty had been killed, he wondered. But then why was there power and air inside the dome? It didn't make sense – unless it wasn't uninhabited after all.

And then, with Ulysses caught up in his musings, they reached the centre of the dome. The echoing silence of the labyrinthine passageways gave way at last to the pulsing *whub-whub-whub* of a fan and the dull hum of living machinery.

Ulysses was the first to peer around the corner of the floor to ceiling opening in the wall in front of them.

"Oh my God!" he breathed. "I don't believe it! Nimrod's it's –" He turned to share what he was seeing with his manservant, his words giving way to shocked silence.

The first thing he noticed was that the Selenites were gone. He had no idea when the three aliens had abandoned them but they certainly weren't there now, leaving him and his weary butler to their fate.

The second was that he and Nimrod had picked up two different hangers-on instead.

Standing in the passageway behind them were a young man and woman. Each was holding a gun, both of the weapons trained on the intruders. Other than for their over-large hand cannons, they looked like any other smart, young couple enjoying the sights of the Moon for the first time.

"Well, well, well," said the woman, stepping out of the shadows, one eyebrow raised, a cruel smile curling her lips and a triumphant glint in her eyes. "What have we here, Mr Chapter?"

"We would appear to have company, Miss Verse," the man replied.

"And unless I'm very much mistaken, it is the redoubtable Mr Ulysses Quicksilver who has deemed to honour us with his presence. You just couldn't leave well enough alone, could you? Well following us here was your first mistake." She glanced around her at the empty corridor. "Not bringing back-up would appear to have been your second."

"And I know you too," Ulysses growled, realisation dawning. "You were on board the Apollo. I saved your life." He turned to the man. "And yours!"

"Oh, I stand corrected. *That* would have to have been your first mistake," Veronica Verse said, pointing her pistol at Ulysses' face. "Still, no hard feelings, eh? After all, business is business. Now turn around and start walking or I'll blow your bloody brains out."

CHAPTER TWENTY-FOUR

Sphere

T minus 21 minutes, 48 seconds

"HANDS WHERE I can see them!" the woman screeched, stabbing her gun into Ulysses' face again.

Never once taking his eyes off her, Ulysses slowly did as he was instructed. If she and her companion had wanted them dead, they would be lying on the floor by now, a tidy bullet hole through each of their skulls.

"And turn around."

Again, the dandy and his manservant silently did as they were commanded. The hitman remained silent, a contented smile playing about his lips.

Ulysses felt the nose of the woman's pistol poke him in the small of the back, even through his environment suit. He grimaced.

His mind was suddenly a focused needle of light. Had he caught up with Barty's killers at last? Had he saved their lives during the incident on board the *Apollo XIII* only for them to murder Barty and now threaten his life and Nimrod's?

"Now move," the woman snapped.

A weapon trained on them each, and their own inaccessible to them beneath their environment suits, with leaden steps Ulysses and Nimrod trudged through the towering aperture and entered the central chamber.

It was hemispherical in form, formed from moulded mooncrete supported by a spider's-web of steel girders, lit by a dozen electro-globes hung on lengths of cable from the roof. The room was ringed by a raised walkway lined with banks of curious equipment that ticked and hummed, dials spiking and lights flickering in response to some unknown process. But it was what stood on the far side of the chamber that had so shocked Ulysses when he had first peered inside.

It stood atop a raised dais, accessed by a wrought iron staircase, and ringed by a bank of Babbage engines. Like some bizarre optical illusion, it looked like a sphere even though it was actually made up from the concentric, yet broken, rings of a giant gyroscope.

The last time he had seen the Sphere had been in the cellar of Hardewick Hall in Warwickshire, eight months ago and a quarter of a million miles away.

And yet, impossible as it might seem, here it sat, squatting upon its claw-footed stand, as tall as a man and half that again, the esoteric machinery limned in a corposant of its own making. But where the device Ulysses had last seen vanish from the bowels of Alexander Oddfellow's house had been gleaming polished metal, the strange artefact in front of him now appeared much older, its surface crazed with a patina of age, the brass pitted and stained with verdigris.

He stared at it, mouth agape, his mind full of questions once again. How had it got here? Was it even the same device? And if the sphere was here...

Ulysses slowly came to realise that there were a number of other people already busy inside the chamber, employed in various different tasks concerning, no doubt, the operation of the Sphere.

Standing before the banks of equipment at the foot of the dais, monitoring the activity of the device, were two men, their backs to the party that had just entered their laboratory.

"Look who we found nosing around," Verse announced proudly, causing both men to turn in startled surprise. "Only Ulysses bloody Quicksilver!"

"Quicksilver!" the taller of the two gasped.

There was something strangely familiar about the man. Ulysses peered at him more closely. He was horribly emaciated and there was something not quite right, it seemed, about the set of his features. He had lost much of his hair and yet Ulysses still recognised him. The pinched face, the round wire-framed spectacles were still the same.

"It's Smythe, isn't it?" Ulysses turned to the other man – an ugly, stooping individual, sporting rodent-like whiskers, with liver-spotted skin stretched taut over a seemingly elongated skull. "Which would make you Wentworth. Am I right?"

The rat-faced man sneered, his top lip pulling back to reveal the blunt points of peg-like yellow teeth. "Quicksilver," he snarled.

"Oh, so you know each other," Verse said, sounding surprised.

Ulysses looked from Smythe to Wentworth and back again, unable to reconcile their warped and aged appearances when he had only seen them eight months ago, looking ten years younger.

"But how can this be?" he said. "What happened to you?"

"You happened!" Smythe snapped, taking a limping step towards Ulysses. Whatever had warped his face had twisted his body as well. "You did this to us!"

A persistent humming that Ulysses had been aware of ever since entering the room – only one of a myriad sounds generated by the whirring banks of machinery – began to intensify. At the same time, the chamber began to shake, a spanner rattling from a console to land with a clang on the grilled plates of the walkway, the glow-globes flickering in response.

"Smythe!" Wentworth hissed. "That bastard can keep. We have work to do."

Reluctantly Smythe turned back to the bank of Babbage engines.

"What's the flux capacitance?" Wentworth demanded.

"Flux capacitance at fifty percent," Smythe replied, "and rising."

"Keep it steady! What's the state of the transmat's containment field?"

"Containment field is stable," another voice replied.

Recognising this one too, Ulysses turned towards its source and was distressed to see Alexander Oddfellow sitting in front of a console on the raised walkway, monitoring a fluctuating oscilloscope.

The expression on the old man's face was one of abject resignation.

"Oddfellow? What's going on?"

Whatever Smythe and Wentworth had over him, Ulysses realised, for the eccentric scientist to be working alongside the very people who had tricked him into perverting his own creation to help them achieve their own dark ends, it must have been something very bad.

So he wasn't surprised when, glimpsing movement, he turned to see Emilia, gagged and bound to a chair in front of another bank of the logic engines with a gun pointed at her head.

With so many unpleasant revelations coming in such quick succession, Ulysses barely even raised an eyebrow when he saw that the man holding the gun was already somebody who he had supposed to be dead.

"Jared Shurin," he said with a sigh. With the industrialist's sudden miraculous resurrection, everything began to make sense at last.

"I suppose that after maniac robots, teleportation devices and building your own secret base on the dark side of the Moon, faking your own death must have been relatively straight forward."

"It would certainly seem that when one has enough money and influence, one can quite literally get away with murder," the smiling industrialist said with a chuckle. "Even one's own."

Ulysses stared at the smug Shurin, a look of unadulterated disdain in his flint-hard gaze.

"I have one question for you, Shurin," he said. "Why?"

Shurin laughed. "It was the easiest way to put myself beyond suspicion when it came to the suspicious deaths of the others, if – as proved to be the case – the police suspected foul play rather than buying the line that all of the deaths were unfortunate industrial accidents."

"No," Ulysses said, shaking his head. "I mean what are you doing mixed up in all this? Why risk everything you've worked for, for," Ulysses gestured at the chamber, "this... whatever it is you're up to here?"

"Watch the hands!" Veronica Verse snapped and the stub nose of the pistol was thrust into the back of his neck this time.

Ulysses found his gaze returning to the bound Emilia and felt the heat of his rage cool, in an instant, to become the cold chill of dread.

Back at the Nebuchadnezzar he had honestly believed that Emilia would be safer the further she was away from him, and yet he couldn't have been more wrong. He had set off in search of the mysterious 'fourth man' Selene had mentioned, only to discover now that the first of the dead industrialists wasn't dead at all and Emilia – along with her father – was in mortal danger.

"Emilia," he said. "I am so sorry."

Emilia said nothing – *could* say nothing – but simply stared at him with glistening eyes.

He could hear the echo of mocking laughter even over the humming of the weird machinery filling the chamber. Ulysses turned, the chill flash-boiling to furious anger once more.

"Why, Shurin?" he demanded, taking another step towards the laughing man.

"Stay where you are!" the woman shouted at him but Ulysses ignored her.

"Why? Why have the others murdered? Why have my brother killed? Why kidnap Emilia and her father? Answer me!"

The explosion of lightning took everyone by surprise – all except Smythe and Wentworth. Emilia gave a muffled cry. Veronica Verse squealed, a sadomasochistic mixture of shock and excitement.

Ulysses heard Nimrod give voice to an earthy oath as he threw up a hand to shield his eyes against the searing flare of actinic light.

The lights in the chamber dimmed, and almost went out, as another juddering tremor rattled the dome to its foundations.

Then the gyroscopic scream of the Sphere became a dull descending whine, before becoming a steady buzzing hum once more. The lights brightened again.

Peering at the dying of the light at the heart of the Sphere, Ulysses could make out the indistinct silhouette of a man, standing proudly at the centre of the whirling device.

As the scintillating glow faded, the dark outline of the figure became clearer until the broken coils of the Sphere slowed and the man stepped clear of the teleportation device.

From his position at the foot of the dais, Ulysses gazed up into the man's face and gave a silent gasp of horror and recognition.

"Does that answer your question?" asked Daniel Dashwood.

CHAPTER TWENTY-FIVE

Frequently Asked Questions About Time Travel

T minus 18 minutes, 36 seconds

IT WAS DANIEL Dashwood, the Nazi agent and Emilia's cousin. Ulysses knew it was – it sounded like him for a start – but it didn't look like him. In his adventures all around the world and beyond, he had never seen such disfigurement as that suffered by this man.

He had once been handsome but now that striking, classical beauty, and his devil-may-care swagger, was gone, replaced by a grinning death's-head.

It looked as if the skin had been burned from his face, leaving seared muscle beneath. His hair was gone too, as were his eyelids. He gazed upon the world with bulging, bloodshot eyes that could never again be closed.

He must be in agony, Ulysses thought, his horror turning to pity. But there was only so much pity he could offer the man. After all, this was also the man who had tried to kill him and who had planned to steal Oddfellow's experimental teleportation device to aid the underground Nazi cause.

Behind him he heard Miss Verse stifle an appalled moan as Mr Chapter swallowed hard to keep his gorge from rising. Dashwood's appearance was too revolting even for a pair of hardened killers like them.

The man's nose was debrided of all flesh and his lips were gone, exposing the yellow enamel of his teeth, set within gums that were bloody and withdrawn. It made him look as though he was permanently smiling when, truth was, he must be in perpetual torment.

And what must the rest of the poor wretch's body be like? Ulysses found himself wondering, appalled.

But as he continued to stare at the Nazi agent, he saw that there was something else. It was as if Ulysses were viewing badly-spliced newsreel footage. Parts of Dashwood's face appeared to flicker and change, or even blink in and out of existence. One minute the dandy was looking at a skinless skull, the next one side of Dashwood's face appeared almost exactly as it had been when Ulysses had last encountered him. Then the skull would return, and a moment later the man's mouth was back, or some of his hair, or he would be looking at Ulysses with half-closed eyes. But always the skull-face would return.

"What the hell happened to you?"

Ulysses looked from the hideously disfigured Dashwood to the withered Smythe, and deformed Wentworth, and back again.

The thing that had once been Daniel Dashwood strode across the raised platform of the dais, never once taking his unblinking eyes from the dandy.

He descended the wrought iron staircase, his breath whistling between the cords of muscle securing his jaw to his skull. He looked like he was wearing what was left of a dinner jacket and matching trousers, although the black suit was in a pitiful state of repair.

Ulysses heard Verse stifle another pitiful moan behind him and felt the pressure of the cold metal against his neck lessen fractionally.

Dashwood came to stand right in front of Ulysses, so close that he could have reached out and touched him. He raised his right hand, and Ulysses saw that he was wearing black leather gloves.

"You did," he hissed in a venomous whisper.

He lashed out with startling speed, striking Ulysses across the face. The dandy turned with the blow and a moment later pain bloomed. He put a hand to his cheek.

Out of the corner of his eye he saw Nimrod tense, but stilled him with a gesture. Chapter and Verse didn't look like they'd need much provocation to pull the triggers of the pistols they were wielding. And Nimrod getting himself gunned down certainly wasn't going to improve their situation.

Ulysses raised his head and looked past the disfigured Dashwood at the device that was spinning slowly to a standstill.

Only he wasn't looking at the tarnished, age-worn device now squatting on top of the platform like some malignant fiend. He was seeing the gleaming golden machine as it had been in the cellar of Hardewick Hall, whirling like a gyroscope, actinic light rippling from it as the air hummed in sympathetic vibration. And he saw himself pulling the bundle of cables free, the sundered wires bleeding sparks.

And then he turned to regard the disfigured Dashwood once more and his face hardened as he recalled what the villain had been prepared to do to old man Oddfellow, Emilia and himself in his pursuit of his fascist schemes.

"What do you want," he simmered, "an apology?"

Dashwood struck him again, harder this time.

"Very well. I'm sorry I didn't kill you properly the last time we met."

This time Dashwood hit him so hard blood flew in a fine spray from his bruised lips. It ran freely from his mouth and he spat a great gobbet of it onto the polished mooncrete floor of the chamber.

And then it all came pouring out of Dashwood, as if he had been waiting a long time to let Ulysses know precisely how he felt about what the dandy had done to him, by causing the Sphere to malfunction when he tore out its power supply.

"Ten years!" he shrieked, his voice suddenly transforming from a whisper to a banshee wail. "Ten years of waiting! Ten years of agony! Ten years with a hatred burning in my heart that was hotter than the pain burning in my eyes! Ten years of harbouring my desire for revenge!"

"Ten years?" Ulysses murmured, incredulously.

"Yes! *Ten years!*"

"But we first met only eight months ago," Ulysses said.

"*You* might have seen me only eight months ago," the warped wretch went on, sounding like some screeching harpy, "but for me, for Wentworth and for Smythe, it's been ten long years of suffering. Although time has done nothing to quell my hatred of you!"

"I don't understand."

"What is he blathering on about, sir?" Nimrod whispered at his side.

"What *happened* when the three of you vanished, along with the device?"

Dashwood leaned in close, his features appearing to run and melt before Ulysses' eyes.

"You couldn't begin to imagine what we went through, what we suffered. I've seen things that would break a lesser man's sanity, that would have fractured your feeble mind."

"But *where* did you *go*?"

Ulysses looked from the monstrous Dashwood to the haggard face of Alexander Oddfellow, seated on the other side of the room, as if hoping the old man might be able to give him the answer he sought. But it was Dashwood who responded.

"That machine," he said, pointing at the Sphere, his tone mid-way between abject awe and disgust, "does not only displace objects in three dimensions. Oh no; nothing so simple. It can also move objects through time."

Ulysses' mouth hung open as he stared at the machine. He looked from Dashwood to his unnaturally aged assistants, then back to the uneasy Oddfellow and the tear-streaked, hysterical expression on the face of the bound Emilia, and lastly the glowering grimace of the man holding a gun to her head in order to ensure her father's compliance.

A curious expression entered Dashwood's lidless eyes, as if he was gazing into the depths of space and time at a place only he could visualise.

"I still don't know where we went to begin with, or for how long we travelled, as the Sphere jumped from one place and time to another at random. All I know is that when it eventually powered down – the energy it had absorbed from the lightning strike finally drained from its power cells – we came to, to find ourselves in the slums of Luna Prime."

"What did you do?" Ulysses said.

"We went into hiding – I mean, what else could we do?"

"If I was you, I wouldn't want to go showing my face in public looking like that."

Dashwood struck him again for that.

"If you think I looked like this then, you are sadly mistaken. Oh, our journey through time and space changed us, there's no denying that – changed us in ways we could never have imagined. But it was ten years of experimentation, struggling to repair and perfect the device – ten years of self-experimentation, using myself as a guinea-pig test subject – that did this!

"But ten years of waiting – waiting for the old man to even invent the machine in the first place – gave me time to think and to plan."

It seemed that now he had himself a captive audience there was no stopping the deranged Dashwood, as he revealed the scale of his audacious and sinister scheme.

"It was a relatively simple thing to get the industrialists on board, with the help of our first convert here." At this Dashwood nodded towards Shurin, who smiled back at Ulysses. "I have always found it more effective to appeal to a man's greed for power and riches than to focus on pandering to his better nature."

"So they set about building you your secret moonbase here, hidden on the dark side, away from prying eyes. What was your price, Shurin?"

"Oh, you know, the usual."

"Money? Power?"

"The others were lured by the promise of greater riches to come, but for me – I have to confess – it was the power." Shurin smirked.

"You disgust me." Ulysses turned his attention back to Dashwood. "While you waited for Oddfellow to carry out his experiments into teleportation back on Earth – and for me to rescue him from limbo, so that..." Ulysses took a moment to order his thoughts as he pieced together the final pieces of the puzzle. Dashwood had most definitely been playing the long game. "So that he could then help you finish your repairs to the Sphere at this point in time."

Something like a smile stretched Dashwood's death's-head leer even further. "Very good."

"The competition they won. That was you."

"Exactly. A mere fiction to get them where I needed them to be. That Alexander Oddfellow might complete his masterwork."

Ulysses dared to turn and look over his shoulder at the noticeably nervous and nauseous Chapter and Verse.

"And then you set about covering your tracks, removing the weak links from the chain."

"Precisely."

"Starting with my brother, because he was onto your little scheme. Even though maybe he didn't realise it at the time."

"*Little*?" Dashwood shrieked. "You call ten years of planning to restore the might of the Third Reich *little*?"

"And just how much longer do you think he's going to let you two live for, now that he's accomplished his insane scheme?" Ulysses asked the assassins, looking Chapter and Verse straight in the eye.

Their guns didn't waiver, but the look in their eyes did.

"The moment you murdered my brother you doomed yourselves."

An expression of quizzical incomprehension clouded Veronica Verse's face. Lars Chapter appeared to sport a never-changing expression of bewildered confusion.

"What is this obsession with your brother?" Dashwood said. "Especially if he's dead."

Ulysses turned to face the arch-manipulator again.

"You heartless bastard! He was just another obstacle to be removed, as far as you were concerned, wasn't he?"

"I don't know what you're talking about." Dashwood said with a dismissive chuckle.

"There's no point denying it now, after all you've done!"

"I quite agree; there wouldn't be. But I didn't have him killed."

Ulysses suddenly felt like the insides had dropped out of him. He turned back to the assassins.

Understanding his unvoiced question, Veronica Verse shook her head.

Everything that had brought him to this point had been motivated by the hunt for his brother's killer. And now he had uncovered an audacious, empire-threatening plan, but at that moment it all seemed for naught.

Dashwood started to laugh. "That's what all this was about, for you, wasn't it? You've been hunting your brother's killer all this time and still he eludes you."

The fires of his hatred and his rage blazed in Ulysses' furious gaze.

"But I'm onto your *little* plan now, aren't I?"

"Your mind cannot fathom the audacity of my master plan!"

"Let me guess. You plan to use the Sphere to travel back in time to the Second Great European War and provide Hitler with the means to win the conflict, and so ultimately conquer Magna Britannia."

Dashwood remained stubbornly silent.

"Am I right?"

"I was right," the other scowled, "you cannot begin to comprehend the magnitude of my scheme."

"So why don't you enlighten me? After all, you have yourself a captive audience, and I'm sure you've been simply dying to boast of the magnificence of your master plan, haven't you?"

"Time travel is only the beginning," Dashwood hissed.

"Fire from heaven, that's the key," Shurin announced proudly.

At that Dashwood whirled around to face his co-conspirator and Ulysses saw the younger man flinch. "Silence!"

"Fire from heaven you say? Interesting," Ulysses said. "Like some modern day Prometheus."

"Perhaps," Dashwood mused. "But that will be as nothing, compared to the might of my army."

"Your army? What army? I'd hardly call a pair of so-called boffins, a coerced inventor, an aspiring megalomaniac and a deranged Nazi-loving freak an army!"

Ulysses tensed, waiting for the blow that was surely to come. Only it didn't. Instead Dashwood began to laugh once more. It started as a ripple of mirth but then swelled into something uncontrolled and less than sane, until the roaring laughter of a maniac echoed from the curving walls of the vaulted mooncrete chamber.

"Here, let me show you," he said, once he had managed to recover his composure. "What army, you say. Fire it up!" he snapped, stabbing a finger at Wentworth and Smythe.

Switches were flicked, levers were pulled and the Sphere began to run up to speed once more.

"Set the temporal jump to one second into the past!"

Wentworth and Smythe, and even Oddfellow, then set about monitoring their stations, focusing on the many dials and cathode ray displays that formed part of the banks of machinery required to run the dreadful device.

Atop the dais the hurtling metal rings seemed to melt, becoming a whirling sphere of light. A pulsing hum filled the air. Under the throbbing force of the vibrations Ulysses felt as though his teeth were rattling inside his head. The walls of the chamber began to shudder in sympathy and Ulysses could now feel the pounding pulse through his feet as well.

"Now, watch this!" Dashwood said and stepped between the whirling rings.

There was a flash of actinic light, and all present were forced to shut their eyes against the glare.

A split second later, Ulysses forced himself to open his eyes a fraction. It felt like the searing light was burning through into his brain and he wondered whether he might go blind if he stared for too long.

But there, in the centre of the dazzling white glare, he could see the silhouette of the man. No, two silhouettes. There was another flash and now there were three. Another flash and, was it a trick of the light or were there really four figures inside the Sphere now?

Only they weren't inside the Sphere, there wasn't room to contain them any longer. They were stepping clear of the light onto the platform. Suddenly there were six. Then seven.

Ulysses blinked.

Ten.

Twelve.

Fourteen.

He was struggling to keep count.

There were so many now that their number blocked the dazzling glare of the spinning Sphere so that Ulysses' vision began to mercifully return to normal. Ulysses blinked away the grey spots from before his eyes and stared in horror at the veritable battalion of figures stepping clear of the machine.

There had to be more than thirty of them now, pouring down the steps, those emerging from the Sphere behind forcing the others down the wrought iron staircase and into the chamber. And still they kept coming.

Ulysses stared in horror. Alexander Oddfellow gave a pained cry of shock.

There were more than fifty of them now but really there was still only one.

They were all the same man.

They were all Daniel Dashwood.

CHAPTER TWENTY-SIX

Armageddon

T minus 12 minutes

ALEXANDER ODDFELLOW RUBBED his eyes and then read the result of the equation displayed on the glowing green screen in front of him again. It didn't change anything.

Behind him the infernal device throbbed with malignant power and he cursed the day, for the umpteenth time, that he ever sat down to create the matter transporter.

There was no escaping the facts, no matter how hard he might wish that he could. If they continued to run the Sphere as they were, the more the very fabric of reality would be weakened. Left unchecked, the final, undeniable outcome was inevitable.

Helter skelter. Total dimensional collapse. The end of everything. Ever.

And it would occur in twelve minutes, and counting.

*   *   *

"TURN IT OFF!" Ulysses heard Oddfellow shout.

The old man wasn't looking at the bank of machines in front of him anymore. He was staring at the ceiling.

Ulysses followed his gaze. A crack had appeared in the structure of the mooncrete dome. As the chamber continued to shudder and shake under the influence of the strange forces being exerted against it, the crack continued to widen.

"*Turn it off!*"

Ulysses flinched as a chunk of masonry hit the floor not three feet away from him.

"TURN IT OFF!" the old man screamed again, flattening swathes of switches at the same time with the flat of his hand.

Another piece of the roof – this one the size of a billiard table – hit the ground with a dull thud, bringing with it a cascade of powdered dust.

Ulysses ducked his head to stop any of the grit getting into his eyes as the dust shower turned his hair even more grey than it already was.

He glanced behind him. The hitman and his female companion were both now more concerned with the crumbling roof above them than the captives in front of them. Their guns were pointed at the floor as their eyes anxiously followed the splintering spider's-web of cracks in the dome.

He looked around for Nimrod, not seeing him at first, until he looked down.

Nimrod lay unmoving on the floor of the chamber, a slab of masonry broken across his back and blood the colour of rich claret oozing from a wound on the back of his head.

"Nimrod!"

His butler groaned.

And then the high-pitched whine of the machine began to drop and the seismic tremors reduced in power. Wentworth and Smythe appeared to have heeded the old man's advice.

Ulysses assessed the situation facing them. The myriad Dashwoods were still piling down the steps from the platform – there had to be over a hundred of them by now – but at least there weren't any more emerging from the Sphere.

The spinning discs of the device were slowing, the brilliant glow fading, although the after image seared onto Ulysses' retinas still remained.

Despite the threat facing his daughter, Oddfellow had obviously felt compelled to act. Certainly, to Ulysses' eyes, it appeared that if the Sphere had kept functioning as it had been, it could have brought the roof down, ensuring the deaths of all present. At least by stepping in to prevent the total destruction of the dome he was giving his daughter a fighting chance – no matter how slim it might be – but was it an opportunity Ulysses could exploit?

Perhaps if Nimrod had not been laid out cold.

Shurin still had his gun pointed at Emilia but the look on his face had morphed from one of supremely cocksure arrogance to that of uncertain anxiety. Was that change in mood something that Ulysses could exploit?

The Dashwoods appeared unperturbed by the cracking of the dome, as far as Ulysses could tell, and were more concerned by the fact that Wentworth and Smythe had shut the device down.

A hundred pairs of lidless eyes fixed on the two cowering scientists.

"Why did you –" one began.

"– turn it off?" another finished.

"I told you –"

"– to keep it running!"

They all seemed to be talking at once but Ulysses only heard one voice speaking.

"The old man was right," the deformed Wentworth said with a feeble sigh. "We had to shut it down or –"

"You disobeyed –"

"– a direct order!"

"Take a look around you!" Smythe wailed, casting his gaze at the cracked egg of the dome and the chunks of masonry littering the floor. "If we'd left it running we'd all be buried under a hundred tons of mooncrete by now."

"You think –"

"– I care –"

"– about that?"

"The device would have been destroyed."

The Dashwoods were silenced by that simple statement.

"You do realise you're weakening the very fabric of reality, don't you?"

The Dashwoods turned to face the old man's challenge. Alexander Oddfellow looked drawn and pale, as if he had aged ten years since Ulysses had last seen him.

"The more you run the machine the more damage you do. I wish I'd never created the damn thing! Keep going like this and it won't just be us you'll kill – the whole of existence will unravel like a frayed piece of string. I'm talking total dimensional collapse. Helter skelter."

The Dashwoods listened to the old man's tirade without saying a word, two hundred bulging, bloodshot eyes boring into him. After a decade of waiting and planning and searching for the means to fulfil his insane scheme, there was no point denying the facts now. Daniel Dashwood might have been driven mad by his long years in the wilderness and his virtual addiction to his use of the Sphere, but he wasn't stupid. He recognised the truth when he heard it.

The mooncrete floor still shuddering beneath his feet, Ulysses took a stumbling step forward and felt a hundred pairs of eyes fix on him.

Where had they all come from? Had Dashwood turned the Sphere into some kind of cloning machine or had he somehow collected them from somewhere?

Even if he had been armed and Nimrod had still been in a fit state to help, he would have struggled to fight his way through the Dashwoods before sheer force of numbers overwhelmed him and put paid to any breakout attempt.

Whatever else he might have had in mind, he would have to deal with the threat posed by this veritable army of Dashwoods first, which seemed an impossible task from where he was standing.

It was the machine that had created the problem. Perhaps the solution lay with the device as well. It had brought them all here, somehow, perhaps it could be used to send them back again.

Ulysses took another step towards the bank of cogitators at the foot of the dais.

"And where –"

"– do you think –"

"– you're going?" the Dashwoods asked.

Ulysses froze. It took him a moment to realise that the Dashwoods weren't paying him any attention. Following their gaze, he glanced back over his shoulder.

Chapter and Verse were already at the entrance to the chamber and showed no sign of stopping, despite the Dashwoods' demands that they do just that. "Stop!" the warped figures shouted with one voice.

And then the freaks were pouring down the steps, spreading out through the chamber, moving after the escaping assassins, screaming in rage, eyes wild, mouths flecked with foam, gloved hands raised as palsied claws.

"Stop them!" the Dashwoods screamed. "Kill them!"

"Sir!" The shout rang out over the heads of the milling maniacs, amplified by the strange acoustics of the chamber. It was Smythe.

The Dashwoods froze and, as one, turned to face the scientist.

"Sir, if we're going to go at all, we have to go now."

The Dashwoods hesitated for a moment. Ulysses was surrounded. He remained exactly where he was, deciding that it was better to watch and wait and avoid doing anything that might draw the freaks' attention back onto him.

"Very well," one of the warped figures said at last.

"Set the target co-ordinates –"

"– and recommence the –"

"– initialisation sequence."

"Yes, sir!" Wentworth and Smythe replied briskly with what sounded to Ulysses like heartfelt relief.

It was clear what they intended to do next. They were back on track with their original plan. They were going to open a doorway to the past, using the Sphere to transport them to the Second European War, that they might hand the Führer the tools he needed to conquer the mechanical armies of Magna Britannia and ensure the Nazi conquest of the world.

It wouldn't matter what happened to the Sphere after that. Dashwood and his henchmen – and perhaps even his army of simulacra too – would be long gone.

And it didn't matter that he was outnumbered a hundred to one anymore either. Ulysses was the only one in any position to bring a halt to such an insane plan.

Ignoring the risk involved in awakening the ire of the multiple Dashwoods, Ulysses sprinted across the chamber. As the Sphere began to run up to speed for the last time, the chamber was bathed in sick white light as arcs of lightning burst from within its whirling coils.

The air was alive with the humming of the machine and the seismic tremors – that had never truly passed – increased in force once more.

Realising what was going on, the Dashwoods began to close ranks.

Ulysses sent two of them tumbling out of his way and was halfway to the Sphere's control consoles before all of the freaks had grasped what he was doing. But a moment later they were on to him in force.

"I said where –"

"– do you think –"

"– you're going?" a trio of Dashwoods demanded as they turned on him.

Ulysses lashed out with a fist as one of them swung a punch at his midriff and batted the blow aside. He ducked another poorly-aimed swipe from a second but then felt a sharp pain in his shins as another two kicked his legs out from under him. He hit the juddering ground hard, immediately struggling to get to his feet as the rest of the Dashwoods closed in around him.

There came a shout from the entrance to the chamber behind him – although he couldn't make out any specific words over the rumble and crash of the shattering dome – and a moment later the Dashwoods' attention was elsewhere entirely.

As they cleared from around him, Ulysses stumbled to his feet, dazed and confused. Before him lay the steps to the dais. On top of the raised platform, rattling like a jar of shaken nails, the Sphere. In that moment, Dashwood's lackeys left their workstations and began to climb the steps, clinging onto the handrails as the force of the vibrations tearing the dome apart threatened to send them tumbling back down to the bottom. And Dashwood was with them, but only one version of the insane Nazi spy, and, Ulysses guessed, the original.

With a crack like thunder the ground at Ulysses' feet fractured, a great void opening between him and the Sphere platform. With another thunderous retort the mooncrete floor splintered again and Ulysses found himself rising as the surface he was standing on cantilevered upwards. Dripping moon rock, the sundered shard of the Moon's crust in front of him dropped away just as abruptly.

As the Moon's crust came apart, Ulysses' thoughts turned from the insane Dashwood to his companions – to his loyal servant Nimrod, to his one true love Emilia, and to her father.

And it was only then, as Ulysses turned to see what had happened to them, that he understood the reason for the other Dashwoods' abrupt diversion of attention.

Pushing their way into the chamber, through the same entrance that Ulysses and Nimrod had used, came a horde of intimidating inhuman figures clad in plates of chitin armour and wielding sharpened bone blades.

"The Selenites!" Ulysses gasped. "They didn't abandon us."

More and more of the alien soldiers were pouring into the chamber and engaging the multiple Dashwoods in battle. The altered Nazis still outnumbered the aliens, but the Dashwoods were brutally outmatched. Fists and feet, and even teeth, backed up with a manic purpose and insane resolve, were still no match for a warrior's training, toughened armour and deftly-wielded glass-sharp blades.

This was the opportunity Ulysses had been waiting for. With the Dashwoods distracted, the dandy scrambled over the still shifting ground to where Nimrod lay, Ulysses shaking him from his stupor.

"You all right, old boy?"

With Ulysses' assistance, the older man struggled to his feet. "I've been worse, sir." He put a hand to his head and winced. "But then I've been better too."

With Nimrod at his side, Ulysses turned to where Emilia sat, bound and gagged, and saw that her keeper had already fled. Jared Shurin was halfway up the steps to the Sphere, close on the heels of the original Dashwood and his pet scientists.

Ignoring the fleeing industrialist, Ulysses ran to free the imperilled Emilia.

"DASHWOOD, WAIT!" JARED Shurin called out on reaching the bottom of the steps leading to the top of the dais.

The hideously disfigured Dashwood hesitated and turned his skinless face and death's-head gaze on the panicking Shurin.

All was chaos around them but still he waited as Shurin pulled himself up the steps.

"Have you got the plans, Shurin?" Dashwood demanded. "Where are the plans?"

"Right here," Shurin panted as he mounted the platform.

"Show me!"

Shurin reached into a jacket pocket and took out the data storage locket that contained the plans for the Icarus Cannon.

Before Shurin could return them to their hiding place Dashwood struck, fast as a cobra, snatching the locket from his hand.

"What are you doing?" he gasped.

"Cutting out the middle man," Dashwood snarled.

Shurin saw the pistol and saw that its muzzle was pointing squarely at his belly.

"You treacherous bas –"

The pistol fired with a puff of blue smoke and the sudden, acrid stench of burnt gunpowder.

Shurin's gasp of shock and pain silenced him and he froze. Clutching his gut, blood dribbling out through the ragged hole in his back, Shurin toppled backwards. He tumbled back down the stairs to the floor where he lay, at the foot of the dais, in a spreading pool of blood as his last breath escaped him in a rasping rattle.

"Right," Dashwood said, pocketing the plans and his pistol, "let's get out of here."

ANOTHER BLOCK OF mooncrete crashed to the ground, shattering against the grilled platform and denting a handrail. That had been too close for comfort, Ulysses thought.

With fumbling fingers he finally managed to undo the last knots keeping Emilia bound to the chair and pulled the gag free of her mouth.

As her father helped her up from the chair, Ulysses pushed them both along the walkway towards the exit from the domed chamber. A figure stood there, in the thick of the swarming Selenites, and yet remaining untouched; someone he felt he should recognise, although he could barely see the man properly between the milling alien ants.

Emilia looked up at him with desperate eyes. Her hair was a mess, hanging in ruffled tangles around her shoulders. Tears streaked her face, her eyelashes clumped together, her eyes ringed red.

"Go!" Ulysses implored her. "You have to get out of here now!"

"But what about you?" she said, grasping him by the shoulders.

"I'll catch you up."

"You're going after Daniel, aren't you?"

"I have to. I can't let him get away again. The consequences would be too terrible to contemplate."

Emilia's own anxious expression sagged.

"Will I ever see you again?"

Ulysses smiled weakly. "Oh, I'm like a bad penny me. You don't get rid of me that easily."

"As if I'd want to."

Ulysses looked across the chamber, trying to discern the mysterious figure through the press of battling Selenites and thcir Dashwood opponents, trying to get a good look at the man hiding in the shadows.

There was something about the man; something he couldn't put his finger on, something that he didn't know how he could possibly know, but he felt that he could trust him all the same.

"Go," he urged Emilia and her father, sending them on their way. "I'll be back, I promise."

The domed chamber reverberated with the strangely insectoid clacking of the Selenites' mandibles, the furious screams of the Dashwoods and the ever present white noise of the glowing Sphere.

"Sir!" Nimrod called from the other end of the curving walkway. "They're getting away."

Ulysses turned from his manservant to Emilia, to suddenly find her lips on his. Taken aback he found himself giving in to the moment.

Breaking contact, Emilia whispered. "And make sure you keep your promise this time."

With a crash of metal and mooncrete, another piece of the fractured dome came down on the walkway, a steel girder coming down with it. Ulysses only just pulled himself back before the debris hit, tearing through a section of the walkway and slamming into the fractured floor of the chamber.

"Now go!" Ulysses shouted, blowing Emilia one last kiss before turning and running for the dais.

EMILIA TURNED AND, grabbing her father's hand, ran. The old man stumbled after her, grunting and wheezing.

Ahead of them, Emilia could make out the strange figure beckoning to them from the entrance to the crumbling chamber, one hand outstretched towards them. Ignoring the terrifying creatures that had swarmed into the chamber with him at their head, she focused only on him, for he seemed to be their only hope now.

And then she was stumbling down the steps at the end of the twisted walkway, still pulling her father after her. She caught a passing glance of a stubbly chin and a black leather eye-patch, before the man took her hand and pulled her after him into the maze of corridors.

As they ran, through the flickering pools of light produced by the shaking glow-globes, she took in the man's mane of lank hair, his battered, poorly-made suit and his scuffed shoes. But still there was something familiar about him; his height, his build, even the feel of his hand in hers.

"Stop!" she shouted, as realisation dawned. "Stop!"

The man ran on, not once looking back.

"*Stop!*"

Emilia's scream echoed away into the shadowed depths of the passageway. The man came to a sudden halt, still facing away from her. He let go of her hand.

"Turn around!" Emilia commanded.

And then, slowly, he did so.

Emilia gasped, putting a hand to her mouth. A feeble whimper escaped her father's rheumy lips.

He might have looked little better than a tramp, his hair long and unkempt, his chin covered with fine grey stubble and one scarred eye-socket covered by a black leather eye-patch, but it was still unmistakeably him.

The butt of a pistol thrust from the top of his trousers.

She made a mad lunge and then the gun was in her hand, the safety off, the muzzle pointed squarely at the man's face.

"Hello, Emilia," Ulysses Quicksilver said. "Well, I kept my promise. I came back."

CHAPTER TWENTY-SEVEN

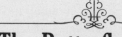

The Butterfly Effect

T minus 6 minutes, 23 seconds

"WHAT'S GOING ON?" Emilia screamed. She had both hands on the gun now. It was pointing directly at the man's forehead.

It was the man she knew, the man she loved – *had* once loved – there was no denying it. But how could it be, when he was still trapped in the chamber with the alien things and her cousin's impossible army? And how could he have the beginnings of a beard, have changed clothes and – if the eye-patch was any indication – have even lost an eye?

"I realise you probably don't want to believe your eyes right now," the aged and stubbly Ulysses began, "but, trust me, we have to get out of here now!"

Emilia didn't take another step. The gun in her hands shook but her aim was still true. Behind her, her father gave another near hysterical whimper.

"You do trust me don't you?" The man sounded desperate now. "I mean I kept my promise, didn't I? I came back, like I said I would."

Still she didn't move. Her pupils were dilated from the rush of adrenaline surging through her. Her breath came in short, ragged gasps. Her bottom lip began to quiver.

"We're not going anywhere until you tell me what's going on!" And then it all came pouring out of her. "How can you be out here and looking like" – she looked him up and down again in appalled disbelief – "like this, when I just left you back there?"

He smiled weakly through the stubble. "It's a long story."

"Well you'd better give me the edited highlights then or we're all going to die here, right here and now."

"Very well," Ulysses said with a sigh. "The short version is..." He hesitated, taking a deep breath. "I must have played this moment through in my mind a thousand times. But no matter how many times I rehearsed it I still couldn't see you believing me."

"Try me."

"Very well. The truth is the man standing in front of you now is the future version of the man you just left behind, although I've actually travelled here from the past."

"What?"

"But don't worry about that now. The important thing is that I'm the same man. The same Ulysses Quicksilver. Your Ulysses."

"Never!" Emilia suddenly snapped.

The man's face – full of hope only a moment before – became downcast.

"You have to believe me!"

"Then I think you have a little more explaining to do, don't you?"

A rumble like thunder passed through the passageway, causing a cascade of dust and rock chips to fall from the roof. All three of them looked up with anxious eyes.

Emilia looked from the shuddering ceiling to the dishevelled man in front of her.

"And you'd better be quick about it."

ULYSSES QUICKSILVER – ATTIRED *in an ill-matching jacket and trousers, and sporting three days' growth of stubble after his journey in Steerage aboard the* Apollo XIII – *watched as Nimrod, Alexander Oddfellow, Emilia and his younger self climbed into the waiting limousine, whilst remaining hidden in the steam and shadows coiling beneath a huge water pipe.*

Ulysses' attention shifted to the girl sat in the cab of the taxi-droid who had just lost out on their business. Her obvious disappointment was clear to see in the girl's innocent and honest expression.

He smiled to himself. Despite everything that he had suffered in the last few months, the pieces were slowly fitting into place. It was all coming together as it should.

Running a hand through his mop of untidy hair and adjusting the patch over his right eye, he hefted his pack onto his shoulder and then, as the car pulled away with all safely ensconced on board, stepped out of the shadows.

Not ten yards away, the two assassins were getting into a steam-cab of their own, refusing the cabbie's help and insisting on loading their many heavy bags on board themselves. Oh how he regretted ever saving their sorry skins when the asteroid attack on the Apollo XIII, *perpetrated by the Martian Separatists, would have sucked them out into the breathless void. It was a favour that they would very readily forget all about in only a matter of – he hesitated and took out his pocket watch, its face cracked now, and checked the date – four days' time, when someone else was picking up the bill.*

They said that money talked. Well, it certainly talked to those two.

He watched them for a moment, a look of resigned hatred in his eyes. He dearly wished that he could intervene but he knew that if he did so at this juncture– just as if he had tried to alter events on the space-liner –he wouldn't have been standing there now. And it was only because he was there now that he had a hope of reaching Barty before his brother's murderer did. At least that was one strand of fate he could change for the better.

Turning away, he wiped the grimace from his face, running a hand over the course grey stubble covering his chin, and made for the droid-cab. The robot's shoulders drooped as if in disappointment. The name 'Rusty' had been stencilled in large yellow letters across its rust-red chest-plate.

"'Scuse me, Miss," he called to the crestfallen girl seated behind the droid's head, "but did I hear you say that you're accepting fares to the city?"

The look of disappointment was instantly transformed into a cheery smile.

"We most certainly are," she declared, beaming at him. "Where do you want to go?"

"Just into the city will do."

It only took him a moment to climb up to the cushioned passenger cab. He patted the hull of the hulking droid as he did so, feeling a sudden warm glow. It was good to be reunited with the automaton that had saved his and Selene's lives again – even if the droid hadn't actually done so yet.

"The name's Billie," the girl said, as the droid rose to its full height and took its first lumbering steps towards the concourse's exit. Turning round she offered the man a gloved hand.

He shook it firmly, feeling the girl return his handshake with a surprisingly strong grip.

"And this is Rusty," she said, leaning forward and patting the droid's head. "What's yours?"

He hesitated before answering. "Wells."

"Very pleased to make your acquaintance, Mr Wells. You been to the Moon before, only you look kind of familiar?" Billie asked as the droid strode along the thoroughfare between the chugging cabs and rumbling haulage wagons.

"Yes, I have," he replied, his eyes glazing over as he recalled the events that had seemed to spin out of his control from the moment he arrived on the Moon and all that had happened in the months since. "This is my third visit actually."

"Really? And what are you here for this time, if you don't mind me asking? Business or pleasure?"

"Neither," he replied sullenly. "It's family."

"Oh, I know what you mean. Can't live with 'em, can't live without 'em," the girl chattered on over the increasing traffic noise and the chugging of the droid's own motive systems. "What

is it they say? You can choose your friends but you can't choose your family."

"Indeed."

"So, whereabouts in the city are you headed?"

"Milton Mansions," he said, suddenly feeling a jolt of nerves pass through him. But then that was hardly surprising, considering the enormity of the task that lay ahead of him.

And with that the droid-cab stomped off along the Humboldt Highway, headed for Luna Prime and a date with destiny.

"THIS'LL DO," ULYSSES said as the lumbering droid turned into Kepler Street.

"Right you are, guv'nor," the girl called back, bringing the droid to a clanking halt, and unfolding the steps again for him to disembark.

"And there you go," he said, pushing a crumpled five pound note into the girl's hand as he descended. The girl's eyes widened as she stared at the note. "And keep the change."

"You really mean that? But that's a ruddy five pound note!"

"I know, and you deserve it," Ulysses said with a smile. "Or, at least, you will do," he added under his breath.

"But I only gave you a lift from the spaceport."

"No, you take it. Buy your droid something nice."

"Right you are, sir! Yes, sir! Very good, sir! If there's anything else I can do for you, you let me know." She handed him a scuffed piece of card with a number written on it in what appeared to be charcoal pencil. "You ever need a lift, you give me a call."

"Oh, you can bet on it," Ulysses said allowing himself a small chuckle. He suddenly felt much more positive about what he was about to attempt – this was his chance to put things right with his brother.

"We could wait for you now, if you like," the girl offered.

"No, it's all right. You get on your way. Besides, I know how to get hold of you now if I need you, don't I?"

"Right you are, guv," Billie said, flashing him her delightful smile once more as she put the droid into gear. "See you round. And good luck with the family reunion."

"Thanks. I think I might need it."

With that, Ulysses turned towards the closed gates of the apartment complex. With the droid's clumping footsteps retreating along the street behind him, Ulysses ran his eye and a finger down the row of bell-pushes positioned next to the firmly locked gate.

Finding the number for his brother's apartment he hesitated once more, his finger hovering over the button.

According to Inspector Artemis's forensic team, in less than an hour his brother would be dead.

His brother's killer might be with him already. Or Ulysses might have beaten him there. He still couldn't completely dismiss the idea that perhaps it was Chapter and Verse or even Jared Shurin who had done the deed, despite all their protestations to the contrary.

And as he stood before the gate another thought crossed his mind – one that he had considered over and over, as often as he had considered how he would ever be able to explain to his precious Emilia what had happened to him after going after her insane cousin.

If he succeeded in preventing his brother's murder, there was always the risk that his younger self would then fail to pursue the investigation that had set him on the path that ultimately brought him to this very moment. But he came to the same conclusion now that he had time and again before. The revelation he was about to make to Barty would set the Quicksilver brothers after Shurin and the others all over again, only this time, working side by side.

Letting out the breath he hadn't realised he'd been holding, Ulysses pressed the buzzer.

There was a moment's silence, the only sound his pulse thudding in his ears, and then the crackle of static accompanied by an irritated voice came through the speaker. It was a voice he hadn't heard in months and one that – at one stage – he had never thought to hear again.

"Yes? Who is it?" Bartholomew Quicksilver asked, his tone suspicious.

"Barty," Ulysses began, his voice cracking as tears coursed down the left-hand side of his face and into his beard. "It's me, Ulysses."

"Ully?" his brother said, surprise apparent in his voice. "What are you doing here? I thought I told you not to come after me."

"And it's nice to hear your voice too. Look, I'd rather we continued this conversation face to face. Can you buzz me in?"

"All right," his brother conceded, sounding like a petulant teenager.

The buzzer sounded and, with a click, the gate swung open.

He darted through it as soon as he was able, slamming the gate shut behind him in the vain hope that it might stop, or at least slow down, anyone with the same intention of meeting with his brother.

He took the stairs three at a time and, in no time at all, he was rapping on the door to his brother's apartment with the bloodstone tip of his cane, his pistol ready in his other hand.

The door opened and Ulysses found himself staring into the face of his younger brother, still very much alive and, as far as he could tell, well to boot.

"Are you alone?" Ulysses demanded, trying to peer past him into the flat beyond.

Barty stared at his brother, his mouth open in surprise, and then, slowly, his gaze was drawn to the pistol which also happened to be pointed directly at him.

"Nice to see you too." Barty said, taking in the state of Ulysses' suit, his gaze lingering on his eye-patch. "What the hell happened to you?"

Without answering, Ulysses pushed past him into the apartment. "You're sure you're alone?" he said, making his way through to the lounge.

"Yes, more's the pity."

"Then lock the door."

"Look, what's going on?" Barty demanded, doing as his older brother had commanded, before following Ulysses into the living room. "And what happened to your eye?"

"Oh, I lost that a long time ago."

"*Really?*"

"*During the war.*"

"*Which war?*"

Ulysses shooed away further questions with a sweep of his hand. He looked his brother in the eye.

"*There's no easy way to put this, your life is in danger.*"

Barty's face suddenly fell, annoyance replaced by red-faced embarrassment; as if he believed he had let his older sibling down.

"*You found out then.*"

Found out what? Ulysses wondered.

"*Come on,*" *he said, holstering his gun,* "*you might as well tell me your side of the story now I'm here.*"

"*Very well. To be honest, it'll be good to share the burden with someone who understands what it's like. There've been enough secrets between us.*"

"*Yes, there have. But that's all behind us now. Come on, sit down and tell me what they've got over you.*"

"*All right, but if we're going to do this I'm going to need a drink,*" *Barty said.* "*And you too, I shouldn't wonder.*"

"*No! I don't want a drink.*"

"*That's not what it sounds like to me,*" *Barty said, pouring two large measures of cognac from a decanter.* "*I mean just look at you, man.*" *He thrust a full glass towards Ulysses.* "*If anybody needs a drink, it's you.*"

"*I don't want a drink!*" *Ulysses snapped, snatching the glass from Barty and slamming it down on the coffee table.*

"*All right, Ully, take it easy,*" *Barty said.* "*Is Nimrod with you?*"

"*No. Not yet.*"

"*And what's that supposed to mean?*"

Ulysses suddenly froze, staring at the full glass in front of him. He then looked at the glass in Barty's hand and watched, the horror of cold realisation writ large in his eyes, as Barty knocked back half of his drink in one go. Fate was playing its hand. Time was running out.

"*Okay, I'm sorry,*" *he said with forced calm.* "*You were saying.*"

Barty crossed the room to the only armchair, picked up the copy of The Times *(Late Lunar Edition)* that lay folded upon it and tossed it onto the coffee table before sitting down. *"Right, well, as I was saying... You know I got into some difficulties – shall we say – back home?"*

"Yes," Ulysses sighed. He knew of his brother's disastrous dalliances with Lady Luck all too well.

"Well it turned out your friend Lord Octavius de Wynter knew about them too."

"De Wynter?" Of all the names he had expected to hear in conjunction with this whole sorry mess he hadn't once thought it would be the spymaster de Wynter's.

But then a memory popped into his head; something his brother's girlfriend Selene had told him. That Barty had been working for the British Government.

"You're not serious."

Barty fixed him with a steely gaze. *"Never been more so. Turns out the great and the good aren't averse to a little blackmail if it gets the job done."*

"And what job would that be exactly?" he asked, even though he already knew the answer.

Barty hesitated and then gestured at a pile of cut-card folders on the table between them.

Ulysses stared at the folders still as much in shock as before. Everything was falling into place. The drinks, the files on the three industrialists, even the newspaper strewn across them. He hadn't managed to change a thing.

"Why didn't you come to me?" Ulysses growled.

"What, and tell you that your boss was blackmailing me to work for him?"

"I could have helped you!"

"You're sure about that, are you? You know, you're not as powerful or as influential as you like to think."

"And what's that supposed to mean?"

Barty's scowl quickly softened into an expression of remorseful shame. *"Nothing."*

Putting his glass down on the table beside Ulysses', rising, he *stepped out through the open French doors and onto the balcony.*

"Tell me!" Ulysses pressed, jumping to his feet and following his brother.

For a moment he caught himself, as his eyes followed the drop to the empty concourse below, suddenly very aware of where he was.

"You really want to know?" Barty shouted. "You really want to know what de Wynter's not been telling you?"

"Yes. Tell me!"

"I told you not to follow me here," Barty snarled, his hands gripping the balustrade, knuckles whitening as his face turned purple with pent-up rage. "I know I've been a fool and that I've made mistakes throughout my life. I know I've hardly been the brother you would've preferred me to be – that business with Screwtape and all."

"But that's all water under the bridge," Ulysses protested, moving towards his brother, his hands held out in an effort to pacify him.

"And then when I try to get myself out of the mess I've got myself into – and try my damnedest to keep you out of it – you have to go and follow me here! Just when I was starting to get my life together you have to come and interfere!"

Ulysses had never seen his brother like this. "Look, Barty, whatever it is you can tell me. Come on, we're brothers. You can tell me anything."

"Can I?" Barty suddenly hissed.

"Of course you can. You know you can."

Barty suddenly put a hand inside his trouser pocket and took out a data storage locket. Ulysses stared at it in astonishment, his mind working nineteen to the dozen.

"It's all on here, you know?" he said, his voice on the verge of mania now. "It's all here. Every sordid little secret, every inconvenient little truth."

"Does de Wynter know you've got this?" Ulysses asked, edging towards his brother.

"Do you know what he said he'd do, if I didn't complete my mission?" Barty said, with a manic giggle.

"*Barty, give it to me,*" *Ulysses said, clearly and slowly, not once taking his eyes off the locket his brother was holding.*

"*Do you know what the price for my silence was?*"

"*Barty, just give me that locket.*"

"*Your life.*"

Ulysses froze. His one good eye locked with his brother's steely gaze. There were tears there now.

"*What?*" *he said, in a voice barely more than a whisper.*

"*And now you've gone and ruined it all by coming here. I should kill you myself!*"

With a scream, Barty sprang at his brother. Ulysses might not have been in the state of peak physical fitness he had once enjoyed, after all he had gone through in the last few months, but his reactions were still far faster than his brother's. He ducked the clumsy punch and Barty's fist sailed through empty air.

But Barty had put all of his strength into that one violent action, lashing out in fury and frustration. Without anything to block the punch, the momentum of it carried him forward.

"*No!*" *Ulysses shouted as he rose from his crouch, reaching for his brother with both hands.*

But Barty was already at the edge of the balcony, his feet tripping from under him as he lost his balance.

Ulysses' fingertips brushed the cloth of his brother's shirt and then he was gone.

His hands grabbing hold of the rail, he almost followed his brother over the edge as he desperately fought against fate, futilely trying to alter events that had already occurred – events that he now realised he couldn't change.

His eye met his brother's terrified gaze one last time as Barty plummeted towards the ground, and then he struck the flagstones below, his body bouncing once before landing, lying like a marionette with all its strings cut, never to move again, the locket falling from his fingers.

EMILIA STARED INTO the face of the man before her, into his one remaining eye, and saw nothing but the reflection of a traumatised soul.

She had been wrong. This wasn't the man she had once known and loved. The Ulysses that stood before her now was broken, the indefatigable confidence and bravura gone, to be replaced by doubt and despair.

"I had gone to see Barty straight away, with the express intention of challenging fate, of changing destiny by saving his life, catching his killer – or so I thought. And yet, by that very deed I condemned him to death."

He sounded hollow, as if something had died in him, when Barty had.

"I know he could be a bastard at times, wasteful and obnoxious to boot, but he was still my brother – my younger brother – and when I was thirteen I promised to protect him, no matter what. And yet, as it turns out, the one person I couldn't protect him from was me."

Slowly Emilia lowered the gun in her hands.

He needed her, she saw that now. And the Ulysses Quicksilver who needed her was the Ulysses Quicksilver she had fallen in love with.

"It was then that I realised that everything that had happened was already pre-determined. I lost myself in a bottle of brandy after that, and a whole day in the gutter with it. Whatever I did would make no difference so I decided to do nothing. It had already happened and so it would happen again. All I could do was let events follow their pre-destined path. But then, when the brandy was gone, I realised at last that I still had a part to play – the part that fate had always had in mind for me. I could be Time's Arrow."

"It was you," Emilia said, with sudden realisation. "You stopped the bulkhead from closing when we were trying to escape from the restaurant on the flight here."

"That's right."

"And those alien things. They're here because of you!"

"I sought audience with their Empress and was able to persuade her that the only way to protect her hive was to stop the Dashwood's evil scheme. I even gave my younger self a helping hand along the way, making sure that the girl and her droid were on hand when a certain gladiator-bot went on the rampage."

"But what about saving yourself now?" Emilia said, grabbing Ulysses' hands and squeezing them tight.

Ulysses looked down.

"If this enterprise has shown me anything it's that you can't cheat destiny. What is about to happen still has to happen for me to be here now, for us to be here now – in order that I might save you and your father."

"But what about Nimrod? What happens to him?" Emilia pressed, ready to believe every word he was telling her.

"I don't know."

"You don't know?"

"I left. I mean I'm going to leave. And I left without him. He stayed behind to destroy the machine."

"So you didn't see what happened to him in the end?"

"No," Ulysses admitted. "I didn't."

"Then how do you know it's not you that saves him now?"

Slowly Ulysses looked up, meeting her red-eyed gaze at last. And there was something there, in his own one-eyed stare, like a flickering candle-flame at the heart of a cyclopean cave. A flicker of hope in the darkness.

And he turned and looked back the way they had just come.

CHAPTER TWENTY-EIGHT

Helter Skelter

T minus 2 minutes, 11 seconds

ULYSSES QUICKSILVER GOT to his feet, the echo of the catastrophic collapse still ringing in his ears. Flicking the hair out of his eyes he quickly scanned the room. The air was filled with dust. Pieces of twisted metalwork littered the fractured floor.

Much of the fighting had abated. Broken bodies of faceless men in dinner jackets lay beneath the fallen ironwork alongside motionless insectoid forms of the Selenite soldiers, a stinking yellow ichor oozing from their cracked carapaces.

The Selenites that remained alive had the last dozen of the warped Dashwoods cornered, offering them no quarter.

Fires had broken out around the chamber and the smoke from these was fogging the air, making it hard for Ulysses to see much at all – least of all where his stricken manservant might be.

And yet, incredibly, the Sphere was still spinning, sick white light shooting beams of radiance through the cloying smoke and dust.

"Nimrod!" he shouted over the throbbing hum of the machine. "Nimrod! Can you hear me? Are you all right?"

"Over here, sir!"

Hearing his aging butler's voice, he felt his heart leap.

And now he could see Nimrod, beyond the tangle of girders obstructing the centre of the chamber, miraculously alive and still in one piece. He was crouched beside one of the consoles Smythe and Wentworth had been working at.

"Don't worry, old boy. I'm coming to get you."

Without a moment's hesitation, Ulysses began to scramble over the sundered, vibrating floor towards the knotted web of reinforced steel.

"No you're not, sir."

Nimrod's words stopped him dead.

"What?"

"It's not your job to save me, sir," Nimrod called back, shouting to make himself heard over the white noise of the humming machinery and the thunderous roar of the collapsing dome.

"But you'll be killed!"

"That's not important, sir. Dashwood's gone through already. You have to stop him, and that means you have to go after him."

"No!" Ulysses railed, tears welling up in his eyes.

"Yes, sir! You do. Otherwise all this, everything we've done, will have been for naught. You have to go after Dashwood and I have to stay behind to destroy the device, thereby ensuring no one can ever use it again. It's what your father would have done!"

Nimrod was right. There was no denying it. His oldest, most trusted companion had spoken the truth. If they didn't go through with this now, who knew what fate awaited the world, in the past or the present?

No matter what his feelings might be for Nimrod, his patriotic duty – the love he bore for his country – had to override all else.

Ulysses returned to the foot of the dais and, once there, started to climb.

The wrought iron staircase was littered with debris and dented where chunks of mooncrete had fallen onto it. Ulysses had to clamber over some of the larger lumps that had embedded themselves within the grilled structure.

At the top of the platform, their broken bodies crushed beneath a twisted iron girder, were Dashwood's assistants. Their master might have escaped, but Smythe and Wentworth were dead. Ulysses barely registered the fact that they lay there, in death, each clasping the other's hand.

Shielding his eyes against the glare of the light pulsing from the whirling rings, Ulysses tensed. The power of the machine was thrumming through his body now. It felt as if the vibrations might unravel the very fibres of his being.

This was it; there was no escaping it now. He had seen what repeated use of the Sphere had done to Dashwood – in both body and mind – but, as Nimrod had said, they had reached too far to turn back now.

Ulysses glanced back down the buckled staircase, the waves of light rippling throughout the chamber as myriad fractures skittered out across the walls of the dome. There couldn't be long before the structure gave way altogether.

His eyes found Nimrod standing in front of the Babbage engine control console. And Nimrod's gaze of steely resolve found his.

"Go, sir!" he yelled, his voice barely audible over the *whub-whub-whub* of the Sphere.

"I'm coming back for you!" Ulysses shouted, the tears streaming down his face. "I'll come back, I promise!"

And then through the waves of light, the tears, the smoke and the dust, Ulysses glimpsed movement on the far side of the chamber. There was someone there – a man – standing at the entrance to the chamber, his hand outstretched towards Nimrod.

And then he turned and, with a mumbled "Here goes nothing!" he threw himself into the retina-searing sphere of light.

EPILOGUE

Somewhere in Time

THE LIGHT FADED and Ulysses Quicksilver suddenly found himself plunged into darkness. His body felt uncomfortably hot and there was the distinct smell of burnt hair and scorched fabric.

With cautious slowness, he stood up. Patting at the environment suit he was still wearing, he felt his pistol, still in its holster under his arm. His cane was still tucked away safely inside as well.

The cold gust of wind took him by surprise.

He took a deep breath, sniffing the air as he did so.

He was outside somewhere and, wherever that was, it had a breathable atmosphere.

He looked up, the all enveloping darkness that had first met his gaze softening to midnight blue.

As he blinked the last of the grey patches from before his eyes he began to make out pinpricks of light in the heavens above. The luminous white ball of the Moon gazed down at him from behind the shadows of clouds.

He took a wary step forward, the vitrified surface of the soil beneath his feet snapping like sugar glass.

Wisps of smoke rose from his suit and, running a hand through his scorched hair, he realised that it was standing on end.

But other than that, and an inexplicable need to urinate, he felt fine.

He took a series of deep breaths, keen to clear the stink of burnt hair from his nostrils. Gradually he was able to make out other scents; the resinous aroma of pine needles, a dampness on the air and leaf mould.

And then the night lit up all around him as half a dozen torch-beams pierced the darkness. Somewhere nearby an engine roared and powerful headlights caught him in their searing sodium light.

"*Halt!*" a harsh voice shouted over the sudden revving and the clatter of rifles taking aim.

It took Ulysses a moment to realise that the voice was speaking German, but once his ear was tuned in there was no mistaking what the man was saying.

"Stop, in the name of the Führer! Raise your hands where I can see them and do not move if you value your life. You are now a prisoner of the Third Reich. *Sieg heil!*"

THE END

JONATHAN GREEN is a freelance writer, with more than twenty-five books to his name. Well known for his contributions to the *Fighting Fantasy* range of adventure gamebooks, and numerous Black Library publications, he has also written fiction for such diverse properties as *Doctor Who*, *Star Wars: The Clone Wars*, *Sonic the Hedgehog* and *Teenage Mutant Ninja Turtles*.

He is the creator of *Pax Britannia* and *Dark Side* is his sixth novel for Abaddon Books. He lives and works in West London. To find out more about the steampunk world of *Pax Britannia*, set your Babbage engine's ether-relay to WWW.PAXBRITANNIA.COM.

Abaddon Books

Now read the exclusive Pax Britannia novella,
Proteus Unbound...

PAX BRITANNIA

PROTEUS UNBOUND

A Ulysses Quicksilver Novella

By
Jonathan Green

Abaddon
Books

WWW.ABADDONBOOKS.COM

~ May 1998 ~

As flies to wanton boys, are we to the gods;
They kill us for their sport.

(*King Lear*, Act 4, Scene 1)

—

Mr. & Mrs. Acrisius Pennyroyal

request the pleasure of your company

at the marriage of their daughter

Constance Beatrice

to

Mr. John Benedict Schafer

at St. Mary's Church, Knightsbridge,

on Saturday 23rd May 1998

at 2.30pm

and afterwards at

The Savoy Hotel

R. S. V. P.

—

I

Bad Dreams

IT HAS TO be a nightmare; there's no other possible explanation, other than that he is awake and that his ordeal is genuine. But that is too terrible to even consider.

But even though he knows it's a dream – is sure it is a dream – he runs on through the cloying London fog, unable to force himself to wake up and unable to bring himself to stop and look behind him, to see what it is that's chasing him.

His lungs heave. Sweat beads his brow. His legs ache. He feels as though he has been running for an eternity but still he hears the beast behind him, panting and grunting. No matter how hard he runs, he cannot shake its pursuit, but neither does the thing ever get so close as to actually catch him in its grasping talons either.

The sounds it makes form a nightmarish image in his mind's eye, the slap of flesh as it scampers through the black puddles that have collected within the alleyway through which he runs, the crack of hooves on the cobbles, the grating of its tail dragging along the ground behind it, the rustle of feathers and fur and the scrape of scales as monstrous slabs of muscle slide under its leathery hide, the clack of pincers, the snap of jaws, and the clicking of hungrily masticating mandibles.

The back-streets twist and turn, writhing through the city like the knotted coils of some gigantic serpent. He twists and turns with them, muscles burning, heart pounding, the dub-dub, dub-dub of the blood rush in his ears loud as an express train.

And all the time behind him, the scratching of claws on stone, the boar-snorts of its laboured breathing, and the wet rasp of its tongue tasting the air before it.

Suddenly he stumbles and falls. He is thrown forwards, arms flailing, and hits the ground hard. He gasps as the wind is knocked out of him and then gags as his mouth fills with the foul black water of a stagnant puddle.

He can feel the beast now, the pounding footfalls juddering through his body with every galloping thud. He can feel its beady black eyes on him, boring into his back with a malignant knowledge of him. He feels a disturbance in the air where it touches his bare skin, as the beast reaches for him with a reptilian claw.

And then he's moving again.

Terror and desperation lend him the strength he needs, the fear-kick rush of adrenalin charging his aching muscles with the energy they need. He takes a gasping lungful of air – he knows not how – and springs to his feet, in danger of tripping over again, his legs stumbling, arms flailing, as he tries to regain his balance and escape his destiny.

A roar echoes through the fog, rebounding from the walls of the alleyway. It is a roar of rage and frustration and, as he runs on, one that is swallowed by the darkness behind him. But still he runs on.

But over the throbbing of his pulse in his ears, he can no longer hear the thing behind him. He can no longer hear the rasp of its breath, the scrape of scales or the snap of pincers.

He falters, ears straining, but, hearing nothing, stumbles to a halt.

He turns quickly but behind him all he can see is the cloying fog, enveloping the street behind him. The only light comes from a gibbous moon, filtered through the smog, giving the mist an unearthly glow.

Eyes straining, he peers into the darkness. Ears straining, he listens.

But there is still nothing. The beast is gone.

He turns again, facing the way ahead of him – looking to his future.

With a savage snarl-cum-howl, the impossible creature leaps out of the fog and the milky darkness, festooned with claws, spines, wings and a multitude of limbs, trailing dirty tendrils of persistent smog.

It lands in a crouch before him and raising its unreal head – part mammalian, part reptilian – it fixes him with its unsettlingly human eyes. Crouched like this, it is still taller than he, as broad across the shoulders as he is tall.

A maw opens, crammed with teeth and tusks and split by a beetle's mandibles, and a voice more akin to beast than man declares, "You cannot run from your destiny!"

And jaws agape, the creature pounces.

Day 8

IT IS NOW a full week since the formula was first administered to the subject and so far the only symptoms observed are such as is associated with the influenza virus, in other words headaches, raised temperature and slight nausea.

However, the subject does appear to be suffering from a worsening sleep condition. My own supposition is that this is being caused by disturbing dreams from which the subject wakes in the middle of the night in a cold sweat.

I shall continue to administer the formula and observe its effects on the subject but I am beginning to have my doubts about the effectiveness of Proteus 12.

II

The Best Laid Plans

"THE TROUBLE IS," Constance Pennyroyal said, perusing the hand-drawn plan spread out on the table in front of them, "we can't have Aunt Grace sitting next to Aunt Agatha, not after what Agatha said about her pug at Little Verity's christening last year. But then we can't sit her next to old Uncle Albert either."

"Would that be Uncle Albert of the wandering hands?" her fiancé, John Schafer asked, trying to sound as if he were actually interested in his fiancée's ridiculous extended family.

"Yes, that would."

"And you think he'd even try it on with your great Aunt Agatha?"

"He'd try it on with anything in a dress, no matter age – or even gender, for that matter."

"The dirty bugger," Schafer smiled.

"John!"

"What? It's not me who can't keep his hands to himself!" He laughed, suddenly grabbing her around the waist and planting a wet kiss in the hollow of her neck.

"Oh is that so?"

"Except where you're concerned, my love."

"Look, you're not helping," Constance said, wrestling herself free of the amorous clinch he had her in. "You're supposed to be helping me finalise the seating plan for our wedding, which I might add, is in only two weeks time now. And there's still so much to sort out. I mean there are the flowers, the bridesmaids' dresses, I have to go for another fitting for my dress..."

"I thought your mother was sorting all that stuff out."

"She is, but it's my wedding."

Schafer's eyebrows knitted in consternation. "I thought it was *our* wedding."

"Of course it is, silly, which means as the blushing bride it's *my* special day. And I want everything to be perfect."

"And it will be."

"Which is why we need to get this seating plan sorted." Constance gave Schafer a look pregnant with meaning.

Schafer sighed. "I thought we were going for a simple ceremony, not too many guests, only close friends and family."

"These people *are* my family."

"They're a ruddy nightmare, if you ask me," he muttered, before having the wit to stop himself.

"Well they're going to be *your* family too, come two weeks today, so you'd better get used to the idea," Constance snapped.

"It's just that I thought I was marrying you, my angel, not the whole Pennyroyal clan."

"Fine. Be like that then. I'll do it by myself, shall I? Seeing as how they're *my* family!"

Schafer took a deep breath, knowing that he was going to have to bite the bullet and apologise. Taking her in his arms again, despite her feigned unwillingness he said, "I'm sorry, it's just that I've not been sleeping well."

Constance's expression of annoyance melted immediately into one of anxious concern. "You are looking a little peaky," she said, putting her arms around him then. Just as irritation had become concern, concern quickly became suspicion. "You're not having second thoughts are you?"

"What?"

"I mean you're not getting cold feet – about the wedding?"

"Of course not!" Schafer laughed. "I don't know what's wrong with me. It's just that I've been having such vivid dreams."

"What sort of dreams?"

"Well it's more a recurring nightmare, really. I don't remember the details, just that something's after me."

"What? What's after you?"

"That's just it. I don't know. Either that or I can't remember, but it amounts to much the same thing. It's like there's something else in here with me," he said, tapping his head with a crooked finger.

Constance met his tired gaze with her own eyes open wide. "It's not malaria is it?"

"Malaria?"

"You said yourself that something had been biting you in your sleep – a mosquito or something."

"Yes, but I wouldn't think for a second that it would be carrying malaria. Not in these climes."

"But it's best to get these things checked out," she persisted. "Why don't you pop upstairs and see Dr Rathbone later? Get him to take a look at the bites and, while you're there, see if he can give you something to help you sleep." A cheeky smile curled her lips as her cheeks flushed rose red. "After all, I want you fit and well for our wedding night."

"Oh you do, do you?" her fiancé said, arching one eyebrow. "Well why don't I give you a taster right here and now?"

"I thought we were going to abstain now, until after the wedding."

"But I could be dead by then, the way you're going on."

"Don't say that!" she chided.

Encircling her with his strong arms, he pulled her close.

"But either one of us could be knocked down by an omnibus tomorrow. We should live each day as if it's our last. *Carpe diem* and all that!"

"*Carpe diem?*"

"Seize the day!" he pronounced, clearing the table of seating plans, guest lists and menu suggestions with one sweep of an arm.

"Oh, John!" she gasped, as he laid her on top of it, parting unresisting thighs with his own body, as she seized hold of something else entirely.

Day 10

In light of recent developments, regarding the subject's disturbed sleep patterns, I have decided to double the dose being administered to see what effect this has on his metabolism. I have already administered the first of the newly increased doses and must now watch and wait, and continue to record my observations, no matter what may now befall.

I have to confess, I feel like a first year medical student all over again. I await further developments with giddy anticipation.

III

Promenade

"I CAN'T PRETEND anymore, John," Constance suddenly announced the following Sunday evening, as the two lovers walked arm-in-arm along the riverbank at Battersea. "I'm worried about you."

As they reached Albert Bridge, she stopped, forcing Schafer to come to a halt as well, and fixed him with that penetrating gaze of hers, that meant he could deny her nothing. The late spring sunset was reflected in the sparkling orbs of her eyes and gave her skin a lustrous orange glow. The call for curfew couldn't be far off.

"I'm all right," he tried to persuade her, "really I am."

"You did go and see Dr Rathbone, didn't you?"

"Yes, last Monday."

"And did he prescribe you anything?"

"Yes; some sleeping tablets."

"And did they make a difference?"

Schafer sighed. Was this constant nagging a sign of what was to come once they were married? "A little. But I'm fine, I promise you."

"Are you eating properly? You're looking gaunt."

"My darling Constance, I promise you, I'm all right. In fact, to be honest with you, I've never felt fitter."

"Well you don't look it."

"So you keep saying."

"It's only because I care," Constance retorted.

"I know," Schafer replied, taking her hands in his. "I understand that, and I love you for it. But I promise you I'm all right. What more can I do to prove it to you?"

"After you drop me home I want you to get yourself off to bed. I want you well rested for next Saturday."

"All right," he agreed, admitting defeat in the face of his fiancée's doggedness.

"You think I'm nagging you, don't you?" she said, suddenly looking shame-faced and casting her eyes at the ground.

"A little."

"I'm sorry, it's only because I love you."

Raising her face to his with a gentle guiding hand, he kissed her. "I know," he said.

Hand in hand, the couple climbed the steps beside the bridge and, once back on the Chelsea Embankment, Schafer hailed them a cab.

"You know something, Miss Pennyroyal?" he said as he helped her into the back of the chugging hansom.

"No, what?" she said, smiling.

"You may go on a bit at times, but I do love you. And there's nothing I want more than to make you my wife come Saturday."

"And do you know something, Mr Schafer?" she replied. "I want that more than anything else in the world."

Day 16

DESPITE THE INCREASED dosage, the subject has not developed any new symptoms. In fact the subject's health appears to be improving, as if his body has somehow become immune to the serum, or the formula has actually enhanced his physical fitness.

I will continue as I have been, however, and, as ever, will continue to observe the subject's progress with interest.

IV

Thick As Thieves

By the time he had bid farewell to Constance at the door to her parents house in Knightsbridge, and feeling truly revitalised, he decided to take a brisk walk back to his flat in Pimlico, keeping to the back ways and the shadows, out of sight of the few patrols of robo-Bobbies he saw. Dusk had already fallen, the moaning cry of the curfew klaxons ringing out across the city, like the mournful wailing of widows.

A preternatural darkness smothered his route home. The prevailing wind was blowing from the east, casting the smoke from the cavorite works upstream over the city like the pall of a funeral shroud. The Smog smothered the street lamps, turning them into glowing will-o'-the-wisps and feeding the shadows that clung to the stanchions of the many pillars that supported the spider's-web of railway lines suspended above the city.

The streets of London, especially those of Pimlico, were no place to be caught after dark. The curfew had been enacted in the aftermath of the Wormwood Catastrophe, when it was realised that those 'changed' by the lethal, transforming rain that had fallen on the city that Valentine's Day, had congregated into great, insect hosts, such as the Locusts of St Paul's and the Cockroaches of Clerkenwell. But many of those with a predilection for crime had turned the curfew to their advantage.

But Schafer wasn't worried. He was only a few hundred yards from home now and he knew these alleyways and rat-runs like the back of his hand.

So, as he turned into Paxton Terrace, he was rather taken aback as three dark shapes detached themselves from the shadows of an Overground arch, and approached with cocksure steps. Their footsteps were accompanied by the hollow slap of a cosh hitting an open palm.

"Well, well, well, what have we here?" the first announced with the bravado born of knowing that there were worse things abroad after dark than Locusts and giant cockroaches, and that he was one of those things.

The three men were all dressed alike, in anonymous black, hats pulled down over their heads, ensuring their faces were left in darkness.

All of them were armed. As well as the cosh in the tight grip of the biggest of the three, Schafer caught the dull glint of a flick-knife and heard the rattle of the chain looped in the hands of the third, who was also the tallest and skinniest of the muggers.

"Look," Schafer said, his tone calm and measured. After all that he and Constance had gone through at the bottom of the Pacific in the company of the dandy adventurer and Hero of the Empire Ulysses Quicksilver, he didn't scare easily anymore. "I don't want any trouble and you don't really want to put yourselves to any trouble, do you, so what say we make this easy?"

He put a hand into his jacket pocket and took out his wallet. The three thieves eyed the leather case greedily. "I've got thirty pounds here, which I'll gladly give you – that's a tidy sum for each of you, for no effort at all – and then what say we go our separate ways?"

"We've got a toff, that's what we've got here," the leader said, as if he hadn't heard a word the young man had said.

Schafer put a hand into his waistcoat pocket and took out his fob-watch. "Look, what say I throw in my father's watch as well? Now I can't say fairer than that, can I?"

"A toff who thinks he can just order us about like we was his lackeys," the thief snarled. "A toff what needs to be taught a lesson, eh boys?"

A slow, rumbling chuckle rose from the big man's chest.

"I'd say about time too, boss," his taller partner in crime sniggered.

Realising that violence was inevitable, Schafer began to slowly back away.

"The thing is, you see, I'm getting married on Saturday and I can't show up at my wedding looking like I've gone three rounds in an illegal bare-knuckle boxing match now, can I? So cut a chap some slack, won't you, just this once? I'm sure you understand."

"Oh, I see," the thief drawled, "well now you put it like that." The thieves continued their relentless march towards Schafer. "Ah, but, you see, the thing is we've got a reputation to uphold and our professional pride to think of. So we'll take the money, and the watch, and anything else you've got hidden about your person that you've not told us about yet, but only when we're done giving you a damn good thrashing. I'm sure you understand."

Schafer turned on his heel to run but the three muggers were off the starting blocks first, the beanpole covering the distance between them in only a few bounding strides.

Links rattling, the chain whipped across the cobbles, catching Schafer round the ankles and yanking his feet out from under him. The young man came down hard on the uneven stones, winded, and winced as he almost bit through his tongue.

Before he could kick his feet free of the chain, the muggers were on him. The cosh caught him across his spine, laying him out flat again. Gasping from the pain he struggled to turn and face his attackers. But even as he managed to manoeuvre himself onto his backside, the cosh fell again.

This time it struck him on the temple, and he fell back onto the ground as his world exploded into darkness.

"You bloody idiot!" Bulldog Drummond growled. "You only gone and bloody killed him!"

"Sorry, boss," the big man apologised forlornly. "I didn't mean to."

"You didn't mean to?" the tall one sniggered. "Oh that's all right then, just so long as you didn't mean to."

"Shut it, Stickler!" Bulldog bit back. "You're the one who's going to have to help Riggs lug the body to the river."

The gangling thief stopped giggling abruptly.

"What's it matter if he's dead, anyway?" Stickler wheedled. "We're still going to rob him, aren't we?"

"Were you born that thick or did you take lessons?" Bulldog retorted. "What difference does it make? Only the difference between the noose and a stretch in the Clink, you idiot, that's what! So get busy emptying his pockets and then you and Riggs can get busy disposing of his nibs here."

"Where's he gone?" the big man asked.

"What?" Bulldog turned from berating Stickler. The street was empty, their victim gone. "Where is he?"

"Don't know, boss," Riggs said unhelpfully.

"Weren't you watching him?"

"I was watching you two. You said he was dead. Dead men don't get up and walk away by themselves," Riggs said in his own defence.

The shrill blast of a whistle cut through the fog and the night.

"Christ! Peelers!" Stickler hissed.

"Get out of here!" Bulldog growled. "And be quick about it!"

Something swept through the foul fog over their heads. They all heard the whoosh of disturbed air and felt the downdraft of its passing.

"What was that?" Bulldog muttered, craning his head to peer through the smog above them.

And then the fog disgorged a horror such as the three thieves had never witnessed before.

Bulldog Drummond was right. There were things worse than Locusts and giant cockroaches abroad after dark, but on this particular night, he wasn't one of them.

ITS SIREN WHINING into silence and the flashing blue light descending back into its helmet, the robo-Peeler screeched to a halt on reaching the slaughter.

It stood stiffly, as its wheels retracted inside its body, and swept the scene with the pulsing red light of the optical scanner hidden behind the helmet-visage of its face-plate.

The cobbles beneath the Overground pillar were slick with blood; a very great deal of blood. Body parts lay like gory puzzle pieces across the alleyway - a jaw here, a few fingers there, a patch of scalp stuck to the bricks of a nearby wall with congealing blood. To say that the scene looked like an abattoir would have been an understatement.

The automaton's Babbage unit working as fast as clockwork, the Peeler droid assessed the scene and determined that the organs and limbs littering the ground belonged to at least three unique individuals.

And not one of the body parts was bigger than a suitcase. A flick-knife glinted dully where it had fallen not far from the slick of blood, although its blade remained unbloodied.

V

Constance Pays A Call

"Take a deep breath," Ulysses Quicksilver told the young woman now sitting in the drawing room of his Mayfair home, "and start again from the beginning."

Constance Pennyroyal fought to master her rising hysteria, taking long controlled breaths, even though her whole body was still shaking.

The last time he had seen her had been when they disembarked at Southampton docks after the Royal Navy frigate *HMS Dauntless* had returned the few survivors of the sinking of the *Neptune* to British soil.

When they had returned to Blighty, Constance Pennyroyal had been arm-in-arm with her fiancé John Schafer. And now, here she was again, ten months on, alone. He hadn't expected to be seeing her until the following Saturday, when she was due to marry her beau at St Mary's in Knightsbridge.

"I don't know to start," she said through her sobs, as she struggled to compose herself.

She had managed to maintain a passable facade of calm collectedness right up until Nimrod had left the two of them alone in the drawing room and at that moment she had broken down in tears. Up to this point all Ulysses knew for certain was that Schafer had broken off their engagement less than a week before their wedding and was refusing to even see her.

"All right, let me help you." Ulysses placed a hand on her knee, offering her his handkerchief in place of her own sodden rag. "Tell me about the last time you saw him."

The anxious young woman, her eyes red and puffy from crying, nodded, took a deep breath and began. "It was two days ago. We had spent the afternoon together and then enjoyed a stroll through Battersea Park. We walked along by the river and then took a cab back to my parents' house in Knightsbridge. The last words we shared were ones of love."

Constance sniffed, dabbing Ulysses' balled up handkerchief at her puffy eyes.

"And you haven't seen him since?" Ulysses spoke gently, in an attempt to cushion the force of his words as much as possible.

She shook her head.

"And had John been behaving in any way that made you think something might be wrong. I hate to say it, but these things rarely come completely out of the blue."

"No," Constance answered a little too quickly and a little too forcibly.

"Really?"

"Well, he's been a little under the weather recently, but nothing more."

"Under the weather?" Ulysses repeated, pouncing on this one small clue as a potential line of enquiry. "In what way, exactly?"

"Well, it was like a bad cold or the 'flu really. That was all. He said he felt fine."

"And how long had that been going on for?"

"A week or two, I suppose."

"And he was still unwell the last time you saw him."

"Yes, but he said he felt fine. He said that I shouldn't worry." At this the tears came again. "But I was right to worry, wasn't I?"

Ulysses waited a respectful moment before asking the next difficult question. "And when did he call off the engagement?"

"The very next day."

"Yesterday?"

"Yes. We were due at the church for a rehearsal that afternoon, but before lunch this came."

At that she handed the dandy an already opened envelope with a shaking hand. Ulysses took it, removed the folded piece of vellum writing paper from within and quickly scanned the letter.

"I see," he said, having considered its contents. The letter was brief and to the point. It stated that he could no longer go through with the wedding, apologising for the upset this would cause, and for wasting her time, and asking that she never try to see him again. "And you received no other explanation from any other source."

"No, none," Constance sobbed. "I went round there to see him after I received the letter but he wouldn't even come to the door. I went round again this morning but all that happened was he screamed at me until I left."

"You poor thing."

"After that I didn't know where else to go."

"You did the right thing in coming here," Ulysses told her.

She looked at him with wide, weary eyes. "The last time I saw him he told me not to worry, that everything would be all right."

"Hush, now," Ulysses said, patting her knee again, in an effort to calm her down. "We'll get this sorted, don't you worry."

"Do you think this can all be explained by the fact that he's been feeling unwell?" Constance managed at last.

"I don't know. Do you?"

"I don't see why a case of the 'flu should stop him from being able to marry me."

"Indeed," Ulysses ruminated.

Constance looked at him with wide, anxious eyes. "Do you think it might be something worse than the 'flu?"

"I don't know. But I think we should find out, don't you?"

Constance continued to stare at him, a disbelieving, delighted smile slowing lightening her face. "You mean you'll help me?"

"I hope I'm going to be able to help *both* of you."

The tears came again then, but this time they were tears of relief, tears of joy; tears of hope.

"Come on," Ulysses said, jumping to his feet.

The grandfather clock at the end of the hall chimed seven. A split second later the whining voice of the curfew sirens could be heard howling their lamentations over the rooftops of the city.

"The curfew!" Constance gasped.

"Don't worry," Ulysses announced, flashing the young woman a devilish grin. "We'll take the Rolls."

VI

Awakening

JOHN SCHAFER SLEPT fitfully, his body twitching beneath the knotted, sweat-drenched sheets, and as he slept he dreamed.

But this time his recurring nightmare had subtly changed. This time he was no longer alone. He saw the sad, desperate faces of destitute men, women and children staring at him with dead, soulless eyes. Then the beast had arrived, as it always did, and the beast had hungered. The people had died, slaughtered to sate its savage hunger.

He woke with a start, and for one blissful moment, it seemed as if it might have all been a dream – the whole sorry debacle.

Then his sleep crusted eyes took in the mess of his bedroom – the piles of broken furniture, the shredded books, and the torn and filthy piles of clothes – and realised, with a bitter taste in his mouth, that it was all true. At least he hoped that it was that realisation that had left the foul taste in his mouth and not something else, too horrible to consider.

There were great gaps in his memory of the last two days, but his rational mind had been able to work out what must have happened in the spaces in between the few bits he could remember.

The last clear memory he had was of the night he had last seen Constance. He had dropped her back at her parents' house in Knightsbridge before heading home on foot. He remembered the thieves in the fog and then...

And then the next clear memory he had was of being at home, with the door to his apartment still locked and the curtains flapping in the breeze coming in through a broken second floor window. He had barely been dressed, the clothes he had worn for his promenade with Constance hanging off him in torn and bloodied strips. And then there had been the wounds that covered the whole of his body. He had no recollection at all of how he had come by them – he had first wondered if it was from coming in through the window without bothering to open it first – but now he wasn't so sure.

What came after that was a patchwork of half-recalled incidents and the pieces of the puzzle he had worked out for himself later. He thought he had slept for much of the time since, although he felt wrung out and exhausted, and then there had been Constance and the reason, hidden deep down within himself, why he had felt compelled to call off their wedding...

And now, as he lay there in bed, stinking like God alone knew what, his body a lost memory map of cuts and bruises smeared with filth and blood – much of which he had a horrible suspicion wasn't actually his – the bedclothes in the same state, his frantically working mind kept coming to the same conclusion and it was enough to drive him mad.

And then there was the constant noise. He could hear the clatter of the Overground, the wail of the curfew klaxons, as the square of light that was his bedroom window faded to purple, and the chugging grumble of steam-engines across the city as people made for home as night fell, as thick and oppressive as the Smog.

The sounds of the city rang in his ears, giving him no peace. He felt terrible. He felt exhausted, even though he had only just woken, although neither did he know for how long he had slept.

But the strident voice of London was nothing compared to the noise coming from upstairs. Dr Rathbone's apartment lay directly above his, but what was the bastard up to that he had to make so much noise? It sounded like a herd of elephants had moved in upstairs. He wasn't usually able to hear anything but now even the tiniest sound was amplified to his sensitive hearing – every footstep on the bare floorboards above a resounding thud, every clink of glass or scrape of cutlery on china was screeching fingernails on a blackboard, every cough as the man cleared his throat the mucus-laced cacophony of a TB sufferer. He could hear it all. And it was slowly driving him out of his mind.

Suddenly leaping out of bed, pulling on a ragged shirt and filthy, shredded trousers from a pile of abandoned clothing in the middle of the floor, John Schafer made for the door to his apartment.

It was time he had a word with the good Dr Rathbone.

And reaching for the door he saw the wounds on the back of his hand open as the bones beneath reformed and a chitinous claw took hold of the handle.

VII

Death Is Now Thy Neighbour

"Is this the place?" Ulysses asked as the Silver Phantom rolled to a halt outside the shadowed tenement building off Paxton Terrace.

"Yes. This is it," Constance answered in a quiet voice.

Together they exited the vehicle.

"Right you are then," Ulysses said, once the two of them were standing at the foot of the steps leading up to the communal front door. "Let's see if he's home, shall we?"

The car window opened.

"Would you like me to wait, sir?" Nimrod asked.

"Yes please, old chap, just hang on there would you?"

"Very good, sir." The window closed again.

"Which number is it?" Ulysses asked, leading the way up the steps to the door.

"Flat C," she replied.

Considering the facade of the house it was clear to Ulysses that the place had once been all one private residence, but like so many properties in the capital it had long since been divided into a number of separate apartments, each one occupying a single storey of the house.

He rang the bell for Flat C labelled with the name 'Schafer' written in smart copperplate on an adhesive label. As he waited for a reply, Ulysses noticed that the smarter brass nameplate next to Flat D was etched with the name 'Dr Michael Rathbone'. Ulysses wondered what the doctorate was for. Was he a doctor of medicine, or merely a pretentious academic who liked to show off his qualifications, having little else in his life of which to be proud?

Ulysses tried the bell again. There was still no response to his constant buzzing.

"Looks like he's out," Ulysses muttered to himself. He turned to Constance, but seeing the forlorn look on her face turned back to the door saying, "But having come all this way it would be good to double-check before we leave."

Ulysses looked at the sturdy door in front of him and then brashly ran a finger over the column of bell-pushes. They rang and buzzed in quick succession.

There was a pause, followed by a crackle of static and then an irritated, elderly, female voice came through the speakerphone. "Yes?"

"Delivery!" Ulysses announced cheerily, holding down the button of the intercom.

There was a second buzz and with a click the door catch released.

"Works every time," Ulysses chuckled as he pushed the door open and then stepped aside, holding it open for Constance to enter the communal hallway ahead of him.

Once inside, however, the dandy led the way up the wide staircase, taking the tiled steps two at a time, so that Constance was forced to jog up the stairs after him in order to keep up.

On reaching the second landing he stopped. "Oh," he said, surprised, the door to Flat C open before him. "Well I wasn't expecting that."

Constance joined him a moment later. "John?" she called out in a wavering half-excited, half-anxious voice, moving past Ulysses and into the flat before he could stop her.

She halted as suddenly as if she had run into a brick wall. "What is that smell?" she exclaimed, putting a hand over her nose.

Ulysses' nostrils flared as the smell of rancid meat and squalor hit him too. He knew that smell of old. It was the smell of death.

Horribly aware of what they might well find inside the apartment, Ulysses stopped Constance with a hand and stepped past her.

"Wait here," he instructed as he moved deeper into the oppressive gloom beyond.

The place was a mess, but it was also currently uninhabited.

It was then, as he was surveying the heaps of broken furniture, the filthy piles of rags and the diamond shards of broken glass covering the carpet, that Ulysses heard a loud thud, followed by a reverberating crash. Constance had heard it too.

"It came from upstairs," she said, staring at the ceiling.

Ulysses sprang into action in an instant. Leaving Schafer's apartment at a run, sprinting up the next flight of stairs, on reaching the next landing he hesitated once more. The door to Flat D was open, just as Schafer's flat had been. And from the open door came what sounded like the last throes of a scuffle.

Approaching the door with slow, cautious steps – unsheathing the rapier blade buried within the blackwood haft of his bloodstone-tipped cane – Ulysses steeled himself as he peered into the strangely lit gloom beyond.

His finely balanced blade in hand, he followed the rustling sounds and the glow of a table lamp to a back room that appeared to be the doctor's study – judging by the framed certificates mounted on the walls and the heavily-laden bookcases filled with medical journals and a plethora of thick, leather-bound books. One bookcase lay on the floor, its papery contents lying in drifts beneath it.

The room was lit by the amber glow of a table lamp that was lying on its side on the floor amidst a pile of tumbled documents. And the reason for such disarray was obvious.

Sprawling in a swivel chair in front of a roll-top writing desk was the body of a man, although all Ulysses could see were the man's blood-soaked trousers and his still twitching feet. Squatting on top of the dying man's chest was something grotesque and hunched, like some demonic incubus captured in oils by a gothic grandmaster, its face buried inside the dead doctor's shattered ribcage.

"Have at you!" Ulysses shouted, lunging at the thing with his blade.

The creature – whatever it was, and his mind didn't want to linger too long on the question of what exactly it was – hissed and recoiled. In the gloom Ulysses could see that it had a vaguely humanoid form but its knobbly hide appeared to be covered with all manner of bony protrusions whilst patches of its flesh gleamed black as chitin.

"John? Is that you?"

The cannibalistic killer's attention was immediately on the woman now standing behind Ulysses. It hissed again and recoiled, as if trying to hide itself in the shadows. And then with a sudden spring it hurled itself sideways, escaping through the nearest window.

The sharp crash of breaking glass and splintering staves filled the study for a moment and then the strange creature was gone, away into the night.

Ignoring the brutalised corpse sprawled across the desk, Ulysses dashed to the window leaning out through the shattered pane as if ready to launch himself after the creature.

He shot glances down the side of the building, to both left and right, but seeing nothing there quickly looked up. And there, nothing more than a black shape now against the shadows of chimney stacks on the roof of the building opposite, he saw the creature again.

"Get yourself downstairs and tell Nimrod what's happened; then wait for me there!" Ulysses instructed Constance.

"What about you? What are you going to do?" she asked, as Ulysses, sword in hand, eased himself out through the shattered window, taking care not to cut himself on a razor-sharp shard, and onto the narrow stone ledge beyond.

"What does it look like?" he said. "I'm going after that thing!"

VIII

Fight or Flight

FROM THE LEDGE it was only some six feet to the building on the other side of the alleyway. Ulysses peered down at the forty foot drop to the cobbled backstreet below and immediately regretted it. He wasn't one of those unfortunates who suffered from an irrational fear of heights. It was the perfectly rational fear of what the fall from such a height would do to him that bothered him. But the longer he clung to the wall and the window dithering, the faster the murderous creature was getting away.

Gripping his sword-stick tightly in his right hand, with a cry of, "Here goes nothing!" he threw himself at the building opposite.

He sailed through thin air for a moment and then his strong, re-grown left hand reached out and grabbed hold of a length of cast iron guttering. He was over. Scuffing his shoes against the wall beneath him as he found footholds in the crumbling mortar, it was a relatively simple matter for the dandy to then pull himself up and over the edge of the building and onto the flat roof beyond.

With only a glance back to the broken window behind and below him, Ulysses turned his attention back to the escaping monster.

He could see it quite clearly, silhouetted against the moon-lit Smog, its backwards-jointed legs taking great galloping strides over the rooftops.

And yet it wasn't so far away that Ulysses felt he wouldn't be able to catch up with it if he gave chase. Despite the length of its stride, its curious, hook-clawed feet appeared to be having trouble finding purchase on the slates.

Even as he set off after it, following his own precarious course across the angled roof-scape, the thing slipped again, kicking a succession of loose tiles free of the roof altogether as it made a desperate grab for a chimney pot with elongated finger-bones.

Ulysses threw himself after the gargoyle, displaying a level of agility not significantly less impressive than that demonstrated by the changed thing he was chasing. He leapt over voids, skidded down sloping roofs and danced along ridges only half a brick wide, every step he took bringing him closer to his quarry.

And then, with the end of the terrace only a matter of yards away, the creature slipped sideways. Ulysses flung himself after it, his rapier raised high above his head, ready to bring it down in a decisive executioner's strike.

The gargoyle-like thing lay sprawled beneath him, in a gulley between two sloping roof sections. It raised its elongated claws over its head, as if ready to block his blow with its arms.

And then the creature cried out, taking Ulysses so entirely by surprise that he faltered and landed awkwardly, his sword-blade dropping to his side. There had been something familiar about its cry.

The creature cried out again, and this time Ulysses was able to make out the words its malformed mouth was struggling to articulate.

"*Pleassse!*" it screeched. "*Ssstop!*"

Ulysses peered at the cowering creature in front of him, trying to catch a glimpse of its face through the shield it had made of its arms.

"Schafer?" he said, his voice little more than an incredulous whisper. "Is that you?"

The kick came out of nowhere, taking the dandy completely by surprise. A distended foot hit him squarely in the stomach, doubling him up and sending him reeling, his sword-stick falling from his hand as he crashed onto the sloping roof behind him, gasping for breath as pain flared in his chest.

Its lithe body taut like a coiled spring, the creature turned its obsidian eyes on the suffering dandy. Its features remained hidden in the darkness, but the orbs of its eyes sparkled like black diamonds.

And the gargoyle spoke again: "*Sssorry!*"

The creature turned away again and, before his eyes the chitin covering its back split apart. With a stomach-churning stretching, tearing sound, flesh and bone warped and distended as a pair of translucent leathery red wings unfolded from its shoulders and the thing – more like a gargoyle than ever now – launched itself from the roof's edge, gliding away into the night.

In a moment it was gone.

IX

Return To Bedlam

AT A LITTLE after nine the next morning, a Mark IV Rolls Royce
Silver Phantom pulled up outside the imposing gates and high
barbed wire-topped iron railings of Bedlam Asylum in Lambeth.

After losing his quarry the night before, as the creature had
become airborne, Ulysses had returned to street level via the
nearest fire escape he could find, still feeling frustrated after
his run-in with the gargoyle. He had been met outside Schafer's
tenement building again by Nimrod and a quivering Constance.

"It was him, wasn't it?" she had asked, shock lending her
cheeks an unhealthy pallor.

"Yes, I believe it was," Ulysses had admitted reluctantly. There
had seemed little point in hiding what he believed to be the truth
from her; especially after all she had witnessed herself firsthand.

To her credit, Constance hadn't gone to pieces at hearing this, but
instead asked the inevitable question. "What's happened to him?"

"That I don't know," the dandy had replied, "but I can assure
you that I won't rest until I've found out."

Opening the rear nearside door of the Silver Phantom, Ulysses helped her into the Rolls. "Do you think he can be cured?" she had asked, her eyes pleading with him as he went to close the car door again.

Ulysses had sighed at that, as though the weight of the world was suddenly on his shoulders, absent-mindedly rubbing at his sternum where the gargoyle-thing had landed its kick. "We can only hope."

The three of them had then returned to the Quicksilver residence in Mayfair, Ulysses insisting that Constance stay, having Nimrod put the call through to her parents that she was safe and well and would see them again on the morrow. Nimrod made her up a hot toddy, the poor girl having little appetite for anything more, before settling her in one of the guest bedrooms.

On returning to 31 Charles Street, the dandy had retired to his study in a contemplative mood. He hadn't emerged again until after midnight, at which point, having already partaken of a nightcap, he had retired to bed.

He had risen again not long after seven the following morning. Possessed of a steely purpose, and having wolfed down the full English Mrs Prufrock had set in front of him and his guest, he set off again in the company of Constance and Nimrod, this time headed across town to the infamous Royal Bethlem Hospital for the Incurably Insane. For it was also there that, since the *Jupiter* Station Disaster, some of the more notable examples of those termed 'the Changed' now resided.

It had been something Ulysses remembered reading in Victor Gallowglass's notebook as he travelled half way across Russia that had set him on his current course. A reference to a component of the weaponised blood agent the haematologist had created that had enabled him to tailor the pathogen to those of a specific bloodline, that changed the chemical structure of the blood-plasma into what was effectively a deadly poison.

After Prince Vladimir's attempt to claim the throne of Russia, Ulysses had recovered Gallowglass's notebook and brought it back with him to England. He had found the reference again as he sat perusing the journal's encrypted contents in his study. Once translated from the code language 'Babel' that Ulysses and the Queen's personal haematologist had a shared knowledge of from their school days, he discovered that the mysterious substance went by the name of 'Proteus'.

During his adventures across the continent, he had thought it was some other artificial agent that Gallowglass had created himself in his laboratory, but now he wasn't so sure.

But that had been only one part of the puzzle. Another clue had come from John Schafer's altered appearance, the nature of the gargoyle-like beast itself. There had been something of the insect about it that smacked just a little too much of the aftermath of the chemical attack Uriah Wormwood had perpetrated against the city three months before.

Wormwood was missing, presumed dead, as was anyone else associated with the production of Dr Feelgood's Tonic Stout, the supposed patent panacea which had in truth contained a portion of the cruel physiology-warping agent. But there was at least one other person he knew of who had studied the effects of the DNA-altering compound firsthand.

"AH, QUICKSILVER, ISN'T it?" the small bespectacled man said, rising as Ulysses and Constance were ushered into the director's office.

"That's right, Professor."

"You were here with another young lady last time, weren't you? A black girl; very pretty."

"That's right. But now I'm here with Miss Pennyroyal."

"Well please, take a seat," the small man said, indicating the two chairs carefully angled in front of his huge desk, the scale of which only served to make the professor appear even more diminutive.

Ulysses and Constance did as they were bidden.

"So what can I do for you this time?" Professor Brundle asked jovially, taking his own seat again. His face suddenly clouded over. "It's not about our mutual friend, is it?"

"No," Ulysses replied, his easy smile immediately putting the asylum's director at ease. "Actually I wanted your professional opinion about something."

"Oh, right you are," Brundle said, regarding the dandy over steepled fingers. "What is it you want to know?"

"Tell me, Professor, have you heard of something – a drug perhaps – that goes by the name of 'Proteus'?"

THE TWO INVESTIGATORS emerged from the hospital building half an hour later, Ulysses Quicksilver with a marked spring in his step, Constance Pennyroyal trotting after him, her fitted skirts making it hard for her to move in any other way.

"Well that was most useful," the dandy announced cheerily as they made for the hospital gates and the robo-orderly on duty there.

"Was it?" his companion challenged him. "Professor Brundle had never even heard of this Proteus thing, or whatever it was."

"No, you're quite right, he hadn't," the dandy said, still smiling. "But he was able to confirm a theory of mine."

"That some derivative of whatever it was that rained down on London on Valentine's Day could have been responsible for..." She broke off.

Ulysses' smile slipped for the first time. He revelled in the thrill of the chase but sometimes forgot that real people with their own thoughts and feelings were involved. "For what we witnessed," he finished for her. "Yes."

"So where do we go from here?" Constance asked as they passed beyond the limits of Bedlam Asylum.

"East," he declared confidently as he opened the door of the Rolls for her. "We're going to ruffle a few feathers. The game is very much afoot!"

X

The Beast Within

FROM HIS ROOST among the statues adorning the aerial Victoria Line, hidden among the pigeons perched there under the track's cast iron arches, John Schafer looked down upon the city with altered eyes and watched the world go by.

From his vantage point he could see a fishwife in Kennington berating her layabout son. He watched a drunken father in Vauxhall chase his five children out into the street, belt in hand. At Hyde Park Corner Overground station, half a mile away, he clearly saw the stolen kiss shared by a squaddie and his girl as the young infantryman boarded the train. It was true what they said; all human life could be found, there in the city. But his gaze lingered on one pair in particular.

He'd not seen the dandy in the flesh since they had returned to Southampton Docks as survivors of the sinking of the *Neptune*, although he had read about some of Ulysses' more recent exploits in *The Times* and watched live footage being relayed via the broadcast screens as the *Jupiter* Station had come down in the

Thames only a matter of months ago.

He had last properly seen his sweetheart only three days before but to him it felt like a lifetime. His heart ached more than any of the open wounds in his flesh from where the beast had emerged to prey on the weak.

He had been trailing the couple since waking that morning to find himself curled in the lea of a chimney stack atop the dandy's Mayfair townhouse. He had been with them ever since, always at a distance, but close enough nonetheless to know that they had met with the hospital director at Bedlam.

Schafer had followed the dandy's car as it headed back across town, stopping first at his apartment building before heading off again. He had watched with interest as the Silver Phantom pulled up outside an unremarkable, dilapidated house, the dandy entering alone, only to emerge, alone still, some minutes later.

In this manner, he had tracked them all day long as the dandy led him a merry dance back and forth across the city. And so it was that he now found himself skulking in the shadow of the Victoria Line, Quicksilver's Silver Phantom pulled up outside Schafer's tenement building once again. However, this time, they had all returned to the scene of the crime to find that the building had been taped off by the police, a ginger-haired inspector in a dull tan trench-coat haranguing his men at the same time as interviewing Schafer's neighbours, demonstrating all the tact of a disgruntled bull.

Throughout the whole day, Schafer had managed to remain hidden, his pursuit of his beloved and the dandy adventurer going unnoticed and unhindered. This had been mainly due to the fact that he had never once returned to street level.

Even now, back in his more familiar, and less bestial, form, he found himself able to perform feats of great agility and possessed of a strength he would never have believed himself capable of.

He was human again – at least as human as he could ever be now – but there were still aspects of his most recent agonising metamorphosis that lingered: the raised ridges above his brow, the protruding knuckles on the backs of his hands, the hard black scales covering his back. And the memories of what he had done whilst in that altered state seemed less dream-like in nature now and, as a consequence, all the more nightmarish.

It wasn't the fact that he had killed those thieves, or that family of beggars, or his neighbour Dr Rathbone, that troubled him the most, it was the cruel recollection of how he had defiled their bodies afterwards that had driven him to the brink of madness.

It had made him vomit the first time he had realised what he had done. But seeing the clumps of hair and a gold tooth at the centre of the red splatter, disgorged from his stomach, weighed so heavily on his soul that he feared for his sanity – what little there was left of it.

The molten orange orb of the sun appeared through a break in the Smog, making him blink and forcing him to half-close his eyes. It would be dark again soon.

His whole body tensed. Would he become the beast again as night fell? Was that how it worked? Or was it some other external provocation that unleashed the beast within? Or was he on a slippery slope now, doomed to descend into a bestial world of madness, mayhem and murder no matter what?

Why had he followed Constance back here, he wondered. He knew that she and him could never be together now, but it gave him some small comfort to know that she was close by, with him watching over her as he had pledged to do long before they ever boarded the *Neptune* on its maiden voyage around the world.

But then another thought struck him. How could he be sure that she would be safe when the beast emerged from within once again? It had taken a supreme mental effort to stop himself from attacking Quicksilver as the dandy pursued him over the rooftops of Pimlico.

Each time he had changed, the alteration to his physical form had become more extreme, had come about more quickly, and had lasted longer. How could he be sure that he would be able to resist the urge to maim and kill next time? And, if he could not control the beast, how could he be certain that Constance would be safe with him around?

Welcome it, an insidious, slithering voice whispered from the primal core of his brain. *Embrace the change!*

"I can't!" Schafer wailed. One of the pigeons perched nearby ruffled its feathers and put its head on one side, giving him a beady-eyed look of avian curiosity.

Why not? Look what you can do already. Imagine what you could achieve if you gave yourself over to the metamorphosis completely. Imagine what you could achieve then. No man could stand in your way.

"I have to keep what I am in mind, before I forget I am a man altogether. It's turning me into an unholy freak – some kind of blood-thirsty, savage animal!"

And what's so bad about that?

"Constance could never love me like that. But if I could be a man again..."

Who says she wants you anymore anyway? the voice cut in.

"How can you say that? We were to be married."

Were you? Perhaps she was only hanging on to you until something better came along. Look how quickly she's taken up with that dandy Quicksilver.

"That's not what's happening here!" Schafer railed against his own traitorous subliminal thoughts.

Isn't it? Look how quickly she's changed her allegiance now that you're out of the picture. See how she behaves around him? What she obviously needs is a real man.

"Shut up!"

But you could be that man, the voice wheedled, not letting him alone for a moment while his ability to resist was at its lowest ebb. *Embrace the change.*

"Shut up!" Schafer raged. "It's making me worse."

Feeling a sudden, sharp pain, like hot needles stabbing into his bones, Schafer looked to the backs of his hands. There was something moving there, beneath the open wounds.

"I'm getting worse!" he shrieked.

You're getting better, the voice said. *Embrace the change. Be the man you've always wanted to be.*

XI

Beauty And The Beast

"Hello, Maurice," Ulysses Quicksilver said, catching sight of the trench-coated inspector on the other side of the police line as he helped Constance Pennyroyal from the car.

Shooting wary glances left and right, as if worried that someone might have heard the dandy use his first name, Inspector Allardyce of Her Majesty's Metropolitan Police jogged over to the barrier formed by the flapping piece of tape where Ulysses stood. They could never have been described as best friends, but since their shared experience in North Yorkshire six months before, they now shared a certain understanding.

"Quicksilver," he said, shaking the dandy's proffered hand. "What brings you out here?" The policeman's expression suddenly darkened. "Don't tell me, you already know that we found a stiff upstairs and that another bugger's gone missing."

"Who do you think called it in?" Ulysses grinned.

Allardyce scowled. "And I suppose you can tell me who the missing sod is and his inside leg measurement."

"His name's John Schafer but you'll have to give me a minute on the leg measurement." Ulysses glanced at Constance who was anxiously observing their exchange. "So, he's not come home yet then?"

"No," the police inspector returned. His features knotted into an expression of intrigue and suspicion. "Why, are you expecting him to?"

"More hoping really."

"You're honestly expecting him to return to the scene of the crime?"

"Well, you never know. Instinct is a hard impulse to conquer."

Constance suddenly gave a strangled cry, causing Ulysses to look up.

Sweeping down out of the purpling sky towards the group gathered before the tenement building was a grim gargoyle of a silhouette, malformed bone and stretched skin forming what looked like a pair of leathery membranous wings.

The thing opened its mouth horribly wide and a hissing shriek escaped its altered throat.

"Down!" Ulysses shouted and such was the vehemence in his voice, not only Constance but also Inspector Allardyce and a pair of jumpy constables did as he commanded too.

Ulysses' sword was out of its darkwood sheath in a second, ready to meet the distended, chitin-edged blade that the creature's arm became, even as Ulysses measured his adversary's approach.

Metal met chitin, denying the beast its killing stroke. But the very next moment, the force of its landing sent Ulysses crashing to the ground, the hissing monstrosity on top of him.

Constance screamed. Nimrod was out of the car in seconds, pistol in hand and levelled at the gargoyle, his knuckle whitening as he applied pressure to the trigger.

Seeing what Ulysses' manservant was about to do the woman screamed again: "Stop!"

Hearing her cry, the monster snapped its head around and hissed, a black, blistered tongue flicking from between its gaping, snake-like jaws. Its face had been disfigured by bony protuberances that exaggerated its features, giving it the appearance of a grotesque more usually found clinging to the crenulations of country churches.

Its disturbingly human eyes narrowed, fixing Nimrod with a venomous look. But then its gaze fell on the young woman, and it took in the look of abject horror on her wretched face.

With the beast momentarily distracted, Ulysses brought a knee up into the creature's stomach. Dropping his sword, he pushed at its knobby shoulders with both hands, rolling sideways as he did so, managing to throw the beast from him.

As he lay there on his back his hand went to a jacket pocket.

But the frighteningly agile creature twisted its spine as it fell and it was on its feet again in a trice, crouched like some lithe devil carved into a church pulpit, before Ulysses was able to even sit up.

Snapping and snarling it came at him again. Ulysses pulled his hand free of the pocket as the gargoyle lunged, knowing that the creature's claws would be round his throat in seconds.

A shot rang out sharp and clear, echoing like a thunderclap from the surrounding buildings.

The gargoyle was punched out of the air and landed several yards away, its scales scraping across the paving stones as it slid to a halt.

A second shot rang out before anyone barely had time to react to the first.

Constance was screaming again: "Stop! *Stop!* STOP!"

Managing to get to his feet at last, Ulysses scanned the fretful faces all around him. "Cease fire!" he commanded.

A suffocating hush fell over the street.

Ulysses studied the faces of the gathered policeman. Nimrod's finger was still tight around the trigger of his pistol, but the weapon remained undischarged. It wasn't the butler who had fired.

Blue smoke curled from the barrel of a gun held in the shaking hand of a policeman standing at Allardyce's shoulder. Ulysses glowered at him.

"What did you do that for?" His voice was like acid in the blushing constable's ear.

"That thing was going to kill you!" the constable protested feebly.

"I would like to have seen it try."

"But you had lost your blade. You were defenceless."

Ulysses held out the closed fist of his right hand for both the policeman and the inspector to see. "No, I wasn't." He opened his hand. "I had this."

Lying there in his open palm was a large syringe with a needle as thick as a pencil, a fluorescent green liquid sloshing within the glass tube beneath the plunger.

"And what's that?" Allardyce asked. "A fast-acting neurotoxin or something?"

"No," Ulysses replied. "A potential cure."

"John!" Constance wailed, suddenly breaking through the police cordon and running to where the metamorphosed creature lay.

The men watched, dumbfounded, as she knelt beside it, heedless of the fact that she was kneeling in a spreading pool of the monster's blood.

"Oh, my poor darling," she said, gently lifting the creature's head from the pavement and cradling it in her lap.

The gargoyle's eyes flickered open. "*Consssstance*," the creature slurred.

"Don't worry," she said, as she stroked the creature's face. "It's all right. They can't hurt you anymore."

And as he watched, in the fast failing light of dusk, it seemed to Ulysses that the gargoyle was morphing back into something more like the man it had once been.

Allardyce stared at the shape-shifting thing in appalled horror. "What is that thing?"

"That is John Schafer – your missing suspect," the dandy replied, with no hint of triumph in his voice.

"But why did it attack like that, with so many police around? It's like it wanted to be killed."

"Suicide by police firing squad, you mean?"

Allardyce turned to Ulysses, his features knotted in annoyance once more, but said nothing.

"I didn't want you to see me like this," John Schafer told his sweetheart, his voice changing along with his appearance. "That was why I called it off. You do understand, don't you? Tell me you understand."

"I understand," she whispered, bringing her face close to his, her lips caressing the bat-like point of an elongated ear. "But you didn't need to have done."

"What?" the shape-shifting Schafer croaked.

"I love you, John."

"But how could you love the monster I had become?" he asked, his eyelids slowing closing again. "How could you have loved a thing like that?"

The young woman's tears splashed onto the man's face, trickling in rivulets from its bony bumps and ridges. "Because it was still you, and I love you," she sobbed.

But her fiancé didn't say another word.

"I've always loved you, John Schafer."

XII

'Til Death Do Us Part

JOHN BENEDICT SCHAFER was buried in haste, three days later, on Saturday 23rd May, the day on which he was supposed to have married his beloved Constance Beatrice Pennyroyal.

At least, they buried what was left of him, which was little more than a husk by the time the undertakers had set to work. Who could have known that the formula with which he had been infected could have caused his innards to decompose so quickly, causing the body to shrink and split along the length of its spine like that?

The undertakers – Morley and Sons – had decided not to report on the condition of the body to the deceased's family or fiancée. It had been decided right from the outset that the family would not be opting for an open coffin, so what was the point in worrying them?

So it was that what was interred in the soil that warm May morning was little more than a shell of the man John Schafer had once been.

* * *

"EARTH TO EARTH, ashes to ashes, dust to dust," the minister intoned, "in sure and certain hope of the Resurrection into eternal life."

The vicar's monotonous tones drifting across the graveyard, Constance Pennyroyal – clad all in black, from her veil and hat to her silk gloves – stepped forward and cast the first handful of dirt into the grave, the crumbling soil skittering across the surface of the coffin lid. Kneeling at the grave-side she let a single black rose drop into the hole to land atop the brass plaque engraved with the words, "*John Benedict Schafer: Requiescat in Pace.*"

"Goodnight and God bless, my darling," she said softly, blowing a kiss at the coffin's lid, her eyes fixed on the rose and the one petal that had been shaken free by the fall.

When it was his turn, Ulysses Quicksilver also took up a clod of earth and cast it into the hole but said nothing, preferring to keep his thoughts to himself that day.

"HOW WILL YOU cope?" he asked Constance as they paced between the grassy hummocks of old graves once the committal had been concluded, genuine concern colouring his words.

"How will I cope?" she asked, turning her gentle face towards his, a soft smile forming on her lips.

"Without him, I mean. Today was supposed to have been your wedding day."

"Oh, John's not gone, not really," she said, unconsciously stroking her belly with one silken-gloved hand. "I feel that he's still there, inside of me."

"You know, if there's anything I can do..." Ulysses began.

"I only need ask," she finished.

And with the sun climbing high beyond the smudges of Smog discolouring the London sky, the two mourners walked on, arm in arm, along the green paths between the lichen-patterned gravestones, where the dead slept.

*　　*　　*

Day 24

DESPITE MY BEST efforts to procure the body so that I might carry out my own autopsy of the subject, on this occasion I was unsuccessful, hence this experiment is concluded.

But Proteus 12 can, I believe, be considered a success and the results observed in this case shall spur me on when it comes to creating the next version of the formula.

Onward and upward!

HIS FINAL OBSERVATIONS entered into his personal Babbage engine, he saved the file and then shut down the machine. A moment later there came a knock at his office door.

"Professor, the trustees are ready for you."

"Thank you, Leckwith. Tell them I won't keep them a minute."

Turning off the cogitator he turned his attention to the device on his desk. At first glance it looked like a mosquito – an overgrown mosquito made of glass and metal – but insect-like in form nonetheless. At barely four inches long it was clearly the work of a master artificer.

Its cylindrical body was the glass receptacle of a syringe, its proboscis the hypodermic needle. But it was more than merely a medication delivery system. Firstly there was the tiny motor that rotated the mosquito's wings a hundred times a second, enabling it to fly, and then there were the twin tiny cameras mounted in place of the insect's compound eyes, a radio transmitter ensuring that its controller saw everything it saw.

Carefully he picked up the delicate device and placed it back in a desk drawer. Closing the drawer again he locked it before placing the key in his pocket.

It was a shame that the first field trial of Proteus 12 had come to such an abrupt end but during the few short weeks it had been in operation he had learnt a very great deal, plenty that could be applied when it came to concocting the next version of the serum. If he could change a man into a monster, then he would surely have the means to change a monster back into a man.

However, he would have liked to have found out whether the old man's cure would actually have worked. But no matter, he would simply have to select another subject and try again, hopefully without Ulysses Quicksilver getting in the way this time.

And so, keeping his thoughts very much to himself, Professor Rufus Brundle left his office, locking the door securely behind him, ready to take the trustees on their annual tour of the hospital. His hospital. Bedlam Asylum.

THE END

Coming soon!

PAX BRITANNIA

ANNO FRANKENSTEIN

By

JONATHAN GREEN

Visit www.abaddonbooks.com for information on our titles,
interviews, news and exclusive content.

UK £7.99 • UK ISBN: 978-1-907519-44-4
US $9.99 • UK ISBN: 978-1-907519-45-1

Abaddon
Books

Follow us on twitter: www.twitter.com/abaddonbooks

Out Now!

The ULYSSES QUICKSILVER

Omnibus

MASTERS OF ADVENTURE FICTION, **ABADDON BOOKS** PRESENT
THREE THRILLING TALES OF VALOUR TO DIVERT AND ENTHRALL

PAX BRITANNIA

UNNATURAL HISTORY · LEVIATHAN RISING · HUMAN NATURE

By

JONATHAN GREEN

Visit www.abaddonbooks.com for information on our titles,
interviews, news and exclusive content.

 UK £9.99 • UK ISBN: 978-1-907519-36-9
US $12.99 • UK ISBN: 978-1-907519-56-7   Abaddon Books

Follow us on twitter: www.twitter.com/abaddonbooks